The Zigzag Kid

By David Grossman

Novels

The Smile of the Lamb
See Under: LOVE
The Book of Intimate Grammar
The Zigzag Kid

Non-fiction

The Yellow Wind
Sleeping on a Wire

The Zigzag Kid

DAVID GROSSMAN

Translated from the Hebrew by Betsy Rosenberg

FARRAR, STRAUS AND GIROUX

NEW YORK

Farrar, Straus and Giroux
19 Union Square West, New York 10003

Translation copyright © 1997 by Betsy Rosenberg
All rights reserved
Distributed in Canada by Douglas & McIntyre Ltd.
Printed in the United States of America
Designed by Jonathan D. Lippincott
Originally published in Hebrew by
HaSifriya HaHadasha/HaKibbutz HaMeuchad Publishing House (Tel Aviv)
as *Yesh yeladim zigzag*, copyright © 1994 by David Grossman
First English-language edition published in 1997 by Farrar, Straus and Giroux

Library of Congress Cataloging-in-Publication Data
Grossman, David.
    [Yesh yeladim zigzag. English]
    The zigzag kid / by David Grossman ; translated from the Hebrew by
Betsy Rosenberg.
        p.   cm.
    ISBN 0-374-29692-8 (alk. paper)
    I. Rozenberg, Betsi.   II. Title.
    PJ5054.G728Y47   1997
    892.4'36—dc21   96-49824

To my children, Yonatan, Uri, and Ruti

The Zigzag Kid

On the eve of his bar mitzvah, Nonny
meets an elderly career criminal while
on a passenger train, and together they
form an unlikely duo, flouting the law
with their petty crimes while traveling
through Israel.

The whistle blew and the train pulled out of the station. There was a boy at one of the compartment windows watching a man and a woman wave to him from the platform. The man waved one hand in a shy little farewell. The woman waved both hands plus a large red scarf. The man was his father, and the woman was Gabriella, a.k.a. Gabi. The man was wearing a police uniform because he was a policeman. The woman wore a black dress because black is slimming. Vertical stripes are also slimming, but if you really want to look slim, she used to joke, stand close to someone even fatter than you, though I have yet to meet anyone quite that fat.

The boy at the window of the moving train, gazing back as though he might never see this picture again, was me. Now they'll be alone together for two whole days, I thought. All is lost.

The mere thought was enough to yank me out the window by the roots of my hair. I could see Dad's mouth forming the grimace Gabi called his "final warning before legal action." Well, too bad. If he cared so much, why did he send me to Haifa for two days, to stay with "him"!

A uniformed trainman on the platform blew his whistle loudly and motioned me to put my head back in. It's a crazy thing, the way men in uniforms with whistles will always pick on me, out of a whole trainload of people. But I would not obey. I stuck my head out even farther, in fact, so that Dad and Gabi would see me till the last possible second and remember the kid!

The train was rolling slowly off through waves of heat and diesel fumes. There was something new in the air, the smell of travel, the smell of freedom. Here I was, taking a trip! All by myself! I presented first one cheek and then the other to the warm caress of the breeze. I wanted to dry off Dad's kiss. He'd never kissed me like that before in public. So why did he do it this time and then send me away?

Now there were three uniformed trainmen on the platform blowing whistles at me. A regular orchestra. Since I couldn't see Dad and Gabi anymore, I pulled myself back in, slow and casual like, to show I didn't give a hoot about their whistles.

I sat down. Too bad there was no one sharing the compartment with me. Now what? It was a four-hour ride from Jerusalem to Haifa, at the end of which I would be met by the grim-faced Dr. Samuel Shilhav, distinguished educator, author of seven textbooks, and, as it happens, my uncle, the elder brother of my dad.

I stood up. Checked twice to see how the window opened and closed. Opened and closed the trash receptacle, too. There was nothing left to open and close. Everything worked. Pretty cool train.

Then I climbed up on the seat, wriggled my way into the luggage rack, and let myself down again, headfirst, to check whether a certain someone had lost any change under the seats. But he hadn't. He was obviously a someone you could count on.

Darn them! Dad and Gabi! Why did they have to turn me over to Uncle Samuel a week before my bar mitzvah? Okay, Dad was Dad, he practically worshipped his brother, the great educator and all that, but Gabi, who called him "the Owl" behind his back? Was this the special gift she'd promised me?

There was a little hole in the upholstery. I poked my finger inside and made it bigger. Sometimes you find coins in such places. But all I found in there was foam rubber and springs. I had four hours to tunnel my way through at least three cars to freedom. I would disappear and never have to face grouchy Uncle Samuel Shilhav (formerly Feuerberg). Just let them dare send me away again.

I ran out of finger long before I got through the three cars. I lay on the seat with my feet in the air. I was a captive here, a prisoner in transit, on his way to meet the judge. Loose change fell out of my pocket. Coins rolled through the compartment. Some of them I found, some I didn't.

Every child in our extended family was expected to submit to one of these sessions with Uncle Shilhav, a form of torture Gabi calls "Shilhavization." Only for me, this was the second time. No one had ever gone through it twice and come away sane. I jumped up on the seat and started drumming on the wall. Then I changed to a rhythmic tapping. Maybe there was another poor prisoner in the next compartment eager to communicate with a fellow fool of fortune. Maybe the train was full of juvenile delinquents on their way to my Uncle Shilhav. I banged the wall again, this time with my foot. The conductor walked in and yelled at me to sit still. I did.

My previous Shilhavization had been enough for a lifetime. I was put through it after getting into that trouble over Pessia Mautner, the cow. Uncle Samuel shut the door of his stuffy little office and devoted two hours of his time to me. He began in a restrained whisper, and even remembered my name at first, but soon he forgot where he was and with whom, and was probably imagining himself on a podium, addressing a crowd of former students and admirers.

But why now—again? What did I do? I was innocent. "It's important for you to hear what Uncle Samuel has to say before your bar mitzvah," said Gabi. Suddenly he was "Uncle Samuel"?

But I knew.

She wanted me out of the way so she could split with Dad.

I stood up. I joggled to and fro. I sat down again. I should never have left them alone together. I knew exactly what would happen. They would fight and say horrible things to each other without me around and I would never be able to get them back together. My fate was being decided there.

"Why don't we talk about it later, at work?" Dad was saying now.

"Because there are always people coming in and out of your office, and phone calls and interruptions. It's impossible to have a discussion there. Let's go sit at a café."

"A café?" asks Dad, astonished. "You mean right now—in the middle of the day? Is it that serious?"

"Don't make light of everything." Now she's annoyed with him. The tip of her nose has turned red, the way it does whenever she's about to start crying.

"If it's the subject we were discussing earlier," says Dad gruffly, "forget it. Nothing's changed since our last talk. I'm just not ready yet."

"Well, this time you're going to listen to what I have to say," says Gabi. "The least you can do is hear me out!"

They get into the police car then, and Dad turns the key in the ignition. His shoulder insignia flicker ominously. His face is stern. Gabi shrinks into her seat. Not a word has been spoken, but the fight has begun. Gabi takes a little round mirror out of her purse. She glances at her reflection, tries to smooth down her frizzy hair. "Monkey-face," she broods.

"Stop it!" I leaped up in the moving train. I forbid Gabi to put herself down like that. I always say, "I think you have a very interesting face." And seeing that she was not convinced, I would add, "The thing is, you have inner beauty."

"Yeah, sure," she would answer. "So how come there are no inner-beauty contests?"

And suddenly I found myself standing by the little red lever next to the window. This was definitely not a good place for me to be, in my present state of mind. Such a lever could stop a train in its tracks, if you happened to pull it accidentally. I read the sign: *In case of emergency only. Persons stopping this train for insufficient reason will be subject to a large fine and possible imprisonment.* My fingers began to itch, at the tips, and in between. Again I read the warning, in a loud, clear voice. No use. My palms were sweating. I put my hands back in my pockets, but wouldn't you know, they popped out again. Someone looking on might have thought, Ho hum, just a pair of innocent hands out for a little air. Now I was really sweating. I touched the chain around my neck and the bullet hanging from it, heavy, cool, and soothing. This bullet was taken out of your father's shoulder, I murmured to myself, and it will always keep you safe from harm. But now I was starting to feel prickly all over.

The old familiar feeling. I knew what would happen next. I'd start rationalizing. The engineer will never guess which of the levers was pulled. But supposing he has some sort of gadget that tells him which one it was? Okay, so as soon as I pull this one I'll run to the next car. But what if they find my fingerprints on the lever? Maybe I'd better wrap a handkerchief around my hand before I touch it.

Why do I get myself into these arguments I always end up losing? I pumped up my back muscles and stood like Dad, sturdy as a bear, telling myself, Relax, relax, but it didn't work. There was this hot place between my eyes which on occasions like this tended to get even hotter: it was happening now, overwhelming me, and at the last minute I bent over, grabbed my legs, and forced myself down on the seat. Gabi used to call this trick of mine "protective custody." She had her own special terminology for everything.

"Look, I'm no spring chicken anymore," she was saying to Dad at the café. "For twelve years I've been practically living with you and Nonny." So far, so good; she's under control, speaking quietly, coolly. "For twelve years now I have brought him up and looked after the two of you and your house. I know you like no one else ever will and I want to move in full-time, I want to be more than your secretary and your cook and laundress. And I want to be there as Nonny's mother all night long, too. What are you so afraid of, would you mind telling me?"

"I'm just not ready," says Dad, pressing the coffee cup between his big, strong hands.

Gabi pauses for a moment, takes a deep breath, and says, "Well, I can't go on this way."

"Look—uh—Gabi," says Dad, his eyes darting impatiently over her shoulder, "what's wrong with things as they are? We're comfortable this way, it works for the three of us. Why change our life all of a sudden?"

"Because I'm forty years old, Jacob, that's why! I want fulfillment, I want to have a family." At this point her voice starts to crack. "And I want us to have a child of our own, I want to see the baby you and I would make together. If we wait another year, I may be too old. And Nonny deserves a live-in mother!"

I could recite this speech of hers by heart. She had rehearsed it with me often enough. I was the one who contributed the touching phrase "Nonny deserves a live-in mother." I also gave her a piece of practical advice: Whatever you do, for God's sake, don't cry in front of him! Because the minute she started bawling, it would be all over. If there's one thing Dad can't stand, it's tears, hers or anyone else's.

"The timing is wrong, Gabi." He sighs and sneaks a glance at his watch. "Be patient. I can't decide a thing like this under pressure."

"I have waited patiently for twelve years. I'm not going to wait anymore." Silence. He doesn't answer. Her eyes are brimming over. Oh, please control yourself, Gabi, you hear?

"Jacob, answer me to my face: is it yes or no?"

Silence. Her double chin is trembling. Her lips twitch. If she starts crying now, she's doomed. And so am I.

"Because if the answer is no, I will get up and leave you, Jacob. This time for good. I mean it!" And she pounds the table with her fist as the tears flow down her puffy face. Mascara trickles over her freckles and collects in the creases around her mouth. Dad frowns in the direction of the window. He can't bear to see her cry, or maybe it's the sight of her swollen eyes and her quivering cheeks that he can't bear.

No, she is not pretty at this moment. And it's so cruel, too, because if she were the least bit attractive, if she had a sweet little mouth, for instance, or a turned-up nose, he might suddenly have fallen in love with her one good feature. The tiniest beauty mark is sometimes enough to win a man's heart, even if the woman in question is no queen of outward beauty. But Gabi has no beauty mark, I'm sorry to say.

"Okay, I understand." She groans through the red scarf, which has recently served a loftier purpose. "What a fool I've been to think you could change."

"Shhh . . ." he begs her, glancing around. I definitely hope everybody in the café is staring at him now. That all the cooks and waiters come hurrying out of the kitchen and stand around with their arms folded over their aprons, glaring at him. If there's one thing that scares my dad, it's a scene. "Look—uh—Gabi," he tries to soothe her. Actually he seems more gentle now, either because of all the people around or because he senses that she's serious this time. "Please, give me a little more time to think about it, okay?"

"Why? So that when I'm fifty you can ask me to give you more time again? And what if you decide to tell me it's over when I'm fifty? Who'll look at me then? I want to be a mother, Jacob!" People are staring now and he wishes he were dead, but Gabi continues: "I have so much love in me to give a child, and to give to you, too! Haven't I done well so far as Nonny's mother? Won't you try to understand my side of it, too?"

Even during our rehearsals, she would get carried away sometimes and start crying and pleading, as if I were Dad. Then she'd get hold of herself and tell me, red-faced, that certain things were inappropriate for children my age to hear, although it didn't matter much, really, since I already knew everything anyway.

I did not know everything, though I was learning a lot.

Gabi rolls up the soggy paper napkins and wads them into the ashtray. She wipes away the last traces of mascara from her swollen eyes.

"Today is Sunday," she says, struggling to keep her voice firm. "The bar mitzvah is next Saturday. You have until next Sunday morning, a full week, to decide."

"Are you giving me an ultimatum? This isn't something you can settle with threats, Gabi! I thought you were smarter than that." His voice is quiet, but the furrow of rage between his eyes grows ominously deeper.

"I don't have any strength left, Jacob. For twelve years I've been smart, and look at me, I'm still alone. Maybe being stupid works better."

Dad says nothing. His red face is redder than ever.

"Come on, let's drive back to work," she says hoarsely. "And by the way, if I've guessed your answer correctly, you'd better start looking for a new secretary, too. I'm going to break off all contact with you. Oh yes."

"Look—uh—Gabi . . ." says Dad again. He can't think of anything else to say. "Look—uh—Gabi."

"Until next Sunday, then." Gabi cuts him off, stands up, and walks out of the café.

She's leaving us.

She's leaving me.

In the train my arms and legs break out of "protective custody." Emergency, emergency, the painted words scream out at me from the red sign above the little lever. The train is carrying me farther and farther away from where my life is just about to be destroyed. I cover my ears and shout, "Amnon Feuerberg! Amnon Feuerberg!" as though someone else were warning me not to touch the lever, trying to save me from myself, someone like a father, or a teacher, or a distinguished educator, or maybe even the head of a reformatory. "Amnon Feuerberg! Amnon Feuerberg!" But nothing will help me now. I'm all alone. Abandoned. I should never have left home. I must return at once. And I stagger toward the lever and reach out. My fingers stretch toward it, because this truly is an emergency.

But just as I am about to pull with all my might, the compartment door opens and in walk two men, a policeman and a prisoner, and both of them stand there, staring in astonishment.

2

I mean—a real policeman and a real prisoner.

The policeman was a wiry guy with a nervous look in his eyes. The prisoner was bigger, burlier. He smiled at me brightly and said, "Mornin', kid! Off to visit your grandma?"

I wasn't sure it was legal to answer him. Anyway, why grandma? Did I look like the kind of kid who would visit his grandma, like Little Red Riding-Hood or something?

"No talking to the prisoner!" barked the policeman, severing the invisible strings between us with his skinny hand.

I sat down. I didn't know what to do. I tried not to look, but naturally, the harder I tried, the more I wanted to. They had an anxious air. Something was wrong. The policeman kept checking their tickets all the time and scratching his head. The prisoner checked the tickets and scratched his head, too. They looked as if they were playing charades, acting out the expression "to rack your brains."

"Why did you have to go and buy separate seats?" grumbled the prisoner, and the policeman shrugged his shoulders. The man at the ticket counter, he explained, didn't say that the tickets were for separate seats. He, the policeman, had assumed they would have adjacent seats, because no one in his right mind would sell separate seats to a pair like them, and as he said the words "a pair like us," he raised his right hand, which was cuffed to the prisoner's left.

It was an odd sort of scene. They looked like a couple of cartoon characters, the prisoner with his striped shirt and cap, and the policeman with his large hat slipping over his eyes. They stood in the aisle together, rocking indecisively to the rhythm of the train. This, for some reason, made me nervous.

At first they tried to sit in their reserved places, the prisoner beside me, the policeman facing us, but they were obliged to lean forward on account of the handcuffs. And then all at once they stood up and started rocking again, which seemed to relax them so much that the prisoner's head drooped down, brushing against the policeman's shoulder, and the policeman appeared to be about to fall asleep. I wanted out of there, fast; I kept wishing there were an adult around, because those two didn't seem quite like adults to me, or like kids either, for that matter; they were sort of undefinable.

The policeman shook himself out of his peculiar lethargy and whispered something to the prisoner. I couldn't hear what exactly, but I knew it was about me, because the prisoner threw me a sidelong glance: "No way!" he shouted in a whisper. "You can't do that! These seats are reserved!"

The policeman tried to calm him, pointing out that since the car was practically empty, it would be perfectly all right under the circumstances to sit in unreserved seats. But the prisoner wouldn't hear of it. "Rules are rules!" he bristled. "If you and I don't obey them, who will?" And as he stamped his foot indignantly, I noticed the ball and chain around his ankle, just like in a book.

I'm getting out of here, I thought. This is not a good place to be.

"Who's going to notice if we sit in somebody else's seat for a couple of minutes?" the policeman flashed back in an angry whisper, with an ingratiating smile at me, the crooked smile of a conscience-stricken jailer. "You won't report us, kiddo, will you?"

I could only shake my head in reply, but I noted the "kiddo" and held it against him.

And they sat down to the right and left of me.

Why, with a whole car to themselves, did they have to sandwich me in like that? Their wrists, double cuffed, were practically on my lap. I was pretty scared. They seemed to be up to something; they were trying to intimidate me, but at the same time they were ignoring me. There was a long silence. My eyes kept darting back to my knees, over which two arms were swinging to the rhythm of the train, one hairy and thin, the other smooth and solid, the arm of the law and the arm of the lawbreaker, with the arm of the law looking distinctly weaker.

What was there to be afraid of, though? I mean, the law was on my side, practically on top of me, in fact, and yet I felt as if I were falling into a mysterious trap, as if those two were implicating me in some conspiracy.

But now they seemed to relax a little. The policeman leaned back and hummed to himself, twiddling his mustache with the fingers of his free hand as he strained to reach the high notes. The prisoner stared out the window at the passing scenery, the rocky hillsides of Jerusalem, and heaved a sigh.

"If someone arouses your suspicion, keep cool and wait. Don't talk too much. Let him do the talking and go about his business while you sit tight. All you do is quietly lay a trap for him and eventually he'll reveal his intentions." That's what I was taught by Dad, my guide in this particular field. I took a deep breath. Here was my big chance to test myself in a real-life situation. I would ignore them, pretend everything was normal, until they made their first mistake.

Look to the right. Look to the left. There they sat. The whole thing seemed like a huge mistake, but I still couldn't figure out what it was.

Okay, I have to get ready for the meeting with Uncle Samuel, I told myself. Because last year he talked at me for two whole hours, and I didn't think I could go through that again. For two whole hours I watched his pouting mouth open and close under his mustache, until I could see it over his mustache, too. I was undoubtedly the subject of every article he'd ever published. For months, for years, he had been sitting in his office, writing against me. I bet he even kept a portrait of me on his desk with the legend: *Wanted Dead or Alive by the Ministry of Education*. And now I would be falling right into his hands—a man like him would never miss such an opportunity. And his stuffy office would fill up with puffy pairs of lips opening and closing and spouting

out more and more uncles of the puffy-lipped variety. Books and jour-
nals fluttered around me and rustled to the rhythm of my name. I was
afraid I might die there of didactic poisoning.

I couldn't make out what he was saying anymore. He seemed to be
accusing me of following the prophets of Baal and Astarte, or of taking
part in the seventeenth-century pogroms of Chmielnicki. He had the
whole of history on his side, and I would have confessed to anything.

Finally, after two mustachioed hours, I remembered Gabi's words of
advice. "Cry," she had whispered in my ear the night before. "If things
become unbearable, start blubbering and see what happens."

Look to the left. Look to the right. Nothing. The policeman and the
prisoner were sitting perfectly still, staring off in opposite directions.
Maybe there was nothing unusual going on here, after all. Maybe I was
simply nervous about traveling alone. Or maybe they, too, had learned
how to wage a war of nerves.

Uncle Samuel, I prompted myself; remember how it was last time you
visited him.

I had never had any difficulty crying myself blue, and with Uncle
ranting at me there, I was pretty miserable. It was easy enough to cough
up the bitter lump of all that had happened to me, or that I had been
told, or that I longed for.

I started sobbing, soft little sobs at first. And to make myself even
sadder, I thought about the things Dad used to say, like, that he didn't
know what to do with me, just when I seemed to be growing up I would
suddenly regress, and how had a man like him produced a son like me?
And he was right, but didn't he know how hard I was trying? Then I
started to cry in earnest, because nothing ever comes out the way I mean
it to. Even my sadness didn't come out the way I meant it to, crashing
into the spectacle of Uncle Samuel's feet in the sandals he always wore
over heavy gray socks, and that tie around his neck, even in summer,
and his Terylene trousers worn ragged by the generations of pupils
reared upon his knees—how sad yet comical it all seemed.

So I found myself laughing and crying, blubbering and sniveling, half
for real, half not, experiencing a strangely pleasing blend of emotions,
as though eating chocolate behind the dentist's back, and I sobbed with

remorse, self-pity, and overwhelming gratitude before this courageous man who was fighting single-handedly to save my wicked soul . . .

Uncle Samuel stopped talking. He gazed at me, his face gently radiant. Through the dimness I could see the glow of an awestruck smile over his mustache. "Well well," he muttered, his hand fluttering tentatively over my head. "I never thought my words would have such an effect on you . . . the simple outpouring of a fervent heart." And suddenly he thundered "Yempa!," which I took to be the victory cry of a distinguished educator over the forces of darkness. He rubbed his hands together and left the room. From the hall he called again, in that same curiously lighthearted way, to his housekeeper, Mrs. Yempa, and asked her to look in on me and help me calm down.

But I had resorted to tears already during the previous Shilhavization. What would I do this time? Gabi had whispered no new secrets in my ear to help me face Uncle today, large as life.

She was alone with Dad now. She was going to leave us.

I couldn't sit still between the two silent weirdos anymore. I had to get up right away, that is I tried to, but startled them to their feet, so that they had to raise their handcuffed fists together to let me by. They stood in my way, swaying drowsily again like a pair of droopy-lidded ducklings, till in my exasperation I blurted, "Hey, why don't we just switch places so the two of you can sit together?"

My voice sounded choked and shrill, yet they smiled happily enough as they twirled me around in an effort to move past without bumping me with their handcuffs. On we danced, arms flapping, until finally they figured out a way to sit together. I collapsed on the seat facing them.

"Quit staring!" barked the policeman, shaking a finger at the prisoner.

"Honest to God, I wasn't staring!" swore the prisoner, hand to heart.

"I saw you eyeing me before!" the policeman upbraided him.

"I swear on my daughter's life, I wasn't looking at you! Did you see me looking at him?"

His question was addressed to me. Why me? What did I have to do with it? Now the policeman leaned forward with him, waiting for my answer, waiting so intently he began to chew on his mustache. Their

movements were disturbingly theatrical, yet strangely fascinating, too.
I wanted to get out fast, but I couldn't move.

"I . . . I think you were looking at him just a little," I sputtered.

"Aha!" The policeman raised a triumphant finger. "You look at me
one more time and you've had it!"

The prisoner stared fixedly out the window. We were passing through
a pine forest. A herd of goats grazed in the underbrush. A she-goat
reared up and started munching on the foliage of a young tree. The
policeman looked away, in the direction of our compartment door. I
was afraid to look in either direction, but I was also afraid to shut my
eyes. I only wished I could disappear.

"There! You looked at me again!" shouted the policeman, springing
to his feet and falling back on account of the handcuffs. "You looked!"

"I swear on my daughter's life, I wasn't looking at you!" cried the
prisoner, likewise springing up and waving angrily, then falling back on
account of the handcuffs.

"You're still looking!" roared the policeman. "You're staring me in
the eye! Stop it!"

But this time the prisoner held his ground. He pushed his big face
right into the policeman's. What was this? What was going on between
them? Some weird kind of staring match: they gawk at each other, then
look away. The prisoner leaned forward, and the more the policeman
tried to avert his eyes, the more the prisoner would squirm around him,
trying to catch his eye. He was practically on top of him now!

"Hey . . . let me go . . ." muttered the prisoner.

"Shut up!" the policeman grumbled back at him. "Shut up and look
out the window! Not at me! Out the window!"

"Let me go . . ." whispered the prisoner in a new insinuating voice.
"It wasn't my fault . . . you know I had no choice . . ."

"Tell it to the judge!" snarled the policeman, and gritted his teeth.

"Give me a break, I have a little daughter . . ."

"Oh yeah? Well, so do I! Out the window!"

And still the prisoner stared fiercely at the policeman, slowly forcing
him to turn his head around. It was a distressing sight, and it filled me

with a sense of foreboding: the policeman kept trying to resist. I watched him as he struggled, hunching his shoulders to avoid the prisoner's gaze. But it overpowered him. It bored into his head until gradually he surrendered, relaxing his shoulders with a deep sigh, squinting at the prisoner and snickering boyishly, till his eyes began to look weary and glazed.

"You've had a long, hard day, Avigdor . . ." cooed the prisoner. "You had to chase me down all those alleys, shooting and yelling, and everything by the book . . ."

The policeman rolled his eyes.

"Sometimes it's hard to be a lawman . . ." whispered the prisoner. "So much responsibility . . . never a moment's rest . . ."

Now I, too, was gaping. That's just what Dad used to say when he came home from work in the evening and flopped down on the couch; those were his exact words whenever he complained, either to me or to himself, "so much responsibility and never a moment's rest." At times like that I used to imagine having a mother who would massage his stiff neck. But we didn't have a mother, we had a Gabi, and she wouldn't dare.

The prisoner reached cautiously into the dozing policeman's belt and pulled out a large set of keys, at least ten of them. He chose one and unlocked the cuff. His liberated hand did a merry dance in the air. There was a deep red imprint around his wrist.

"It was worth being cuffed just for this," he said.

Then he pulled off his striped shirt and prisoner's cap and set them down on the seat beside me. And I froze. He was going to bolt now, I would be an eyewitness to a prisoner's escape, yet for all my experience and training and my dad and that, I couldn't so much as move a finger.

"Would you please hang on to this for a second?" he addressed me pleasantly, and handed me the black gun he had just taken from the policeman's holster.

I recognized it at once: a Wembley service revolver. Dad had one just like it at work, one I'd held in my hand at least a thousand times. I'd even shot blanks from it at the firing range, but I had never been in a

situation like this before, facing a real criminal with a gun in my hands.
What was I supposed to do? Kill him? My finger twitched on the trigger.
How could I shoot him? What did he ever do to me? I had only one
wish—to see the round face of Uncle Samuel as soon as possible. I
would run straight into his arms, transformed forever into a model
citizen.

"Thanks, kid," said the prisoner, taking back the gun and sticking it
in his belt. And then he carefully unbuttoned the sleeping policeman's
shirt and slipped it off, as though he were a baby. The policeman,
Avigdor, slept on in his undershirt and never even dreamed of waking
up. You could nudge him, shake him, bounce him around—and still he
went on sleeping! I was furious: Dad hadn't been late for work in
twenty years, he always took on the most dangerous cases, even when
he was sick with a temperature, while this crooked cop here . . .

The prisoner dressed him quickly in the striped shirt and set the
prison cap on his head. Then he slipped free of the ball and chain,
locked it around the policeman's ankle, squeezed himself into the uniform, put on the police hat, and turned to the window.

"A good detective thinks like a criminal." I knew that, too, and I
knew exactly what would happen next, that he would open the window
and jump out of the moving train, to freedom. Do something! I ordered
myself. Jump! I told myself.

But nothing happened.

The prisoner looked out at the hilly countryside rushing by, then took
a deep breath of freedom, heaved a sigh, and sat down beside the obliv-
ious policeman. Gloomily he slipped his hand back into the open cuff
that dangled from the sleeper's wrist and locked it. Once again they
were bound together.

"Wake up! You fell asleep!" blared the former prisoner, nudging the
policeman with his shoulder.

The policeman sat bolt upright and glanced around bewilderedly.

"Huh? What happened?" he asked. "What did I do?"

"You fell asleep," shouted the former prisoner, drawing closer, with
his visor in the policeman's face.

"I did not fall asleep," muttered the policeman. He fumbled with the handcuff, then felt down his leg to the ball and chain, stopped in astonishment, wrinkling his brow in an effort to remember something, gave up and slumped back in his seat like an empty sack. A few more ghastly moments went by, and the ex-policeman turned to the man in the uniform sitting beside him.

"Let me go . . ." he whispered.

"Shut up!" barked the big former prisoner.

"I'm innocent," pleaded the ex-policeman. "You know I never . . ."

"Tell it to the judge," drawled the other indifferently.

"The judge?" repeated the policeman. He sat hunched over on the seat with a drooping mustache. It suits this guy to be a prisoner, I thought. This was the most profound thought I could dredge up just then.

"Give me a break . . ." he started again with a mournful smile. "You know, I have a little daughter at home . . ."

"Oh yeah? Well, so do I." The retired prisoner cut him short, glanced at his watch, and said, "Get up! 'Tenshun! Make it snappy!"

"Where to?" asked the policeman, turning pale.

"To the courthouse!" ordered the prisoner. "Forward march!"

"Already?" whispered the policeman, shuffling his feet. The prisoner bullied him out of the compartment and closed the door behind them. There. It was over. I still couldn't move. For a second I saw the former prisoner's face again, framed in the glass of the compartment door—a smiling face, a friendly face, in fact. He looked back at me and put a finger to his lips, as though asking me to keep mum about all that I had witnessed. One moment he was there, the next he was gone.

That was that.

Even now, some thirty years later, the memory of that moment troubles me, and I'd like, if I may, to let off some steam and tell you that in the next chapter I plan to introduce something new: from here on in, every chapter will have a name, a name that hints at its contents.

Or a nickname.

I wished the train would turn in its tracks. I wanted to go home, to

Gabi and Dad, especially Dad. I mean, he is an expert on crime, and I wasn't up to this sort of thing yet, sorry to disappoint you.

And then I saw the envelope on the former prisoner's seat. But what was it doing there? It wasn't there before they entered the compartment. And the weirdest part was that I saw my name written on it in a large, familiar scrawl.

3

Tenderhearted Elephants

"Greetings to the Bar Mitzvah Boy, and may the gods grant you length of days and brevity of nose. I hope you were not too upset by the little prank we played on you, your dad and I, and that even though it may have been somewhat alarming, you will, ere long, forgive us, your unworthy servants."

What was I supposed to do? Scream? Stick my head out the train window and shout, "I am such an idiot!" Or write a letter to UNICEF complaining about the way Dad and Gabi were treating me?

"But before you write your letter of complaint to the United Nations," Gabi went on, "consider this: first, the good folks there are tired of deciphering your hieroglyphic scribbles, and second, it is customary to give the accused a chance to speak before sentencing."

The words danced slowly before my eyes. I had to stop reading. How did they do it, she and Dad? How did they think this up? When did they find the time to plan such a caper? And where did they come up with those two, the policeman and the prisoner? Could it be that . . . But . . . I am such an idiot . . . I leaned back and shut my eyes: what if they were only actors . . . I could run through the train and search the other cars . . . but they'd most likely changed out of their costumes by now, so I wouldn't recognize them among all the passengers.

I turned from the letter and stared out the window at the scenery. The whole thing was Gabi's idea, that much was certain. I felt a little guilty for being so ungrateful after the trouble she'd obviously gone to, but I just sat there, stunned, and kind of gloomy, though I didn't know why.

Maybe their extravagant surprise hadn't left enough room in me for gratitude. If Gabi had had children of her own, I mused, then stopped myself. It wasn't nice even to think something like that. But she really did seem to enjoy shocking people at times, and liked to say the wickedest things and embarrass them half to death. Dad once remarked to her that it must get kind of tiring, having to be so special all the time, and Gabi flashed back that he spent so much energy keeping a low profile, he was half erased by now.

Gabi has a dangerous mouth on her, but Dad's no slouch either: a few well-chosen words from him would cut her like a knife, you could tell how deeply from the look on her face and the way she gasped and flapped her hands, breathless and speechless. And the words would still haunt her years later, no matter how much Dad tried to reassure her that he hadn't meant it, he had just been angry. But she couldn't put the insult behind her. He had called her insensitive, said something to the effect that she had the hide of an elephant, too. It was this "too," this unfortunate allusion to another elephantine feature that made her leave.

This sort of thing would happen once every few months. Gabi would run out of the house and disappear. At work, she would be inordinately courteous to Dad and about as friendly as a cold fork. She would follow his instructions to the letter and type his reports, but there were no smiles between them, no familiarities. Behind his back, she would phone me twice a day so we could work out strategies. Normally it would take him about a week to break down. First he would start grumbling about the food in the cafeteria, and then he would complain that the shirts he ironed himself were a disgrace to the department, and that our house was filthier than a jail cell the morning after. I knew he was trying to drag me into the fight, so I held my tongue. I refrained from pointing out that Gabi was not our servant, that she only kept house for us out of the goodness of her heart (and because she was allergic to dust). It was obvious to me that he missed her a lot, not merely as a cook or a laundress but as our Gabi; he was used to her being around the house, to her never-ending chatter, her emotional outbursts, and the jokes he tried not to laugh at.

And he also missed her, I knew, because she made it easier for him to be with me.

Why this was so, why the two of us needed Gabi to feel close to each other, I can't explain. We both just knew it was good to have her there, because she made us, him and me, into a kind of family.

So then we'd have a few more days of sulking and grumbling. And eventually Dad would try to find a pretext to engage her in friendly conversation at work, and she would harden her heart and say that unfortunately his subtleties were lost on her, due to a certain pathological condition of her hide. And he would beg her to return and promise to be nicer, and she would answer that his request had been duly noted and that he could expect her final decision within thirty days. And Dad would shout, "Thirty days, that's insane! I want to make up with you here and now!" And Gabi would roll her eyes and announce in a voice like the one over the loudspeaker at the supermarket that before entering any agreement, she would present him with her NRP's, or New Relationship Provisos; whereupon, with head held high, she would exit the room.

And phone me right away to whisper that the old grouch had surrendered unconditionally once again, and we would all be going out for dinner.

On these peacetime evenings Dad seemed almost happy. His eyes would shine after a few beers as he recounted the old stories we knew so well, like the one about busting the Japanese con man with the fake jewelry, or about the time he had to share a kennel with a dog for three days, a boxer bitch from Belgium with a pedigree and a million fleas—so he could catch a dognapper who'd crossed the sea to steal the priceless canine. From time to time Dad would interrupt the story and ask suspiciously whether he'd ever told it to us before, and we would shake our heads and say, No no, please go on, and as I watched him I could see that once upon a time he had been young and adventurous.

I sat in the train, thinking it would take me weeks to absorb everything—the policeman and the prisoner entering the compartment, raising their handcuffs over me, asking me to decide whether the prisoner had looked into the policeman's eyes or not, and handing me a gun, and the way my finger twitched on the trigger when I thought the prisoner was about to escape through the window.

In short, I felt like a couple of kids coming home from the movies, saying, Remember when this, remember when that.

But unlike these young film buffs, I was not at all pleased. And the more I thought about what had just happened, the more furious I grew. How could Dad stay with a person like Gabi for so long, I wondered. If Gabi had been a real mother, she would have understood what such a prank might do to a kid like me.

My pride was injured, too, not so much because she had fooled me but because I suddenly realized I was still a child, and grownups could plan things behind my back.

Dad was definitely an accomplice. While Gabi directed the performance and wrote the actors' lines, he was in charge of production. First she'd had to convince him that it could be done, and when he remained skeptical, she said it truly amazed her to see a man like him getting so worked up about such a simple operation. I'm sure she used the word "operation." She knew that would get him. And still he hesitated, I know he did. In some respects he knows me better than she does. I mean, I am his blood, after all. He must have told her that this grand production might be too much for a kid, that the humor would be lost on me. And she laughed and said he should only have one quarter of Nonny's sense of humor, and that before he got to be such a stick-in-the-mud, he had earned himself a certain reputation—or were all those stories about him just a lot of hot air? So what could he do, he had to prove to her that he was still the dashing young man who used to tear through the streets of Jerusalem on a motorcycle with a sidecar and a tomato plant; and they went on and on, never asking themselves how the poor bar mitzvah boy felt about any of this.

There was a sour smell of perspiration in the compartment, the lingering smell of the policeman and the prisoner. I wondered how they had planned this escapade. Was it hard to learn the lines, I wanted to ask, and where did they find those costumes, and the ball and chain, and how much did it cost to put on a performance just for me, and how about train fare, the tickets must have been pretty expensive, too, maybe Dad and Gabi had reserved every seat in the compartment to prevent any hitches. This was some big operation.

Gradually I felt better. After all, they had meant well. They only wanted to make me happy. They'd tried so hard, it was really nice of them . . . Wasn't this fun. I sat there, muttering to myself, till I felt calm enough to pick up Gabi's note again, and then I saw that the writing had changed.

"As usual, the whole idea was Miss Gabriella's," scrawled Dad in big black letters. "Only, once she'd convinced me that you were going to have a perfectly wonderful time, our valiant Gabi suddenly got cold feet—what if it proved too much of a shock for you, and I told her—well, you can probably guess what I told her."

That at my age he was already running his father's business, and that life is no insurance policy.

"Right!" exulted Gabi's small round letters. "And since your father, being a member of the Israeli police force, does not even have a quarter of a business to leave you, but only a fat pile of bills . . ." (here Gabi sprinkled three drops of liquid on the paper and drew a balloon around them with the words: "The tears of the crocodile amanuensis") . . . he is therefore duty-bound to toughen you up as your bar mitzvah draws near, in order to prepare you for the struggles, challenges, and dangers of life. But first, my little fledgling, I must inform you that the meeting with your uncle, the esteemed Dr. Samuel Shilhav, will not take place today as planned. And at this point I shall pause to let you commune with your grief." Outside, a white-haired farmer with a sunburned face riding across the field in a mule cart was jolted suddenly by the loud whoop that came from the boy at the train window.

"I am sorry, my dear neglected child, for having cruelly misled you to believe that you were heading for Haifa and the talons of that eminent educator, your uncle. We only resorted to such baseness in order to heighten the surprise and allay your suspicions, and for this we humbly beg your pardon."

I, too, bowed humbly before a fleeting image of my big, clumsy dad cracking his knuckles, and Gabi, curtsying like a ballerina with laughing eyes. I was utterly confused by the changes of the last hour: my misery about the trip to Haifa and the trick they had played on me quickly gave way to a thrill of anticipation. I felt like that tank filling up and emptying out in the famous algebra problem.

Tight, dark letters invaded the bouncy round ones.

"Thirteen is a special age, Nonny, the age when you assume responsibility for your actions and behavior. When I was your age, because of the catastrophes that befell the Jewish people, I . . ."

A long, crooked line across the page here indicated that a certain plump hand had snatched the letter away from the pen, which was becoming lost in reminiscence.

"Your father forgets that this is not a police briefing," Gabi's writing continued, "and I sometimes wonder whether he is in fact so different from his brother Samuel . . ."

"Once you reach the age of thirteen you are no longer a child," Dad's black pen reiterated, "and though I wish I could be certain that you'll undergo your transformation precisely then, unfortunately . . ."

Here there were three blank lines. I could imagine them arguing in the kitchen, what she said and what he said. Gabi losing her temper and stamping her foot, and Dad insisting that they had to use the opportunity to teach me a lesson, and the winner, as usual, was the stronger of the two.

"Having persuaded your father to fix himself a cup of coffee, I can now continue uninterrupted," she went on in a feverish scrawl.

"Dearest Nonny, your grouchy old dad is right, as usual: thirteen is a special age that marks the beginning of adulthood. I only hope you will be as nice an adult as you are a child."

I knew that here she would write: "says Gabi fawningly," or "says Gabi groveling at the feet of the heir to millions," as she usually did after expressing affection. Only this time she didn't.

"And we both wanted to plan something very special for your bar mitzvah, in addition to the shindig on Saturday and the camera your father promised you. We wanted to give you something money can't buy, something to remind you of the three of us together, you, your dad, and I, while you were still a boy."

Those words, "the three of us," reminded me of the trouble that was brewing: did "the three of us" mean we were going to be a permanent unit from now on, with Dad's consent? Or was there a note of farewell in her words? I read them over. Everything seemed momentous to me. I couldn't quite make up my mind. On the one hand, it was encouraging that Dad and Gabi had managed to plan such a complicated operation together, without any help from me. That seemed a good omen. Well done, bravo! On the other hand, the words had a parting tone I found alarming. "Something to remind you of the three of us together." What did she mean by that, I wondered. Weren't we together anymore?

"And so we came up with this idea. That is, I came up with a modest idea, which in typical fashion your father developed into a major operation, oops, there he goes, pulling the letter away from—"

The writing changed again. The tug-of-war was over, leaving a large coffee stain in the margin.

"Justice has triumphed!" proclaimed Dad's big ugly scrawl. "Let us not waste words! On this journey, anything can happen! Why, you may never get to Haifa! You may end up having the most incredible, hair-raising adventure of your life!"

It was touching the way Dad imitated Gabi to make me like him better, kind of like a trained bear trying to dance the hora, and though he never laughed at my jokes, I was generous enough to smile.

And he continued: "Perhaps you'll meet new friends, or old enemies! Or maybe you'll meet us! Get ready, get set, go!"

"But first, how about a little scratch between the ears?" Gabi slipped in, very tiny.

Nice girl, nice Gabi. I remote-scratched the frizzy hair between her ears, and Gabi purred with her legs crossed in the air and her tongue hanging out, and jumped up to write the following in a single breath:

"The adventures we've planned for you are about to commence, if you so desire. But if, God forbid, you do not, just stay put for the next four excruciatingly boring hours, all the way to Haifa, and when you get there take the next train back to Jerusalem and you'll never know what you've missed.

"But if you are a valiant youth, rise up, O Nonny the Lionhearted, and boldly meet your fate!"

Gabi writes the way she talks. Sometimes I think Dad and I must be the only people in the world who understand her.

"Should you decide to embark on the perilous course we have painstakingly laid out for you, step down to the third compartment on your left (on your left with your back to the window, Columbus, let's not discover India by mistake!). And what awaits you there? God only knows (and He'll keep mum, as usual). You will be met by someone, though we cannot divulge to you whether this person will be male or female, young or old, or give you any kind of description. Seat number 3 will be empty and waiting for your little tush. Sit down there, and check out your fellow passengers. Choose one of them to be your partner in the adventure, approach, and say the secret password."

"What secret password?" I asked aloud.

"Shh!" scolded Gabi. "The walls have ears! No . . . that's not the password. The password is a question. Choose someone and ask, 'Who am I?' That's all there is to it."

"Who am I?" I muttered a couple of times. Nothing easier.

My God, I shuddered again: look what they've cooked up here, and without any help from me!

"If you make the right choice, the stranger will tell you what your name is, entitling him to act as your guide for the rest of the adventure. He will be eager to regale you in his wild and mysterious way, and as soon as you recover from this episode, you will be sent to your next stop in this game of ours, where you will be awaited by yet another character whose only desire will be to amuse you till your little ears perk up more sharply than ever, and having achieved this, you will be sent to the next stop, and the next, and the next—whereupon . . . you will find a real surprise!"

I put down the letter and took a deep breath. Everything had happened so quickly that only now did I begin to grasp the full scope of their plan. How many days and nights had they spent making these arrangements and coaching the actors? Maybe they even wrote a special part for each of them to perform for me, and just for me . . . Ah hah! I gasped. I tried to read on, but couldn't, my eyes were getting bleary, and I knew that Dad had planned this the way he planned his police operations: studying every angle, every contingency, every possible and impossible course of action . . . and I felt proud that they had gone to so much trouble over me, and kind of amazed, too, because I'd always believed they needed me around to communicate with each other, and that without me, they wouldn't know how to behave, and that it was my responsibility to keep them from fighting, yet now, all on their own . . .

"Nonny the Lionhearted," wrote Gabi. "Nonny, my Nonny, if you use your intelligence and the discerning eye of the world's foremost detective to identify the character who awaits you in each car, you will enter one of the most fabulous adventures ever fabulated for a boy of thirteen. And when you leave this train at journey's end, you will be truly worthy of your age, a high-spirited youth who has passed through an ordeal of cunning and courage. In short—"

And here Dad grabbed the paper and tooted his own horn in big ugly letters:

IN SHORT, YOU'LL BE LIKE ME!

"The important thing is to be yourself." Gabi closed with a doodle of a kiss, Dad's square face, and her own round one with a pair of rabbit ears, surmounted by a halo.

I sat awhile, wondering how Gabi and Dad had managed to transform this creaky old train into a mobile funfair. At this very moment, persons unknown, young or old, male or female, were waiting for me to find them in their respective cars, according to plan. Yes, they were waiting for me, little me, with faces so inscrutable that the passengers next to them would never guess for whose sake they had boarded this train, would never dream that the entire journey was taking place for the benefit of one boy. But if I did not approach and ask my simple question—because suppose I turned out to be not so very brave and high-spirited after all—then they'd sit there in vain, the whole way to Haifa . . .

4

My Debut in a Monocle

I walked out of the compartment. The left side is the side you wear your watch on (Dad taught me that), the side your heart is on (Gabi), so I turned to the left. Slowly I walked—don't run—trying to keep a low profile. Craggy hills flew by the window, the rocks nearly grazing the train; as we rounded the bend I saw the caboose behind us, then it disappeared. In those days, the trains on the Jerusalem–Haifa line had closed compartments, four to a coach, linked by a corridor so narrow, a man standing there to look out the window would completely block the way. I, however, being slim, would have had little trouble getting by such a person, who would no doubt have watched me pass out of the corner of his eye, disappointed that I'd hindered him in the performance of his traditional role.

Farther along the corridor I had to struggle with the door, a heavy iron door that stubbornly resisted me. I had to push with my hands and feet. When I finally forced it open a crack and squeezed through, I found myself in the passage to the next car, where I was suddenly knocked over by a terrible booming, clanging, creaking, and screeching, and under my feet there were two black plates that locked into each other like wrestlers in a stranglehold. I didn't dare step over them, so I jumped with my eyes shut and nearly fell, because they tried to throw me, bucking under my feet, because maybe I'd made a mistake, maybe passengers weren't allowed to pass from one car to another while the train was in motion, so I hopped from foot to foot to avoid staying on either plate for longer than a second. Who would have believed such perils lurked so close to where the passengers were talking peacefully? The wind whistled all around me, and through the cracks I could see the ground speeding by and hear the noisy rumbling of the wheels and the creaking and shrieking of iron and steel: one wrong move and down I'd go.

I couldn't think straight. Noise confuses me. And such awful noise from every direction, it was enough to drive me crazy. I didn't have enough protective skin suddenly to keep out the world, and I might be sucked into the whirlpool of noise and burst down the middle, and I'd never even realize that I was the one who was screaming.

Let me through, I screamed at the heavy door, damn you, let me through, and I pounded and kicked and butted with my head. There were times when I could butt at an iron door without getting hurt. At school they had a special name for that, but on the train it actually worked, Mount Feuerberg erupted and the iron door opened a crack, but even that was enough. I was light as a scream, so I managed to squeeze through and close the door, leaving the whirlpool behind me, good riddance.

I took a deep breath. The din subsided. It was a "comin' round the mountain" train again, though from that moment on I would look at it differently.

And so—

Who am I?

I began to mutter, rehearsing my line.

Who am I? Who am I? Who?

First compartment. I walked by without a glance. Second compartment—without a glance. Third compartment. I paused outside the door.

This, I believe, was when I became aware of a small problem.

Suppose I went in. Suppose seat number 3 was empty, as Gabi promised. Suppose I could even identify the person waiting for me there. How would I find the nerve to turn and ask, Who am I?

What would the other passengers think? I could just imagine them glaring at me.

One of Gabi's typical schemes, I grumbled. Dad would never have gotten me into this fix. He would know how embarrassing it is.

Who am I?

I think it's time to tell you a little about myself.

When all this took place, exactly twenty-seven years ago, I was a few days shy of thirteen, a perfectly normal kid, in my opinion, though there were other opinions, so let me present the undisputed facts:

Name: Nonny Feuerberg. Place of birth: Jerusalem. Family status: single (naturally), and likewise: one father, one Gabi. Best friend: Micah Dubovsky. Distinguishing features: a deep scar on the right shoulder. A bullet on a chain around the neck. Other particularities: my hobby.

My hobby was the police. By age thirteen I'd memorized the shield number of every police officer in the Southern District. I was familiar with every type of police weapon and vehicle. I had my own collection of wanted posters at home dating back five years. And I had another collection, possibly the largest in Israel, of missing-persons notices. In addition to this, I was able—in ways best not divulged—to get my hands on all the top-secret documents that Gabi typed, including autopsy reports of famous murder cases, crime scene sketches, and photocopies of forensic files. Twice I spoke to the Police Commissioner himself, on the steps of district headquarters and at the wedding of a superintendent. At the wedding he called me—everybody heard him—the district mascot.

Who am I? Who am I?

And what if I picked the wrong guy?

Would I have the nerve to approach anyone else after that? In the same compartment?

Better cool off awhile and think it over.

The first thing you do—I addressed myself in Dad's voice—is learn everything you can about your opponents. Pick up information. That's what he taught me: Knowledge is power. How many times have I heard him say those words: "Knowledge is powerrrr!," making a fist and pounding it for emphasis. I could never be sure which was more important to him, knowledge or power.

Who am I?

Here was compartment 3 already. This train was going too fast for me.

First try—I hurried past in such a dither that I hardly dared to look in. But straightaway I turned in my wobbly tracks and made a second attempt, forcing myself to peek inside this time. There were five people in there and one empty seat between them marked off with a red ribbon and a tag that said: *Reserved.*

Ho ho!

I went back for a third try, taking it more slowly this time. I could see that there were three men and two women inside. A man with glasses was reading a newspaper. The women were both slender: the elderly one wore her hair in a bun, the other wore bangs. There wasn't much I could deduce from that. I walked by again. The elderly woman nudged the man sitting beside her, indicating me with her eyes. She had a sour expression that reminded me of my grandmother Tsitka, but I was beginning to make a little progress just the same: I noticed a man wearing a tall black hat. Very strange: he looked like a diplomat. Or an executioner. A chilling question entered my mind: What was an executioner doing on the train to Haifa?

I stopped. Pivoted sharply. Turned back. Didn't stop this time. But I needed a cover, some excuse for all the scurrying back and forth outside their compartment. Because the secret of a successful stakeout—according to a certain person—is to believe your own cover; i.e., if you go out disguised as a beggar, do it with all your heart, despise cheapskates and bless the generous. When you dress as a woman, be a woman in every way: your walk, your gestures, your preference for one display window over another. Make a wrong move and you give the whole show away, Dad would tell me, narrowing his eyes till the crease between them darkened ominously. "Listen, Nonny, when an actor flops, all he gets is a bad review, but a blundering detective is liable to end up with a bullet in his head!" And he inadvertently touched his shoulder, as I touched the bullet on the chain around my neck. We looked into each other's eyes. He had never told me the name of the person who shot him, and I didn't dare ask. There were certain subjects we didn't broach, subjects that called for a manly silence.

Again I walked by the compartment, for the fifth time in a row, maybe, frowning with concentration, my arms folded over my chest.

Was I ever lost in thought! That's how it is for a young genius like me, on the verge of inventing the pendulum.

But then, despite my excellent cover, all five passengers in the compartment sat forward to take a better look at me, and due to their exaggerated attention, I was unable to turn up any more clues regarding my suspect, the man in the executioner's hat. I did recall, though, that he had been wearing a red bow tie. I stopped. To change my cover? Was I, perhaps, too young to pass for a young scientist? Or did they suspect that the pendulum had already been invented?

Time was running out. Soon we would be pulling into Haifa station. There and then I changed my cover, turned on my heel, cursed Gabi, and walked by the compartment again, this time as a young actor in the role of a tormented Ping-Pong ball, but they all turned to the window—including the executioner—and started whispering together. , Actually, they may have been talking out loud, or even shouting angrily, only I couldn't hear them through the glass.

No good. How many more times could I walk past them before they pounced on me and dragged me screaming into the compartment? With bated breath I stood at the door. All five of them turned to glare at me. Blinking courageously, I entered the compartment, and nearly fell over them, under them, and between them. I stepped on every foot in sight before groping my way to the empty seat with the red ribbon and the *Reserved* sign, where I sank down, finally, frozen with fear, though my ears were burning hot.

Five pairs of reproachful eyes were upon me, surprised that the seat of honor had been taken by a child.

Five pairs of reproachful eyes?

But wasn't one of them supposed to know I was coming?

They all looked so stern.

I didn't have the nerve to look back at anyone.

And then, cautiously, I took a peek . . .

Casually . . . glancing this way and that . . .

She'll be comin' round the mountain . . .

Bangs . . . bald head . . . glasses . . . top hat . . .

Who am I? Who am I?

The train is rattling and shaking like me. I've never asked a stranger who I am before. Who am I? . . . Who-am-I? . . . WhoamI?

But suppose the man in the top hat turns out to be the Swedish ambassador on a sightseeing tour of the country, what then?

Or a chef in mourning? I quickly looked him over: a tall, grim, tight-lipped character, someone who might slap your face for asking an impertinent question.

But wait a minute!

That roly-poly guy sitting next to him . . . the baldy with the red face, wide round nostrils, and fat lips; he looks like a pastry chef, or maybe a balloon inflator. He's staring out the window, muttering to himself, possibly rehearsing the big scene when I turn to him and ask the question!

Or the girl in the blue jeans. I broadcast her description over my imaginary radio: blue patch on left knee, green T-shirt. Brown hair, cut short, with bangs. Small khaki bag. Distinguishing features? None. What a boring face. End of description, over and out.

Or that old lady who looks like Tsitka, Dad's mother, and also my grandmother, I regret to say, but that's another story—could she actually be in on the game?

Maybe Dad had a secret motive: four hours of this was surely worth a month of training . . . an accelerated practical course . . . and to pass it, I'd have to use every trick in the book . . . What a bar mitzvah present, I thought with some dismay, though a Swiss watch wouldn't be so bad, either.

One face, another face, a smile, a nose, a mouth. Dad used to say that every face is like a book, you only have to learn how to read it. And a real pro can tell just about everything from a person's face and lines and wrinkles. For my tenth birthday he made me an IdentiKit, just like the one he had at the office. He drew all the transparencies himself, the noses and chins, the beards and eyebrows, and the eyes and ears—everything that goes on a face— Handing me the kit, he said, "Here—read this, the most interesting book in the world."

Time was passing, the train sped on, and still I couldn't decide who my man was, though more and more I suspected the top hat, who sat rigidly erect, his eyes under a bushy awning and his mouth set in an angry scowl. Though I was pretty certain he was the man, somehow he frightened me more than the others. Or was it this very fear that Dad and Gabi hoped I would overcome? I cast an anguished glance his way. Please, sir, smile at me. Even a hairline smile would help me get started. But he wouldn't budge. He looked like Dad when I try to make him laugh.

I failed. I was a coward. Why didn't anyone offer to help?

They just kept staring, staring at me shamelessly. How did I look to them? Like a skinny blond kid with a short haircut (the only style the police barber knew) and big blue eyes, widely set, which could be disconcerting if you tried to look into them both at the same time. Yep, that was me. The unobservant might take me for a goody-goody. "Ah, you're the picture of an angel," Gabi would sigh. "But in your heart lurk the seven deadly sins!" Because the picture didn't show the vein throbbing in my neck so hard it hurt, or the burning in my cheeks, or my fluttering fingers, or the way my eyes would dart anxiously around: Who wants to hear how I (almost) caught a pickpocket single-handedly once? Anyone interested in buying a used compass or a dog whistle? Want to hear a joke?

"This kid has ears like an elf," Gabi would add, touching them in wonder. "See how pointy they are? Who are you, a boy or a wildcat?"

WhoamI, whoamI . . .

I couldn't. I just couldn't ask them who I was. A hundred times I tried to whisper the words, but they crumbled in my mouth. What would Dad think of me now? He would snort with contempt because I'd failed him again. Here he had planned such a wonderful surprise and I wasn't even enjoying it.

Before I realized what I wanted to do, Mount Feuerberg decided for me, spewing me out into the corridor like lava.

Now what? I couldn't go back. Should I just give up the adventure? Nonny's a coward, a rabbit-hearted coward.

I walked away. Standing by the window at the end of the coach, I hated myself. I knew that the mystery man Dad and Gabi had posted in the compartment would report how I had disgraced myself and Dad.

Who am I?!

But now that I'd worked up my courage, now that it was bursting out of me, I didn't want to lose momentum. Over and over I whispered, WhoamI? WhoamI? and went on whispering as I slowly turned around and doubled back to the third compartment, afraid that if I stopped for even a second I would lose my nerve, and after every tiny step I thought, I'll just close my eyes and walk in without looking, and ask that guy over there, and whatever happens happens, and still whispering to myself, I shuffled along, but noticed that every time I asked the question, I felt a sharp pang inside, as though there were somebody knocking in there to get my attention, and the more I whispered, "Who am I?" the more bitterness I felt in my heart.

It was strange that I had never asked such a simple question before. I knew who I was, everybody knew, I was me, Nonny, the Jerusalem district mascot, with a father and a Gabi, and a best friend named Micah, and future plans to work with Dad, but just then, for some reason, I had a feeling maybe there were a lot of other answers, maybe things weren't so cut-and-dried, and my heart sank, weighing me down till I almost didn't care anymore about this adventure, and wondered glumly, What's the matter with me, who am I? . . .

Just then I caught sight of someone gazing at me through the glass partition with a strange look in his eye, as though he didn't really see me. I stopped; that is, I was stopped in my tracks by the expression on his face. I knew, I just knew I reminded him of someone, because he kept looking at me with a dreamy, faraway smile. I stood directly in front of him, keeping perfectly still. He seemed to want me to stand there and pose so he could concentrate on his memory.

Then his eyes focused sharply. They penetrated the bewildering reflections in the train windows and stared directly at me, yes, me, with quizzical affection, as his long leg jiggled over his knee, and he fished something out of his pocket, a round piece of glass hanging from a fine gold chain. He put the glass to his eye, wedged between his cheek and his eyebrow. I had seen something like this in a movie once: a monocle, that's what it's called. The kind English gentlemen wear.

Hey, I'm being watched through a monocle! I realized happily, raising my head high and thinking noble thoughts to improve my reflection, because it isn't every day an Israeli kid makes an appearance in a monocle.

But even as he watched me, I did not neglect my professional duties: I guessed he must be seventy or so, with a deep tan and the handsome face of a stranger from a distant land. His eyes were blue and clear and smiling, the eyes of a baby in a manly face, with sun-baked wrinkles radiating from the corners and a distinctive pair of bushy eyebrows overarching them; in between there loomed the nose, and what a nose! A stately nose, a monumental nose, a nose of such grandeur one was prompted to bow down before it. And fine white hair that curled down behind his ears, making him look like a distinguished old painter.

He was alone in the compartment—of course he was, because there was no one else like him on the train. He wore an elegant white suit and a tie as bright as a tropical bird. And that's not all: there was a fresh red rose in his lapel and a handkerchief folded in his pocket. To this day I remember every detail. There weren't many people in Israel in those days who dressed that way. Who could afford to buy a suit back then? And anybody who happened to own one certainly wouldn't wear it on a train, least of all the Haifa train.

Yet I knew at a glance that the suit belonged to him, that he wasn't an actor wearing a costume. It was as much his own as the rose he had picked for his lapel. There was an ease about the man, as if his clothes felt good on him.

And another thing: for a minute he resembled Dad. Though not physically. I don't really know why he reminded me of Dad just then. Maybe because of his solitude in the compartment. In every other way he was completely different. Most of the time Dad looked—I have to admit it—like an SOS, as Gabi used to say (a sweaty ornery slob). And this man seemed happy, like someone who enjoys life, who knows how to relax and has time to take a lively interest in everything and everyone around him. But there was also an invisible line setting him apart from his surroundings. Maybe that's a sign of true nobility, because he definitely had that. And the feeling inside me was so strong by now that without a second thought, I opened the door to his compartment; I did so in direct defiance of the letter from Dad and Gabi setting forth the rules of the game, because I didn't care, I could always catch up later; I walked straight over to him and asked in a loud clear voice, Who am I?

And he beamed an even bigger smile, and crossed his other leg, and took a long look at me, and the scent of his aftershave filled the compartment, and his cheek muscle twitched and the monocle dropped into his waiting palm and disappeared into his pocket; it was unbelievable, like in a movie. But he hadn't answered my question yet. I tingled with anticipation, that pleasant excitement you feel sometimes when you're about to solve a riddle. He, too, I could see, was savoring the moment. I truly hoped he would know the answer. Here was the partner I wanted for the game.

"You are Amnon Feuerberg," he said at last. His voice sounded surprisingly high-pitched, and he had a Romanian accent. "But at home you are called by your father—Nonny."

5

Wait, Is He a Good Guy

or a Bad Guy?

I was speechless. I held out my hand and he shook it. Then he said, "Begging your pardon, I forget to mention: Felix is my name!" And I thought, Gee, I hope I have hands like his someday, long and strong and finely shaped. And I began to bubble inside like boiling milk. I don't know what got into me, maybe it was the way he looked. I held my hand out again, and again he shook it, probably realizing that I needed to touch him one more time in order to imprint his strong, slender fingers, so that when I grew up, I would be able to duplicate them together with his regal nose and lion's mane and crinkly blue eyes, and his nobility and everything else about him.

Had I been less shy, I would have shown him I could climb into the luggage rack and hang by my ankles, or do a handstand in a moving train. But it took all my strength just to put on a civilized front and assume an upright stance.

"Please to sit, Mr. Feuerberg," he said gently, as though he sensed my inner turmoil and wished to help me relax. I sat down. I wanted him to give me more things to do so I could show him how obedient I was. Whereupon he pulled a black-and-white photograph out of his suit pocket, studied it carefully, looked back at me, and said, smiling, "Just like in picture, only better."

He handed the picture to me. It was one I'd never seen before, showing me on my way home from school in a billowing gray coat. Dad must have taken it from the car when I wasn't looking.

"Shot with a telephoto lens, right?" I said to this Felix character, to show him I know what's what. "He gave it to you so you'd recognize me, right?"

A manly blue smile flashed from his crinkly eyes. I thought I would faint. He looked like a movie star. I returned the smile and touched the corners of my eyes, but couldn't make anything crinkle. How many years would it take for me to get those three deep wrinkles there? His looked as if they'd been there all his life. He was still poring over the photograph. I suddenly realized that there might be others on this train carrying pictures of me for identification purposes! I couldn't believe the lengths Dad had gone to over me!

I leaned forward to get a better look, and a better whiff of Felix's aftershave, too. My best friend, Micah Dubovsky, was in the picture, standing two steps behind me, openmouthed.

"And this is your friend," said Felix amiably, though he didn't sound too pleased with Micah. Micah looked kind of goofy there, catching flies.

"He's not such a close friend," I quickly explained. "I mean, we play together and all. Actually, he's my deputy." At home we called him "my man Friday," and Gabi used to make fun of him sometimes, but he was okay, I guess, as a deputy.

"You wish to tell me more about him?" asked Felix, crossing his arms over his chest as if he had all the time in the world to hear stories about Micah. "What's there to tell?" I answered. "He's just this kid I know who's been with me for years. He thinks I'm his friend, but I only hang around with him out of pity," I added with a giggle, wondering why we were wasting so much time on Micah, though Micah was an okay guy, I guess.

"So, your best friend is who?" Felix wanted to know. "From what you tell me, I think it is Micah!"

Oops, now I was in trouble. Maybe Dad had provided Felix with detailed information about me, and because I was afraid he wouldn't like Micah, that Micah wasn't worthy of someone as noble as Felix, I put him down when actually he was okay.

"Micah is uhm . . ." But I didn't want to talk about Micah. What was there to say about him? Just that he was the type of kid who was always around.

"Actually, he's my bodyguard," I started to explain, and then, before I knew it, I heard the buzz in the middle of my forehead, the sound of the motor heating up in there. "But the truth is"—I went on earnestly, listening to my tongue roll in my mouth so I would know what to say next—"my number-one best friend is Chaim Stauber. He's a real friend. He's special. I mean, he's a genius. We've been friends for years. Boy, the things we've done together!"

And there was Micah staring out of the picture, looking like such a dope, with his mouth hanging open. He always stared that way, as though he were in a trance or something, whenever I started talking big and telling terrible whoppers. But he never corrected me in front of the other kids, never said a word. Sometimes it drove me crazy; I could do anything I wanted, tell lies about him, things he had to know were lies, and he would just listen to me with his tongue hanging out, like a lazy dog.

And now this handsome, well-dressed man was listening to me, too, but not at all stupidly. He nodded, deep in thought, till I felt he was looking into my heart and that he knew all there was to know about me and Micah, and about my recent betrayal.

But I couldn't stop myself. The buzzing between my eyes felt good. It was like being tickled there with a feather to stimulate the invention center of the brain. "Wow, Chaim Stauber, too bad you've never met him! What a kid! He knows the whole Bible by heart! And he plays the piano! And he's been everywhere, even Japan! And he skipped two grades!" Most of this was true, but I wanted to make sure Felix knew that I, too, had friends who were men of the world, that they weren't all jerks like Micah. Only, Chaim Stauber wasn't really my friend anymore. After the episode with Mautner's cow, we had to sign a note for the principal and Chaim's mother promising not to exchange another word until after we graduated.

My mood turned glum. Why did I start off this new friendship with lies and betrayal? He seemed so sweetly innocent, smiling like a big baby. Well, too bad. I felt as if I were getting nowhere fast. As if I were missing something, not to mention the game, because soon we would be pulling into Haifa station. So what should I do, I asked the mysterious Felix. Should I start over and play it again, move by move, until I found him? I didn't really feel like doing that, to tell the truth, but Dad and Gabi had gone to so much trouble, and there were people waiting for me, people who'd rehearsed their parts.

Fortunately for me, this person named Felix was no stickler for rules. He smiled a little smile of what seemed like contempt for them, and I smiled, too, though I had no idea what I was smiling about, maybe I just wanted to try his smile on for size, and then he pulled a fine chain out of his trouser pocket, and I could barely refrain from reaching out to touch it: this time it was a silver chain with a big pocket watch. The only one like it I'd ever seen was in a movie called *Pimpernel Smith*. Felix's watch had large square numerals on a white face with a golden ring around it. If I had a watch like that, I thought, I would put it in a safe and only take it out at night, when I was alone. He shouldn't keep something so valuable in his trouser pocket. This Felix character was much too trusting. Hadn't he heard of pickpockets? Or thieves? I could certainly teach him a thing or two, if he'd let me.

Felix closed his eyes and moved his lips as though thinking aloud. "Is like this, perhaps," he said at last in his heavy Romanian accent. "You come earlier than expected, or, another way of saying, your time is coming soon."

I didn't understand a word of this.

"Time now is ten minutes after three o'clock, young Mr. Feuerberg, and we must to arrive at our car by three and thirty-three o'clock. That's right."

"What car?" I asked.

"Oh, did I say car?" He threw up his hands. "Beg pardon! Poor Felix, he grows old! Saying aloud what must to be kept secret! Young Mr. Feuerberg will please to forget everything he has heard and wait patiently for big surprise. Surprises are important, but even more important is to wait for them, not so?"

In those days, the word "secret" was enough to set my right foot trembling, and the word "surprise" would make my left foot positively twitch. Felix didn't know what he was doing when he used those two words in a single sentence.

"Why this hop-hopping, Mr. Feuerberg?" he asked, bending down to pull a brown leather traveling bag from under his seat.

I didn't explain the cause of my strange frenzy.

"My valise is made of leather, made-in-Romania!" He gave the bag a friendly pat. Each time he spoke, his voice surprised me: it sounded old and shrill, and reedy, not the right sort of voice for someone so distinguished. "Ha, my whole life I go everywhere with this valise," he said as he carefully buckled the strap, and then chuckled. "My only friend is this."

As he was speaking, I tried to guess where Dad knew him from and why he'd never mentioned Felix to me. Maybe he was somebody from Special Operations, or one of those legendary detectives sent overseas under a false identity to work with Interpol and the FBI. Sometimes one of them would whisk through the corridors at District Headquarters while home on leave, spreading a trail of mystery behind him. Everyone whispered, A *Shushu* is in town—a secret agent—and then all the secretaries would scurry out on one pretext or another to take a peek. Even Dad used to tense up when a *Shushu* walked past his office. "Remember you saw him," he would say to me, indicating the agent with his eyes, and quickly add, "Now forget you ever saw him," in case I was kidnapped by blackmailers who wanted to squeeze secret information out of me. But the one *Shushu* I happened to catch a glimpse of looked pretty normal in his civilian clothes—he was a short, bald guy with pale arms.

And this Felix character, who was he? What was he? One minute he seemed perfectly innocent, and the next he was peeking out into the corridor, left and right, with the expertise of an absolute *Shushu*. And then an astonishing thought occurred to me: Suppose Felix had once been a bad guy who changed sides and joined the good guys. Why not? Dad had all sorts of connections. It was truly amazing how many people greeted him whenever we walked down the street.

"Come, Mr. Feuerberg," said Felix. "We must to go now."

"Why do you call me Mr. Feuerberg?" I asked. It sounded funny, but kind of annoying, too.

"So how I must to call you, please?"

"Nonny."

"Non-ny?" He tried my name out. "No, no, I cannot call you Nonny . . . We are not major friends yet."

"Why not?" I know, that was stupid of me. It was true that we weren't. But I wanted us to be. So we wouldn't have to waste time on details. That's the kind of person Felix was, he made you want to trust him right away.

"But everybody calls me Nonny."

"Then I must to call you Mr. Feuerberg, because God forbid Felix should do what everybody else is doing, correct?" He looked at his reflection in the window and adjusted his tie.

"Perhaps later," he said, "when two of us are major friends, it is possible I call you Amnon. Only then. Because too close is not good. A person must to have boundaries, yes? For now you will be Mr. Feuerberg to me, and afterward we see, all right?"

Let it be Mr. Feuerberg, then. Somehow, coming from him it sounded fine. I had a teacher once who used to call me that in class, as though she were holding my name with a pair of tweezers. But there was a big difference between her and Felix.

The memory of this teacher brought out the chutzpah in me.

"So why do I call you Felix? Don't you have a last name?"

He turned to me with an approving smile. "It is enough for now, till we get out."

"Out of where?"

"Out of here, this train, this locomotive."

"How are we supposed to get out of the locomotive?"

"We cannot get out of locomotive until we get into it, correct?"

Something cold and white fluttered around my heart, touched it for an instant, then passed, so quickly I didn't have the chance to figure out what it was. A twitter of alarm, perhaps, or a warning. One painful spasm, and that was all; I forgot.

We hurried out of our compartment and headed toward the locomotive. Felix walked quickly ahead of me, alert and catlike. More and more I suspected him of being a *Shushu*. He kept glancing around all the time, like the bodyguard of some VIP. Only I was that VIP, apparently. It was fun to trail behind him with a blank expression on my face, hoping some cold-blooded assassin would come after me and give Felix the chance to pounce on him and knock him out, and then, as I coolly made my way past the cheering crowds, I would whisper to my followers, Such a bore, these assassination attempts.

But it was not an assassin who approached me, it was the man in the top hat. I saw him get up as we passed compartment 3, his mouth opening in a soundless cry and his hand raised as if to stop me. All at once I understood: he had been waiting for me patiently, thinking I had disappeared because I didn't have the nerve to play this game, and suddenly here I was again, but instead of turning to ask "Who am I?," I walked right by and continued the game without him!

Felix noticed him as well. A single glance, sharp as a whip, was enough for him: he grabbed my hand and yanked me past the door of the compartment. He looked so determined, so stern and tough, that for a moment I thought maybe it was no simple prank Dad and Gabi had planned for me but something far more meaningful and important, practically a matter of life and death.

But there was no time to stop and ponder what was going on. It all happened so fast. I was hurled down the corridor, past the the man in the black top hat, though I couldn't quite figure out why I was supposed to run away from him, why Felix didn't simply stop and explain that young Mr. Feuerberg here had decided to skip phase one of the game; and what's wrong with that, Mr. Feuerberg is a free agent!

I looked around and couldn't believe my eyes: there was Felix, leaning against the door of compartment 3 with the silver chain in his hand. No mistake about it: it was his silver watch chain. With one vigorous pull, he managed to tear it out of his pocket and wind it around the door handles, with the watch still attached to it! His hands moved so nimbly, it crossed my mind that he would have made an excellent pickpocket, or perhaps he had been one in the past—and here I'd thought to warn him about pickpockets! I stared at him round-eyed: he couldn't have cared less about the people he was locking into the compartment. As he wound the chain tighter he pursed his lips, and a fine shadow of cruelty played over them, the cruelty of a predator.

And the same shadow appeared over my own lips. It emanated from me, in a fine white line that rose to the surface, like a scar. My brow, too, was creased with effort, like a pro's. Even our hands moved in sync, and I could actually feel the sensations in his fingertips, their tingling nerves, because I had touched them.

The people on the other side of the glass stared at him uncomprehendingly. They were transfixed. The man in the top hat bent his knees as though he couldn't make up his mind whether to stand up or sit down, with one hand hanging limply in midair and his mouth forming a mute, astonished O. The other man, the roly-poly bald fellow, gawked at Felix with a silly smile of disbelief. From behind those two, the woman who looked like Grandma Tsitka peered out, her lips stretched tight with amazement, just like Tsitka, though unlike Tsitka, she didn't say a word.

And neither did I. It was the most fantastic thing I'd ever seen in my life: here was an adult, an old man, in fact, doing things that would have gotten a kid like me permanently expelled from school!

And maybe this is what was so thrilling about it: that someone could be like me and still be an adult.

Felix had no time to waste on the passengers. He made sure the doors were chained fast, grabbed me by the arm, and pushed me toward the locomotive, flashing a smile like blue lightning. "Everything all right now! We must to go!" he said.

"But—but," I protested, "the people in there are . . . They won't be able to . . ."

"Later, later! In the end will come explanation! Hi-deh!"

"What about the watch?" I groaned. Please, let him take the watch at least.

"Watch is not important! Time is important. Not to waste it! Hi-deh!"

"What does hi-deh mean?" I shouted as we ran.

Felix stopped in surprise. "Young Mr. Feuerberg does not know what hi-deh means?"

We stood face-to-face, both panting. The train rocked as we rounded the bend. Sounds sort of like Heidi, I thought, but wisely said nothing.

"Hi-deh is like ho-pah!" Felix laughed, grabbing my hand and bounding ahead with me. "Like 'Go go go!' Like 'Giddyap!' "

"Ah." I understood at last. "Like 'Yempa!' "

We ran through car after car, as the scenery went flying by, outpacing us on the wooden legs of the electric poles. A long green line of eucalyptus trees rushed past, and then a field of sunflowers, and mounds of earth, and straight ahead, more corridors and cars and doors. Sometimes the passengers seemed to glance up and raise their hands in a mute cry of surprise. Maybe they were the people Dad and Gabi had sent to meet me, only I couldn't stop, Felix was pulling me so fast, not that I wanted to stop, and suddenly we were in the very last corridor, where a sign on the heavy door said: ENTRANCE STRICTLY FORBIDDEN, and Felix, who may or may not have known how to read Hebrew, pushed the handle till the heavy door gave way, and there we were, inside the locomotive.

The noise there was even louder. A giant in a filthy undershirt was standing with his back to us, leaning over a big steel box.

He didn't turn around as we entered but only roared, "Engine's running down again! Second time today!" Felix closed the door behind us and bolted it shut. It was blazing hot and right away I started sweating. And the noise, I already told you how noise affects me.

Felix winked at me and tapped the engineer on the shoulder.

The engineer raised himself heavily, turned around, and gaped in surprise.

He must have been expecting somebody else, an assistant or a mechanic or someone, and he demanded to know who we were and why we had barged into the locomotive. He had to shout to make himself heard over the din, and Felix smiled at him so bewilderedly, it was enough to break your heart. Leaning toward the engineer, he shouted in his ear that he was truly sorry, he knew he had broken the rules, but what could he do when little Eliezer here begged to see just once, for the first and last time in his life, what a locomotive looks like.

Those were his very words. And as he gently smoothed my hair, I saw him give the engineer a significant look, with a nod in my direction.

At first I didn't understand what he was saying. He seemed to be lying to the engineer, lying through his teeth, pretending I was, say, a kid he was taking on a farewell trip around the world, to grant my last wishes before I died, God forbid, of some dread disease.

Impossible, I told myself: the noise in there must have made me hear wrong. I smiled at my own stupidity, a nervous little quarter-smile, because how could such a distinguished gentleman concoct a ridiculous lie like that. I mean, as far as I knew, I was a healthy devil with only the mildest of allergies to grass. But when I looked into the engineer's eyes and saw the dismay there, I began to think perhaps I had been right in the first place, perhaps Felix really had said those terrible things in his amiably gentle, sincerely plaintive way.

As for me, I was gone, glued to the side of the locomotive, with the engine roaring up from my heels into my brain. The heat had melted what remained of my wits. It didn't occur to me that my father would never have allowed Felix to involve me in something like this. I trusted him implicitly. Nor did I shout at him to stop, or tell the engineer he was lying. I merely stood there, gazing at him as though I were in a dream.

How did he make up an excuse so quickly and tell such a bold-faced lie?

It would take me years to learn how to control my face the way he did: people can always tell straight off when I'm lying, except Micah, maybe, who for some reason finds my lies extremely fascinating.

But Felix was an adult—and he had told a lie! And a whopper at that, big enough to stun the engineer. Definitely the wrong kind of lie to tell, if only for superstitious reasons!

I stood there, frozen.

But I had to admire him.

Against my will, albeit aghast at his chutzpah, I admired him.

That is the bitter truth.

I was outraged at what he was doing, yes, but also humbly resigned to it. It was as if I had been obliterated, completely wiped out, together with all I'd ever learned and every single finger that had ever wagged "No, no, no!" in front of my nose, and the ghastly furrow between Dad's eyes that grew ominously deeper whenever he was angry, and loomed over me like a permanent exclamation mark. At the last moment, a faint cry seemed to escape my lips, "No! It isn't so! This is all wrong!" But just then a joyful squeal went through me, to the accompaniment of the roaring engine and the rattling locomotive, as if I had been whisked off to another world where such things were permitted, where everything was permitted, where there were no stern-faced teachers or forlorn-looking fathers, and you didn't have to make such an effort to remember what you were and were not allowed to do all the time.

In fact, no effort of any kind was required of you. As soon as you said a thing, it came to be.

Like when God said, "Let there be light," and there was light.

Yes, I admired Felix for tying those people in there, behind the door, just like that, and wasting an expensive silver watch, and for daring to go through a door marked ENTRANCE STRICTLY FORBIDDEN, and for telling the engineer such a horrible lie, the kind of lie it's wrong to tell. As if it was all a game to him and the only law was his law.

But I didn't know the half of what he was capable of yet.

He was deep into his lie by then and believed in it completely, which is the way to lie if you want others to believe you, like a detective working undercover, and as I watched him, I could feel the heat of the buzzing between his eyes. For the first time in my life I sensed that itch in somebody else, and Felix was lying with so much conviction now, looking at me so pityingly, that I, healthy if mildly allergic imp that I was, began to go into a decline; the morbid gray veil in Felix's eyes floated around over me, cloaking me in blissful languor.

That was how it started, the new sensation, the pleasant lightheadedness that nearly made me faint. I wish I could say I fought it off for a while, that I displayed more strength of character. But I didn't fight off or display a darn thing. In a matter of minutes, Felix had made me his accomplice. He didn't even have to train me for the role; it was as if he knew me so well, all he had to do was blow the dust off the real Nonny. The false one, that is . . . Who am I?

I leaned back against the wall. Felix was staring at me, and so was the engineer. I grimaced with pain and shrank into myself. Life, my own precious life, was ebbing away. I felt cold all over. It was sweltering hot inside the locomotive, yet I was shivering. I had converted the shiver caused by Felix's astounding lie into a shiver of sickliness, of melancholy and gloom. I was heartbroken over this terrible disease which even now was consuming my body, and by the velvety black curtain closing on the stage of my young life. My right hand began to tremble like a little animal in the throes of death, a symptom of my illness, no doubt, and totally spontaneous, while my arm flapped at my side, what a trouper, who would have believed it, too bad Gabi wasn't there to see, not that I was thinking about her just then, I put that in just to cover my embarrassment, though I was not in the least embarrassed at the time; in fact, I was proud of myself for having put on such a wonderful act. Felix's eyes grew wide with wonder as I writhed and grimaced and gasped for breath. I was proud that Felix was so pleased with me, as though I were his prize pupil. At long last I was somebody's prize pupil; I mean, acting is an art, isn't it, and writers make up stories, don't they? And isn't a story a kind of lie? I felt the blood throbbing in my temples as the train chugged on, and I gazed feebly at the engineer, pardoning him in advance for thwarting me, with a look that said, "Yes, I know there are rules and regulations, Mr. Engineer, and I don't blame you, friend, for not wishing to bend the rules and bring a little happiness to a child like me. I mean, what is one child's suffering compared to rules and regulations, rules and regulations make the world go round and the sun shine and trains depart on schedule, and there are so many kids like me at death's door, but only this one, very special locomotive." "Oh, thank you, thank you, kind sir," whispered my parched lips when the engineer reached out in the nick of time to stop me from collapsing and offered me a bench, because a lie doesn't have a leg to stand on . . .

It worked. The engineer believed me. I was filled with exhilaration: he believed me! He believed me, Nonny—though hardly anyone ever did, even when I was telling the truth!

Yempa and hi-deh!

The engineer mopped his bald head and face with a sooty blue rag, leaned back in his seat, which was bolted to the floor, and shook his head, not daring to meet my eyes. Instead, he stared at Felix, unaware that in so doing he had sealed his fate. In a low, gruff voice he began to explain how the engine worked, how much power it had: "1,650 horsepower," he declared with a pout and a sideways glance in my direction. He was a clumsy, heavyset man with curly hair growing on his back and arms and even out of his ears. Though no great talker, he tried his best on account of my condition. He even offered me his seat, and leaned over me cautiously, pointing out every switch and lever and gauge, with occasional glances at the door, lest the conductor walk in and discover that he had allowed strangers into the locomotive.

Felix asked him questions, too. Like where the brakes were, and how do you pick up speed, and blow the whistle? The engineer, delighted, even flattered by Felix's interest in the train, forgot his worries for the moment and told us more and more. He showed us the main brake that stops the whole train, and the smaller brake that stops only the loco-motive; he let me pull the whistle switch, and a mournful wail re-sounded, as though the train were bemoaning the deception, but I was sad about something else—nobody in my class would ever believe that I got to blow the whistle—and I knew I had no choice but to leave the whistle part out if I wanted to convince them that the story was true.

Then the engineer showed us how to speed up to 120 kilometers per hour, and Felix recalled how as a boy in Romania he loved to lie on a clifftop and watch the trains go by below, and hold his breath when the steam blew up around him, and the engineer reminisced about the old-fashioned steam locomotives back in Russia, not like these modern babies, with their twelve-cylinder diesel engines made by General Motors, no sir, and in Russia once, in the middle of our regular run, wouldn't you know it, the engineer got drunk, so I, though still a fireman, had to come to the rescue, *tfoo!* (He spat out the window for luck.)

Under Felix's caressing gaze, the engineer became loquacious, describing the wonders of his locomotive, which weighed a hundred tons, while all the other cars, including passengers, came out to another hundred. A heavy responsibility, he said, showing us the soiled and crumpled letter of commendation he kept in the pocket of his overalls. At this point, I started worrying that the trip would be over before I could get on with the adventure Dad and Gabi had planned for me.

But then:

"What say, Mr. Engineer?" Felix beamed his enchanting smile at him. "You like to let this boy here drive train now?"

Some Personal Reflections on Driving Locomotives;

and the Difficulty of Breaking the Habit Thereof

No, I thought, he doesn't really mean it, and I put on the old quarter-smile, knowing that if the engineer consented (oh, if only—God forbid—if only and God forbid), then I would have to drive the locomotive. Felix repeated his question. The floor groaned beneath my feet. The locomotive raced guilelessly on. Disjointed thoughts clattered through my brain: there are cars attached to the locomotive. There are people in the cars. These people have done me no wrong. Felix may not realize how inexperienced I am at driving on rails. No child should be allowed to drive a locomotive . . . I sank down on the side bench, at the mercy of sickly Eliezer.

"God forbid!" The engineer was frightened, too, and firmly shook his head. "Something the matter with you, mister? You must be crazy! Are you an adult, or what? I could lose my job!"

I sent a faint smile of encouragement his way, but Felix was smiling at him just then, too, and the way Felix smiled, you had to smile back, even if you did not feel particularly cheerful. The engineer was anything but cheerful, and yet, when Felix flashed his smile at him, a smile that expanded slowly from his lips to his eyes, and the three creases around his eyes smiled, too, making him look like a movie star who had alighted from the screen to visit mortal kind, and his smile grew even brighter, with the radiance of a sunrise, suffusing everything in its light, then slowly, and unaware, the lips of the engineer formed an answering smile.

Luckily for me there was more to the engineer than his wimpy lips.

In one angry motion, he wrenched his gaze away from the blue glow of Felix's eyes, shouting, "Look, mister, no offense—but that's all! You take the kid out of here right now or else!" But Felix was no quitter. He beckoned him closer, and when the engineer shrank back, as though in response to an indecent proposal, he beckoned again, this time with his long, slender forefinger, and the engineer stared as it drew him closer, till before he knew it, he was huddling with Felix, his bullneck, dirty undershirt, and fiery bald dome against the leonine head with the wavy white mane.

They were whispering together. The engineer kept shaking his head. A muscle bulged out on his arm. Felix tapped the rebellious biceps, soothing it with a barely perceptible touch. The engineer was listening now, his bullneck calm, his shoulders drooping. I knew that something had been settled between them, though Felix continued to whisper sweetly into the big, hairy ear that was more accustomed to the din of screeching brakes.

The engineer observed me sideways through his little left eye with its network of veins, looking so weary that he seemed to be on the verge of surrendering to some mysterious force.

It was there, inside the racing locomotive, that I first saw Felix use this dark magnetic power. In the days that followed I was to have several more occasions to witness the phenomenon, and years later, when I conducted research on the subject, I heard many more such stories about Felix and his power to overwhelm people—there's no other word for it—and bend them to his will.

The amazing thing is that he rarely used violence—quite the contrary, in fact: it was almost as if he were able to create a chasm between himself and others, cushioned with kindness and the caring smiles people need so much that they let themselves float off in a fairy-tale trance. And that's when Felix would zip the chasm over their heads, leaving them to wake up at the bottom of what was now a trickster's suitcase.

And me? Why did I go on believing his story? And what did I feel? I felt as if I'd been split down the middle: One part of me tried to cry out to the engineer and deny all the lies Felix had been telling him. And as I've already admitted, there was another part of me completely under the spell of Felix's flashing blue daredevil eyes. Still a third part of me (I guess I was split in three) kept thinking, What an idiot you are, Nonny; has any other kid in your class ever driven a locomotive? Who else do you know who'll get a chance like this! What would Dad say if he found out you wasted it after all the trouble he went to for you?!

"Okay," grumbled the engineer, straightening himself up with difficulty, "but only for a little while, for half a minute, no longer, it's against the rules . . ."

He was still leaning heavily against the wall in front of me, shaking his big bald head, but his arms hung limply at his sides and his eyes were in a fog. "But only for a little while. This isn't right . . ." he mumbled, nodding vigorously, as though to cancel any memory of the deed.

"Now, Eliezer"—Felix smiled happily—"please to drive engine."

I sat down on the driver's swivel chair with my right hand on the throttle. I kept my left hand on the emergency brake, as I'd seen him do. He stood over me, tightening my grip around the brake, but I didn't need his advice. It seems I had memorized his movements, as though guessing in advance that Felix would offer me this chance to drive. I picked up a little speed, and the engine obeyed with a roar. It was too abrupt, for a beginner, at least. I pulled down the brake that stops the engine, let some air out through the one above it, and suddenly I knew how to drive. Dad's like that, too: get him into any vehicle and he'll drive away in it, though I doubt that he's ever driven a locomotive.

But I wasn't thinking about Dad just then. If I had been, I might have realized that there was something really weird going on. All I could think about was having to skip this part when I told my adventure to the kids at school. They would never believe it. But at least the story about blowing the train whistle could go back in, now that it seemed like a relatively easy thing to do.

I remember this little window where the grime and dust had been wiped away, and through it I could see the tracks rushing at me before they disappeared below. The engineer leaned on me with the full weight of his lifeless body. His hand grasped mine around the brake, as if all his vitality were concentrated in this crucial limb. Felix, though, was positively glowing. His eyes shone like sapphires. He was so happy to be giving me this incredible gift. We were passing through the coastal plain. Banana plantations whizzed by us, fields of loamy soil, cypress trees, and furrowed sand . . . and on our right, a road, where I remember a red car moving slower than I was.

And then it happened: There was an explosion inside me; the power of the locomotive, the roaring, the grandeur, the speed that made my hands tremble and sent the trembling up my arms and into my chest; I couldn't contain it all, and I started screaming; here was this hundred-ton locomotive, like a great drum pounding in my chest, what a heart had been given to me, and I pulled the throttle till the needle jumped on the dial and "hi-deh!" A hundred-ton locomotive, plus a hundred tons worth of railway cars, not to mention the poor passengers who knew from nothing! If I felt like it, I could leave the rails and go racing through the fields where no one would be able to stop this chariot of mine, drawn by 1,650 horses, and I, who until a moment ago had been an ordinary passenger on this train, not even bar mitzvahed yet, was suddenly summoned from among the multitude and chosen to sit in the driver's seat, where I was doing a pretty good job, Dad would be proud of me, me, Nonny, driving a train, and all because I didn't chicken out this time, there was nothing I couldn't do, there were no limits, no laws . . .

With all their might Felix and the engineer tried to pull me away from the control board. I don't remember what happened exactly. I only know I struggled as hard as I could to keep driving. I was like a wild animal: stronger than the two of them put together, because I was getting power directly from the locomotive with its 1,650 horses.

They won, of course. But it took their combined strength to drag me away. Felix held me so tight that it hurt. He was very strong for his age. He threw me down on the bench, and they both stood panting at my side. Sweat trickled down the engineer's forehead and onto his cheeks and neck. He stared at me with revulsion, as if he'd just noticed something disgusting about me. "Go," he said, his barrel chest rising and falling. "Please, I'm asking you, get out of here," he said again, his voice breaking into a scream.

"Oh yes, yes, of course," said Felix absentmindedly. He looked at the clock on the panel, mumbling calculations. "It is exactly time. Thank you very much for everything, Mr. Engineer, and please forgive us if we cause some harm."

"It's pure luck nothing terrible happened," howled the engineer. He grasped his head with his hands. "What have I done? Oh no! . . . Enough . . . just get out of here. Enough."

"There is just one little problem," said Felix. By now I was familiar with the quiet, catlike tone beneath his surface politeness, and I felt a little uneasy. The engineer's face turned redder.

"Because we two must to get off from train before Tel Aviv," Felix explained apologetically. He took a handkerchief from his pocket and fastidiously blotted a drop of perspiration which had formed on his brow during the struggle with me. There was a faint smell of perfume in the air.

"In half an hour we'll be getting to the station. Go wait quietly in your car!" shouted the engineer. His fingers turned white on the handle of the brake.

"Beg pardon!" Felix corrected him patiently. "Perhaps you do not understand me, because my Hebrew it's not so good: we must to get off train before Tel Aviv. Before that forest. In maybe three kilometers."

I peeked through the dusty window. The train was now traveling through a plain of yellowing fields. Something dark loomed ahead, a clump of trees, apparently. I glanced at the big clock on the wall: it showed 3:32.

"Now is only two more kilometers," said Felix amicably. "You must to slow down, Mr. Engineer."

Suddenly the engineer veered around. He was a big man, but his anger made him even bigger. "Unless you two get out of here this minute . . ." he said, and the veins on his neck swelled like muscles.

"Now is only kilometer and half," said Felix calmly, peeking out the window. "*Nu*, our car is waiting for us, Mr. Engineer, please to start to stop."

The driver turned to look out the window, and his eyes grew wide with amazement. There by the tracks was a long black car with yellow doors. I, too, was amazed: Felix had mentioned earlier that a car would be waiting for us at 3:33, but who would have believed something like this could happen, in the middle of nowhere . . .

Like two mechanical dolls, the engineer and I turned slowly back to Felix. Then we saw what he was holding in his hand. No! I thought. It can't be, this is just a bad dream! The engineer realized how bad it was before I did, but it was definitely no dream. Heaving a sigh, he reached for the brake and set about stopping the train.

He must have pulled the emergency brake, because I nearly jumped out of my skin. A burning smell filled the locomotive. Compressed air escaped with a shriek. Sparks flew. The brakes screeched, the train lurched forward and groaned, and then everything was still, except for the hissing, whooshing sound of the engine.

No one moved.

Not a sound came from the cars behind us. People were too stunned to talk, I guess. Then somewhere in the distance a child began to cry. I looked out the window and saw that we were in the middle of a new-mown field. There was a row of gray beehives in the area, as I recall.

"Come, we are in hurry," said Felix apologetically, pulling me up from the bench and leading me toward the door.

My legs wobbled. He had to bolster me up, and with his other hand, the one that held the gun, he pulled the door open, and I slowly made my way down the steps. Again and again I felt my legs buckle under me as though my knees had been temporarily removed.

"Goodbye for now, Mr. Engineer, and thank you for all your help," said Felix, smiling at the dumbfounded man, who leaned back against the instrument panel with two growing pools of sweat under his arms. "So sorry if we inconvenience you." He approached the radio transmitter hanging next to the engineer and, swift as a snake striking, tore it down from the wall and cut the coiling black wire.

"Come, Mr. Feuerberg," he said pleasantly. "Our car awaits."

Mischief in the Toy Department

Shiny black. With lemon-yellow doors. And big, biggest I'd ever seen. It was parked obediently beside a dirt road in the middle of the field, like some huge dog waiting patiently for its master. There weren't many cars like it in Israel at the time, not a one, in fact. It was brand-new, sensational. I thought it must be a Rolls-Royce, but it was something even better.

"Come, please, I open door now for Mr. Feuerberg!" said Felix, and he ran ahead, spry and light-footed, and opened the door to a glorious world.

I slid into the car, buoyed up on the plushy seat. Dad and I had once owned a vintage car we used to tinker with together. It was a Humber Pullman from the forties, like Queen Elizabeth's automobile and the one General Montgomery raced in through the desert. We called it the Pearl. Dad had found her scrapped at a junkyard and spent years restoring her piece by piece; I got to help him as soon as I was old enough. In the end, we had to give her away. A sad, sad story. But compared to Felix's car, our Humber looked like a jalopy. I wasn't much to look at either just then.

Because of the shock, the commotion.

Gabi used to say that I rated a nine out of ten on the IBS (International Brat Scale), and that at the mere mention of my name in the teachers' lounge, twelve men and women would start stamping and snorting and furiously pawing the air. Yep, that was me. But on the train with Felix, and those people he'd locked inside the compartment, and the engineer and all, I had passed beyond brattiness into a world of grownups and guns and real crime, like in real movies, and I just floated through the storm in a trance.

With a sudden screeching of tires, Felix took off. A cloud of dust rose up around us, and we emerged from it, black and shiny.

The car was spick-and-span on the inside, too, with red velvet upholstery and a mahogany dashboard. There was a glass partition between the front seat and the back, and a fine silk curtain on the rear window. Never before had I been in such a car, or taken command of a passenger train, or experienced so many "never befores" in a single day.

"The black button," said Felix, pointing.

I pressed it. A little door swung open and a light went on inside, revealing a sandwich on a plate wrapped in cellophane, a quartered tomato, and slices of melon. There were also slices of some other fruit I didn't recognize at the time, probably fresh pineapple, which as far as I knew grew only in books and cans. I carefully picked up the plate. It had a gold rim around it, like the gold rim around Felix's watch. I ran my finger over it: for the first time ever I was touching gold.

"I thought maybe you will be hungry, and prepared for you sandwich. Cheese, this is kind you like, no?" I nodded limply. The contrast between the train hijacking and this cheese sandwich really slew me.

"Are you taking me to Haifa?" I asked.

Felix laughed. "Oh-ho, you are too impatient! But we have bigger plans for you!"

"Who's we—you and Dad?"

"Ah yes! We two. Each looking after his own end of plan."

We drove in silence for a while. What exactly did he mean? I had hundreds of questions and didn't know where to start; everything had happened so fast, it was utterly fantastic: how could my dad have planned something which involved breaking the law, like hijacking a train, at gunpoint no less! Okay, supposing he went along with Gabi's modest first proposal (not very likely, but supposing he did) and started developing it into a kind of action film for me, then why didn't Gabi intervene? "A hair-raising adventure," he'd written in the letter, but wasn't this a little too hair-raising? There's something wrong here, I thought to myself, this is too dangerous for a kid my age.

I listened, but didn't hear Dad say that at my age he practically ran his father's factory. Maybe he realized he'd been carried away. A sudden wave of fear numbed my face and body. Because what if I was making some terrible mistake?

"If you are worried, I take you back right away," said Felix.

"You mean, back to Jerusalem?"

"In just one hour. This is a Bugatti, fastest car in Israel today."

"And will that be the end of the game?"

"If you wish, I take you there later this evening. Or perhaps tomorrow evening, if you wish. Is for you to decide, me to obey, yes sir!" He saluted with a wink.

"Is that what Dad said?"

"Soon you have your bar mitzvah, young Mr. Feuerberg, and then you will be grown-up man!"

But not quite yet, I thought. True, I had secretly smoked a couple of cigarettes down to the butt, and inhaled, too, and true, I had kissed three girls in my class, only on a dare, though, and then Semadar Cantor went and told her giggly girl friends that I'm a two-timing wolf. But sitting next to Felix in that car, leaving a whole trainload of people behind us in a state of shock and indignation, I knew I was only a thirteen-year-old boy, or would be, come Saturday, and that this weird adventure was a bit over my head.

Those last moments on board the train started flashing through my memory: the look on the engineer's face when he saw the gun in Felix's hand, the way his eyes nearly popped out when Felix slashed the radio transmitter so he wouldn't be able to call for help. And then, after we jumped off the locomotive, Felix took something tiny out of his pocket and tossed it in the air. I didn't really see what it was, I only noticed the glitter of gold as it spun around in the sunlight, and then I heard a faint tinkle, like a coin hitting the floor.

We drove on in silence. The tires stirred up more dust on the path, but inside, the car was cool and fresh. We turned down a narrow road. The car spanned all the way across it. We passed through a small village or kibbutz, I didn't really notice. I was deliberately slacking off on Dad's training. I didn't read the road signs, or make a mental note of landmarks, or check the speedometer to see how many kilometers we'd driven so far, or invent memory aids using the initials of the turnoffs north and south, etc. I was angry with Dad and his wild ideas. I wanted to betray him the way he had betrayed me. And there was this rumbling inside me, telling me that a bar mitzvah surprise should make a kid happy, not scare him half to death.

"You wish to go home, no?"

"No!"

I barked the answer, and Felix peered at me and began to slow down, till the car was hardly moving. He stared silently at the road ahead.

Okay, I told myself, this is going to be tough, and you almost gave up just now. Try to be stronger. It's true you've just been through a lot, and you're still out of kilter, but actually, nothing so terrible has happened. Here you are, riding around in the most beautiful car in the world, nibbling pineapple (apparently) and cheese from a gold-rimmed plate, and if you're brave, this Felix person will take you on adventures no child has ever had before. And I don't mean fantasy adventures either. So enough of your whining. Sit up straight. Put a smile on your face. Don't pretend to be a man. Start by being yourself, Nonny, as Gabi put it in the letter.

I liked these little pep talks. I used a special voice for them, a gruff interior voice that addressed me in staccato slogans, like a general transmitting orders during battle. It helped sometimes.

Really it did.

I stretched out. There was plenty of leg room in the car. I devoured the sandwich, and fed on the fabled pineapple, allowing the taste to melt on my tongue. I pulled my shoulders back and sat up straight. And I whistled softly to myself. There was one thing I knew for sure: nothing would ever be the same after that pineapple.

Felix drove on, glancing at me quizzically in the rearview mirror from time to time, as though wondering whether perhaps Dad had misled him, and I wasn't really mature or brave enough yet to participate in what he had planned for me. The next time Felix looked my way I

looked steadily back at him. The way Dad taught me: Steady eyes are
a declaration of self-confidence. Like making a muscle. That was a very
important trick for a skinny kid like me. It worked on Felix. He smiled.
I smiled back. He pressed a button, and over my head the roof opened
slowly, revealing the vast blue sky. Never before, etc.

It was warm and pleasant outside. I turned on the radio without
his permission. American music filled the air. I felt American. I smiled
like an American. Felix threw his head back and laughed. Finally, a
grownup who thought I was funny.

"We have a Humber Pullman," I told Felix.

"Ah yes! Fantastic auto! Six-cylinder engine, yes?"

"Yes, and it's black, like this car."

"A Humber Pullman is always black! And only black!"

Except the fenders, which were striped white, because the car came
from England during the Blitz, when roads were dark during the black-
outs and people had to put special stripes over their car fenders so
pedestrians would see them approaching at night.

"Dad found her in the junkyard. Before I was born."

"How did this Humber get there?"

"Dad thinks it must have belonged to a British officer during the
Mandate. Maybe he got drunk and smashed it up."

"Yes sir! Anything is possible! British soldiers like to drink! Johnnie
is always shikker!"

"Dad and I work on her every Tuesday," I lied. Because we did once.
We used to.

"That is important! Cars like that need work! You drive her often?"

"Yes . . . but only behind the house, up to the fence and back. Dad's
afraid to take her out on the road."

He used to be afraid, that is. We used to drive her up to the fence
and back. We used to work on her. Everything in the past.

"She's a real pearl."

She was a real pearl. That's what Dad called her. "Come on, Nonny,
let's polish the Pearl," and out we would go with our rags and buckets
and baby shampoo. Working together, two hours at a time, we rarely
spoke about anything except the car. When we'd start her up, the sound

of the motor was like music to our ears. Dad could really make her sing when he put his heart into it, and then the three-meter ride to the gate and back was like gliding on velvet wheels. Or sometimes we'd dip into our savings and call Roger, an ace mechanic from Nahariya who specialized in vintage cars, to come up to Jerusalem and adjust the brakes and the shock absorbers.

It gives me a pang to remember the effort we put into her. Once we took a trip to Tiberias just to buy special desert tires from a rare-car dealer. But that's all in the past. To this day I feel guilty about what happened. I think Dad must have aged ten years the day he had to turn her over.

"But why you never drive your automobile on the road?" asked Felix in surprise.

"Dad says that a car like that . . . it wouldn't be right to take her out on the bumpy streets of Jerusalem. In our back yard she's protected."

"Aha!" said Felix mockingly. "Is safe to drive Humber in desert, but too dangerous in Jerusalem?"

"I guess so."

I, too, had found it strange that our Humber never left the gate, as though we had to keep her caged in the yard. When we gave her to Mautner in compensation, he had no fears about driving her, but he didn't know how to treat her, either. The first time he took her out of town, she went out of control and rolled over. He told the neighbors she'd gone wild like an animal the moment she hit the open road, and no matter how hard he pressed on the brake, she raced ahead, a car with a curse, he swore to everyone, and Dad heard him and smiled bitterly, as though he'd known all along what would happen. I wince just thinking about it. Mautner sold the Pearl to a used-car dealer. We haven't heard anything about her since. Or spoken about her. That was that. She was dead.

"This car is Bugatti," Felix said again. "You never hear of Bugatti before, eh?"

I admitted that I never had.

"There are six cars like it in all this world," he explained, "built by genius sculptor named Ettore Bugatti! Every car is specially designed! Unique!"

I took a closer look at this masterpiece I was privileged to be riding in.

"And Mr. Bugatti himself decides who will buy his six cars. He decides: kings are worthy enough so his first Bugatti he sells to King Carol of Romania, who once I saw touring in his private car!"

"And this one? Which king was this one for?"

"This one? For King Feuerberg II. Felix brought you this car by ferryboat, one month to get to Israel, very long trip!"

"For me?" I was astounded. "You mean you brought this car here for me? A car like this?"

"No, I am sorry to say, it is not present for keeping, only for today. So we will have lovely time together. To make our trip special."

"You mean to say you brought a car here for one day? For me?"

"Oh, that. Someone in Italy owed to Felix debt of honor. Also another gentleman in France, his former partner. They think Felix is dead. For ten years they hear nothing from me. Suddenly comes telephone call: *brrring brrring!* Got to hurry! Old friends run here, run there, for debt of honor! So this Bugatti arrives in Israel for one week, then it goes back to museum, and no one any wiser, good day, thank you, and shalom!"

My lips were dry. Maybe there's a special prayer you recite the first time you ride in a Bugatti. Too bad no one in my class could see me now. Too bad there had been no photographer following me around all day. Because I knew that even if they believed me about driving the locomotive all by myself, and blowing the whistle and stopping a train, no one, not even Micah, would believe that the automobile of a real king had been sent from overseas just for me! A convertible, yet! Who cares if they don't believe me, I thought angrily. Why should I have to impress them? Does a king have to impress anyone? He's the king, that's all.

"He sure was scared, that engineer . . ." I said with a forced laugh, because every time I thought about what happened in the locomotive I'd get this wave of anxiety again.

Felix shrugged his shoulders. "And gun was only toy," he said.

I was relieved. "Only toy?"

He shrugged his shoulders, took the gun out of his pocket, and handed it to me. It was a small gun, fairly heavy, as heavy as a real gun, its handle inlaid with mother-of-pearl. I'd seen a real one like this once in a display of impounded weapons. Dad took a long time inspecting it, caressing it, peering through the sight. When I asked him what it was, he quickly put it back in the case and sneered, "It's only a woman's gun." But I didn't tell Felix that.

In this pleasantly expansive mood, I ran my fingers over Felix's toy. It was the second gun I had held in my hands that day, the first being the one the fake policeman carried. Ho-hum, what a boring life this was.

We were still driving over back roads. I raised myself up on the seat and stuck my head out through the open top. I waved to an oncoming truck, and the driver waved back, staring at our big black car with admiration. Too bad I didn't have a cowboy hat. That would really have completed the picture. I said so to Felix, who threw his head back and laughed. Again, for an instant, he looked ferocious to me, like a panther: an elderly one with droopy jowls, that still had a glint in his eyes, and I began to imitate his changing expressions, and the fierce blue of his flashing smile . . . or have I already mentioned my silly habit of trying on a person's expression in order to feel it inside out? I can't decide whether that means I have a flair for drama, or a flexible nature, but at any rate, Felix noticed it. He could see right through me. He sized up my character in a matter of seconds, and I didn't mind a bit, because I saw by his smile how much he enjoyed my mimicry. He, too, was something of an actor, as was clear to me from his scene with the engineer, and I felt a special rapport with him, an instinctive warmth; what pros we'd shown ourselves to be in that locomotive, with me sensing what Felix wanted and improvising accordingly, and how about the way my arm started twitching, nice touch, huh?

Felix stepped on the gas and winked at me conspiratorially. We knew—we both felt it—that this was the start of a special friendship between two adventurers, and he grabbed the toy gun from my hand, aimed it at the blue sky above us, shouted, "Hi-deh!" and pulled the trigger.

The shot reverberated through the air. I was aghast. Suddenly I felt miserable and cold. A wispy trail of smoke rose up from the gun barrel. I slid back on the luxurious seat. All the air in my lungs escaped with a whistle, blowing out the fun of the adventure and the joy of our new friendship.

"But you said . . . a toy . . ." I mumbled.

Felix held the steering wheel with one hand and sniffed the gun barrel. He looked at me with his baby-blue eyes, shrugged his shoulders, and smiled. "So what you think, young Mr. Feuerberg—someone in toy department was playing michievous trick on me?"

9

We Fugitives from Justice

Gunsmoke wafted over my head through the open roof of the Bugatti and up to the sky. I could smell it, scorched and heavy.

"Maybe we should go home now, back to Jerusalem," I whispered.

There was a look of disappointment in Felix's eyes. "*Pardon*," he said. "Forgive me, please, that I frighten you when I want just to make you laugh." His triangular eyebrows peaked in distress. "I am perhaps too old to make children laugh, yes?"

I said nothing. What a team we made: an old man who can't make children laugh and a child who can't make grownups laugh.

Sulkily I asked whether he had any children.

Again he hesitated, weighing the answer in his mind, as though there were no such thing in this world as "reality" or "truth" and you could give several different answers to any question, depending on what the person asking it had in mind at a given moment.

Then he decided. The familiar smile spread over his face. "One child," he answered, "grown up now. She could be your mother."

I said nothing, out of pure courtesy. I mean, really, how could anyone be my mother, except Gabi, that is.

"I did not know her so well in childhood," said Felix, "because I was traveling always, for work and such. This is great pity, no? So much I miss, no?"

I didn't feel like answering. The truth is, he didn't strike me as capable of raising a child. He seemed more the type who could be nice and have fun with a kid for an hour or two. I was sure, for example, that he knew how to make shadow puppets with his fingers and do three or four simple magic tricks, or tell the kind of story that would grab a child's attention. But actually to be there for the child, giving discipline and care and comfort, the way Gabi is for me—that's something else again.

"Why—why you looking at me like that?" stammered Felix with an awkward smile. I stared at him unswervingly, to let him see that I was angry.

"I do love children . . ." he mumbled uneasily, apologetically. "Everyone says always—Felix is great hit with children! Children adore him . . ."

Uh-huh. Just as I thought.

Cruelly I held my tongue.

"What's this?" murmured Felix. "Cat has got our tongue, Mr. Feuerberg?"

I could see that my silent scowl was troubling him, shaking his confidence. I had a feeling he could read my mind. Fine, then, I thought, go ahead, read on, here's what I think of you, Mr. Felix: you are a vain and self-indulgent man who delights in raising himself as his only eternal child!

It worked. Maybe it was mean of me, but that's how I got even with him for the gun. Though I must confess, I am not the author of the wonderfully cutting line about the man who delights in raising himself as his only eternal child, et cetera. Gabi had said that once about her favorite actress, Lola Ciperola, and it was engraved in my mind forever. How strangely appropriate to Felix the words seemed now: his eyelids fluttered, his cheeks blushed red. He grasped the steering wheel with both hands and stared out the window, speechless.

The silence lasted several seconds, and when Felix looked at me again, his eyes were utterly changed. Gone was the glint I had noticed in them earlier. I knew that something had passed between us, that we had fought a kind of duel, which I, for reasons unknown, had won.

"You are clever boy, young Mr. Feuerberg," said Felix quietly. "But now we see if you are brave enough to continue on journey."

So we drifted along in the big black car. I had to decide whether to say "Enough," in which case it would be over, like some pleasantly confusing dream, an eerie dream which had just begun and would lead who knows where. I closed my eyes and tried to decide, but there were too many thoughts running around my head. In my heart lurked a nameless fear, a cold and heavy fear about what I was doing here with this Felix person, though I realized maybe I shouldn't try too hard to get to the bottom of it, in case the solution turned out to be more frightening than the riddle itself.

"Let's continue," I blurted.

"Very well." He sat upright behind the wheel. I could tell he was relieved, overjoyed in fact, that I was willing to continue our journey, despite what I had learned about him. I, too, sat up and looked him straight in the face. I was feeling rather proud of myself, though I didn't fully understand what I had done to bring about this change both in him and in me.

"But first we must to switch over to Beetle, yes?" he said.

This was a surprising turn in the conversation. And in the trip. I asked no questions. I literally bit my tongue and waited to see what would happen. We parked the massive car near an orange grove. We got out. I didn't know where I was, or where he was leading me. He opened the trunk and took out the brown leather suitcase. He closed the car door and began to walk away. I followed him into the orange grove. I was still forcing myself not to ask where we were going. With Felix, I now realized, there was no predicting. Everything could change from one minute to the next: situations, plans, the future . . .

We stepped through the trees and into the orange grove. On and on we traipsed, past the muddy watering ditches. There were red rags tied around the tree trunks here and there. When I turned to look, I couldn't see the Bugatti anymore. Or the road either. We were surrounded by the trees and the silence. Him and me.

And then, between two rows of orange trees, I saw a huge frog: that is, a green Volkswagen, called a Beetle, though it looks more like a frog. I could hardly speak. I was amazed again at the magnitude of the operation they had planned, and yet one little thought kept nagging me:

Couldn't they have chosen a simpler present? Like maybe a regulation soccer ball? More and more I felt as if I were floating downstream. I followed Felix. He walked at a quick but easy pace. It was beneath his dignity to rush ahead. He moved to a special rhythm, which naturally infected me as well. He opened his door, I opened mine. He got into his side, I got into mine. He started the car. I cleared my throat. We were silent. I liked that manly silence. The car went up and down the ditches, found the dirt road, and away we drove.

"It was important for me to start our trip with black Bugatti," he explained. "Special car gives style, no?"

He pronounced the word "style" as though tasting something sweet. But what would happen to the luxurious car he had shipped all the way to Israel for a half-hour drive? He had left it just as he had left his expensive watch with the silver chain. He never even bothered to lock it. Apparently Felix was the richest man in the world.

"But black is eye-catching, and with yellow doors, would take no more than few minutes for police to find it. This is why I arrange for us this Beetle car. There are so many in Israel, no one will notice. If we drive past police station, policemen will only tip their caps and say, 'Good day, thank you, and shalom.' "

I maintained my stern, professional silence. What Felix had said about the police began to sink in, and gradually, through the fog, an interesting thought occurred to me.

"You mean we're running away from someone?"

"From police, I believe, who may not care for what we did on train," said Felix with a shrug, clicking his tongue three times like a witness to police impropriety. "Sometimes they are old-fashioned this way." And he added with a chuckle, "Not your father, of course, oh no no no! Your father is true champion, but the rest are not. You listen to me, your father is best detective in all of Israel!"

And then two things happened:

1. My young soul positively crackled with joy that someone else thought as much of Dad as I did.

2. I suddenly understood the true meaning of Dad's plan.

That is, I almost dared to understand it.

"You mean, the two of us, you and I, are now . . ." I asked hesitantly, afraid of his answer, "fugi . . . fugitives from justice?"

"Ah, this is lovely way to put it." Felix smiled. "Yes, yes, we are fugitives from justice." And he murmured the words to himself again.

"What about . . . tomorrow? Will we also be . . . fugitives from justice then?"

"And also day before yesterday . . . I mean day after tomorrow. It is up to you until when. What you wish is my command, like Aladdin and his jinni, yes sir!"

And he gave a salute.

Just then, the ringmaster of my inner circus raised his whip and I heard a deafening crack in my ears. The band struck up a lively march while inside me, thirty-two acrobats, three fire-eaters, two magicians, a knife thrower, clowns, monkeys, lions, elephants, and five Bengal tigers all leaped into the spotlight and circled round and round . . . Yes, it was one of those incredible moments when an entire circus runs away with a child, and the euphoric voice of the ringmaster resounded in my shell-like ears: Ladies and gentlemen, beloved audience, let's hear it for me!

I sank back in my seat and closed my eyes, hoping these shenanigans would drown out the cool warning whisper that tried to tell me I was wrong and that I didn't understand what was going on, but I didn't want to hear any more: Shut up, quit spoiling everything. Felix drove unhurriedly, humming a comical tune syncopated with little clicks of the tongue like a one-man band. I rolled down the window and let the breeze wash over my face. Very refreshing. I sat up straight again. There. That's better. Everything will be all right now. Everything will return to being clear and simple. At last, after so much confusion and resentment toward Dad and Gabi, the whole plan was coming into focus, the angle, the method, and the audacity of it all: so this was my bar mitzvah present! And this was the man Dad had chosen for the role! Again I gasped at Dad's ingeniousness. You'd never guess from his outward appearance who and what he is, and how brilliant he is when he wants to be. Sure he keeps a low profile when he's out on a case; so low, in fact, Gabi claimed it was becoming his second nature, but even I hadn't guessed he could be so bold and reckless. How I wished I could have heard what Gabi said when he told her his idea.

She would never leave him now, not after an idea like that.

I looked at Felix in a new light, too: for Dad to have entrusted him with such a mission, he had to be someone pretty special. The honorable Mr. Special, meanwhile, had put on a pair of simple black sunglasses, without a trace of monocular elegance. He drove with self-assurance, his eyes narrowing behind the shades, though I could tell he never missed a thing. More and more he reminded me of Dad. They were so different, yet so alike. I swallowed hard, trying to control what I would say from now on, but I could scarcely control the trembling of my fingers.

Because what if this turned dangerous? Or even more unlawful?

What if I disappointed both Dad and Felix?

What if we were caught?

The plan unfolded before me now in all its grandeur and absurdity: the risk Dad had taken! To let me do something that was clearly illegal, like the crime I'd committed on the train? Because if the police caught up with me and learned what really happened, Dad would lose his job, and his crooked partner would take over, and what would Dad have to live for without his work, without the force? "I won't squeal," I swore to myself. "Even if they torture me in the interrogation cellars, I will never betray him to the police!"

No, no, I couldn't imagine it. I didn't dare. I took a deep breath. I got ready to ask a long question, to clarify things once and for all:

"Wwwwhat wwwill . . . ?"

I gagged on the words. I sat there shamefaced. Felix smiled wanly.

Nu, I told myself, go on!

"And wwwhat wwwill . . . will we do together?"

The pipsqueaky voice that hovered in the air was mine apparently.

"*Oi*, Mr. Feuerberg," said Felix, waving his hand. "You and I do things you never dream of!"

"And . . . if they catch us?"

"They will not catch us."

It was now or never. "Hey—uh—Felix . . . did they . . . I mean . . . the police, ever catch you?"

He went on humming as though he hadn't heard me. It was a while before he turned to me and answered: "One time, once and no more."

He smiled to himself, but only his lips were smiling now, and the cruel line I had seen over his mouth before stood out again.

"How many years have you known my dad?"

"Oho! Ten years, maybe!"

I hesitated, carefully wording my next question to avoid insulting him. "You know each other—professionally?"

Now the wrinkles around his eyes smiled, too. "Professionally. Yes, you put this very well."

He speeded up and concentrated on his driving, whistling a jolly tune. Now and then he would hum with glee. "Professionally!"—accompanying the word with a "pam pam—pam pam pam." He was always whistling or humming, I noticed, filling the air with chirping or buzzing noises. Maybe this is what happens to grownups who were like me when they were young, I mused.

But in spite of my uncertainty and confusion about him, I still got a good feeling whenever I looked at his hands. They were long and calm and manly. The only thing that bothered me was the ring, the big gold ring he wore which suggested a kind of flashiness and self-indulgence I had never met with before. The stone was black, black as a tunnel under a prison wall, shiny as a gun barrel, black and shiny as flashing dark secrets.

So I kept my eyes on his right hand. It gave me courage and made me like him and want to stay with him. The right hand was the good hand. It kept me safe, and reminded me that Dad was watching over me from afar, that he had chosen Felix for this mission with the utmost care. A single glance at Felix's right hand made you see that he was like the legendary *Shushu*s who don't know the meaning of fear. Or a criminal with a heart of gold.

"Dad's a champion, isn't he?"

"First-rate detective. *Número uno!*" he said.

Too bad Dad wasn't around to hear this. He'd lost so much confidence after falling out with his buddies on the force. None of the other detectives wanted to work with him anymore. There was even an article about him in the morning paper, saying he had bungled every big case that came his way, and that his hatred of criminals made him charge into the most delicate investigations like a raging elephant. I was hoping Felix hadn't read that paper.

"Only, he's been having some trouble recently," I ventured.

"Ach, it's all goulash what they print in newspapers!" said Felix dismissively. "They do not see that your Mr. Father is no ordinary, run-of-mill detective! It is in his blood! He is not like others, office clerks in uniform! He is real maestro, he is among detectives like Bugatti among cars!" And for emphasis he raised a finger, the one with the ring, which no longer bothered me somehow.

"But this one reporter," I said embarrassedly, "wrote that whenever he has to deal with a criminal, he goes berserk and blows the case."

"Ach, they are crazy in head!" Felix was furious. "I also read what those stupidiots say! Do they think fighting crime is children's game?"

"And he hasn't been promoted for such a long time," I confided uneasily, knowing it was wrong of me to divulge a thing like that. We of the police are not supposed to hang our dirty linen out in public, but I was full of resentment at the way Dad had been treated, and I knew that Felix was on our side.

"Is swinishness!" grumbled Felix, slapping the steering wheel. "They resent your father because he is fantastical!" he said, locking his mouth nearly up to his nose.

I tried to remember his exact words so I'd be able to repeat them to Dad the following day. I only wished Gabi had heard, too. For some time now she'd been annoyingly critical of Dad's work, and I couldn't understand why he put up with her insulting remarks, like that he should quit the force and start looking for another job. She was blunt, all right.

"Another job?" Dad's jaw dropped. "This is me you're talking to!"

We were standing in the kitchen, the three of us, fixing supper just then. I froze in front of the frying pan. Dad was beginning to swell up over the macaroni pot. Gabi waited for an outburst from him, and when none seemed forthcoming, she worked up her courage: "Quit the job. Enough already!" Dead silence. Dad, amazingly enough, controlled his tongue! Gabi went on cutting the vegetables with a trembling hand. "You've given nearly twenty years of your life to the job, and a lot more than that. It's high time you tried something different, something more normal, with regular hours. And no guns, no shooting, no risking your life day after day." Here she glanced around. He still hadn't opened his mouth. She took a deep breath and blurted, "I suggest that you retire early, with severance pay. I'll retire with you; we'll put our savings together and open a restaurant. Why not?"

From crooks to cooks? This was a pretty astounding idea. Dad croaked like a frog who'd dug a tunnel in England and popped out in a kitchen in the middle of France. "A restaurant? A restaurant you say?!"

"Yes! A restaurant! With homemade food. I'll be the cook, and you be the mana—"

"And maybe I'll put on a nice pink apron and help you cook, huh? Maybe you think I'm too old to be a detective? Go on, say it, say it!"

I could see what we were heading for. I tried to change the subject fast, but I couldn't think of anything to say. Now they would fight. Then she would leave. And every temporary departure brought the final one that much closer. I couldn't live this way, in the midst of so much uncertainty.

"You used to be a good detective," said Gabi in a quiet voice that boded ill. "You used to be the best, and everybody knows it. But that one episode and what you went through as a result of it have made you lose all sense of proportion. You treat your work like some private vendetta against crime. Don't you see that it's impossible to maintain professional objectivity that way?"

Silence in the shambles. No one could say a thing like that to Dad and hope to come out alive.

But still he didn't answer! He didn't answer her!

"You're in such a fever to get back at every petty criminal, you wind up giving yourself away!" More silence. Slowly and deliberately, Dad stirred the macaroni. Gabi was so tense, she kept chopping the same poor tomato into tinier and tinier pieces. She could tell that Dad was listening to her for real this time, and here was my chance to say something that would shut her up. What did she know about being a detective? What did she understand about the eternal battle between the police force and the dark forces of crime?

But then a memory flashed through my mind. Something which happened while Dad and I were lying in wait for some car thieves recently. It was the way he acted, like Gabi said. He had spoiled the ambush, and it was lucky I just happened to be there with him.

I went on quietly scrambling the eggs in the pan. A new situation was developing, it seemed.

"I really blew up when they called me a raging elephant," said Dad quietly. "Imagine how you'd feel if they called you an . . . um . . ."

With heroic effort, Gabi managed to ignore this lame remark. "It's true the article was vicious," she said. "But there were one or two points you ought to consider if you want to change your life!" At last she set aside that tomato, glared briefly at the red pulp on the cutting board, and turned her vengeance on a cucumber. "You're so blinded by rage whenever you come across any petty crook that you lose the patience you need to trap him! Or your timing goes wrong during the interrogation! You don't have enough perseverance to make use of the simplest strategies!" And she slashed the cucumber three times for emphasis.

We were back to back, the three of us, but I peeked around out of the corner of my eye.

"And I bet there's not a single drop of iodine in the whole damn house!" she shouted suddenly, dropping the knife and rushing to the bathroom to stop the blood that dripped from her finger. Dad stood motionless, his back like a cast-iron wall. I couldn't decide whether to go after her or stay and comfort Dad. My loyalties were divided. He hadn't seen what I saw: that Gabi deliberately cut her finger. Grimacing with self-hatred, she had cut her own finger with the knife.

"She's right," said Dad in a faraway voice. "Everybody's telling me, but I never listen. She had to say it to my face because it hurts her and she really cares about me. She's right."

"No, she's not," I protested, my mouth dry with fear. What did he mean, she was right? Dad was the greatest detective in the whole country. He had to stay on the job until I could join him so we could be a team.

"Wait here, Nonny," said Dad, his voice so gentle I barely recognized it. "I'll go bandage her finger."

How I wished that Gabi were beside me in the car, listening to Felix talk.

"And perhaps he is best not only in Israel," Felix continued, nodding his head for emphasis as he repeated the words, "not only in Israel!"

I inhaled deeply, taking in what he had said. The only interruptions to our manly silence were the humming and muttering noises Felix made. I was feeling peaceful, dreamy and peaceful, almost as if I were listening to a story about myself, a kid whose dad, a high-ranking detective, arranged an adventure for him in honor of his bar mitzvah, a voyage to the darker side of life, as a special gift for his coming-of-age so that he would know both sides of life, and remember that even his dad had another side—a side that was wild and free and happy.

Or had been, once upon a time.

When he was young. Before he married Zohara, before he joined the force. I knew. Gabi had told me about it, or hinted, rather, and Dad's cronies would sometimes recall with a wink the rapscallion he used to be. He had two friends, the Three Musketeers, people called them, army buddies who started a furniture-moving business in Jerusalem, not that Dad ever mentioned any of this; for him the mere thought of happier days seemed to desecrate his mourning over Zohara. But I collected bits of information from Gabi and pieced them together in my heart: once upon a time in Jerusalem there were three famous hooligans with hearts of gold, chief among them, Koby Feuerberg, with his cowboy hat and horselaugh and daredevil exploits, like dancing a waltz with a refrigerator strapped to his back, or stealing a zebra from the Biblical Zoo and riding it through the streets; and sometimes in the evening, after work, the Three Musketeers would comb their hair with brilliantine and crash the fancy parties in the better neighborhoods, where one of them would cut in on the belle of the ball and whirl her around till she nearly fainted, while the other two stood guard to make sure no one else cut in, and they would suddenly vanish and turn up at another party. A lot of ladies were after him in his bachelor days, and he would sweep them off their feet, but never fall in love with any of them, he always said no woman alive could catch a man like him, she'd have to hunt him down and shoot him first, if she really wanted him, that is, he would laugh. Yes, that's how Dad used to be a million years ago, whizzing through the streets of Jerusalem on his motorcycle with the little sidecar where a tomato plant grew so luxuriantly that he could pick a fresh tomato and eat it as he drove, and people called him the Tomato Cowboy, and whenever a policeman pulled him over for reckless driving, Dad would bribe him with a luscious tomato, and everyone would laugh and sigh, What can you do, a cowboy is a cowboy . . .

Where was he now, the man he used to be? Why had I never known him? Why had he never peeked out at me from behind Dad's eyes? Where was the prankster who liked to steal cars and mount them with square wooden wheels? Why did grief come and dig that terrible crease between his eyes with an iron claw?

Felix drove on, still humming, and I only hoped I would be able to keep my heart from bursting through my teeth. I kept touching my lucky charm, the bullet Dad had taken out of him. Some criminal had fired a gun at him, but Dad kept shooting till the guy surrendered. I wore that bullet on a chain around my neck and never took it off, even in the shower. It came out of his body, and it would stay with me for the rest of my life. We're together, I reflected, I'm here with Dad. Everything I do now I do with him, even if I break the law; his spirit is with me in the bullet I wear around my neck. All of him—even the long-lost cowboy—is with me, next to my heart.

This was a moment of rare insight. I didn't always realize how close we were, Dad and I, closer than twins, even closer than two pros working side by side who understand each other without saying a word. Sometimes I'd get this lacerating fear that I would grow up to be different from him. But just then, in the speeding Beetle, I felt that I was growing, growing with him, getting to know him to the depths of his soul, perhaps for the first time ever. Because only now had he revealed himself fully to me, and given of himself with unflinching generosity, and this was his greatest gift for my bar mitzvah.

A police cruiser with a wailing siren was heading our way. Heh heh heh, I chuckled inwardly, like an old crook. Maybe the cops in the cruiser are hot on the trail of the hijackers in the black Bugatti! I checked myself: no, I wasn't afraid, not much. What did the cruiser have to do with me? Actually, I kind of wished they would come after us so we could lose them in a thrilling car chase. Of course we would lose them. We were fearless, lawless, a couple of wild animals. And with Felix beside me, everything would turn out right. He had experience, he had nerves of steel. No one would catch me under the spell of his deep blue gaze, at least for a day or two, then I would forget everything and mend my ways, I would be a good little boy, and never tell lies or misbehave, and only sometimes, alone in the night would I remember this day or maybe two, and all that happened in reality, though it will seem like a dream: the hijacked train, the black Bugatti, and the wailing sirens of a hundred police cars chasing after me, till I lose them and escape. Because I am swift and sudden, I buzz and sting and fly away. A master of crime is Nonny Feuerberg, soon to be the best detective in the whole wide world!

My heart was pounding. I pressed my knees together and bent over in the protective-custody position. For a moment I felt confused and scared, because, who am I anyway?

10

A Chapter I Prefer to Leave Without a Title,

Particularly a Humorous One

Gabi's been with us forever, I told Felix; that is, as far back as I can remember. She came to Dad and me after my mother died, which happened when I was very young, like at the age of one. I paused briefly, because this was usually the point where people started asking all sorts of stupid questions, like what she died of, and did I remember her. Felix, however, said nothing.

I was a little perplexed. Why did he show no interest, why didn't he care about this motherless child, this virtual orphan? I decided to conceal my surprise from him, though, because as I explained earlier, ordinarily it was the other way around, people were always bugging me with questions I didn't feel like answering, so I could just pretend it was the same this time.

I told him more about Gabi, that she'd worked as Dad's secretary since the old days when he was deputy chief of the bunko squad, and then transferred with him to the felonies division, and stayed on when he became a detective. Wherever he went, she went.

"I am the thunder, as it were," she would say, "if we mistakenly assume for the moment that your dad is the lightning, that is."

"She is kind of thundery," I explained to Felix. "She's big and fat, and has a booming voice, but let me tell you, Gabi's the greatest, I don't know how we would have managed without her. [Brief pause] Especially after my mother died."

Silence. Okay. He had a right to be silent. Even though, in my opinion, when a kid says, "After my mother died," it makes him sort of special. Or maybe not. Felix turned down a narrow road that led us to the sea and the sunset. The green beetle rolled slowly on, as though there were no policemen anywhere.

"She's always trying out new diets," I confided, "because she's sworn not to give up the battle until her body is fit for human habitation. But she loves to eat, she's a chocolate freak, and then Dad and I cook these big wonderful meals, so she has to join us."

She eats and then she hates herself. But when the onions sizzle in the olive oil and Dad throws in some mushrooms and stirs the macaroni, how can she be expected to control herself? Sometimes I suspect Dad of doing it on purpose: of cruelly tempting her so she'll get even fatter and he'll have an even better excuse not to marry her.

"But Zohara was really beautiful," I told him for no particular reason. "I saw a picture of her once."

Silence. He drove along the shore.

"Dad kept only that one picture. A picture of him and Zohara. He wanted to throw all the rest of her things away after she died." I stressed the word "died," in case he hadn't heard me the first time. But he didn't respond this time either. He just hunched over the steering wheel, with a long, tense face.

So be it. There's no law that says you have to discuss a dead woman, even if she was the mother of the person you're talking to. Because that person may not be so interested in talking about her himself. He hardly knew her. He was only a year old when she died, and she's hardly ever mentioned at home. She just died and that was that.

"And what about Gabi?" asked Felix out of the blue.

"She doesn't talk about her, either," although occasionally, in the middle of a conversation, Gabi would fall strangely silent, as though she sensed a presence passing through the room and we had to pretend not to notice, and then Gabi would pick up with "Now, where were we?" I knew that Dad had forbidden her to mention Zohara in our house, because every time I worked up the courage to ask about her, Gabi would say, "Anything you want to know concerning Zohara, kindly ask your father," and then seal her lips, though I knew very well that she was bursting to tell me things.

"No, you did not understand," said Felix. "I meant, why is it Gabi came to take care of you?"

"Oh, that."

All right, then, I thought, if this guy has no respect for the dead, if all he wants to talk about is Gabi, we'll talk about Gabi. In any case, there's not that much I can tell him about Zohara, since I know next to nothing about her. She's a stranger who happened to give birth to me, whereas Gabi's invested so much in my upbringing.

"When Dad married Zohara, he took a leave of absence from the police department; he wanted to try a different life. But after she died," I continued, "he decided to rejoin the force, just when Gabi was thinking of quitting. She was fed up with working as a secretary. Gabi has loads of talent. She could succeed at anything."

"Like what, for example?"

"Like what? Like being an actress maybe, or a singer! And she's a fabulous organizer, she organizes the holiday shows for police force kids, and she writes skits for the department ball. And she's terrific at crossword puzzles, and she's a real film buff, we go to see at least one film a week, and she does these hilarious impersonations of people in the news, and let's see, what else? . . . She has a great sense of humor. Practically perfect."

Felix smiled.

"You love Gabi, don't you?"

"She's the best," I said. Too bad I couldn't convince Dad of that, on account of her looks—or on account of Zohara . . .

"The trouble is that she is not pretty enough for your Mr. Father," reflected Felix. I thought of something Gabi used to say: "Oh, why did my parents have to give me such a patty-cake face when I was meant to be Brigitte, the femme fatale!" I, personally, felt glad that Gabi had never resigned herself to her looks, otherwise she might have turned into some dumpy woman, with nothing interesting about her, when the opposite was true: she had a razor-keen wit and a zest for life—and suddenly I wondered whether maybe Gabi was Gabi not because of any genetic trait, and not because of her education, but because her soul had chosen to fight her form and face, and that was why she was always trying to be so smart and special, and then I understood how hard she'd had to struggle all her life, without anyone's help, without anyone to confide in.

"Why she wanted to leave the police department?" Felix asked quietly.

"Because she was sick and tired of typing reports about corpses and murderers and organized crime."

"And you know what I hated most?" she would ask me. "Seeing your father's sour face every morning." (I didn't mention this to Felix.) She never heard a word of praise from Dad, and he would fly off the handle if she missed a day of work.

"Silly fool that I am, I thought this was his clumsy way of showing how much he needed me," Gabi would say with a sigh whenever she told me the story.

"Once she almost left him," I continued, "but she decided to stay on a little longer."

"Because he looked so sad and so defeated, I couldn't leave, and I couldn't stay with him, either," recalled Gabi, as we discussed it for the umpteenth time, over a cup of hot chocolate at a café after the movies, and later at home, in the kitchen, just the two of us. "The circles under his eyes were darker than ever, if you can imagine, and still his idiotic pride wouldn't let him admit the pain he felt to anyone." Here she narrowed her eyes as she drew me closer, and said in a chilling whisper, "The sadness simply flowed out of him. He was the embodiment of human tragedy."

"And then one day she saw him trying to diaper me on his desk at the office," I told Felix, smiling to myself, because I could imagine him doing it.

"And when I watched him searching frantically for the pacifier, which was stuck in his gun holster . . ." At this point, her eyes would always turn misty, and her voice get hoarse and low. "Well, seeing him that way, as lost and helpless as his bawling baby, I realized that I loved the guy, that I had loved him all those years we worked together, without knowing it, and that I was the one who would bring a smile back to his grieving face."

Then we would both fall silent in deference to her tender feelings. I liked that story.

"I guess I've seen too many movies where the widower marries the children's governess," she would grumble.

"I wasn't allowed to call her Mommy," I told Felix as we parked the green Beetle near the beach and made our way over the hot sand. Even before I could actually see the water, and only smelled it, I began to chatter. The sea always has that effect on me.

"She explained that she wasn't my mother, she was Gabi, my friend and Dad's. But I was too young to understand the difference."

Because Gabi was always there with me. Except at night, when she went home to sleep. Or sometimes when Dad was out on a case, I would stay with her in her little apartment, and she would read me her favorite bedtime stories, and it was Gabi who chose my babysitters and my nursery school, and attended PTA meetings, and took me to the clinic when I was sick, and stayed with me for all my shots and vaccinations (because Dad, the hero, fainted when he saw the needle). And she kept a special baby book of what I'd learned and all the cute things I said. And it was Gabi who talked Dad into giving me a promotion, though he wasn't sure I'd earned it yet, so that, thanks to her, I made sergeant second-class, and she . . . and she . . . and me.

And once a month or so, when my homeroom teacher, Mrs. Marcus, expelled me from school, "this time for good," it was Gabi who would fly to the teachers' lounge for the inevitable ritual of pleading with her to give me one last chance, after which, laying a hand on my shoulder, she would ask in her booming voice how they could possibly give up on such a wonderful boy, and Mrs. Marcus would answer with a smirk that she supposed a week's suspension was reasonable punishment for a boy like me, for a shallow pond like me, for chaff before the wind like me—back then teachers put a lot of thought into their insults, not like today—and that maybe Gabi ought to accept the fact that I needed a different sort of framework, better suited to my limitations. Rest assured, Gabi didn't let that pass in silence: "What you may see as limitations, I happen to consider advantages!" She swelled larger in front of Mrs. Marcus, like a cobra protecting her young. "The advantages of an artistic soul! That's right! Not all children fit neatly into the square framework this school provides, you see. Some kids are round, some are shaped like a figure eight, some like a triangle, and some"—her voice dropped dramatically as she raised her hand high in the style of that famous actress Lola Ciperola playing Nora in *A Doll's House*—"like a zigzag!"

And my heart, as they say, went out to her.

My earliest childhood memory is of Gabi (we were sitting on the balcony one evening, and she was feeding me cream cheese out of a green pepper, when a man in sunglasses walked by, took a good, long look at us, and tipped his hat). She's always there in my baby pictures. To her I would run with my childish secrets, and she's the only person who ever saw me cry.

I stopped talking and let the sand trickle down between my fingers. We were sitting under a red beach umbrella by the nearly deserted sea. A black dog stood barking at us from the dunes. He must have smelled me from afar. The sea was smooth and blue. I could barely stop myself from diving in. Gabi says that I'm a fish who landed on shore by mistake, and it's true that as soon as I step in the water, in the waves, I feel much better, and I close my eyes and whisper things that I would never dare say anywhere else, all my most precious thoughts, all the questions I would never utter on land, and the secrets I could never remember there, these I would shout into the waves and let sink into oblivion, though I knew they would ripple on to infinity, preserved like a letter inside a very large bottle.

There by the sea, I wanted to tell Felix about her. Not to say "My mother died" to create an impression, but simply to talk to him about her. Because while I was talking about Gabi earlier, telling him how she fell in love with Dad, I felt a strange new sadness.

I couldn't figure out why Felix was keeping so quiet. He didn't seem bored by my story, though he also didn't try to draw me out. He had a special way of listening, unlike that of any other adult I knew, including Gabi. And I began to feel that I might have been mistaken about him before, when I thought he didn't want to hear about Zohara. Maybe he just wanted me to feel free to talk without interruptions.

It may have been the way he listened to me that made me grasp certain things I had never really thought about before. For instance, that Zohara was a real person, not just a stranger whose name could go unmentioned for so long. She had existed once upon a time, as a woman with a face and a body and moods and childhood memories, and a voice and thoughts of her own, and she had wandered through the world, with a smile on her lips when she was happy and tears in her eyes when she cried. She had been alive.

And she had also been the wife of my father. Yes, suddenly it was clear to me: Dad had loved her. Maybe she'd been the only love of his life, and he could never love another woman.

Strange that I hadn't understood it this way before. Maybe because I'd always heard the story of their love from Gabi, and in Gabi's stories she was the central character, she and her love for Dad, and her disappointment in him, and her hope that he would stop mourning for Zohara one day and come back to life, or rather, to her. But it was only then, on the beach with Felix, that I realized how unhappy my father was. He was the sad, lonely one, the one who was in mourning for Zohara, even today. And these were not mere words from Gabi's story, words she'd recited so often even she forgot how painful they were. Then a question began to torment me: Why did he still never mention her, even to me? Wasn't I grown up enough to know about her with my bar mitzvah coming?

And why had I never questioned him? He might have told me about her if I had. Yes, maybe to me he would talk. Maybe he was just waiting for me to ask. I could have brought it up, starting with some silly topic, in the days when we used to work on the Pearl. I could have crouched down by the tires with the white stripe from the days of the Blitz and asked him something, like where had he met my mother, for instance, and what they used to do together, and how she died; and if he didn't want to answer, he could pretend he didn't hear me. So why didn't I ask him then? It's hard to start asking questions after a silence of thirteen years, and maybe it was too late now.

"I don't know anything about her," I reflected. Felix leaned closer, but didn't say a word so as not to disturb me.

"Nobody ever told me anything."

I felt a pressure in my throat, as if someone were choking me, and a sharp pain in my eyes. Maybe if I dipped my head in the cool blue water it would go away. I had never talked about such things on dry land before.

Once, when I was four or five years old, Dad and Gabi had this huge argument about whether or not to tell me. I was in another room, and I heard Dad say angrily that some kids aren't happy even though they have a mother, and that I would just have to get used to it, and Gabi said maybe a child could never get used to a thing like that, and he said that for me it was normal to grow up without a mother, that I had practically been born without a mother, and if I started brooding about it I would end up feeling sorry for myself, and if there's one thing my dad can't stand, it's self-pity, and a lot of his friends were killed in war, but he tried not to dwell on them, because that's the way it is, you get no insurance in this life, and not everyone makes it to the end, and those who do must never look back.

He doesn't know I heard him, that I faithfully obeyed his command. I wasn't going to disappoint him. I rarely thought about her. And when she did steal into my thoughts sometimes, I would shut my eyes tight as I could and gently but firmly push her out. I had a special voice for this, a kind of humming noise I made inside my head and between my teeth to stifle any thought of her. I was very good at this, except in the sea, as I mentioned before, when I dived into the waves, and I would feel something circling me, nestling against me; but then I would come out of the water and dry myself briskly and just forget. Only, this time a new thought occurred to me: What if he still loves her? What if he, too, sometimes looks back?

"I know that she died young. At the age of twenty-six."

Twenty-six was only twice as old as I was, I realized to my astonishment. Thirteen plus thirteen was not so much older than I was that day.

I hugged my knees and bit the inside of my cheeks, and dug my fingernails into the palms of my hands. I stayed this way for a few seconds, till I felt a little calmer. I didn't say a word, didn't even wipe the sweat from my forehead. My back and shoulders were as stiff as a board. I was afraid that if I opened my mouth now and pronounced her name, my neck might snap. Felix gazed at the spot on the horizon where the sun was setting. The black dog on the dune would not stop barking in my direction, with his head toward the sky and his tail pointing out behind him. I dug into the sand with my finger, searching for the place where the sand gets wet. A light breeze was blowing, and a flower fluttered its pale white petals.

"If only . . ." I began, choking on the words. If only I had known her as a little girl. There, that's what I wanted to say.

All at once this became my most pressing task in life; everything else was irrelevant and annoying. I couldn't understand why I had never wondered about her before. It was as though I had been living in a dreamworld or something, and I couldn't figure out why I had awakened just now to ask Felix, this person I barely knew.

"So where were we?" I asked uneasily, but couldn't go on.

His silence was oppressive. I didn't have to look at him to feel it grow heavy and deep, too heavy and deep. His breathing sounded wheezy and harsh to my ears. It suddenly occurred to me that a change was about to take place and that I had better start paying attention. I turned to him and saw a tiny muscle twitching like crazy in his cheek.

Something inside me turned hollow and pale.

"Why?" I asked feebly. "Did you ever meet her or something?"

11

Stop in the Name of the Law!

Shortly after we left the beach, as we were driving down a country road, another police car passed us with flashing lights and whirling siren. The policemen inside ignored us, since they were on the lookout for a black Bugatti with yellow doors, not an old green buggy. A prince as opposed to a frog. But as soon as they were out of sight, Felix reached for his leather suitcase and started rummaging around in it as he drove. He pulled out a pair of heavy glasses and something else I couldn't identify, a hairy gray switch, all limp and disgusting, which for a moment I thought was a live animal, or one that used to be alive.

"Close your eyes one moment, Mr. Feuerberg," said Felix. "Now we will put on Purim costumes, because I see police are getting nervous."

I closed my eyes and kept them closed for five minutes or so. The Beetle swerved right and left. I figured he'd taken his hands off the wheel.

"Is okay now for you to open."

I opened my eyes. There beside me sat an old man with a bowed back and heavy glasses. His pointy chin stuck practically into his chest and his lower lip pulled down to the right in what seemed like a constant tic. In place of his wavy white hair, there was a mat of wispy gray. He had changed out of the white suit with the rose in the lapel into a threadbare jacket, had sprouted a drab mustache, adopted a feeble smile, and let his jaw hang loose as though he were toothless.

"Under your seat you will find your Purim costume," said Felix. Even his voice had changed and sounded squeakier than ever.

Like an idiot I almost asked, "Is that you, Felix?"

He had changed his entire character. He wheezed and he panted, and even his nose looked different, longer and redder. Felix the panther with the gleam in his eye was barely recognizable. I reached down and pulled a big paper bag from under the seat. I peeked into it and saw a skirt and a blouse and a pair of girl's sandals. And a black wig with a long pigtail.

"I'm never putting that on!"

Felix quietly shrugged his shoulders. I touched the wig with disgust. There was no way of knowing where the hair had come from. Why, it might even have belonged to some dead girl. How could anyone wear a thing like that?

Another police car went by with a loud wail.

"Tsk tsk tsk, very nervous, our police . . ." said Felix. "They are all in fuddle. Perhaps I tell them now what really happened in the train?" He gurgled with silent laughter.

I was still fretting over what Felix had revealed to me earlier on the beach. "I knew your mother very well," he had said. "I knew her even before I knew your father!" Your mother and your father. He had joined them together in a single phrase, and all of a sudden I had two parents who were husband and wife.

"Your mother was very strong woman," he said, "and very beautiful. She was strong like only very beautiful people are." He seemed to be choosing his words with care, not paying her a compliment. There was too much caution in his voice. I didn't dare ask why. "Very strong and very beautiful," he said. What did he mean by strong? Physically strong? Spiritually strong? "And very beautiful." So Gabi didn't stand a chance. "She was strong like only very beautiful people are." What did he mean by that? That she was tough or something? Tough like Dad? That she liked to be independent and do things her own way? I didn't ask, and Felix said nothing. In the only photograph at home she really did look beautiful: seated with Dad peeping out behind her, her face animated and her long black hair falling over it, as if the wind had been blowing while the picture was snapped, and her wide-set eyes with a childlike twinkle, dark and radiant.

Because of the strangeness of her eyes I began to think that perhaps it wasn't a photograph at all but a drawing. Someone had cut the chair she was sitting on out of the picture. But why? Why were there so many secrets? Sometimes when I was rummaging in Dad's drawer, I would find that cutout picture facedown, always facedown. But was it a drawing or a photograph? Because the eyes seemed exaggerated, the way an artist might have drawn them. But the rest of the face seemed alive. A photograph? Who cut it out? And why did they cut it out? And what kind of strength do the very beautiful have? I didn't ask. I sat beside Felix in the car and said nothing. My fate lay in his answers to my questions, yet I didn't dare ask him. And Dad was in the picture, too, with his arms around her, looking not at the photographer but at Zohara, at her mouth, his hesitant smile unconsciously mimicking her irrepressible laughter, as though he, too, wanted to be wildly happy, with her help . . . The sun set and disappeared. Felix was silent. So was I. All I had to do was ask a few more questions and then I would know everything. But suddenly I didn't feel strong enough to know everything.

"If you want, I will tell you . . ." Felix began.

"Later," I interrupted, standing up. "And you can tell me why you said she was tough—but later."

"But I didn't say 'tough.' "

"Fine, whatever. We'll talk about it later."

Felix, still sitting on the sand, looked up at me. "Yes," he said, "I, too, think it is better to wait awhile for this story. After dinner, perhaps?"

"Yes, I'm getting hungry. Let's go," I said, because I was tired of standing there; my heels were burning.

"It is for you to decide when you hear this story," said Felix, watching me closely. "Is your story, after all."

"That's right. And later you can tell me everything."

"About their castle and horses and everything, later."

Oh no.

"Horses?"

"Certainly! Their house was like castle. On lonely mountaintop, not far from border, your father built castle for Zohara."

"A real castle?" My knees buckled under me, and I sat down facing him.

"Not like castle of Napoleon or King Carol of Romania, but for them it was like castle."

I can't take this any more, I thought. Now he'll start telling me what they were like together, what Dad was like while she was still alive, and I realized that not only was I completely ignorant about my mother, I knew very little about my father, too. What a lousy detective I was. For hours, days, weeks, and months I had thought about nothing, I had neglected the important questions. All those afternoons when I lay in bed, just staring at the ceiling. What exactly did Dad build for her, and why did he build it on a mountaintop, near the border, and where did they get the horses?

"You see, it is very strange story I have to tell you," said Felix, and as he spoke he took a fine leather wallet from his pocket and began filling it with sand. "Your father took Zohara to lonely mountaintop not far from Jordanian border, and all around were only mountains and wind and wolves, and there he built their home; she was queen and he was king, and no one ever came there, because it was dangerous, and your father watched over Zohara . . ."

His face looked almost tender now, and I curled up and listened.

"And they kept horses there and nanny goats for milk, and sheep for wool," he said, and put the sand-filled wallet back in the pocket of his jacket. I asked nothing and understood nothing. I didn't have the strength to take in all he was saying and all he was doing. "And they wanted no electricity, no telephones in their Garden of Eden . . ."

No no. I shook my head, shook everything out of me, the story, the exhausting surprises. I didn't want any of this. Not now. It was too frightening to think of them that way, of Dad that way. I wasn't ready yet. I needed time. It takes me a while to understand things, and this was tearing me up inside, the suddenness, the longing—

"And how she galloped on horseback, she would fly—"

It wasn't a chair, stupid Nonny, it was a horse your father cut out of the picture. He cut out the horse together with the mountain and all the rest of his life with Zohara.

Like a whirlwind the images swept around me. Their Garden of Eden. Why had he never told me about it? And why had he never taken me there?

"Why did they go so far away?"

Felix reached over and touched my forehead with his finger, right on the boiling point, which burst with a flash inside my head, and I shouted, "Were they running away from something?"

"You want perhaps to hear whole story here and now?"

He moistened his lips with his tongue, and his eyes darted to and fro. He wanted to tell me the story. He couldn't wait to tell me. Which was strange. Why was he so eager? We had just met, we barely knew each other, what did he want from me?

"No! Tell me later," I said abruptly, my final decision. I got up and stood over him.

He was startled for a second, as if I had awakened him out of a dream. "When later? Maybe there will be no time later!"

"Later. Not here." I wanted to go, to be on the move. No more sitting around. "Come on. Let's get out of here."

He looked at me, then sighed and reached for my hand. I helped him up.

We brushed the sand off. We covered our tracks in case anyone was following us. We'd both had practice covering our tracks, each for his own professional reasons. From time to time he would look at me in astonishment. I couldn't explain to him what I was going through. I'd have to hear the story later. I covered my tracks with both feet as well as with a branch I found lying on the ground until no trace remained. He could tell me the rest later. Why rush? There was time. Time to get used to it . . .

Slowly we walked away. The black dog of the sand dunes began to trot along, at a safe distance. It wouldn't stop barking at me, but Felix said I shouldn't worry about the dog barking at him, because dogs always barked at him. I didn't feel like getting into an argument, telling him about all the dogs that had attacked me for no reason, as though it was something about me, a smell I had, that drove them out of their doggy minds. But actually it was this dog that made me like Felix again, and I figured we would gradually get used to each other, and that it wasn't absolutely necessary to blurt out all our secrets right away; the important thing was to know there was a secret, a secret we shared.

We zigzagged over the white sand, and I could almost feel her walking with us. I even looked back once to see if she had left any footprints between his and mine. I think Felix understood what I was looking for, because he smiled at me and put his arm around my shoulder, and that was how we walked back to the Beetle, he and I, swaying with laughter like a couple of drunks.

Very strong and very beautiful and tough.

Tough? The way a professional has to be tough? Wait a moment: maybe she worked with Dad? Maybe she was a detective, too? My mother the detective?! Maybe it was because of her that he was so determined to fight crime. Why had I never thought of that before?

I curled up even tighter. Better not think about that in the midst of our journey, the midst of the adventure. Later on there would be time. Tonight. Or tomorrow.

So he built her a castle. A home on a mountaintop not far from the border. With nanny goats and sheep and horses. No electricity, no telephone. Maybe he wanted to be alone with her there. In purity and innocence. Like Adam and Eve in the Garden of Eden. He even gave up the force for her sake.

A police car passed us with a screaming siren. It startled me.

"Mr. Feuerberg," Felix reminded me, "this will be our last chance."

If they catch me now, I thought, I'll never get to hear the story about her, and them.

I pulled the clothes out of the bag. A red skirt and a green blouse. Bright colors, a bit on the loud side. How could I put on a girl's clothes? I'd die of shame. I'd vomit. It would be easier to hijack another train than to put on a skirt. Some things are not a matter of courage but a matter of . . . what? What do you call it?

I climbed into the back seat to change my clothes as we drove on. For a minute I saw my face in the rearview mirror. I looked like someone who was about to swallow a particularly bitter pill. Once my father had to dress up like a woman. He was working on a case involving a

con man who had promised ten different women he would marry them
in order to get at their money. Dad, for all his professional experience,
was so disgusted at the sight of himself in a skirt that he talked Gabi
into being the bait instead, which is how, says Gabi, she got three pro-
posals: the first, last, and only. I took off my trousers. I put on the skirt
backward, naturally. How was I supposed to know? I twisted it around
my hips. At least you didn't have to take a skirt all the way off to turn
it around. I put on the delicate sandals with the twisted straps. There
now, I was wearing my disguise. So what? It went with the job. And if
I did fool someone with the disguise, would that mean I was more of
a pro than Dad? Or less of a man? Because I'd always thought that
being a pro meant being a man, but now I was confused.

And all the while I kept trying not to think about the girl these clothes
had belonged to. They were a perfect fit, only they looked kind of old-
fashioned, not the style girls in my class wore. I wanted to ask Felix
where he had picked up the clothes, but I didn't. Why didn't I? Why
didn't I demand an explanation about where an old man like him had
found girls' clothing? But I just kept still and fought off the evil thoughts
whirling inside my head. If I hadn't known Dad trusted Felix, I might
have worried, not frantically or anything, but I might have been just a
little wary. A light chill emanated from the clothes. They had a peculiar
smell, too, the smell of a cool, dark, secret place. Maybe they had been
folded up for a long time in a cupboard.

I tried on the wig. The lining was leather, or maybe rubber. It was
like putting the inside of a soccer ball over my head. My scalp started
itching. I was sure the wig was full of ants and that they were crawling
all over my head. The rubber gripped the roots of my hair and pulled
out one after another. If this kept up, I was afraid I'd never be able to
go without a wig. The pigtail made the back of my neck itch. I pulled
it out of the collar, but the minute I turned my head, it slid back in. I
tugged at it, and again it bounced up and then settled in again. And all
this time I kept thinking, What would Micah say if he saw me now?

"Hey, Nonny, you've got a pigtail!"

I climbed into the front seat again. Felix regarded me admiringly.
"Perfecto!" he said. "To achieve success you must to go the limit!

Change all rules! Do and dare! Courage! This is what means to be brave!" He scowled till he looked like the old man again with the lower lip pulling to the right. And then he muttered in his new voice: "Grandpa Noah and little Tammy are going to picnic. Goody-goody-good!"

Tammy?

I was dumbstruck. The wig was killing me. It made my head sweat. Under far less trying circumstances I might have gone crazy by now, but when I looked down at my legs peeping out under the skirt, I saw that they were thin and smooth, and my feet looked different, too, in those sandals, like the feet of a girl.

If I'd had a sister she would have looked like me.

And if I'd been born a girl this is what I would have looked like.

And I would have moved like a girl and grown up to be like my mother, not like Dad.

These thoughts were irksome.

Five days from now I was supposed to turn into a man, and here I was being turned into a girl. It was downright insulting that I could switch this way. A boy in my class named Samson Yulzari shaved already, and here I was, wearing a pigtail.

Still, if I had been born a girl, this is what I might have looked like.

A girl. A little sharp-featured, but a girl all the same.

And I would have led a completely different life.

It was frightening to me that if a boy could impersonate a girl so well, maybe a part of her would stay in him forever.

Felix cast another glance at me, and for a moment he almost forgot he was holding the steering wheel. This was exactly how he had looked the first time he saw me through the window of his compartment on the train: like a person who sees someone who reminds him of someone else, and enjoys the nostalgia.

Who am I? I wondered. I was perplexed, a stranger to myself. Who am I?

The black pigtail, dry as straw, bounced against my back till I felt as though someone behind me was trying to make me turn around. The clothes fluttered out, brushing against my skin, caressing me and blowing away with the breeze, which taught me that when you wear a skirt the wind can get in from below.

And then—

A large black motorcycle suddenly appeared at Felix's window, and the driver, a policeman wearing a helmet, waved him over to the side of the road.

"We've had it!" I whispered, bitterly regretting that we had been caught, that the strange adventure was ending almost before it began.

"Enjoy yourself," said Felix in his normal voice, as we watched the policeman stride toward us like a cowboy trying to make an impression.

12

I Uncover His Identity:

The Golden Ear of Wheat and the Purple Scarf

"**L**icense, please."

As the policeman came closer we saw that he was a lanky young guy whose nose—like the rest of him—was long and thin, and whose cheeks were covered with pimples. He didn't look so tough in his overlarge uniform with the fraying insignia. He reminded me of the fake policeman with the prisoner I'd met earlier that morning, a million years ago, and for a moment I hoped that he, too, was only acting a part in the performance Dad and Gabi had planned for me, but alas, he was only too real.

Felix presented his license. The policeman studied it.

"This is my granddaughter Tammy, Mr. Policeman," said Felix in his doddery voice. "We are on our way to beach for picnic. I didn't break any driving laws, I hope?"

The policeman looked him over and smiled. "No, you drive just fine, Grandpa. But I doubt this car of yours will last very long." And he fondly tapped on the door of the Beetle.

"I have this car already fifteen years." Felix chortled so gaily that bubbles of saliva sparkled in the corners of his mouth and dripped from his gray mustache. It was kind of disgusting, but amazingly convincing, too.

The policeman took off his helmet. He had wispy hair that fell over his pimply forehead. "You didn't happen to see a flashy black car go by, did you?" he asked.

My heart skipped a beat.

"Black car?" Grandpa Noah didn't grasp the question, and cupped his hand to his ear, the better to hear him.

"A big black car!" the policeman shouted in his ear. "The kind they have in America!"

"Did you see this car, little Tammy?"

Somewhere inside me, the word "no" was rattling around, trying to find its way out. I shook my head twice. The pigtail bounced against the nape of my neck.

"Something like a new Chevrolet. Or a Lark. The kind of car you don't see a lot in Israel. With a man and a boy inside."

"Ah!" Grandpa understood at last. "It is their car?"

"No. Seems it was stolen. A strange thing happened: it was parked in an orange grove where witnesses saw it last night, and today a man and a boy drove away in it, after they jumped off a train."

"Jumped off? How can that be!" Felix feigned surprise, and his eyes opened wide behind the heavy spectacles.

"We don't know for sure yet. It seems the man forced the engineer at gunpoint to stop the train. The boy got off with him. The engineer is still a little confused, and we haven't managed to get a clear statement from him yet. It was a kidnapping, apparently. Our guess is that he kidnapped the boy and used him as a hostage to stop the train, though we still don't know for certain."

In spite of my fear, I could barely keep from laughing: a kidnapping, that's rich!

"And where are they now?" asked Felix, brushing a speck of dust off the policeman's sleeve.

"God only knows," grumbled the policeman, with a hand over his eyes, as if to shade them from the sun, when actually, I noticed, he was trying to conceal his pimply forehead. "We found some other suspicious characters among the passengers," he said, and snorted with contempt. "Grown men in costume! Would you believe it? On the regular Haifa run?"

"Costumes?" gurgled the old grandfather in utter amazement. "You mean, Purim costumes?"

"Purim in summertime." The policeman chuckled, leaning against the window so that we could see him only up to his eyebrows. He really had to plan ahead to hide those pimples, with endless little acts of deception. "We found a couple of clowns, an acrobat, and a magician."

So that's it, I thought, the magician must be the man in the top hat, the one I called the executioner.

"And a fire-eater, and a juggler, and a contortionist, an entire circus . . ." He chuckled again, as though embarrassed by these silly things he was telling us.

For a second I regretted all the surprises I had missed by landing at the end of the game with Felix. Not that I'd missed anything really important. You can see clowns and fire-eaters in the circus any old time, but there was only one Felix.

But how did Gabi and Dad organize it all? When? And where was I when they met the fire-eater and the contortionist? What else in their lives did I not know about?

"This is an all-out investigation," the policeman reported mysteriously, and I knew it was the admiring, helpless look in Felix's eyes that was making him feel so mysterious. "I happen to think it was a setup," said the policeman, lowering his voice to a secretive whisper. "I'm telling you, the circus bit was only a way of distracting the passengers' attention from the guy who threatened the engineer . . . My nose tells me we have a mystery here," he said with a finger to his nose. "And this nose of mine never lies!"

"What is this country coming to?" said Felix, spreading his hands in sincere dismay and rubbing his lips over his gums as though he were toothless. The policeman could easily have seen that Felix had teeth, but he didn't. "What is this country coming to? I tell you, Mr. Policeman, things have changed! In old days someone simple like me could leave his door unlocked and nothing happened! No one would steal from you anything! But today? Today?!" he croaked with distress, till even I forgot for a moment that far from being "someone simple," Felix was the very type thanks to whom Mr. Simple couldn't leave his door unlocked anymore.

"The little girl, your granddaughter, shouldn't she be in school to-day?" asked the policeman as he returned Felix's license.

"It's August, summer vacation!" said the old man reproachfully. "Somebody must to listen to Grandfather's boring stories, eh, my little Tammy?"

I smiled my brattiest smile, and played with my pigtail. I was beginning to enjoy this.

"Ah, she is shy." Grandpa smiled. "But her report card: all A's! She is good, sweet little girl!"

"My wife is expecting," said the policeman all of a sudden, and a blush spread over his cheeks. "In two months, our first child."

He didn't have to tell us. Felix never asked him. He volunteered the information. It burst out of him spontaneously and landed like a gift in Felix's outstretched hands. I'd realized by now that this is how it always was with Felix: people confided in him almost immediately. His eyes, his smile, made you want to entrust something valuable to him, your most cherished secrets. The way the policeman blurted out the story of his expected child, or the way I told him about Zohara, and even the engineer, though he tried to fight it, eventually agreed to let me drive the locomotive. And I couldn't understand it, because—how shall I say this without offending him—Felix is sort of a con man, you know? And what if Dad was wrong, what if you can't read a person's character in his face? But why should someone with such a trustworthy look about him choose the life of a con man?

And what of me, with the seven deadly sins in my heart and the face of an angel?

Felix's cheeks melted with pure pleasure. "Yes, Mr. Policeman, your life will be transformed after this first child is born!" A nostalgic smile lit up his face.

"Yes." The policeman smiled with him. "All my friends with children say the same thing."

"I tell you from my own experience, young man," continued Felix, radiant with joy, "once your child is born you are someone else. Someone new. Something changes in here, in here!" He hit his narrow chest with a trembling hand and immediately started coughing.

The policeman slapped him gently on the back, still smiling shyly at all the things that Felix had told him. It was only then that I noticed what nice eyes he had, big almond-shaped eyes with long lashes. He stood leaning over Felix's window, and you could sense how much he was enjoying the closeness, as though he believed that in some strange way this wise old man could pass on his life experience.

It was the kind of moment you can't time with a clock, only with the beating of your heart. Even I felt left out of the warm bubble that enveloped them. I completely forgot that Felix was only acting. That he'd told me himself about the terrible way he had neglected his daughter, and how sorely he regretted it. I had forgotten. I didn't want to remember.

The policeman savored the moment, and then with a sigh he looked into my eyes and said, "Have fun with Grandpa!"

"This Saturday is my bat mitzvah," I chirped.

I didn't have to say that. No one asked me. But I said it just the same. I blurted it out, and in the appropriate voice for Tammy-with-a-pigtail. The policeman threw me a smile, tapped Felix on the shoulder, glanced again at his driver's license, to remember his name. "All the best, Mr. Glick," he said with a wave, then mounted his motorcycle and zoomed away.

Mr. Glick?

That was the name the policeman said.

He had read that name on Felix's driver's license.

Glick. Felix Glick.

"Mazel tov on your bat mitzvah." Tammy's grandfather chuckled as he started the Beetle. Oh my God, I thought, I'm on the road with the one and only Felix Glick.

The man with the golden ears of wheat.

"I never knew you have so much talent," said Felix.

"What talent?"

"Acting talent," he said. "Perhaps someone in your family was once actor?"

"Uh-uh, don't think so," I said, averting my eyes so he wouldn't see how excited I was. Felix Glick had once been the most notorious criminal in Israel. He had squandered his millions, after robbing banks all over the world and swindling governments and shaming the police. He had had a private yacht, a thousand mistresses.

And it was Dad who finally caught him.

"And also fine talent for lying. You were cool as cucumber just then, my boy. Perhaps there is future for you. Do you often tell lies?"

"Sometimes. Not too often."

Like now, Mr. Glick.

"But you see, policeman as good as invited us to lie," said Felix. "So what is wrong? You tremble at your own courage?"

"Why? Why do you ask?"

"You are looking pale. You want we should stop? Feeling ill? Must to vomit?"

"No, I'm fine . . . Drive on. Keep going . . ."

Whenever Felix Glick struck, he would leave a fine ear of wheat made of gold at the scene of the crime. This was his trademark, recognized by police departments the world over. Time after time he'd risked getting caught on account of it. Gabi, incidentally, had her heart set on owning one of Felix Glick's trademarks, the golden ear of wheat; that, and the purple scarf belonging to her favorite actress, Lola Ciperola. "Someday, when those two things are mine," Gabi would say, "I'll close my eyes and make a big wish, and then we'll see if miracles still happen."

"Where are we going?" I managed to squeeze the question through the excitement choking my throat.

"Out for dinner, to finest restaurant in Israel. The Bugatti of restaurants! This is your day!"

I looked away. It was typical of Dad not to mention Felix Glick to me, although Gabi (also typically) used to tell me things about him from time to time, quite a lot of things, in fact: about his escapades, and his legendary wealth, and all the women who had loved him, and how people used to say it would take someone with two brains to outwit

Felix Glick. The whole of Interpol was on his track, a host of detectives investigated his every crime, yet he always managed to get away, to slip like a shadow out of every trap they set, and only Dad succeeded in laying his heavy hand upon him. That's right, they do know each other professionally! I thought, almost choking with laughter. And how they do!

I stretched my legs out, still looking the other way. I was afraid Felix would see everything on my face. I took a deep breath of fresh air. Dad's plan was beginning to seem even crazier to me now, and better: I almost cried, it was so touching that twenty years later, he and Felix had joined forces to entertain me on the occasion of my bar mitzvah. And I could just imagine how it happened, how Dad made contact with Felix and met with him to talk somewhere, and how Felix said, "We must to forget past, Mr. Feuerberg. We had fair fight, and you won. You are true pro, and I admire you. You caught Felix, and because of this, you are top detective in all of Israel, perhaps outside Israel, too. We both know how it is lonely at the top, and for this reason I think is natural you turn to me, it is great compliment that you wish me to guide your son through world of crime. You will never find better guide than Felix, yes sir!"

And my sad-eyed father shook hands with him, and his face turned red.

This so moved me that I almost jumped up and gave Felix a hug.

"At least he left us very nice present," said Felix, suddenly mischievous.

"Who?"

"That boychik policeman."

He raised his hand and displayed the policeman's watch on his wrist, the big Marvin all members of the force had received as a gift last Passover.

"How . . . ? When did you . . . ?"

"Who knows? I see it there and I take it. My fingers think faster than I do."

I didn't know what to say. I didn't quite know how I felt about him now. On the one hand, Felix had actually stolen something, but here he was, looking at me sheepishly, knowing full well what I thought of him.

"How silly," he blurted at last. "You are right. It was mean to take it from him, that nice young man."

"So why did you take it?"

Felix slowed down, his head between his shoulders. Now he did look old, and the pitiful mustache seemed to be really his.

"I think perhaps . . . don't laugh, but I think that perhaps I wish to impress you . . ."

"To impress me? How?"

"Well, I don't know, maybe by showing you I can steal watch of policeman . . . I lift it while he is checking my license . . . for prank, for joke, you see, to laugh at later, you and I . . ."

I was annoyed with him for stealing the watch. For me this petty theft marred the noble understanding between him and Dad. Again I could feel the cold blade twisting under my heart, cautioning me that I was mistaken, that there was something I had yet to discover about Felix. But then I looked at his remorseful face, at his penitent lips muttering silently, and I felt sorry for him. He was only trying to make me happy, I thought. He would have danced for me if he could have, or sung if he could sing to make me happy, but all he knows is how to cheat and steal and shoot a gun. So first he shot the gun, and now he put on this little pocketpicking demonstration for me.

"Maybe we could return the watch to him?" I suggested.

"Maybe . . . yes. We will leave it in car when we abandon it."

"Why are we going to abandon it?"

"Because we must to keep changing everything, cars, Purim costumes, cover stories. Otherwise police will catch up with Felix, and then no more game! But never you worry! I am used to this," he said with a glum little chuckle. "All my life I am changeable this way."

"Hey, wait." I had a sudden suspicion. "Is this car legit?"

Felix Glick shrugged his shoulders. "No, it is not, young Mr. Feuerberg," he said, "nothing in this entire game is legit. The only question is: Do you still want to play?"

I thought about Dad, about his meeting with Felix after twenty years, and how he entrusted me to his care and shook his hand. And I thought about the story of Zohara, which Felix had agreed to tell me. And then I sat up straight: You bet I want to play.

13

Are Feelings Touchable?

We drove on in silence, as though we were both sad for the same reason, a reason I couldn't quite explain. It was as if we had failed in some way. But it was Felix who stole the watch, so why did I feel this bitter pain? Maybe it was because I saw the way he lied, I saw how easy it was for him to lie, and I knew he was capable of cheating me as well. Or maybe it was the way he winced like a child caught doing something naughty—childish shame in an old man's wrinkles; and just then an unhappy memory recurred to me, the memory of Chaim Stauber, and the way I had tried to impress him and make him like me, and what had happened as a result to Mautner's cow, so maybe I wasn't any better than Felix, and who could say where I would end up after such an unpromising start?

I closed my eyes. I pretended to sleep. I went over what happened with Chaim relentlessly, so it would hurt. I thought about the day he moved into the neighborhood, and the way his eyes glowed with a little sunrise over the pupils whenever he became excited about something, and how before him, the only friend I had was Micah, who wasn't really a friend, as I realized all along, except I didn't have anyone else, and he never argued with me and hardly ever talked, and whenever he listened, his face looked dark and dull, till sometimes I suspected that he wasn't listening out of friendship but the opposite—it almost gratified him to see me carried away by my own tall tales.

But when Chaim arrived on the scene, everything changed. My whole life was transformed. He came in the middle of the school year. The week before, they started telling us about this special new kid, the son of a famous professor, who would soon be joining our class; the kid was an absolute genius, and a concert pianist, too.

A few days after Purim, in the middle of an arithmetic lesson, the school principal knocked on the door and introduced Chaim to our class. We looked him over. He seemed normal enough, though he did have a big head, as befitting a genius. There was something strange about his forehead, too: it was high and tan where his thick dark hair was brushed back. That looked unusual. The teacher sat him next to Michael Karni and told us to be nice to the new boy.

At that time I used to hang around with a little gang of kids who always did things together. We had a password and a hideout and a tree house, and we would go on secret missions, and there was this enemy spy we used to pester—some poor guy named Kremmerman who lived upstairs. (I should probably point out here that in those days, children played together, not through a modem.)

During recess I suggested that we let the new boy into our gang, so he wouldn't feel lonely.

The new boy was only too happy to join us. We played soccer and we made him goalie, only he wasn't so good at it, a real butterfingers. I did like his spirit of self-sacrifice, though. I remember saying to Micah, See those suicidal leaps of his? And Micah answered dully, Yeah, but what's the point of leaping if every ball goes straight into the goal?

After school we walked home together, me, Micah, and Chaim Stauber. They walked, that is; I roller-skated. In those days I virtually lived on wheels. I hardly ever stepped out of the house without my big, clunky skates. On the way home from school, Micah would walk while I skated circles around him, talking to him first from one side, then the other, enjoying the way he kept looking for me where I wasn't anymore. The day Chaim joined us I skated even wider circles. I gave a casual demonstration of what a professional skater can do. A few little whirls, death-defying leaps from the sidewalk, and a long, pensive slide on one foot between two disruptive cars—my usual routine. Chaim Stauber devoured me with his eyes. This was the first time I saw his eyes light up as if somebody had struck a match inside them. There really was a little sunrise over each eye. I could tell he was bursting to ask me for a turn, and I started planning how much to charge him. He was obviously rich. We walked him home. He lived in a big house not far from our building. As we all stood chatting outside his gate, his mother ran out calling, "Chaim, Chaimke, how was your first day at school?" And Chaim said quietly to Micah and me, "Don't tell her I played soccer with you," and he stood there letting her cuddle him like a baby.

"Are these your new friends?" she asked, regaining her composure and scrutinizing Micah and me as though she were trying to see under our skin in order to determine whether we were good enough for her son. So I promptly put on my angel face and cooed, "How do you do, Mrs. Stauber," extending my hand, which she pressed with a little smile of surprise. And what a hand she had . . . ! Warm, soft, silky, with slender fingers and manicured nails, and though I didn't want to let go, I quickly pulled back my own filthy mitt, sullied by filchings and fist-fights and crawling on the floor. Luckily I had enough sense to hide my left hand behind my back, as well, the hand with the long pinky nail, probably the longest pinky nail in my class, in the whole school, even.

That was our first encounter; she was so pretty she took my breath away, and I didn't dare open my mouth for fear of blurting out that Chaim had played soccer, though I didn't really see what there was to hide.

"It's because of the piano," Chaim explained the following day. And when we didn't quite understand the connection, he explained that he had to be careful, his mother was anxious about his fingers. Micah laughed his slow, stupid laugh, while I—God knows what came over me—replied at once that his mother was right, that maybe he shouldn't play soccer, after all. Chaim Stauber said that his mother would have liked to keep his fingers safely in her own hands forever and only let them out to play études and concertos. Then suddenly he gave a whoop, jumped high in the air, and clapped his hands, and I peered around to make sure no harm had come to the fingers his mother wanted to keep in her hands.

And then I heard myself telling him again that his mother was a hundred percent right, and that now that I understood all the facts, I intended to keep him out of trouble, because his future, and maybe that of the entire country, depended on his piano playing; decent soccer players aren't hard to find, but a concert pianist is one in a million.

Micah was startled by what I had said, and so was I. I mean, who appointed me guardian of Chaim's fingers, and what did I care about his fingers anyway; as soon as the words were out of my mouth, I knew I had said the right thing, the noble and virtuous thing, and it was one of the few times in my life when I felt I had principles, something important I was willing to fight for, even though there was nothing in it for me. To demonstrate my seriousness, I quickly removed my roller skates and carried them as I walked at Chaim's side like a bodyguard. Chaim, who seemed fairly amazed that I was taking him under my protection, asked hesitantly whether I, too, played an instrument, and I laughed and said, What, me play an instrument? and Micah said, Yeah, sure he does, he plays on people's nerves. I must admit that from the moment Chaim Stauber joined us, everything Micah said or did seemed dumb, crude, and annoying to me, and I only hoped that Chaim wouldn't hold him against me.

Nevertheless, the following day at school Chaim insisted that we play soccer. I walked over nice and friendly, took him aside, and tried to explain that it was too dangerous, but he said he didn't care. I tried to talk him out of it, I even tried to bribe him, but he wouldn't listen. The others started clamoring that recess was almost over, and I had no choice but to give in. I also had to relinquish my position as center forward that day so I could concentrate on defending his goal. I didn't budge from the penalty area the whole game. All I did was stop the other team's attempts to break through. I was such a great defense, Chaim Stauber could dawdle around safe if empty-handed. I can't remember a more exhausting game.

And so it went. He would insist on playing goalie, and I would protect him like a precious *etrog* packed in wadding. I would kick the shins of any player who came near those invaluable fingers. I was getting to be more like a professional bodyguard than a soccer player. As soon as I got rid of a player trying to kick the ball into our goal, I would turn to Chaim and smile, flushed with devotion. Sometimes even my best defense was not enough to stop a rival player, so I would be forced to watch breathlessly as Chaim risked his whole future with a furious lunge at the opponent's feet, and I would shut my eyes and tremble, feeling his mother's warm, slender fingers closing tenderly around my heart.

Apart from these nerve-racking soccer games, there were good times, too. I don't know what it was like in his old neighborhood, since he never talked about it, but with me and the gang Chaim really started to enjoy himself. Once a month we'd go through this ordeal of courage in the valley behind the building to prove our friendship. The ordeal consisted of crawling through a thirty-meter sewage pipe, no longer in use, until you reached a deep underground cesspool, where you then had to turn around and crawl back. It was pretty scary crawling there in the dark. There was no guarantee that sewage wouldn't start gushing through the pipe again and flood the cavern. Simon Margolies swore to us once that a big black snake had slithered by him inside (the week after, naturally, I spotted a viper, over one meter long). And finally when you crawled past the big hole, you could hear the water flowing below, all black and putrid. But for me the scariest moments were when Chaim crawled in there alone.

He insisted on going through the ordeal with us, and even yelled at me when I tried to talk some sense into him. The others started teasing me, saying I treated him like a grandmother, and even Micah giggled about it.

So what could I do? I stood aside, chewed grass, and pleaded silently with God to extend His influence over the cesspool, though mostly I prayed to Chaim Stauber's mother, joining my hands with hers to warm Chaim's fingers now that he'd decided to be a roughneck.

He emerged from the pipe with dirt all over his face and his hands covered with scratches, but you could see he was one happy kid. Simon Margolies asked how he felt in there, and he said that it was a little scary, especially while he was over the cesspool, but otherwise it was fun. That was all. He didn't brag or tell us that his heart was in his underpants or that he'd seen a ghost like I did one time; he merely observed that it was fun, and that he wanted to go in again next week.

He was driving me crazy, this Chaim. Anything I told him not to do, he couldn't wait to try, just to provoke me. Sometimes I felt like the babysitter of a severely disturbed child. In class I would stare at his back, groaning under my latest worries. I mean, it had gotten to the point where Chaim Stauber offered me money for a turn on my roller skates and I declined. Even Micah. Micah, who was made of steel, told me bluntly that I was overdoing it with Chaim, but I think he was only jealous.

And he had good reason to be. Chaim Stauber, in spite of his plans to drive me nuts, was truly a smart and interesting kid. He had an encyclopedic mind. For hours I would sit around listening to his stories about the Aborigines and Eskimos and Indians. He'd even been to Japan once with his parents, and said that the houses there are made of wood and that they grow miniature trees. He would say the most amazing things in his modest way, quietly and simply, without being a show-off. He wasn't trying to impress me, he was just telling me the facts. But his facts were more amazing than anything I could have imagined. And lying in my bed at night I would try to mimic the matter-of-fact way he told me, for instance, that "in Japan we went to a place where they serve chocolate-covered ants. I didn't eat mine because Mommy wouldn't let me."

That was the main reason I admired him: he had the guts to say his mommy wouldn't let him. I mean, if it were me telling a story about chocolate-covered ants in Japan, I'd make a big megillah out of it; I'd say I devoured a kilo of ants, that they tickled all the way down, and that the ant-chef swore he'd never met a kid like me.

And Chaim's mother. I've already described her hands, but everything else about her seemed wonderful, too. She was very tall, taller than Chaim's father, with a porcelain complexion and honey-colored hair that fell in heavy curls down to her shoulders. She would blink her blue eyes at you like a doll, as if any minute she might open them again and say "Mama," but instead she would say, "Chaim." Like this: "Chaim?" softly, liltingly, as if she had to make certain each time that he was alive and breathing and hers. Whenever I was there, she would keep coming into the room with a different excuse each time: to turn on the light so he wouldn't strain his eyes, or to bring him a special vitamin to strengthen his bones. I rarely spoke when she was around, and if the buzzing started between my eyes I would just hang my head and bite my cheeks till they bled. I used my very best language with her and, of course, never alluded to my rich experience with law and crime, because I sensed it might put her off.

Had it been possible, I would have stayed at his house from morning till night. But Chaim always wanted to go out. He said it was stifling at home, that his mother drove him crazy. I couldn't understand what drove him crazy. She was just concerned about him, like a mother should be, and it didn't bother me a bit that she came into the room every other minute, slowly blinking her blue eyes like a doll, saying "Chaim?" or sometimes "Chaimke?" I even looked forward to her intrusions and to the way she would ask us in her soft, deep voice if everything was all right, if we wanted a glass of freshly squeezed fruit juice or a plate of cookies. And I was so attuned to her maternal devotions that I could predict to the second the next time she would walk into the room.

The best days were the days when Chaim was sick. I would go over to visit him and watch as he lay in bed, with his high forehead and black hair on a big white pillow, and his face so pale, it was almost transparent, looking handsome and weak, but also safe from all the dangers out there. On such days I would sit in class with super-Nonny concentration, writing down every word the teacher said and copying the homework assignment from the blackboard so that I would be able to report in full to Chaim after school, particularly when his mother was in the room with us. She would come in every few minutes to smooth the sheets or plump his pillow, and being so weak, he had to submit. And she had a special way of covering him and tucking the blanket around him, till he was swaddled like a baby up to his chin. Sometimes she would take his temperature, not with a thermometer, but with her lips on his forehead, closing her eyes as Chaim's closed, and they would stay like this awhile, until eventually she would open her eyes and say, "You're still running a little fever. I think you'd better sleep now. Amnon can come back again tomorrow."

She was forever testing me. Chaim said she always did that to his friends. Anyone deemed unworthy was banished forever. That's how it had been wherever they lived, both in Israel and abroad. On the other hand, if his mother approved of you, you had a chance of being invited for Friday-night dinner, which was apparently a very big deal.

I was intrigued by this Friday-night business. Chaim told me that they set the table with special china from Switzerland. They always had interesting guests for dinner, mostly colleagues of his father; each member of the family would choose a meaningful passage to read aloud, and after dessert, Chaim would play the piano.

The words "a meaningful passage" made me laugh, but on Sundays (Chaim wasn't allowed to play outside on the Sabbath because that was a family day) I would rush over to ask him about the Friday-night dinner, about who came and what they'd talked about and which "meaningful passages" everyone read. Sometimes I would go out on Friday nights—because, in any case, that's when Dad and Gabi took care of all the stuff they'd put off during the week—and I would roller-skate past Chaim's house or climb up into my tree house and try to peek through the heavy curtains and see or hear a "meaningful passage."

On other days, between four and five-thirty, I would listen to Chaim practice the piano. It amazed me that nobody had to force him to play. He wanted to, of his own free will. When I don't practice, life feels empty, he would say. But how could a boy who knew so much and who had traveled all over the world say life felt empty unless he plunked on the piano for an hour and a half each day. I asked him to explain to me in simple human terms how playing the piano fulfilled him. I just wanted to understand what he meant, so maybe I could find fulfillment playing piano, too.

But he couldn't explain it. He said there were no words to describe a thing like that. And I got mad and said, At least try to explain. You know how to talk, don't you? Make an effort to explain in simple Hebrew how musical sounds can fill a person's life. I mean, are they made of cement? Earth? Water?

And Chaim nodded pensively, and wrinkled his high forehead, and said he was sorry but he just couldn't explain, it was something that happened deep inside so it was impossible to describe it to someone outside. At which point I stopped asking. Because if to him I was someone outside, then I wasn't interested anymore. Besides, I'd learned from Dad to be suspicious of such things. Dad used to say, "I can only believe in what I see and touch! Have you ever seen love? Have you ever seen emotion? Have you ever held an ideal in your hand? Me, I come from a line of simple peddlers, and all I know is: you have to touch the merchandise!"

And yet, deep in my heart, I knew that Chaim wasn't lying to me, that he wasn't trying to convince me of anything. That's what drew me to Chaim, but it depressed me, too, because I was always trying to convince people I was telling the truth, even when I was lying (especially when I was lying), while Chaim was exactly the opposite. For him it was enough that he believed himself, he didn't require others to think as he did. Others who were outsiders, that is.

I made a habit of climbing up to my tree house every afternoon to lie down between four and five-thirty. And there I would listen to Chaim practice the piano, and think, or fall asleep, or reflect on the meaning of an empty life—was it like a vast hall you wandered through with nowhere to rest, or like a huge unfurnished room where every word you said echoed back to you. And aren't I lucky, I thought, that my life is so full, with such a lot to do: my hobbies, and police investigations, and calisthenics. I didn't waste my time on useless thoughts, did I? And supposing there were dull, empty days from time to time; now, thanks to Chaim and our friendship, each day was full and exciting.

Sometimes I would ask myself why a genius like him was so keen on a kid like me. I mean, compared to him (artistically speaking), I was kind of backward and still had a lot to learn. Even then I realized with an aching heart that I might never become like Chaim, that I might live my whole life as a lowly soccer player, a climber of telephone poles, an artiste of make-believe.

Sometimes Micah would join me in the tree house and ask what the matter was and why I always kept to myself. I would silence him with a wave of my hand and point to the source of Chaim Stauber's music. And Micah would shake his heavy head and say that music bored him. Once or twice I flew into a rage over his contempt for meaningful things, but eventually I gave up and just felt sorry for him.

The minute Chaim Stauber finished practicing he would come flying out to play with me. All the culture and serenity would fade away. His mother had no inkling of what happened to him when he left the house. Thanks to my face and my cautious behavior whenever I paid them a visit, she was sure I was a mild-mannered, responsible boy like Chaim. From Chaim's stories I gathered that eventually she would make friends with the neighbors and start to ask them questions about me, and when she found out who and what I was, she would realize I had been putting on an act around them, pretending to be a sensitive, dependable child, when in fact I was just the opposite.

Though not really the opposite, I felt, and even cried out in protest against the inevitable verdict, and wished I could explain it to her: because in non-opposite reality I am like that, even though I'm not like that. I could never be sure what I was going to be next. And yet whenever I was at their house, I was truly good, almost innocent. Unbeknownst to her, the week before the final contest I clipped my pinky nail. A wave of devotion and responsibility would engulf me whenever she walked into Chaim's room and asked us softly whether we'd like a nice drink of fresh-squeezed juice now and a plate of butter cookies.

I knew she'd find out, though. It was a miracle that she hadn't already.

But Chaim Stauber had.

No, not that I was wild, and sometimes more than just wild. That he liked, which may have been the problem: that was all he liked about me. Once I'd finished showing him everything I could do, and taken him to all my secret places and taught him how to crawl through the sewer pipe, and scare drivers with death-defying leaps from the sidewalk, how to swipe cakes from Sarah's store, and how to glue a dog and cat together with rubber cement, and how to take money out of the charity box in the synagogue, and how to make a yellow scorpion commit suicide, and a hundred and one other tricks I knew—then he got a little tired of me.

I have to write the truth about it, even though it still hurts.

He got tired of me, all right. It didn't take him long to explore my depths.

I realized this before he did. I had long prepared myself for the moment of abandonment. And when I saw his eyes go blank when I started to tell him something, I felt awful and empty and unwanted.

My mind started working overtime. For example, I came up with the idea of going over to the university and catching some gambusia fish in the pond outside the Canada building. Is that allowed? asked Chaim Stauber, and when I answered no, he asked, a little disappointed, "Is that all, just no?" I immediately answered that in fact it was absolutely against the law, it was stealing from a scientific institution, and he said, "Cool—let's go!"

So we went off to catch gambusia fish with nylon bags, and poured them into the big fountain at the entrance to the university where the tourists throw coins. We did it five or six times, and a month later the fountain was so full of gambusias, they had to change the water.

Great, that was over; now I had to think of something new to light up his eyes. Because that's what he wanted, for us to share adventures, and ever more daring exploits; only, it got too complicated, because all I wanted was to be with him, to listen to him talking about the Civil War and the Incas and Mozart and the Gypsies, and all the other things he would tell me in his calm, gentle way, without showing off. I wanted to look at the thick black hair combed back from his high and handsome forehead. That's all I wanted. That and no more. I think he must be the only boy I have never tried to sell or rent something to for an hour. If he expressed interest in something of mine, I'd just give it to him as a present. For me, his friendship was a present.

I blush to remember the pranks I planned to keep Chaim with me. If Dad had discovered some of the things I did, he would have sent me to juvenile court. One night Chaim and I sneaked out and poured sugar into the gas tank of our principal's car, which ruined the motor, and for years the car stood dead in front of his house with a dead motor, a sign of our wickedness.*

But I couldn't help it. Chaim found new friends who were apparently more interesting. Maybe they could talk to him about Mozart and the Incas. Maybe they understood what he meant by "a full life."

And I was stuck with Micah. I was mean to him. I tormented him. He didn't understand what was going on, or maybe he did. Maybe he liked my tormenting him because that made the ugliness in me stand out even more.

One day in class, Chaim Stauber said something about bullfights, that in Spain there are six bulls killed in every bullfight. When I came home that day I did what any decent citizen would do after hearing a thing like that—I called the police.

I told Gabi to stop whatever she was doing and tell me everything she knew about bullfights.

Gabi took a cab to the public library. She came home with a sheet of paper on which she had copied out what the encyclopedia said. We hurried to the kitchen, where she read it to me. She didn't ask any questions. With one swift glance she saw the whole story on my face, muttered, "Knowledge is power, eh?," and went on reading. I closed my eyes, letting her every word imprint itself just where my brain was sore with jealousy.

Next morning I found an opportunity to tell Chaim that the little sword they plunge into the bull at the beginning of the corrida is called a banderilla, and that it's shaped like a bee's stinger so it will pierce the hide and be hard to take out. Chaim listened earnestly and said he didn't know that, but did I know the difference between a matador and a torero?

Gabi worked hard to solve that one. She called up some friends and

* Should Mr. Aviezer Carmi, our retired school principal, ever read this story, I hope he will forgive me, and of course, I'll gladly compensate him for the damage. Please understand, though, Mr. Carmi, I had no choice. The fear of Chaim Stauber leaving me was utterly unbearable. It was his friendship that saved me, I don't know from what, maybe from being like Micah Dubovsky, another ordinary kid. When I was with Chaim, I felt there was more to me, that I had the chance to learn something else. And when Chaim began to get tired of me, I could feel myself falling back into Micah's gaping mouth.

even one of her old professors, and the conclusion was that a torero is anyone who participates in a bullfight, but only the matador kills the bull.

The next day at recess I blurted the information out to Chaim, explaining that in Portugal they don't kill the bulls, and in Spain an outstanding matador receives the bull's ear as a prize, sometimes both ears, and if he's absolutely tremendous like Paco Camino ("the greatest of them all," I added), he receives the tail as well. There was a flickering in Chaim's eyes. He said his father had promised to find him postcards of a real bullfight which he would then be able to show me. And I made the innocent suggestion that he should look for postcards showing the banderillas, because "they're really spectacular" (I swear, that's what I said!), so we'd see the bright paper ribbons hanging from the barbed darts.

And I walked off.

And Chaim followed me.

And then cautiously, in a roundabout way, he returned.

Day after day we would exchange useful information about the corrida, the costumes, the different sorts of knives and lances. He would finish practicing at five-thirty and hurry to my tree house, where we would spend a couple of minutes, limiting our conversation to a single topic. This was the suitable thing to do. Our revived friendship was too shaky to overburden now. Maybe Chaim sensed how raw with pain I was.

There was an unspoken pact between us, a pact of mercy, and we were careful not to speak of things he knew about but I didn't. He truly was one of a kind.

We would chat about the famous matadors I knew of from the material Gabi found for me, or about those tragic instances when a bull killed a matador, or the various methods of thrusting a sword. With a shiver of delight, we would savor names like Rafaelo di Paula, Ricardo Torres, and Luis Machaniti, and quiz each other on their famous fights and where they got an ear or a tail and where they had surrendered their glorious lives . . . And after a few minutes of such small talk, flimsy as a cobweb but iridescent in the light, Chaim would politely take his leave, and I would recline on my back for an hour, content and benevolent enough to tolerate Micah's face slowly rising through the branches.

"What's happening, Nonny?"

One week, two weeks. A fine thread. If it tore, I would plummet to the end of time, I could not endure another such blow. Gabi worked like a demon. Every day she would phone the cultural attaché at the Spanish embassy and pump him for more information. She went to visit her parents in Nes Ziona and came back with a book of poems by García Lorca, who wrote about bullfights; I, meanwhile, began to spy on Pessia, the cow our neighbor Mautner brought with him when he left his kibbutz. Pessia had never been dehorned, so she now boasted two splendid bony protuberances which were of no use to her whatsoever. Pessia had a quiet, easygoing nature. She loved to stand in the little meadow behind Mautner's house, chewing the long grass with a sideways movement of her puffy lips, so dreamily content that her black eyes shone with something nearly human. One day I ran before her, waving a red towel I had swiped from the clothesline. As she watched bewilderedly, her tail started swishing like a pendulum, and I wondered if maybe she had some Spanish blood. That evening, in a mood of sublime pathos, Gabi recited "The Goring and the Death" from Lorca's "Lament for Ignacio Sánchez Mejías," a poem in memory of a dead matador. There were lines like "The bass strings began to throb at five in the afternoon. The wounds burned with the heat of suns at five in the afternoon. Horrifying five in the afternoon!"

Gabi finished reading. Her face was dark. Her hand trembled, and her head fell backward as though it had been severed with a sword. I shivered under the covers. Lorca's words passed through me like a heady wine. I pulled the blanket over my head and my bed seemed to burst into flames. Later, after the horrible incident, Gabi remarked that if she had foreseen how Lorca's poem would affect me, she'd have stuck to *When We Were Very Young*. But all that night she let the words resound through the room and flash blood-red behind my dreaming lids . . . The next day, at the water fountain, I announced to Chaim and Micah that I'd made up my mind. I had decided on my goal in life:

To be the first Israeli matador.

Silence. The skies of Spain turned red above me.

"You've got to be kidding," whispered Chaim in awe. "You're going to break into Mautner's yard?"

"Yeah, sure, why not? I'll fight that bull if it's the last thing I do."

And it probably would be. Because Mautner was a very tough character.

"She's a cow," observed Micah. "Pessia is a cow."

A wave of terror, terror of myself, washed over me. The little motor in my head was buzzing like a wasp.

"Well, she does have horns," Chaim answered slowly, beginning to grasp that what I was proposing here was the wildest, wickedest exploit yet, the ultimate proof of my friendship.

"So, are you guys in?" I asked. "I'll need two picadors with swords."

There was a moment's silence. Gory visions whirled through my brain with piercing cries and shrill admonitions. But then Chaim's eyes lit up like torches, and we both began to titter nervously. Micah looked on with contempt, or maybe glee, because he'd already guessed what would happen. I ignored him. I didn't want to see his boring face anymore. What did he know about courage, and madness, and friendship, and thrilling escapades, and a life of meaning? Chaim and I joined hands and started jumping up and down and screaming, but quietly, lest his mother turn up and see my seven deadly sins upon us.

14

Wanted: Dulcinea

"**A**h, what a meal!" said Felix, setting his fork down and smiling with contentment.

A rosy dimness spread over the restaurant. Petal-pink candles illumined every table. My tummy was round and full, and on my plate were the remains of the best dinner I had ever eaten in my life. For an hors d'oeuvre, Felix ordered goose-liver pâté, followed by cream of asparagus soup and duck à l'orange. I could barely resist the juicy steaks I saw on passing trays, but I controlled myself and dined on rice and fried potatoes instead—incredibly delicious rice and fried potatoes! Twice I asked for a second helping, and then I ordered fresh mushroom soup and stuffed peppers with almonds and pine nuts, and three servings of chocolate mousse for dessert, and when Felix asked what I thought of the food, I answered sincerely that the chef at the police cafeteria had a lot to learn.

"Best of all, today and tomorrow you and I will do great things!" rasped Felix in the voice of Grandpa Noah.

"Like what?" I asked warily, and immediately repeated the question in Tammy's voice so no one would suspect anything.

"Perhaps we make this world more exciting." He laughed. "When people hear what we did, they will say, 'Oo-la-la! Such finesse! They were so daring, those two!' "

"But what will we do?" I whispered.

"I don't know. You decide. Anything. There are no limits! No laws! Only courage! Nerve! You must to dare."

Hah. I must to dare. Easy enough to say. But what do I really want? To sneak into the movies? To break into the teachers' lounge at school? To steal the skeleton from the science room? I realized these wishes would sound pitiful to a man like him. I had to try harder, to liberate myself, to be worthy of Felix, to take risks, to be crazy, to be a criminal. I must to dare . . .

Should I climb up to the roof of one of the embassies and change the flag, as Dad did once before he joined the police force? Or steal a zebra from the zoo and ride away on it?

I wanted to do something new, something all my own.

The heavyset waiter who had been serving us approached our table again, leaned over, and removed the bottle of pink champagne from the bucket of ice water. He poured more sparkling wine into Felix's glass. I was still on my first. The bubbles danced in it. I'll never forget the moment at the beginning of the meal when the waiter popped the cork with a loud bang and champagne gushed out of the bottle . . .

Life sure is different at home, I thought. If I were home at this hour, Gabi would already be gone and Dad and I would be in our rooms, with everything peaceful and quiet. I would be playing table soccer against myself or leafing through a catalogue of service revolvers and police equipment, or doing calisthenics, or just lying in bed, sucking candy, thinking of nothing at all, deep in reverie, with my eyes closing and my finger tracing the scratch on the wall—I could almost feel it with my fingernail now—a scratch the shape of a thunderbolt, which I had put there, and which I would dig into whenever I felt the need to cry; Dad would be in his room, reading the paper (he'd started to wear reading glasses of late, but didn't like being seen in them), or working on his case files, or phoning headquarters every five minutes to check on the patrols. Then one of us—usually me, because I was always hungry—would start to fix supper. When it was just the two of us, we ate simply: mushroom soup from a mix, canned corn and chickpeas (and meatballs for Dad). Side by side, in contented silence, we would work at our respective tasks, listening to the Hebrew-song radio program we both liked so much. Sometimes I would tell him things that happened at school, but he never really listened. I could tell him things that didn't happen, make up children's names, lie to him, and he would only look at me distantly and sigh. It was hard to imagine how I would feel the next time I was home at this hour, now that I knew how exciting life could be in places like this restaurant.

"I see you have trouble deciding, little Tammy?"

I smiled at him dreamily. "Yes, there's so much I—"

"Fine. Think slow. No hurry."

Again I drifted off, slowly stroking my pigtail. What should I ask for? How far would I dare to go? I was totally unprepared for this, for a fairy godfather like Felix to come along and offer me three wishes. Every time I tugged at the pigtail, my wig would stretch, right over my forehead, and that felt good. It tickled. Now what should I ask him for? What did I want to do most of all?

To stay here in the dream. To sink into it as though it were a featherbed. And to feel a little homesick.

Because on the days when Gabi stayed with us, the days she didn't have classes in cinematography or beginner's French or how to feel full and lose weight fast—in short, on a Sunday or a Wednesday, we would all be in the kitchen together, fixing supper, eating and talking, and arguing. Sometimes I would just sit there and let them go at each other. That's when they seemed most like a real couple. Dad would start nearly everything he said with "Look—uh—Gabi," as if he had trouble remembering her name, or as if her name were "Uhgabi," and she would get back at him by calling him "dearest" or "apple of my eye" or "flower of my youth." On rare occasions, Dad would tell us about his problems at work. Once, Gabi helped him solve the case of a diamond polisher who kept getting robbed. (It seems the diamond polisher was using Dad's coat pockets to hide the stones. As soon as Dad carried out his daily search of the other employees, the diamond polisher would pick his pockets, sell the diamonds, and claim the insurance money, to boot.) After supper we would wander into the living room to read the papers, and Dad would put his feet up and smoke the daily cigarette Gabi allowed him. And she would go back to the kitchen to make the special Bedouin coffee you have to bring to a boil seven times, and from there she would inform us noisily about the latest world news, and then she would corner me and ask about school, who liked whom in my class, and whether we did the latest dances at parties yet (as if I knew). That was the kind of thing that used to thrill her when she was a girl.

Then at around ten o'clock, by which time Dad and I were already exhausted, she would suddenly decide to tackle our closets and take out the winter clothes or the summer clothes and sort them in piles for ironing, folding, mending, and the house would be filled with flying, floating, and flapping garments, and Gabi, her pants rolled up to her knees and her cheeks flushed, would sing Beatles songs as she loaded the washing machine, or ironed, or mopped the hall, running to the kitchen between chores to fix us the treat rated seventh on the international YUMTUM scale (yummy in the tummy): instant chocolate pudding, which only Gabi knew how to make so smooth, without the yucky lumps. And meanwhile, she would order Dad to wash the dishes and hang out the laundry and throw away the old newspapers that were cluttering up the house; me, she would send to straighten the big mess in my room, and Dad and I, like chastened slaves, would grumble about her and make faces behind her back whenever we met between the hall and the bathroom, but what choice did we have, born for a life of toil, hooked on the instant pudding only she knew how to make without lumps, and at midnight the three of us would collapse, with the house fit again for human habitation and the silence broken only by our three spoons scraping the last drop of pudding from the bottom of our dishes, and my lids would droop, and Dad would forget himself and put a hand on her shoulder and kiss her forehead as though I weren't there, but what did I care, let him kiss her, I wished he would, and now the day was over and I curled up on my chair so that he would carry me to bed in his strong but (for me) gentle arms, and now I am sound asleep, but who just kissed me so tenderly and was that an expression of friendship between two pros?

As though from afar I heard Felix whisper: "But now you must to dare! You must to think big, my Tammyleh! Think in color, like cinema, like theater!"

As he pronounced the word "theater," a firecracker went off in my head: what a jackass I'd been, or rather, what a jenny ass. But I didn't dare tell him my new idea. I was afraid he might think it was stupid, that I was a real jerk for blowing my chance to become a daring criminal and requesting presents for a girl instead.

"Presents for someone, perhaps?" asked Felix with a smile that made me worry he could see everything on my face; but if I had such a thin skin, how come he didn't realize that I knew who he was?

"Yes . . ." He smiled, leaning back contentedly. "I see everything on your face—is something for your lady you want. How lovely! Like what was his name, Don Quixote, who fought for Mistress Dulcinea!"

Even I, who'd never bothered much with books as a child, knew that once upon a time, a not so beautiful lady in the village of Toboso had inspired Don Quixote to set out on his adventures.

"So what you say, Tammy?" Felix pressed me with a sly twinkle. "Have we decided yet who will win your courage? Who is your beautiful lady? Felix can keep secret!"

"Gabi," I blurted.

"Gabi?" he burst out, aglow with laughter. "I expected to hear you name prettiest girl in your class, not your stepmother!"

"Gabi is not my mother, step or otherwise. She's Gabi!"

"Gabi, then. Beg pardon. So you are her champion."

"Well, first I thought of Zohara," I lied, "but Zohara is dead, and no one else has offered to be Gabi's knight, so—"

"I understand!" Felix raised a finger. "Gabi you say, Gabi it is!" I felt childish and silly. Why didn't I name some girl I knew, like Semadar Cantor, or Bathsheba Rubin, the rival queens of the class. But I didn't like either of them or want to serve in their name.

But Zohara. Why hadn't I thought of her first?

"You give me big surprise!" said Felix. "You are very fine gentleman for Gabi, her true knight. Ladies will love you for this, take it from Felix . . ." And then he added: "You make me feel new, I am like new man."

Me? Him?

"So we offer our courage for Mistress Gabi." He shook my hand across the table. "What special present would you like to bring her? How about small diamond or modest cruise to Cyprus?"

"No . . . she gets seasick, even at the beach . . ." I mumbled, and as for a diamond, that would be too grandiose for Gabi. I stared down at the table. I shrugged my shoulders as if to say I had no idea what she might want. Because I didn't know how to tell him without feeling like a total idiot.

"But surely there is one thing above all that she wants," Felix prompted, and by now I recognized that tone of his which said: "Don't be ashamed to dream, ask for everything, for what is possible and for what is not. You must to dare!"

I started to giggle. "I know this is silly, but . . . No, never mind, it's ridiculous."

Felix leaned toward me. His eyes lit up. "Ridiculous is my middle name," he said guilefully. "I am world champion at being ridiculous."

"Well," I said offhandedly, "actually, there is this actress Gabi likes, I mean, she's a great fan of hers."

"Actress, you say?"

"Yes, in the National Theater. Lola Ciperola."

A spark of light? A warning flash? What was that sudden gleam in his eyes? And did he really prick his ears like a panther?

"Lola Ciperola? Ah yes—I know this name—I even met her once." His eyes looked like narrow blue slits now, and I knew he was withdrawing into a lively dialogue with himself, a vigorous debate. But soon he was back again.

"Yes, Lola— She was famous even in my time! When I was young, she was queen of Tel Aviv." And his arms swayed over the table in a graceful dance as he sang: " 'Your eyes shine / Di-a-monds / From the quay, you wave farewell—' Ah yes, Lola sang as well as acted, and she danced, too—she could do everything!" Again his voice faded in contemplation. "Only I didn't know she is still popular with young people like Miss Gabi—"

Here was my big chance: I stretched my legs and told him that Gabi did a great imitation of Lola Ciperola, that she often made me laugh and cry with scenes from Lola's plays. There were a number I even knew by heart, thanks to Gabi.

"So, Miss Gabi is great fan of Lola's?"

"Yes . . . and she sings 'Your Eyes Shine' just like Lola, same movements and everything, you can hardly tell the difference. Anyway, Gabi says that if she had a—uhm—a scarf—no, forget it."

"No!" His voice resounded and his smile grew wider. "We forget nothing! You must to tell me everything! Now what about this scarf? This scarf is Lola's?"

Oh the hell with it, what did I care?

"Sometimes Gabi says, jokingly of course, that if she could somehow get hold of Lola Ciperola's scarf, she, too, could become an actress or a singer, anything she wanted. Oh, never mind."

"Lola's scarf?"

"You see," I endeavored to explain, "Lola Ciperola always wears a purple scarf in her pictures, whether she's at home or at the theater or anywhere, it's her trademark."

"Yes, this I know. It has always been so—Lola's purple scarf— Did you see it once?"

"Once?" I beamed. "Eleven times!"

"Oho! And how is that?"

"Mostly at the theater," I answered. "Three times Gabi took me to *Romeo and Juliet*, twice to *Crime and Punishment*, once to *Blood Wedding*, and four times to *Macbeth*. And once I actually met her in person, on the street in Tel Aviv."

"You meet her by chance?"

I hesitated. This was supposed to be our secret, mine and Gabi's. Not even Dad was allowed to know.

"By chance. We were waiting near her house, and she came out."

"By chance you wait near her house?"

"Yes—we just happened to be—"

We had waited for her maybe fifty times before, but she appeared only that once.

"And did you speak to her?"

"We almost did. Gabi asked her what time it was, but she didn't hear. She was in a hurry."

How Gabi's hand on my shoulder fluttered as Lola Ciperola walked by! We had been waiting for an hour and a half by the bushes in front of her house in Tel Aviv. We almost froze, it was so cold, the clouds were low and heavy, but suddenly the whole world turned to gold, and there she was in the back of a cab, wearing a broad-brim hat. She waited for the driver to open the door, put a long, shapely leg out of the cab, declined his hand, and said in her hoarse, majestic voice: "You may charge it to the theater." And away she went, like a queen, with her purple scarf floating out behind her. For almost a whole minute we stood within touching distance of her, which is why we waited for her so many times after that, spending hours in the heat and cold and rain and wind, our umbrellas blown inside out and our hearts pounding with disappointment, but we never stopped trying on our excursions to Tel Aviv.

"And did Lola not speak to you?"

"No, she was in kind of a hurry." Gabi had pushed me right in front of her, but a woman like Lola Ciperola is too busy to notice what goes on at her feet. She didn't even glance at us, but strode ahead, dignified and stately, and we forgave her and didn't take it too much to heart, because she was Lola and we were only us.

Felix reflected a moment, hiding his mouth behind his shapely hand. Now that he knew, I couldn't hold back anymore. "Gabi said that there's a secret charm in Lola Ciperola's scarf, but she was only joking, I'm sure." Even her name tasted sweet to me, like white Swiss chocolate.

"But exactly what is this charm of Lola's?" asked Felix pensively. I was amazed at how familiarly he pronounced her name.

"Her charm in being an actress of such"—I groped for Gabi's word—"such genius."

The heavyset waiter with the puffy face brought us a tray of coffee. He kept trying to ingratiate himself with Felix, hoping to get a nice fat tip from the elegant gentleman. Looking at the prices on the menu I calculated how much the meal would cost and nearly fainted: it amounted to half Dad's monthly salary. Maybe being a waiter wasn't such a bad profession. Maybe Gabi's idea of opening a restaurant was a good one, after all. Slowly I sipped the black coffee, which tasted horribly bitter, though I tried not to let it show on my face so Felix wouldn't guess I'd never drunk black coffee before.

Felix was lost in thought, and I began to wonder about Lola Ciperola's admirers, the poets and artists of her circle, and how once in an
interview in the evening paper *Maariv* she declared she would never
marry, because marriage was a form of bondage and she could not
conceive of letting any man dominate her body and soul. "No man on
earth would be worth it," she said in an interview with *Woman's Mag-
azine*, "and no man alive has ever loved a woman the way a woman
can love a man." That's the kind of unabashed statement she made all
the time.

"I could kiss her every word," said Gabi, licking her lips. "If I had
one fourth of that woman's courage, I would be happy."

The waiters carried a cake with lighted candles to a pretty woman
sitting in the far corner, and everyone in the restaurant sang "Happy
birthday to you." I felt nice and warm. Candlelight flickered on the tall
glasses. My cheeks burned. Now that I had disclosed my idea to Felix,
I felt quite exuberant, easily able to switch back and forth between
Tammy and Nonny by smoothing down my pigtail and tugging at it
like a bell rope to summon up the little Tammy within. My gestures
and expressions stayed pretty much the same, and all I had to do was
shift the center of feeling, as it were, from one square of my heart to
the other with a barely perceptible click.

Then Felix pulled the monocle out of his pocket, stared at me curiously, and nodded till his face grew gentle and happy; it didn't bother
me a bit that he was aware of my clicking back and forth. I was so
delighted to see my reflection in his monocle again, because it made me
feel omnipotent, as if I had been dipped in a magic potion and could
turn into anything or anyone I wanted, even a girl, no sweat, I was a
pro, a master. A prodigy of change. With a few days' practice, I could
be like Felix. His double even. His heir.

Felix put the monocle back in his pocket, raised his champagne glass
as if to toast my performance, and drank it down. "Excellent meal,"
he said, licking his lips. "Many years ago, when Felix was still Felix, at
least one night of week I would reserve this restaurant for me and my
friends. In those days I had money to pay for meals." He smiled
broadly. I hadn't listened too closely. I should have, but the excitement

went to my head. He wiped his mouth with his handkerchief: "And does Mistress Gabi also wish to be great actress?"

"At one time she did, but now she only wishes she had Lola Ciperola's courage to follow her desires, no matter what people think." And to be independent like Lola, and strong like Lola, and to drive men crazy the way Lola does, instead of being hurt by them, and to get Dad to take her seriously for a change and beg her on his knees to marry him. That's what Gabi really wanted, though of course I didn't tell Felix that.

"And what does Mr. Feuerberg, Sr., have to say about this?" asked Felix, who read me like an open book.

"I hope he never finds out. That's our secret, Gabi's and mine."

"That Lola is Gabi's idol?" Felix inquired.

"Yes. And that we met her in Tel Aviv and went to see her plays." Gabi had made me swear not to say a word to Dad about this, and never to mention Lola Ciperola's name in the house. I probably shouldn't have mentioned it to Felix, either.

"You won't tell, will you?"

Felix pledged secrecy with a hand to his heart and a fluttering of his long lashes. "I promise you."

"No—swear to me."

The flames of the guttering candles danced in his glasses. "Know this," he said, "when Felix swears, he cheats you. But if he promises, he keeps his word. That is how it is. So, now I give you my criminal's word of honor."

I hesitated, and agreed to this.

Maybe because what he said about cheating reminded me vaguely of something else. "What were you just telling me?"

"When? I tell you many things."

"Before, about not having money to pay for the restaurant."

"Ach, she is great lady!" cheered Felix. "She is superb!"

"Who? Lola Ciperola?"

"No, our Mistress Gabi-Dulcinea. I am very pleased with her." I was so glad he said that, I forgot what I wanted to ask him. Then he mumbled something to himself and asked, "Does she wish to have Lola's scarf?"

"Yes."

And also your golden ear of wheat. But I didn't dare say so aloud.

"And what else does Miss Gabi want? Do not be ashamed. Tell me everything!" He went on speaking with an air of amusement, though I noticed how fast his fingers fluttered.

"How did you know that she wanted something else?"

"I am waiting, Mr. Feuerberg."

Then I realized that he knew already. I looked down at the table. It was life or death.

"A golden ear of wheat; one of yours."

"I knew you will say this," said Felix, unsmiling.

My heart was beating fast. It's all over, I thought, my wonderful dream-come-true with him. He toyed with a matchstick and casually asked, "So you know who I am all along?"

"No, only since this afternoon," I confessed, "when the policeman read out the name on your driver's license."

"I did not know you were paying attention," he mumbled, slumping a little in his chair. "I thought that police fellow was too young to remember my name, and I thought you were not listening . . ." He bent the match back till it snapped, and I began to tremble. "All this time you keep it in your heart, when you know that I am Felix Glick. I think one day you will be best detective in world."

But his voice had a harsh ring to it suddenly, as though he were speaking across a barricade, and again I sensed the danger in him.

"What do you know about me? What else did Miss Gabi tell you?"

"Uh, more or less what you told me yourself while we were eating. That you were once very rich but you wasted your money. That you were the king of Tel Aviv, and that you traveled all over the world and that you—did things: you robbed banks and outsmarted all of Interpol." In order to spare his feelings, I refrained from mentioning that I knew how he and Dad had met the first time.

"And she has never spoken of this in front of your father?"

"Never. It's our secret."

"She is very special person," said Felix wistfully, running his finger over the black ring on his right hand. "She is more clever than Felix, more than your Mr. Father, too, I think. Real smart apple!"

"Do you mean it? You really think she's special?" Living with Gabi for so long, and seeing the way Dad treated her, sometimes made me forget how smart and special she truly was.

Felix thought awhile and selected his words with care: "I think, if I understand her plan right—I say, Bravo, Miss Gabi! You are real smart apple!"

I felt as if I'd been redeemed. As if the whole trip had been salvaged, and now Felix and I could carry on. But I didn't dare believe it.

"So we are agreed? We will try to . . . to take scarf?"

"Right, and the golden ear of wheat, too."

Praised be the Lord and glory hallelujah!

"And by any chance did our Miss Gabi mention why she wants my ear of wheat?"

"Not that I remember."

But I was lying. I was afraid he'd be insulted.

Because Gabi used to joke that if she'd been blessed with a criminal nature, Dad would surely have fallen in love with her, seeing that his one true passion in life was crime. Maybe I should have told Felix that. He might have taken it as a compliment. Gabi used to say, "Felix Glick and Lola Ciperola! There's the winning combination! Bring me the purple scarf and the golden ear of wheat, Nonny, and with my one fairy-tale wish I will overcome the ill fate of my patty-cake face and win the prince's reluctant heart! Canst thou find them, O my knight?"

And she would flutter her eyelashes.

Felix said, "Maybe Lola will ask favor in return for giving us something so important to her!"

"Let her ask! It will be our task!"

"But maybe she will ask something very difficult!"

"You must to dare!" I reminded him, nearly bursting with joy.

Felix smoothed down his pasted mustache. "So perhaps I, too, ask something in return for ear of wheat, eh? And it will not be easy."

A warning bell sounded inside me. "What . . . what do you want?"

I had spoken too sharply, as though he were a stranger.

"Don't be afraid, Mr. Feuerberg!" he replied. I sensed he was insulted. "Have you no faith in Felix?"

"I was only asking . . ."

"No! Don't speak. Don't lie!" And all at once he blew his top. "Felix never lied to you! Why you must to always make sure about him? That is unkind. It is great pity, too."

He fell silent. His lips were pale with anger, his brow was furrowed, and the little pouches at the corners of his mouth began to twitch. He was a fairly old man, but humiliation turned him into a little boy again.

I was ashamed of myself. Repentantly I explained, "I just wanted to know what you want me to do for you."

"Not yet. First I must to know that you are truly ready." He crossed his arms over his chest and looked at me.

"I'm ready, okay? I'm ready now!"

Felix shook his head. "No, no. You are still suspicious, always making sure about me!" He had totally forgotten the Grandpa Noah disguise and spoke to me in his usual voice. "Don't you see that Felix is making you special offer? This is your big chance to think like Felix, to live tales of adventure! But only if you believe me, even my lies, then you will be worthy of my law!"

What could I say? I wanted desperately to please him, but at the same time I was kind of scared. Maybe I didn't believe him all the way. Maybe I didn't have it in me to be an out-and-out criminal, not even a pretend one, because I always scare myself.

"Finish your coffee and we go," he said, and added, "It is not necessary to drink the grounds, you know. Come, we have much work to do."

I put down the cup and we looked into each other's eyes. He seemed a little calmer now. I hoped one day he would forgive me for insulting him.

"Do you know where we are going?"

"To take Lola Ciperola's scarf?" I answered in suspense. I could scarcely believe I had uttered those words. I wanted him to be aware that I was changing before his eyes.

"Bravo," he said wearily. "You are quick learner."

"Come on." I jumped up eagerly. I wanted to infect him with my joy, my exuberance, so he would forget what had just occurred. "Let's go!"

"One moment!" He frowned as he sat before me, but a sly new gleam entered his eye with a look both pious and reproachful. "Is that any way to behave, Mr. Tammy Feuerberg? We are in restaurant here! First we must to dodge our bill!"

15

The Bullfight

"But what if she isn't home?" I asked a few minutes later as we drove away.

"She will be, she will be," muttered Felix, and began to hum again, clicking his tongue in syncopation and tapping the wheel. "She is maybe at theater still, acting in play, but later she will go directly home."

"What if she decides to go somewhere else instead?"

"No, she must to come straight home."

It annoyed me that he was suddenly such an expert on Lola Ciperola. I had devoted a lot more of my time to her than he had.

"Why must she come straight home?"

"Because that is law of things, what will be will be. And Lola Ciperola must to come home and give you her scarf. That is that!"

"Whose law?"

"Law of . . . of our adventure. It is special law! You will understand it by-and-by."

I didn't understand, though. I felt comfortable in the seat of the old Beetle. I leaned back, snug as a bug in a rug (Gabi), too tired by now to be afraid of either the heavyset waiter we had left behind in the parking lot, shouting and waving his arms, or the two police barricades we passed through easily, without arousing suspicion. I had a hunch this was my lucky day.

But who was I?

A fake, an impostor. A boy disguised as a girl. Walking out of restaurants without paying the bill. Which is stealing, you know. And still—there was a subtle yet painfully intense sensation between my eyes that fluttered sweetly through my head and down my spine . . . the thrill of Felix's perfect caper—the way he persuaded the waiter to give our car a push, and how he left him behind holding the heavy wallet, heavy but empty, or rather, full of sand . . . I'm skipping some of the details, but they're not important. Or maybe I'm ashamed to tell what I did, the part I played in the cruel little hoax.

Dad will probably get here tomorrow and pay the bill, I suddenly realized, and felt relieved. Too relieved. I didn't want to think about it. I tore the wig off and scratched my head with all ten fingernails. Enough is enough. I'm me, Nonny, and I don't want any more of this tammyrot. Dad will show up at the restaurant tomorrow morning with a fat wallet—not that I've ever seen him with a fat wallet—and with a smile and a pat on the shoulder he'll apologize and explain and work things out and pay the bill, and leave a fat tip, hey, suddenly everything is fat, and by the time he leaves they'll all be smiling and happy again, even the fat waiter we cheated, and everyone will say, Yes, that was a great caper, he's a real pro, who wouldn't forgive such a brilliant performance, and then Dad will hurry on to the scene of Felix's next prank, where once again he'll put things right.

Nitwit, Nonny numskull.

"But you still owe me something, Mr. Feuerberg," said Felix. "You promised to tell me why you are vegetarian and don't eat meat."

"Do you really want to hear?" I asked, because what was that compared to his escapades?

"Do I want to hear?" He laughed. "I want to hear all your stories! I want to know everything about your life."

Again I wasn't paying enough attention. I assumed he'd said what he did to flatter me, to open me up. Only later did I realize he'd meant every word. He really did want to know everything about me, every detail of my boring life. I was just too dumb to believe him, and I had no idea what he meant.

We joggled up the coastal road. The air was sultry, summery. Cars whizzed by us on their way to Tel Aviv. Jerusalem was fast asleep at this hour, but here, life was just beginning. Felix stopped humming and listened to me, but I was so quiet, he turned on the radio. Soft, breathy jazz poured into the Beetle, the kind of music Gabi loves. I closed my eyes and thought about home and her and Dad, and about not having called all day to tell them how I was and to thank them for coming up with this crazy idea. And I wondered how Dad had found it in himself to let me go through such an experience, in the midst of his life-and-death war against crime?

And then, half-dreaming, I started to talk.

Not right away, though. My tongue was too thick and my brain too slow. I wasn't quite ready to tell him the whole Chaim Stauber story. I began with my Israeli bullfighter idea, described then how me and Chaim and the other guys rigged up banderillas out of broken rakes decorated with crepe paper from the sukkah, and used broomsticks for the horses with heads made of old army socks stuffed with rags, and how we roamed the neighborhood, stealing anything red we could find on the clotheslines—skirts, shirts, dresses, towels—I mean, how else are you supposed to rouse a bull?

And these are the children of Israel who did the work:

> Banderilleros: Simon Margolies and Avi Cabeza.
> Picadors: Chaim Stauber and Micah Dubovsky.
> Matador: me, Nonny.

"How nice that you were matador," Felix remarked.

"Why nice?"

"I like for you to play leading role. I like for you to be like me."

Then, at five o'clock sharp, Lorca time, we all sneaked through the hole in the fence into Mautner's yard, where Pessia was quietly grazing. She looked up at us with unsuspecting black eyes and went on chewing. She was a big old cow, covered with black and white patches. Mautner took good care of her. He had her artificially inseminated every year and sold her cute little calves without compunction. Having no wife or children of his own, he was probably closer to Pessia than any other living creature. I would say she was his soulmate, if I believed he had a soul.

Mautner was a big man with bristly, ginger-colored hair. His face was always red, as though he were about to explode or something, and he had a little mustache, from under which he emitted short phrases in an angry staccato. Every Thursday at four-thirty on the dot he would get into his Ford Cortina, wearing a khaki shirt covered with army decorations and khaki shorts, and drive away to the weekly meeting of the veterans of the Haganah. And every time Dad and I polished the Pearl, Mautner would march up, slap himself stiffly on the thigh, and ask Dad why he didn't have the nerve to take the Pearl out on the road like a real car. It was their weekly ritual: Dad, still crouching, would only say, "This is no ordinary automobile, Mautner, and if I take her out, she might get a whiff of freedom and go haywire. A car like this needs a lot of space. She's not made for the kind of roads we have in Israel!" And Mautner would sneer and say that if Dad would sell her to him, he was sure he could train her to wheel like a real sweetheart. At which point, with the same gesture every time, Dad would point to the grease-stained palm of his hand and say, "Sure, I'll let you drive her—when hair grows here."

And it did.

At five in the afternoon I stood before Mautner's cow. I was wearing a red poncho made from a towel with four red socks hanging from the corners like the rays of a big red sun. This was my *muleta* to wave at the bull. Simon Margolies and Avi Cabeza wore their best clothes for the occasion, Terylene trousers and white shirts. Avi, who was past his bar mitzvah already, put on a black bow tie as well.

But Chaim Stauber was really spiffed up: he wore a black suit (he was the only kid I'd ever met who owned one) with shiny trousers, a white shirt, and a jacket with pointy tails.

"It's for concerts," he explained. "Dad bought it for me when we were abroad. I'm not allowed to get it dirty."

We all shook hands, looking earnestly into each other's eyes, mounted our wooden horses, and began a slow, solemn lope around Pessia.

"A murmur of excitement runs through the crowd," I broadcast, and added with a shout, "Yes, ladies and gentlemen, the toro has a murderous glint in his eyes, and now he stamps into the bullring!" Pessia Mautner, that gentle soul, nodded her head as she chomped on a blade of grass.

"And now, the banderilleros," I announced with a flourish of my hand, stepping back ceremoniously.

Simon Margolies and Avi Cabeza rode quickly into the ring. According to the rules of the corrida, they should have been afoot, but as they both considered this an affront to their dignity, and threatened to form an Israeli guild of banderilleros to protect their rights, or worse, to quit the fight, I was forced to submit.

With shouts of "*Olé!*" they urged each other on, wildly waving their truncated lances. Avi, the more daring of the two, galloped all the way up to Pessia, whereupon, with a will of iron, he reined in his steed right in front of her nose. The noble steed reared up and whinnied, and Avi struck Pessia lightly on the back with the lance made out of the handle of a hoe.

A nervous giggle was heard. Chaim Stauber stood beside me, pressing his legs together.

"You touched her," said Micah in a slow bass voice. "Mautner's going to slaughter us."

But Avi Cabeza, who was drunk with pride by now, galloped around the ring, loudly cheering the Jerusalem soccer team, and once again struck Pessia, this time on the rump.

The big cow stumbled back a step. She raised her head and gazed at us in astonishment. Sunlight refracted against the tips of her horns in sudden anticipation of her terrible fury.

But her fury had not been roused yet. It was still dormant, inside her horns.

And to this task, the picadors, Micah and Chaim, charged swiftly with their yellow screwdriver lances, and did their bee dance around the cow. Micah was no great picador. He lacked (to put it mildly) a certain deftness and eccentricity. It was only out of friendship that I let him have the job. Chaim Stauber, on the other hand, was truly magnificent. He rode in full tilt on his stallion Death and circled the cow like a fearsome falcon, lurching at her unexpectedly and screaming in her ear, with his coattails flying out behind him. One time he even ran his screwdriver down her back.

Pessia started and gave a good strong kick with her hind leg.

In a flash the fight was over. Picadors and banderilleros huddled together, their faces pale, their fighting spirit gone.

"Are you going to let one lousy kick scare you to death?" I asked as I stepped forward, waving my red poncho around my face. It was a bath towel someone had swiped from a hotel in Tiberias.

Chaim Stauber stepped forward, too, panting and puffing. He eyed me quizzically. He had the most remarkable eyes I've ever seen, eyes that seemed to breathe, dilating and contracting in moments of excitement.

"You have the guts?" breathed his eyes.

"Do I have a choice?" answered mine.

I went down on my knees and prayed for the help of God. And being the first and only Jewish matador in history, I made the sign of the Star of David instead of the cross, and froze in this pose, like Paco Camino, Rafael Gómez, and Juan Belmonte. Maybe I could sense what was about to happen and wanted to savor the last few moments. And then slowly, momentously, I approached my good horse.

I began by slowly circling the cow. She was nervous by then and followed my movements with her oblong head. She looked pretty scary from close up, really big, too, a whole head taller than me and about as broad as a four-door closet. Then I galloped right in front of her wet black nose and saw her nostrils flare, and just as I was passing her, I smacked her near the tail with my open hand.

It sounded like a whip cracking. My whole hand ached, and Pessia looked back at me with a plaintive moo.

I was stunned by her mooing, but also stirred somehow. It was so real, just like she mooed when Mautner took her calf away each year. For a few days she would moan and cry, exactly the same way she'd mooed at me a moment before. And suddenly I was overwhelmed. I turned around. Pessia, too, turned around, with surprising grace, and stared right at me. Her milk-swollen udders sagged heavily. I stamped on the ground. So did Pessia. I lowered my head. So did she. I waited for her to moo. I was dying to hear that terrible sound again. But she played dumb. She refused to cooperate! And then, with a loud whoop, I galloped straight at her, swerving off in the nick of time and smacking her again with my open hand. And again she kicked at me and mooed, but I sheered away from her.

This was getting serious. The others were huddled by the hole in the fence. They were about make a run for it. I couldn't see their faces, but from time to time I would catch sight of Chaim's brightly burning eyes, and I knew that he was mine forever. That this bullfight was our covenant, because there was nothing more he could ask of me, nothing I could give him, beyond the madness I had whipped up for his sake.

Torrents of blood flowed through my brain, and then came that feverish buzzing between my eyes, with the tall tales, and the lies, and the need to impress people with how special I am . . . On one of my next forays I took a tumble at Pessia's feet, and it was a real miracle that I managed to roll away in time, as she lunged forward, stepped on my horse, and snapped its spine as though it were a matchstick.

Without my horse I felt small and vulnerable. I ran out in front of her, waving my arms around like propellers and screaming at the top of my lungs, and I knew the time was fast drawing near when I would have to fight her to the death.

She, too, must have sensed it, the way she stamped her hind legs, raised her tail, and let out a steamy jet of piss. She stank of urine, sweat, and fear, as she nervously trampled the fresh mud. Like a speeding bullet I flew toward her. I saw her head go down and the black of her horns, and her startling agility as she butted me.

I'd never caught it so bad before. Pessia's massive head, which was solid as a rock, bashed into my shoulder and down my arm, knocking the wind out of me. I flew up and landed in the thick of Mautner's grapevine. The others rushed over to me. I could barely see, with my left eye swollen shut and all bloody, and there was blood spurting out of a gash on my right shoulder, where I would have a scar for the rest of my life, and still I got up. I tottered but I was standing.

Now I was drawn into the fiery ring of battle. Slowly I pulled out Dad's screwdriver. I couldn't speak, my jaws weighed a ton, so I signaled Micah to lend me his horse and began to shamble around the cow.

The sun had almost set. Pessia turned full face toward me. She followed my every movement. Now and then she lunged and tried to gore me again. Her eyes were red with rage, and her lips foamy white. Three times I waved the red poncho in front of her nose, wondering whether the massive head with the horns would come at me from the other side.

My wounds were bleeding. My shoulder was a bundle of pain, but still I went on fighting, beyond pain and fear, beyond all reason.

My poncho flapped in the air, and the glare of the sun was like the reflection of a thousand pairs of binoculars trained on me; but more than that, the buzzing between my eyes bored deep into my forehead like a giant drill and, with it, a sense that what I was doing no kid before me had ever done nor should have done, and that I was both the greatest and the most despicable kid in the whole world.

And as the sun spewed forth its dying rays, I charged one last time.

I galloped full speed, rolling my eyes with terror and brandishing the screwdriver at Pessia from afar. She lowered her enormous horns. I flew at her. I jumped higher than I'd ever jumped before, up over her shoulders, and I stabbed her flank with my screwdriver and rolled over in the mud.

"With your screwdriver?" asked Felix, accidentally stepping on the brake and jolting us both. "You mean, just like that?"

Just like that. Her right flank, all the way down.

Blood spurted out of her, blackish red and very hot.

Pessia was suddenly still, and then she turned her head toward me in bewilderment, or sorrow. We stood there staring at each other in disbelief.

And then she mooed.

And her eyes filled with madness. They shone blacker than ever. She mooed again, and raised her tail, and started to run around in circles.

It was an awful sight. She went crazy. She charged at Mautner's house and gored down the door. She threw her hulking body against the brick wall and crashed through. Into the house. It was astounding. I lost sight of her. All I could see was the doorway and part of Mautner's living room; a mad cow was on the rampage in there. I could hear furniture crashing and glass shattering, and deafening booms; maybe she was only looking for the way out, maybe she didn't mean to wreak havoc, but in a very short while she managed to tear down Mautner's house, smash the furniture, and dent the refrigerator . . .

Then the noise stopped. I glanced right and left. My friends weren't around anymore. I was standing alone in the middle of Mautner's yard. From the house I heard a long moo, and Pessia trampling in a daze through the ruins, bumping her shanks and horns into the chairs and tables. You might have thought she was rearranging the furniture. After a while she appeared in the doorway. Her imposing head, her monumental shoulders. Then she lumbered back out to the yard. She stared at me blindly, as if I didn't exist anymore, and started to graze again. There was clotted blood on her hide where I'd stabbed her.

She munched with zeal, with rapt attention, as though trying to remind both me and herself what a cow looks like and what she does.

A heavy silence filled the car. Felix glanced at me out of the corner of his eye with a new expression.

Silence. I was sorry I'd told him the story.

"And then?" he said, both hands on the steering wheel.

As a result of the corrida, my friendship with Chaim Stauber was over, and our little gang split up for good. Dad was obliged to compensate Mautner with the Humber Pullman. There was no more Pearl, and worse yet, no more Tuesday-evening ritual, with Dad and me talking man talk. And incidentally—it was then that they sent me to Haifa for the first time, to hear a sermon from my uncle.

But there was more. One day Mautner drove home with a truck, heaved Pessia onto it, and took her back to the kibbutz. He told the neighbors that he hadn't been able to go near her since the stabbing. That she'd let him down and he didn't want anything more to do with her. The kids at school started avoiding me, and quietly leaving me out of things, though it was nothing official. They all seemed frightened of me. Or disgusted. They were careful not to touch me, as though I might infect them with my evil. Only Micah stayed faithful; well, not exactly faithful: actually he seemed to derive a strange pleasure out of constantly hanging around to remind me with a little sneer of that ghastly experience.

I changed. First of all, I became a strict vegetarian. I calculated that if I gave up hot dogs and steaks for ten years, I would spare the life of one cow and atone for hurting Pessia and driving her crazy, and causing her banishment from home. And I began to be scared of myself. Because I knew that what had happened to me was completely out of my control. That I was in the grip of a sort of madness, that an alien self might pop out of me any second, a stranger who had chosen to possess my soul for some inexplicable reason.

These were things I'd never said out loud before the night Felix Glick and I drove up the coastal road. I told him so he would know I was completely in his hands now, for better or worse. Or maybe this was my way of saying, Take care of me, please, you are leading me on this wild escapade, and I'm all confused. I don't understand what's going on or who you really are, I'm completely in your hands now, so remember Pessia and what I might do, and how fast I might do it. And please, keep me safe, don't let anything bad happen to me, now that you know who and what I am.

Felix said nothing. I knew he had heard my unspoken plea, because he was listening to me as no grownup ever had.

The car cruised along silently. The lights blinked orange, and all the traffic seemed to have passed us while I was telling him the story. The soft jazz on the radio whispered comfortingly. The streetlamps cast yellow halos around us. I told Felix that Gabi had stayed loyal even after the Pessia incident. She was the second grownup, after Chaim Stauber's mother, who arrived on the scene of the crime. Even when I was muddy and covered with blood and paralyzed with fear, Gabi hugged me and said, "Don't worry, Nonny, I'll protect you from your father."

Because Mautner eventually calmed down, but my father almost killed me, and in a fit of rage, for the first and only time, he said something about Zohara, and about the curse which had, it seemed, passed down to me.

16

A Brief Moment of Light in the Dark before Dark

A subtle perfume filled the air. Light from a small Chinese lamp-shade rose like mist, spreading through the room. I sank into an easy chair and tightly clutched the armrests.

Felix was calmer, but then, Felix is always calm in times of danger. He sat in an armchair facing me, with his legs crossed and a glass of wine in his hand. In the course of the evening he had polished off a bottle of champagne, three glasses of whiskey, and now wine.

My trembling soul cried: Let me out!!!

I raised my feet off the carpet to avoid dirtying it and kept my eyes discreetly lidded, so as not to desecrate the room with my naked stare.

Out. Let me out of here. This is too much already.

One wall was covered with framed photographs hanging side by side, like in a camera shop display. Only, here it was the same woman in every picture—Lola Ciperola—now with a famous actor, now with a government minister, now alone, holding a huge bouquet of flowers in her hand; and there were pictures of her at crowded parties, or posing dramatically on the stage; or alone again in an empty room, her face turned wistfully toward the light, resting her chin on the palm of her hand, reminiscing no doubt about a long-lost love, the one fortunate man she might have married because he wouldn't have tried to control her body and soul.

Every picture had a few words scrawled on it. On one I made out the autograph of Elizabeth Taylor herself, and there was one from David Ben-Gurion, and another from Danny Kaye, and even one from

Moshe Dayan. With all those famous people in the room I felt intimidated. Gabi would have given anything to be here with me, I knew, after all the hours we'd spent waiting outside this house together, trying to imagine what it looked like inside. And here I was, without her. I supposed I ought to memorize every piece of furniture, every picture and every plant in the room, so I could describe them to her later, but I didn't dare: as though anything I might imprint in my mind here would be an invasion of Lola Ciperola's privacy. A breach.

"Lady of the house is late tonight," observed Felix, glancing at the big clock on the wall.

"There's a lot of applause when the curtain goes down," I explained in a whisper. "And after the play, people come backstage to ask for her autograph . . ."

"And you, did you ask?"

"No, I was too shy. Come on, let's get out of here."

"What? You mean, without her scarf?"

I was so terrified, my stomach did a flip-flop. I almost threw up all over the big, beautiful carpet.

"Let's go already. It isn't right to walk into a person's house like this."

"Like what?"

"Like this, the way you . . ." I was trying to come up with a tactful explanation, "just walked in without . . . you know, by picking the lock."

"Only because our noble lady locked her door and left no key."

"Right, to keep strangers out!"

"What, are you and Felix strangers?" His eyebrows arched sharply. "How can she think we are strangers if she does not even know us?"

I turned this question over in my mind, but couldn't quite grasp what he meant.

"We make our lady's acquaintance"—Felix continued to reveal his cold-blooded intentions—"and then ask if she wants us to visit her home. If not—we get up and go, Good day, thank you, and shalom. Felix never forced himself on anyone!"

"But what if she calls the police?"

"That would be sure sign she does not want us here," Felix conceded. "But why decide in her place what she does or does not want? I hear she is liberated lady who will allow no one to make decisions for her."

He got up and poured himself a drink from the bottle standing on a round table in the corner. The clock ticked loudly. Felix went to the window. A minute passed and then another. I was petrified each time I heard footsteps in the street. Felix heaved a sigh.

"Once I, too, live in beautiful house like this."

As though he were talking to his reflection in the glass.

"Let's go outside," I tried again. "And you can tell me about it there."

"Why outside? Outside is too dangerous! Better here inside. Ach, if only Felix knew enough then to build warm home for the time of his old age, instead of just place for parties." And he added with a wave of his hand around the room that was now suffused in a pleasant glow and at the cozy armchairs and the embroidered tablecloths, and the leafy green plants, "You see, this is what Felix lost. This house he could have had, and he lost it. Why was he hungry to travel everywhere? To run so fast! And lots of money, ach, for what?!"

Felix leaned against the windowsill, looking bowed and withered.

"*La dracu!*" he suddenly spat, and though I didn't understand the words, I knew he was cursing in Romanian. But it wasn't like him to curse. I felt a little nervous.

"That is Felix for you!" He shook himself and raised the glass to his reflection in the windowpane. "Sometimes down, sometimes up!" He tried to smile. "Today all I have is wallet filled with sand for running away from fat waiter, but tomorrow I will be Felix of great wide world! Beloved Felix! Felix who dances . . ."

With a sudden groan he collapsed in his armchair. I jumped to my feet. He signaled me not to approach, not to touch him. I felt as if an invisible circle had been drawn around him, the way I do when Dad gets sick and starts to shrink into himself. He fights the pain and suffers inwardly. So no one will see, so no one will try to help him.

He groped in his pocket with a shaking hand and took out a little round box. He swallowed first one pill and then another, and closed his eyes. Beads of sweat broke out on his forehead. His face turned sallow and he started muttering over and over, "So old . . . and sick . . . Who will cry when Felix is no more?"

I moved closer. Then away. I didn't dare. He looked so helpless and alone there, so utterly withdrawn. His face was no longer that of a pro, and you could see he was afraid to be alone beyond the invisible circle, but I crossed over to him, come what may. I knelt beside his armchair and cautiously touched his hand. Felix was stunned. He opened his eyes and made an effort to smile at me, and far from pulling his hand away from mine, he clasped it with the other. I could see him struggling to catch his breath. He wanted to say something, but he couldn't. I breathed along with him, to remind him how, in case he'd forgotten, while he kept trying to smooth his wrinkled shirt. Maybe he was ashamed to be looking so disheveled, so unlike Felix, and all I could do was sit there in dismay, shaking my head to let him know how wrong he was, that even though I'd known him for only a short while, less than twenty-four hours, in fact, I would never ever forget him. Today had been a day like no other, and we had forged a special bond between us.

We sat this way for several minutes till he caught his breath again. Sitting up in his armchair, he loosened his tie and looked at me with a wan smile.

"Beg pardon . . . it was just stomach cramp probably . . . Now everything is fine! Back to normal again, yes sir!" He tried to speak in a loud, clear voice.

I went to the kitchen to fetch him a glass of water. How could a famous star like Lola Ciperola live so modestly? Her kitchen was cramped and antiquated. The refrigerator was shorter than I was. There was a half loaf of rye bread on the counter. She had left the light on. Dad would have given her a demerit for that. I poured a glass of water and took it to Felix. He was somewhat recovered. Or at least, pretended to be.

"Okay, now tell me," I said, "tell me about the olden days."

So he would forget his weakness, and I, my fear.

"Sit here, don't go away." He clasped my hand and peered into my eyes. "You are good boy, Mr. Feuerberg. I feel you are boy with heart. Like Felix used to be. Only, Felix learned to conquer his heart. Beware. You will have difficulties in life if you are too good. Beware of people, people are bad. Like wolves."

"Tell me," I asked again.

But still he couldn't speak. He tried once, he tried again, and then he stopped. He took a sip of water. His false mustache had come off on one side, but he didn't notice. A few moments went by. Again and again he pressed my hand. It occurred to me that if Felix died, there would be no one left to tell me about Dad and Zohara.

"In olden days," he said feebly, "I get everything I desire. Mercedes car? Sure! Small ship, sailing yacht? You bet! Most beautiful woman in world—she, too, is mine! And in my salon would gather celebrities of Tel Aviv, actors and singers and beauty queens, and *giornalistas*, and people who are rich and powerful. Everyone knew—Felix's parties are the best!"

Slowly the color came back to his face. Let him keep talking, I thought, let him find comfort in happy memories and forget what happened here. He sipped his wine and flashed me another blue smile, just to show he could still crinkle his eyes with the three creases, and I smiled back politely, because he could no longer put me under a spell, the way his lips were trembling—

"Ach, such feasts I would serve my guests on Friday night!" Felix bragged hoarsely. "So elegant, flowers everywhere, everywhere burning candles. No electric lights—not in your life! Only red candles—that's style!—and white tablecloths. And in center of table was challah, maybe one meter long, baked especially for me by Abdullah in old Jaffa. And dishes with gold rim and my monogram, also gold: F.G. for Felix Glick."

My cheeks were aching by now, but I was afraid that if I stopped smiling for even a minute he might break down and cry. I don't know, I just had this feeling that he desperately needed my reassurance, and to reassure myself I thought, All right, so maybe he is a little weird, but aren't I kind of a weird kid myself? I could easily have had someone like Felix for a grandfather and be sitting at his feet like this, listening to him reminisce, say, about the heroic days of the War of Independence, with minor exaggerations and a bit of boasting . . .

"And behind where guests sat was special counter, called buffet, with platters of lovely fruit and delicious sausages—not kosher, God forgive me—and shrimps, tiny ones flown in fresh from Greece, and this, remember, was in Days of Austerity after War of Independence, when even if you have money to go to restaurant, all you can get there is dry old chicken. But at Felix's table, oho!"

"Wait," I interrupted. "Did everyone know that you were a . . . uhm . . ."

"Criminal?" Felix smiled. "Go on, say this word. It will not bite you. Of course they know. Maybe it was for this they came to me. You see, sometimes rich and cultured people like to get close to crime, to rub shoulders with it, if it's dressed in smoking jacket and kisses ladies' hands that is . . . not that they know all information about me. Why tell people everything? It isn't polite. Imagine them eating bouillabaisse, when suddenly I tell them how once I rob big bank in Barcelona and have to shoot two guards who get in my way? Not so pleasant, eh? Spoils appetite."

"Did you really shoot two guards?" My plan to adopt Felix as a grandfather was taking an unfortunate turn. Why wasn't he just a nice old guy?

"What must I to do?" Felix shrugged. "It is their job to catch Felix, and Felix's to get away. No Felix, no job."

"Were they killed?"

"Who?"

"The guards!" I barely refrain from shouting.

"Killed? Heaven forbid. Felix was great marksman in his day. He could shoot cigarette from housefly's hand. But Felix never killed, heaven forbid! He only took money and left his golden ear of wheat, and then *whish!* No more Felix!"

I swallowed hard. The moment had come to ask him. "Could I . . . could I maybe . . . have a look at one?"

"At ear of wheat?" He gave me a long, penetrating look, reached into his collar, and pulled out a fine chain with a heart-shaped locket, the kind for keeping a picture in. What interested me, though, were the two golden charms dangling from the chain, glittering in the lamplight. I touched them gently. I didn't dare press them. Thousands of policemen the world over had striven in vain for this: to apprehend Felix with an ear of wheat.

"Once, fifty years ago, when I start out in this profession, I go to goldsmith in Paris and order from him exactly one hundred ears of wheat. Yes! Even before I was famous, I plan Felix's style of life." He jiggled the golden ears around in his hand, blew over them, and polished them with his sleeve.

"One hundred there were. And then I order another hundred. And another . . . three hundred ears of wheat found all around world: in banks and vaults and palaces, ocean liners and pocketbooks . . . Wherever Felix went, whenever he pulled off special job that called for great courage or great love, he left his ear of wheat behind. Souvenir from Felix."

And then it hit me: "Like today, when we got off the train!" That flicker of gold in the air, the faint clink, like the sound of a coin falling . . . I had witnessed Felix in action!

"Like today. Stopping train, that was special, that was style. It is first time for me, so I leave ear of wheat behind, my signature, like Picasso's on painting, yes? And how many are left? Only two. You see? This is sure sign that Felix's days are numbered."

I wanted to touch them again but didn't dare. I began to see them through his eyes now: like the last grains of sand running out of his hourglass.

"Aiii," groaned Felix. "You're through, old man. Kaput."

"But what about all your friends?" I tried to comfort him again. "The ones who used to come to your parties . . ."

"I have no friends!" He stuck the chain back under his collar and wagged a finger at me. "Sure they come, they come to have good time and dance. That's okay by me. And I send fine gifts on their birthday every year! But true friends? Friends from my heart? There is only one woman in all this world who is my friend, though no one knows it."

"Did you marry her?"

"Marry her? Heaven forbid!! That would not be good for me, or good for her. But she loves Felix, yes . . . he is her knight, like Robin Hood, who steals from rich to give to poor . . . And she loves that I am like him, romantic, charming, brave, and also that I am not like her cultured friends. Because I do more than make pretty speeches and recite Shakespeare, I fight and punch and carry gun. And I can keep secrets. And my lady friend knows that others may hang around her like flies, but only Felix . . ."

I was listening. Gabi had never told me about his true love.

"As for others—they were only interested in good times, in dancing and laughing. That is okay by me, but listen to this old man who has seen everything and knows truth: it is not good to get too close to another person's soul. Once you do, you cannot simply enjoy being together anymore, and dance and laugh and forget your troubles. You see within too many of each other's wounds, too much darkness, so is it worth it?"

He gulped his wine, spilling a few drops on his trousers.

"But Felix doesn't need friends. He likes to be alone," he pronounced in a heavy, loud voice. "So he was not disappointed when police caught up with him finally and took him to trial; it was written up in every newspaper; they called Felix Glick world's greatest swindler, arch-criminal, and other fine names . . ." Felix made an effort to smile as though he had just recounted a pleasant anecdote, but the corners of his mouth were trembling. "Think of it," he said, "so many came to my parties, shared Abdullah's challah with me, took my presents—and all forgot me. Very nice, eh? And they tell reporters they never met me, they only go to Felix's party by chance! And others say they laughed at Felix and said that Felix is big fool, trying to impress everyone, thinking he can buy friends with money . . . But that's okay by me! Yes sir!" His broad smile looked like a mask about to tear.

"And that woman," I asked, "the one you said was a real friend?"

"That woman . . ." He sighed again. "She alone was true to me . . . but is difficult for me to talk about these things, you see, even after so many years . . . And for her, too, is difficult to be with me . . . too much pain, she said, too many wounds . . ." He held the cool glass to his forehead.

"That is price Felix must to pay. To be old and alone. And sometimes I think maybe it is people who spend their lifetime breathing stale air who are really strong! Because they have endurance; they can spend fifty years doing one job, married to one woman. Maybe that is greatest strength people can have, who knows? Maybe Felix is weak, like spoiled child who wants what he wants when he wants it: travel, adventure, money, stories. What do you think?"

I didn't know what to say, but managed to come up with a good answer: "So why are storybooks always about people having adventures?"

Felix smiled gratefully. "Yes . . . you're good," he mumbled to himself. His Grandpa Noah wig had slipped, revealing his hair. The mustache was hanging askew. He looked miserable and rather comical, but touching, most of all.

"You see, you, too, went into your corrida wanting something like my dream, not so? That's why you did it! I know! And I created my own world, so people will remember that once there lived this man—Felix . . . and wherever Felix went, he left some light, for people who are still intoxicated . . . dreaming of more beautiful worlds . . ."

I looked up at the clock. It was almost midnight, time to get him out of there, I thought, while he was totally absorbed in himself. Gently I said, "We'd better leave now. She isn't going to come." I only wished it were true.

He was so distraught he didn't even hear me. "Do you ever look at people's faces on morning bus? You must to take good look one day—and you will see how sad they are, how without joy, without hope, living like dead! I say, we have one life to live! Sixty, seventy years—and all is over! We must to be happy! We deserve to be happy!" Here his voice climbed up and broke into a shrill shout. It was as though he were defending his entire way of life, and I felt like a witness to a most peculiar trial, where Felix would be presenting his own past deeds, his sins, and his character, only why was he doing it in front of me, I was just a kid he hardly knew, and as he drew closer, he cried out from the depths of his heart, "Because before we are born we all lie in darkness for millions of years, and when we die it will be same! Here is darkness, there is darkness! All our life is brief interlude—*whish*—between this first darkness and last darkness!" He gripped my shoulder and shook it. "And this is why Felix says, if we are really like actors walking across stage for one moment, then Felix will put on magnificent performance and write every part! He will write play with lighting and color and orchestra and applause. It will be great performance; like circus with one star under spotlight, Felix Glick. Is that so wrong?"

Then he let go of my shoulder and tried to catch his breath. He stared fixedly at my lips as though waiting to hear what I had to say. In the silence I realized: Felix had decided to make me his judge.

I could barely concentrate on what he was saying. What, me? His judge? Who was I, anyway? I just wanted this to be over so I could go home, yet I also wanted to stick around and hear more. No one had ever spoken to me like this before, and I'd never been allowed so close to the fear and darkness in a grownup's life, so that even Gabi's stories about herself seemed tame all of a sudden compared to Felix's life and the torment he had endured . . . And as he went on, I tried to remember everything that had happened that day, everything he had told me and shown me . . . Yes, as in a carousel slowly coming to a stop, the blurred images gradually separated, coming sharply into focus, and I understood that since the moment we met, Felix had been trying to make me like him, to make me understand him. And forgive him.

But why me? Why had he chosen me of all people to be his judge?

I felt a sudden chill from my toes to the top of my head: because what was I supposed to forgive? What had he done? And did it have something to do with me, something I didn't know about yet?

He read my face. There was nothing I could hide from him. My fears, my pleas to stop mystifying me with his electric transformations and tell me the truth for once.

"And there is something else you must to hear," he said, looking aside, "this is very serious business: before, when I had attack of . . . when I had stomachache, you did not run away."

"Where to?"

"I don't know. I thought, seeing an old man this way, maybe this boy is afraid, or disgusted, and he will run away. That is possible! So I say this: Mr. Feuerberg decides he will not eat meat for ten years to make up for cow in corrida. Correct so far?"

Correct, I answered. I didn't understand what he was driving at.

"And Mr. Feuerberg is plenty fond of meat. I saw this at restaurant, how you look at steaks when they go by, but you must to control yourself another eight years, yes?"

"Eight and a half."

"So, I make you business proposition: Felix will take on five of those eight years. What you think? We have deal? *Nu?*" He held out his hand for me to shake.

"I don't understand," I muttered, though I did by now.

"Listen: for five years—if I live another five years—I will not eat meat, I will not even touch it! *Nu,* this way I will help you make up eight and half years still left."

"Well . . . that's a nice idea, but . . . it won't work." I didn't have the strength. Because once again, a few words from him and I was completely confused, and ashamed of having suspected him, and—against my will—I felt my heart swell with admiration.

"Won't work?" shouted Felix. "Why? What is wrong? Felix can spare more than one cow in five years! He can spare whole herd!"

I didn't know what to say. I sat there, hunched over, realizing I'd never received such a generous offer before.

"Think about it," he said. "I merely return your favor. Felix does not like to be in anybody's debt."

But we both knew it was a little more than that.

And just then I heard footsteps climbing the stairs, approaching the door. Felix sat up straight and smoothed his hair. He also tried to smooth his rumpled jacket. "Here she comes," he whispered hoarsely.

The key turned, hesitated, and stopped. Maybe the person at the door noticed that someone had used a screwdriver on the lock. The door was shoved open. There in the doorway, tall and slender, stood Lola Ciperola. The hall light behind her illuminated her long silhouette. A purple scarf was draped around her shoulders. When she moved, Felix rose slowly, as though coming alive.

17

The Infinite Distance Between

Her Body and His

"**W**ho's there?" she asked in a deep, loud, almost manlike voice.

"Uh . . . friends," said Felix from the depths of his armchair, not bothering to turn around and face her.

She stood transfixed, uncertain whether to stay or flee. But even I could tell she was incapable of running away from danger.

"I don't recall inviting anyone tonight," she added with misgiving. Her gloved hand still rested on the doorknob.

"Just this old man and this boy." Felix spoke into his wineglass.

"A boy?"

I nodded feebly.

"I don't know any boys, and I don't want any here. Send him away."

I jumped to my feet, prepared to clear out immediately.

"He is not just any boy," said Felix, motioning me to sit down again. "This boy you want."

It was strange, there was an air of playfulness between them. They were like two actors reciting their lines. Lola Ciperola hadn't moved from the doorway and Felix was still sitting with his back to her.

"And why is this boy dressed up like a girl?" asked Lola Ciperola.

Holy cow! I'd forgotten I was wearing a skirt!

"Because he, too, is playing his part," said Felix.

Now she hesitated, carefully choosing her words.

"And . . . does the boy know which part he's playing?"

Silence.

"An actor only knows he is acting," said Felix reflectively. "He does not know what others see in him." I couldn't work through so many riddles.

"That skirt . . ." Lola Ciperola groaned, and as she approached, I saw a look of shock in her eyes. What could be so alarming about a skirt? I tried to pull it down over my skinny legs. Lola Ciperola veered toward Felix. "You . . . you . . . you'd do anything, wouldn't you."

"There is no law to stop me," agreed Felix, unperturbed. "As it happens, this boy is great fan of yours . . ." He stood tall, facing Lola Ciperola, very close to her. They gazed into each other's eyes. She tilted her head back slightly, as though submitting to him, then straightened herself up again and looked at him sharply. She began to say something, but Felix took her hand, held it fearlessly in his, and led her to the armchair. "Please to sit down!" he ordered, and Lola Ciperola sat obediently down as though about to swoon.

"Pour me a drink," she said weakly, taking off her shoes. Felix went to the corner table. He looked over the labels and poured her a glass of thick purple wine. Lola Ciperola nodded to him.

"So one night an old man comes to my door with a boy," she muttered to herself. Her trembling fingers groped for cigarettes in her pocketbook. Felix whipped out a gold lighter. A tiny flame flickered between them. Lola Ciperola took a long puff, her eyes still fixed on Felix. Already he's mesmerizing her, I thought, just as he did the engineer, the policeman, and me. I was disappointed to see her give in so easily.

"Perform for her, son," whispered Felix, still gazing at her.

Perform what? Did he expect me to recite something, me, in front of Lola Ciperola?

"I'm . . . I'm not . . ."

"Amnon."

Maybe it was hearing him call my name at long last, or maybe I just didn't care about anything anymore.

"Yes, perform for me, Amnon," said Lola Ciperola, drawing out each letter of my name.

"I can't . . . I . . ."

In the corner, among the plants, a prodigious shadow loomed and flapped its arms at me.

"Yoohoo!" called Gabi. "Go on! Recite something!"

"I can't!" I moaned.

The shadow of Gabi galumphed around me, tearing at her frizzy hair. I vehemently shook my head. The shadow considered a moment, then stood up straight, one hand high in the air, the other covering her eyes, the way Gabi does when she imitates Lola.

"But she frightens me!" I pleaded.

"On your feet, Nonny the Lionhearted! I shall help you!"

"Oh sure! It's easy for you to be heroic—you're not even here! But I saw the way *you* trembled when she was standing in front of you!"

"Shut your mouth and pay attention: we're about to begin!"

My knees wobbled as I slowly stood up, looking steadfastly away from Lola Ciperola. I tried to forget that she was there, that she had kicked off her majestic pumps and now sat barefoot, with her common, ordinary feet tucked under her; that I was dressed up as a girl in a skirt and blouse and sandals; and that nothing made sense anymore. I stared into the corner where the plants were. I tried with all the powers of my imagination to drape the shadow with Gabi's everyday dress, black, because black is slimming, and because she was forever mourning the thin woman buried underneath the ripples of fat; and over the black dress I set the patty-cake face with the red potato nose and began to envision her suddenly dropping her mop or the onion she happened to be peeling, to heed the silence, as though a distant voice were calling her, and I, of course, knew what would happen next, and would watch her, all smiles, as she raised her hand high, stood up straight, and declaimed in a hoarse, majestic voice: "Oh, withered gardens . . . benighted larks . . ." and she would curtsey like a princess, modestly holding out her dress and covering her eyes, which were tearing from the onion. "The prince has departed, Your Highness, he has gone far, far away in a dark chariot, and how should he call me 'faithful' when I have stayed behind, when I have not accompanied him beyond the border?"

I'm not sure exactly when I chimed in. At first I felt like choking after every word, but then my voice leveled out and I overcame my shyness, and even got a little carried away and dared to wave my hands around like Gabi does, impersonating Lola Ciperola . . .

How did I do it? Where did I get the chutzpah to perform like that in front of her? At a certain point I heard an armchair creak and the clinking of a bottle against a glass. I saw nothing, I never once opened my eyes. I just went on and on and on. Maybe I was too tired to be shy, though it probably helped to have Gabi speaking out of my mouth and watching over me, blending into the figure of Lola Ciperola, softening her as she sat across the room, and asking her, woman to woman, to take care of me in her absence. Yes, I think after a whole day with the bewildering, exhausting, dangerous, and unpredictable Felix Glick, it was actually a relief to be in the cool, serene presence of Lola Ciperola.

I didn't stop until the scene where Aharon Meskin, in the role of the old king, replies to Lola Ciperola. That's when I collapsed on the chair, utterly spent and astonished at myself. I was ready for bed.

And then I heard her clap three times.

Lola Ciperola was applauding me.

She was sitting in the chair with the footstool, a tall glass on the table beside her. There were tears in her eyes, not like the lone tear in the photograph of her that hung on the wall, but tears in great abundance flowing down the gullies of her made-up cheeks, and suddenly I realized she wasn't so young anymore.

"You are very talented," she said in her loud, manlike voice. "You're a born actor, my boy." And she turned to Felix. "Did you ask him where he gets his talent?"

And Felix replied, "I asked, but he does not know. There is nice woman named Gabi, his father's friend, who teaches him to act. Perhaps his talent comes from her side, who knows?" he said, looking innocent.

I wanted to explain about Gabi, but hesitated to waste Lola Ciperola's precious time on such personal matters.

She stood up with the Chinese lamp in her hand, trailing the cord behind her as she padded around me in her bare feet, studying my features from every angle. I was afraid to move, and a little disappointed, too, as I recall, to realize that she wasn't so young anymore. For some reason I'd always imagined her about Gabi's age . . . "Never idolize anyone, child," she said, her face half-lit by the ring of yellow light. "No one deserves to be idolized, Amnon." And she wiped her nose on the back of her hand the way a child might, only she was wearing a glove of purple silk.

How can she be unhappy, I wondered, when she's so famous and popular and successful?

"Damn my success!" she roared, then laughed bitterly. As she passed by, I felt a light, electrifying touch: her scarf had brushed against my cheek.

"The most dangerous professions are those involving emotion . . ." she said, pouring wine from her glass into Felix's, sending him a stagy smile. "Would it not be easier to be . . . an acrobat? Or a fire-eater? Or a mountain climber? The body . . . the body speaks a single language. The body is truthful. It never lies . . . But those who use their passions to quicken the feelings of others are liable in the end to lose their own . . ."

She put her hands over her mouth and sat down. Was that a speech from a play, I wondered, and was her smile a signal for me to applaud her? I restrained myself.

"I never asked, who are you?" her voice resounded. "I mean, what role have you chosen to perform for me tonight?"

"This boy is—Amnon, and I am, as usual, your strolling player, magician, thief, safecracker, heartbreaker."

"Oh, you are a thief, sir?" asked Lola Ciperola wearily. "You'll find nothing worth stealing around here anymore. Only memories," she said, with a sweeping gesture at the photographs on the wall.

"Memories cannot be stolen," answered Felix, "only counterfeited. And for me is enough I must to counterfeit my own."

"Explain!" demanded Lola Ciperola, waving her glass and kicking her slender leg out.

"What is to explain?" Felix laughed. "Who wants bad memories? I take bad times in my life and paint them brighter. I paint beautiful women I loved even more beautiful, and I stretch truth about money I rob from banks . . ."

They barely exchanged a glance as they spoke. They talked into their wine, yet there was a great if shy intimacy between them, as though they had known each other for years. And all the while I could sense, without actually knowing what was going on, that they were trying very hard not to sound like two ordinary people who had met after a long separation.

"And the boy—how did you ever manage to bring him here, Felix?"

I didn't remember Felix mentioning his name, or perhaps I wasn't paying attention. Suddenly Lola Ciperola sat up straight and stared at him in alarm.

"Is it all right, Felix? Bringing him here? Did you have permission to do it this way? Or have you relapsed into . . ."

"Him? He came along of his own free will . . . Right, boy?"

I nodded. I didn't have the strength to go into a whole long story about how Dad and Felix had met and exchanged a manly handshake, and all the rest.

"Felix," said Lola Ciperola, and her voice was cold and cutting now. "Look me in the eye, Felix: will you take good care of him? You won't harm the boy, will you? This isn't just one of your crazy games, you know! Answer me, Felix!"

A long silence followed this strange outcry. Felix hung his head. I smiled at her reassuringly, but I could still feel her voice inside me, twisting like a knife, and I thought, If I could have just one uneventful moment, I might be able to figure out what's been bothering me for the past few hours, and catch the questions buzzing around in my head about Felix and this escapade, and why Dad chose him in the first place, and where exactly they met and shook hands . . .

"Don't worry, Lola," said Felix with a little sigh. "I spend day or two with Amnon, we kick up our heels, have great time, fooling policemen, but only in play, Lola, and I'll be careful with him."

I couldn't understand why she was so worried. She observed me with a disquieting gaze. A wrinkle arched over her eyes.

"I am taking good care of him, Lola," repeated Felix softly. "We are only playing . . . not like before . . . nothing will happen this time . . . and whenever he's ready, I take him straight home . . . It's my last performance before final curtain. I have waited long time for this. And in few days is Amnon's bar mitzvah, so I thought, Now is time for us to meet, Amnon and I."

"Yes," murmured Lola Ciperola distractedly. "This week is your bar mitzvah . . . August . . . August 12 . . . yes." How did she know? When did Felix tell her? I'd been in the room with them the whole time, so had I fallen asleep for a moment or something? Lola turned to Felix: "What was that you said? The final curtain? Are you quitting the profession?"

"The profession, yes," he said with a wry smile.

The actress regarded him, and suddenly frowned. "Is something wrong, Felix? Are you sick or unwell in any way?" she asked, a different sound, warm and tremulous, now issuing through the cracks of her theatrical voice as queen of the stage. She had reached out to him, traversing the infinite distance between her body and his, till at last she was touching his shoulder, and he bowed his cheek to her caress; and as they gazed at one another, there was no doubt left in my mind that the two of them were old acquaintances, and that they had to restrain themselves from rushing into each other's arms.

"Everything will be okay, Lolly," said Felix. "It's just old age. And heart trouble. This old heart is broken. Ten years in prison is no holiday. But everything will be okay now."

"I see . . ." she said with a bitter laugh, "everything will be okay. No, nothing is okay. We can never get back what we lost, Felix . . . What a mess we've made of life . . ."

"But now we fix it," said Felix. "I come here to fix everything, everything that is wrong."

"You can't fix anything," whispered Lola Ciperola.

"No no," he replied, gently stroking her hand. "I'm Felix, your fix-

it man . . . Where Felix passes, there is light . . . People are like drunk-
ards . . . dreaming of better world . . ."

Lola laughed softly, but she seemed to be crying, too. "You're hopeless," she said. "But I want to believe you. Whom should I believe if
not you?"

"Never believe anyone but crooks. This is true."

"Swear it."

"You know I can only promise, never swear."

Again she laughed. Her face was in semidarkness now, and a soft
light fell on her silver hair. She stubbed out her cigarette in the ashtray. And then, as though playing Anna Karenina, she entered the
spotlight, and looked up at Felix like a young woman looking at a
young man. Her weary eyes were suddenly filled with a smile of
love.

"Where have you been all my life?" she asked.

"Gone too long," he sighed. "I would come to visit and run away.
Then for ten years, I had urgent business, you know . . ."

"You're telling me?" She sniffled and leaned back in her chair. "For
ten years, day after day, I cursed you and I longed for you. But I was
glad you got such a stiff sentence. You deserved it." She spoke quietly,
averting her eyes. "And then as the years went by, five, six, seven, all
the hatred vanished. How much can a person hate? Hate is as weak as
love, and anyway, it's all a game. How did you use to put it? A brief
moment of light in the dark before dark. L'chayim!"

He raised his glass. "To your life, Lolly. To your beauty and your
talent."

"It's strange." She smiled with tears in her eyes. "I finally meet someone who seems real and he introduces himself as a great impostor."

And gracefully removing her hairpins one by one, she let down a
cascade of heavy silver curls. "Tell me a little more about yourself,"
she said. "Tell me the whole story again . . ." Felix caught a lock of
her hair and began to stroke it. No one else would have dared do that
to Lola Ciperola, I thought. She offered no resistance. She bowed her
head and bit her lip, and he ran his fingers through her curls and started
humming a sentimental melody she, too, joined in before long. They

were like a couple of elderly children singing themselves a lullaby, and the whole room was filled with a dreamy sweetness.

My eyes were beginning to close. I thought it would be a good idea to call home now, to tell Dad and Gabi where I was and thank them for their brilliant idea. I also wanted to ask Gabi how she could have missed the connection between Lola Ciperola and Felix Glick, the purple scarf and the golden ear of wheat? Or maybe she knew about it and deliberately withheld the information. And how come a famous woman like Lola Ciperola knew my birth date? Who told her? What was going on? Why did I feel like a marionette being pulled to a certain destination. And who would be waiting for me there?

I woke up with a start to the clanking of heavy blinds. For a moment I thought it was morning already, but it was pitch-dark outside. I was still curled up in the armchair. The clock on the wall struck two. Felix and Lola Ciperola were standing by the open window, looking out, her hand on his shoulder, his arm around her waist. It was so embarrassing, I wanted to hide.

Lola pointed outside and Felix nodded. Then I heard her say she had been robbed of the sea. He pressed her shoulder comfortingly. She rested her head on his shoulder and said, "People like you exist only in fairy tales, Felix."

"The way our world is, maybe that is only place where you can really live."

I coughed to let them know I was awake. Lola Ciperola turned to me with a smile, a wonderful smile. It wasn't the smile of an actress anymore, it was the smile of a woman gazing at a beloved child.

Felix asked, "And if Amnon and I succeed, will you give us your scarf?"

She was still smiling at me, caressing her scarf.

"If you succeed, yes, I will give it to you."

"Succeed at what?" I asked sleepily.

Gently, as though I were very fragile, Lola reached out and caressed the air in front of my face. I sat perfectly still, full of longing, though I didn't know why. Then she stroked my face, resting her warm palm on it from my chin to my forehead. Her skin was soft, very unlike the voice she used in her roles. Lightly her fingers rested on my eyes, barely touching them, and then she pressed the spot between them, but I didn't hear or feel the buzzing like a hornet. I only felt my eyes grow wide at the gentleness of her touch, becoming clear and pure at last.

"Bring me back the sea I was robbed of," said Lola.

I couldn't speak. I didn't understand. I nodded my head under her palm. I would have done anything for her.

"Tell me, Lady Ciperola," said Felix, having thought it over a moment, "is there bulldozer around here?"

18

Like a Creature of the Night

Lola Ciperola scratched her head. "A bulldozer? Yes, I think I had one . . ." She hurried to the refrigerator, opened it, and called from the kitchen, "Ah no . . . I forgot, I just threw the last one away . . . How silly of me!"

"Perhaps in your drawer . . ." muttered Felix, opening his traveling bag, rummaging through it, and pulling out a particularly hideous wig. This he put on, and soon sprouted a matching mustache (from a whole kit he kept in one of the side pockets) plus two moles on his chin. Lola took one look and hurried out of the room, returning with a tattered shirt and a pair of patched trousers, mementos from some play of hers, and a moment later Felix had transformed himself into a beggar, stooped with age and dragging his lame left leg. "How are we doing, Amnon Feuerberg? Are we too tired to go out on little job tonight?"

I was pretty tired, but I didn't want to miss anything. "Where are we going?" I asked.

"I explain everything on our way. Later we come back here for scarf, and for Lola."

"Don't forget," Lola cautioned, seductively swirling the scarf over his face. "I will give you my scarf in return for the sea—the sea, the whole sea, and nothing but the sea!" She was suddenly as blithe as a young girl. Her body seemed to dance of its own accord. I'd never seen her that way onstage.

"Hrrrr!" roared Felix, and winked at me. Pointing two fingers over his head, he made ready to charge at the purple scarf, and Lola gave a whoop and jumped aside. Felix ran past and Lola knelt by her chair, flaunting the scarf in a great purple arc over her head. Felix stamped his feet and howled with laughter, until he saw the look on my face.

"Beg pardon!" he called to me, suddenly solemn. "I was only making joke! I completely forget!" He smacked his forehead.

"That's okay."

"Is anything wrong?" asked Lola, standing up and draping the scarf around her shoulders again.

"I am so stupid . . ." grumbled Felix. "All I want is to see Amnon laugh, but every time I spoil it, and he gets sad instead."

Lola didn't understand, of course. She glanced from him to me and said, "So, you two have secrets already." She smiled. "Very nice." She threw her arms around us both and kissed me on the forehead.

There were no photographers present, no flashing lights. It was only Lola Ciperola kissing me. Gabi would have fainted. She would have embalmed my forehead as a souvenir. Now Lola kissed Felix on the forehead and on the mouth. She kissed him with her eyes shut.

"Felix has no friends," I remembered him saying, "except for one woman." And they hadn't seen each other for ten years, the ten years he had apparently spent in prison. Lola Ciperola was that woman, his only friend. Things were beginning to come together like the pieces of a jigsaw puzzle, only the connections remained mysterious, and more frightening than the puzzle itself.

"Wonderful!" cheered Felix. "Amnon and Felix will now set off to bring you back your sea! What hour of morning does her ladyship rise?"

"I tell the press I never open my eyes before ten, but that's only for effect," Lola purred. "The truth is, I'm awake by five. Old people like me don't sleep very much."

Neither do young people like me, I thought, and hiding behind an armchair, I took off the blouse and skirt and changed back into my normal clothes.

Felix threw me a look of astonishment. "What if someone sees you like this?"

"It'll be easier for me to run wearing pants and my own sandals."

He thought a moment and shrugged his shoulders. It was okay. Then he turned to Lola. "At six o'clock tomorrow morning Amnon and Felix will bring your sea back. Now turn off lights and go to sleep."

"Don't you order me around!" she retorted in her queenly voice. "I happen to have big plans for tonight while you two are off on your escapade."

She walked us to the door and blew us kisses.

We emerged on a cold, dark street. The trees rustled softly. The moon was pearly white and almost full. I thought of all the people I knew who were sleeping just then. The ordinary people, the amateurs, were dreaming peacefully in their beds while I walked down a darkened street with Felix Glick, the fabled criminal.

"Here's what we do." Felix stopped me. "I walk first. You walk fifty paces behind me. If there is hitch, policemen come or something, then whoosh, you run and hide. Then go back to Lola's house. Don't wait for me in street!"

"But where are we going?"

"We go to sea. There is problem there. We look on beach for bull-dozer. It's easy. You come, you do it, good day, thank you very much, and shalom."

"But wait a minute, I don't understand: what's the problem?"

"Later. I explain to you later! Now we must to go!"

And he vanished—even before his "hi-deh"—into the darkness.

But only to reappear farther down the street, I don't quite know how. Did he run there? Or fly? Suddenly he was on the corner, limping slowly along, dragging his leg.

I followed cautiously, staying a fixed distance behind him. I glanced furtively around to make sure no one was tailing me. It was kind of strange, following someone who wanted me to follow him, while at the same time keeping a lookout in case someone was following me.

I walked as quietly as I could, feeling nervous. Maybe the police were already on my tail. I tried to think like them: they were searching for an old man and a boy who had jumped off a train. I wondered if they'd figured out yet that the hijacker was Felix Glick. It would be typical of them to take an interminable amount of time putting a composite to-

gether and comparing it with the mug shots of known criminals, and
only later to recover the distinguishing ear of wheat Felix had deliberately left on board the locomotive.

But he had shown his real driver's license to the pimply-faced
policeman.

And had stolen his watch.

Only to amuse me?

No, it wasn't only that. With Felix, nothing was "only" anything.
There was another, deeper motive.

But what was it? Why had he let the policeman see his real name?

So he would suspect something and try to remember the old man's
name.

I could just imagine the guy scratching his pimply forehead. The name
Felix Glick sounds vaguely familiar, but he can't quite place it. After
all, he was only a kid playing cops and robbers when Felix went to
prison. So he waits an hour, finishes his shift, goes home to his pregnant
wife and tells her what the old man said about children changing your
life. Then he asks her if she's seen his watch around by any chance.
He's almost sure he had it on before the meeting with the old guy and
his pigtailed granddaughter. Again he tries to recollect where he might
have come across the name Felix Glick. Could he have seen it written
somewhere, perhaps in print? He becomes irritable and impatient, tells
his wife he'll be home soon, and drives to the precinct. Maybe he left
the watch in his locker. But the watch isn't there. He steps into the
office of a certain captain, who's been on the force so long he can
remember things that happened twenty years before. Someone from
Dad's generation. "Uhm, tell me something," he asks the older policeman, "does the name Felix Glick ring a bell?"

And the case explodes in a huge display of fireworks and a great
machine is set in motion.

Felix wanted the police to know he was the one. He always enjoyed
an escape more with somebody in pursuit. He needed a little danger to
spice things up. I watched him admiringly as he limped up the street,
looking quite pathetic. What an actor. Dad had certainly known what
he was doing. There were things only a criminal like Felix could teach

me, and tests I could undergo only in a situation involving real-life danger. Maybe the only way for me to become the best detective in the world was to learn such things, like how it feels to be alone in the dead of night on your way to commit a crime with the police after you and nothing to rely on but your instincts, your cunning, and your courage.

Dad could count on me, I knew. My whole life he'd been priming me for a night like this, I suddenly realized. It was all part of the training, preparation for the work of a detective and the struggle to survive. For example, we'd be walking to the grocery store together, talking about this or that, when suddenly he'd say, "You see this street," and right away I recognized that special tone of voice. "For eight people out of ten it's just a place where they shop, meet friends, and catch the bus, but the remaining two have an altogether different agenda. One of them is the criminal; the other is you, the detective." (Meekly I stood up a little straighter.) "The criminal sees hiding places, pockets to pick, open handbags, loose locks, and, above all, you, Nonny, the plainclothesman; you, on the other hand, survey the street and ignore the innocent citizens, who interest you about as much as your grandmother's shopping list." (Here a vision of Grandma Tsitka mounted on a broomstick, ignoring the innocent citizens, flitted past my eyes.) "What you see is a kid with darting eyes or a couple of dubious-looking characters pressing up against an old lady in the bus line, or someone hurrying by with a suspicious package in his hand. No one else exists for you! The war you're waging is with them!"

I loved to walk down the street with Dad. It filled me with a sense of responsibility to nod at passing classmates and continue on my way, afraid of being distracted from my duty. Sometimes my heart went out to those ordinary people, the eight out of ten innocent ones going about their business without any inkling of the dangers lurking around them, or of the duel of wits taking place over their heads. They may have been older than me chronologically, but when I walked down the street with Dad, I felt like their father.

I'm running too fast, getting too close to Felix. Uh-oh. See how tense I am. Can't let anybody notice that. Can't let anybody see I'm on duty. Me, I'm just some kid hurrying home late. It's a good thing I'm wearing my own clothes. A girl alone at such an hour would draw a lot more attention. Besides, it feels good to be a real boy again.

Not that it was so terrible being that girl. I was beginning to get used to her.

Where's Felix? I've lost him. There he is.

A dog is barking at him, a scraggly pooch in somebody's yard. Not good. He'll attract too much notice. Felix limps quickly away. But other dogs start barking, too, indoors and out. A curtain flutters on the second floor. Maybe someone is peeking out to see what's going on. Felix says dogs always pick on him. I myself have been bitten at least ten times. Even the most well-behaved dogs start going crazy when I walk by. I've even been attacked by a Seeing Eye dog!

Okay, let's go. Never mind. The whole city's barking at us. My feet start running of their own accord. As if someone's calling, beckoning: Come to me . . . maybe because I feel so lonely now, away from Felix, away from Dad, and overhead the big white face in the moon has changed expression, and I go forward. But where? To whom?

Zohara surges up within me. She was very beautiful. A tough cookie. How old would she be if she were alive today? Thirty-eight. Like the mothers of most of the kids in my class. What would my life have been like with her? We wouldn't have had Gabi, but I would have had a mother. Not that I feel I missed anything. I've done just fine through the years. There are only a few small details I'd like to find out, so I can wind up the investigation I began today.

The dogs calmed down. A hush fell over the slumbering city. I was a panther, fierce and silent. A creature of the night. Children fast asleep in their houses never dreamed what a boy their age could do.

A little outlaw. A little law unto himself.

Just thinking of it gives me the chills.

At the end of the week was my bar mitzvah. The entire police force would be on hand. And Dad promised to give me my promotion then. We had this deal. Over the years I'd made sergeant second-class, and this Sabbath I'd be promoted to first sergeant! We would go through the usual ceremony, with me drinking a whole glass of beer like a man, and him pinning on my insignia. About time, too. A year and a half had gone by since my last promotion, because of that cow business.

Suddenly I stopped in my tracks. There was a police cruiser parked on the sidewalk ahead. Like a flash I dropped down and disappeared into a nearby garden. Seconds later I peeked out. There were two policemen in the cruiser, leaning back in their seats and talking together. A bored blue light revolved on the car roof. The radio was tuned to the music station. Two overgrown patrolmen, shooting the breeze. Bad cops. But there was no way I could get by without their noticing me. I glanced right and left. The streets were bare. I looked up. In case there was a sentry on a roof somewhere. The coast was clear. I emerged from the garden, edging close to the fence. I ducked past them, a fugitive from justice. So easily. Like a dark shadow I whisked by them—lazy shlubs.

Idiots, I chuckled inwardly.

At the corner I stood and walked normally, with my hands in my pockets. Felix, too, appeared out of the darkness. We'd both used the same method of slipping past the policemen. I whistled quietly to myself, feeling great all of a sudden. "Exhilaration," our Gabi calls it.

It was almost as if Felix and I were the only two real people in the world now and everyone else was an actor in our play. We ordered them to sleep and they obeyed. Even the ones who weren't asleep weren't actually awake, either, maybe just hallucinating. Or dreaming they were awake. Whereas Felix and I were sharply watchful as we skulked through the streets like shades of night. To them we were strangers, a different breed, with only a fine line separating us from each other. A child waking up just then, in his pajamas, looking out the window at me, might have thought he was dreaming, or that I was Batman. Or a navy frogman. I stepped lightly. I kicked the tire of a parked car. For no particular reason, my leg just kicked out at it. So what. Now everything was mine, the streets, the city. I lurk in the darkness while you sleep, dangerous and unpredictable. If I get a mind to, I'll destroy half your city, burn it right to the ground, and who will know? You poor innocent babes. Good night. Don't worry. I'll do you no harm. I'm good and kind.

But say I took a nail and scratched my name on a whole row of cars—"Nonny was here last night"—you'd be absolutely horrified.

Maybe I ought to have a special signature. Like Felix's golden ear of wheat.

Sleep, sleep in peace, little families with a daddy and a mommy and two children. What do you know about real life, and how easy it would be to crumble your world? What do you understand about the struggle for survival, and the everlasting war between law and crime? Hush, go to sleep now, pull the covers over your ears.

I stole along like a spy behind enemy lines. Whenever I heard approaching footsteps, I would duck into a yard or building entrance and wait there patiently. People brushed by me unawares. Once, in a darkened stairwell, a woman stood only a few centimeters away, groping in her purse for her keys. She looked right through me at a couple of bicycles and didn't see me there.

Slow down. You're always running.

About a year ago I happened to be present one time when a kid like me got arrested. Dad and I were on our way home from a special dinner at Gabi's, I don't remember what the occasion was, maybe she'd succeeded in one of her diets. As we were driving home that night, we heard over the police radio that two boys were attempting to break into a car parked near the Ron Cinema. Dad swerved around and headed there directly. He shouldn't have taken me with him, but he was afraid that if he dropped me off at home first he'd miss the collar, and God forbid Dad should ever miss a collar.

We zoomed away so fast I was glued to my seat. Then we were held up behind a long line of cars, and Dad huffed angrily and pounded on the steering wheel. We didn't have a siren or a revolving beacon, so we just had to sit there, stuck in the traffic. I was keeping my mouth shut because I could see the veins about to pop on his neck and forehead, when suddenly he took off from behind the line of cars.

The tires screeched, the motor groaned, and Dad wheeled around and charged head-on against the traffic! He cut between lanes, drove up a safety island, and just about crashed into an oncoming car . . . All I could do was sit there, mute and frozen with fear. I was sure we'd both be killed on the spot, but what frightened me most was the look on his face, and the power he had to break all laws at once, even his own sacred laws, and though I knew his motto, "A bodyguard doesn't apologize to the Prime Minister for knocking him down when an assassin is pointing a gun at him," it was scary nonetheless to see him change so abruptly, like some huge steel spring coiled up so long that the second it's released, it goes berserk.

And in the midst of this joyride he explained to me curtly, in an official-sounding tone of voice, what I wasn't allowed to do, like make noise, or leave the car, or act conspicuous in any way. As if I didn't know. Glancing at him out of the corner of my eye, I thought he was a stranger, somebody new who had suddenly popped out. He faced tensely ahead and licked his lips. There was a dangerous glint in his eyes: as though he was enjoying this crazy game of defying death and continuing the wild games of his youth, now, albeit, within the confines of the law. Over the radio we heard details from the detectives lying in wait near the movie theater. They said the smaller boy, the lookout, was casually standing in the middle of the street, making sure no one spotted his friend, who was about to break into a car. Little did he suspect there was a detective posted on the roof, reporting his every move over a walkie-talkie.

Sounds like I had a pretty wild childhood, right?

Actually I didn't. But I don't feel like interrupting the current case in order to describe how my childhood really was, police operations and guns aside.

Some other time, when I get around to it.

We pulled up at the corner, where a lot of other cars were parked. All at once the dangerous stranger with the glint in his eyes disappeared. I could feel the spring coiling up again inside him. He threw a civilian sweater on, took out a small pair of binoculars, and peered through them at what was happening. I knew that look on his face. He turned to me as though suddenly remembering that I was there with him and that I wasn't a fellow policeman but only his son, and he gave me a sad little smile, a smile from the heart, and touched my cheek.

"I'm glad you're with me, son," he said, and I was completely dumb-

founded to hear something like that from him, in the middle of an
operation. What on earth made him say it? My cheek burned at his
touch, and wanted more.

The detective on the roof reported that the car thief had just walked
by the yellow Fiat for the third time and peeked inside. Whenever a
pedestrian passed, the thief would hide behind the car, while the lookout studied the movie posters.

"Seventy-two to seventy-five, over," Dad whispered into the radio,
the consummate pro once more.

"I read you, seventy-two," answered the voice on the radio.

"Nobody make any unnecessary moves until he's actually inside the
car. So he won't try to run for it, and so we'll get plenty of FP's, is that
clear?"

"Roger," answered the voice. FP's was short for fingerprints.

Several moments of suspense followed. A couple walking down the
street stopped to embrace next to the Fiat. They must have wanted to
be alone, never guessing how many pairs of eyes were upon them. The
whole world was abuzz with binoculars and walkie-talkies, and those
poor innocents didn't even know it.

"Okay, they've finished," reported the detective on the rooftop.

"Like an outdoor movie, eh?" a detective hiding in the bushes jested
over the walkie-talkie.

"Shhh!" scolded Dad. "No joking on the job!"

Another minute went by. Dad tapped nervously on the steering wheel.
His eyes squinted narrowly. He was ready to pounce.

"He's taking out a screwdriver," reported the detective on the roof.
"He's opening the lock." And a few seconds later: "He's in."

"On the count of ten go after him," Dad whispered into the radio.
"I'll grab the lookout. Seventy-five, you go after the thief. Seventy-three,
block the escape route. Let's move!"

He said it so perfectly, just like a movie cop.

Then he quickly slid out of the car, forgetting all about me, he was
so involved in the operation. I watched him, studied him. The way he
casually walked down the street with his hands in his pockets. The
lookout also studied him out of the corner of his eye and decided he

was okay. He appeared to be an ordinary passerby on his way home after a tiring day at work. His shoulders slumped as he trudged along, just as Dad's did when he left the precinct building every evening. Maybe he didn't look forward to going home. I was there—but the house must have seemed pretty empty to him. And the person he wanted to see was gone.

Thirty more steps, twenty more steps; my mouth went dry. There were just fifteen meters between them now, and still the boy suspected nothing.

And then suddenly Dad rushed at them. Like a raging bull he bellowed, "You dirty bastards!," wildly flinging his arms. Even I knew he had made a big mistake, that he should have waited till he closed in on the boy and only then pounced on him!

But he just couldn't wait; he hated criminals so much he would have torn them to pieces with his bare hands.

"Your war against criminals is getting too personal," said Gabi in the kitchen one night. "And that's why you louse up your investigations."

What did she mean by getting too personal? What did he have against them personally?

"You're in such a rush for revenge that you end up giving yourself away." Revenge for what? What was she talking about?

The lookout gave a cry that sounded like an animal howl. He tripped over his feet, recovered almost instantly, sprang up, and then ran away so fast he barely touched the ground. He got past Dad without any trouble at all, dodging him like a nimble-footed soccer player. I saw Dad turn, looking heavy, angry, clumsy, hurt, waving in a fury. The buddy who had broken into the car saw what was going on and immediately fled in the opposite direction. I saw the detective in the bushes come out of hiding and spread his hands in anger and frustration. The lookout, who had slipped away from Dad, was running toward me now. A hundred meters separated us, and I knew exactly what to do. Slowly I got out of the car and walked nonchalantly toward him. I wasn't even nervous. My body acted like a well-greased machine and did the thinking for me. I didn't look at the boy, and he didn't look at me: a kid like me was nothing to worry about. He was afraid only of grownup detectives. In less than a minute he had run all the way up the street and was about to pass me, I could see his eyes nearly pop, and I lunged at him just right, the way Dad had shown me so many times at the gym—I threw myself on the ground and tripped him.

It happened in a fraction of a second. He was moving with so much momentum that when he fell he rolled into a parked car and lay there, stunned. A moment later two detectives were handcuffing him.

"Is that Feuerberg's kid?" said Detective Alfasi, and recognizing me, he added, "Isn't he the mascot?"

"What are you doing here, Nonny?" asked the second detective, the one with the beard.

All the detectives in the district knew me.

"I saw him running away, so I tripped him."

"Hey, you did great! You saved the day!"

Dad came running over, huffing and puffing.

"Sorry. I misjudged the distance," he grumbled. "I jumped him too soon."

"Never mind, sir."

"Never mind, sir."

The two detectives busied themselves with the boy's handcuffs so Dad wouldn't see what was plainly written on their faces.

"The other one got away, sir, but your son caught this kid, and he'll help us write out a nice invitation to his friend. Right, buster?"

The detective, whose nickname was "Blackbeard," gave the kid a swift kick in the butt, but we all knew who it really was he wanted to kick.

We stood there awhile longer. Dad was waiting for the forensic unit to arrive and dust the car for prints. A small crowd gathered nearby, and the detectives ordered them to move along. People were pointing at me, some of them whispering to each other. I stayed cool, walked around with my hands in my pockets, checked for FP's, searched for any other bits of evidence that might help the investigation, did just what the situation demanded.

The kid I'd caught was lying on the sidewalk with his hands cuffed behind his back. The streetlight shining on his face made him look like a small hunted animal. I dared not look into his eyes. His whole life was probably about to change, and I had been his doom.

Yet his eyes were seeking mine. He squirmed on the sidewalk, trying to get a look at me. I didn't move. Let him look. I thought I saw an expression of disdain on his face, disdain for the brat of the law. He gave me a smile, a hateful smile, but it was also a kind of bitter salute to me for having apprehended him.

You see, that's how we are, we professionals: we always acknowledge our opponent's skill. It's part of the professional code of honor. Like Felix and Dad shaking hands that time, or reaching an agreement for my sake, which strikes me as pretty incredible now, though I'm sure they did, because what if they didn't?

Dad said goodbye to the other detectives and we drove home in silence. It was downright embarrassing that he almost blew the whole thing and that I was the one who came to his rescue. I wanted to say it was just a coincidence, that my success had been unintentional, that a kid my age has faster reflexes, but that he was clearly much smarter and more experienced as a detective. I decided to keep quiet in the end. The worst part of it was that I was afraid he might take back what he'd said to me earlier in the car, before the bust.

I hadn't thought of that incident for a whole year. I didn't even discuss it with Micah. I just wanted to forget that terrible silence in the car. Neither Dad nor I had ever referred to it again. And Gabi, who learned what happened from the report she typed, also kept mum about it. It was only tonight that it all came back. The vicious smile on the kid. Maybe he'd grinned at me that way to show his contempt for brats. Maybe he'd sensed something about me even then.

But what did Gabi mean when she said his war against criminals was getting too personal? What did they ever do to him to make him fight like that? Why did he want revenge?

To tell the truth, I was beginning to understand. I'd guessed the answers already, but I forced myself to be cautious. Not to draw hasty conclusions. And I posed my questions in a systematic way, according to protocol, questions which had been buzzing around unasked all my life: Who was behind his personal war against criminals? Had they harmed him? If so, how? Did they kill someone he knew? Was it because they killed her that he was fighting this war? By now I'd forgotten I was running away and that I had to be careful. I went on muttering my questions, moving my lips, unconcerned about anyone noticing. But why did they kill her? Was it something she'd done to them? Maybe they killed her to punish Dad. And who was the killer? And did the punishment stop after her death? Or would they now try to get at somebody else who was close to him?

Maybe that was why he had trained me from such an early age to keep my eyes open, to suspect everything and everyone. But maybe I wasn't professional enough in my suspicions. Take Felix, jogging ahead of me there, for example, what did he have to do with any of this? Did he and Dad really shake hands and come to an agreement for my sake? And why did I feel so drawn to him and want to stay, in spite of my fears; maybe it was time to run away and save myself . . .

By now I was trudging along, scared and depressed, moving forward, though I felt a constant backward tug. As if I'd been allowed a glimpse at something kids my age aren't supposed to see. At Dad, standing in the dark, with his muscles and the bulging veins in his neck, gritting his teeth and fighting crime. He had to protect the world from the villain with a thousand faces, but mainly he was protecting me, preparing me for the eternal battle. Alone and forlorn, he waged a war against the entire world of crime, never asking anyone's help, never compromising.

There, I was running again.

≈ **19** ≈

Riders of the Sands

nd suddenly I could feel the sea. It assaulted me with its wet smell and the clash of the waves. The sea! I had been away only a few short hours and already I longed to be there again. I loved the sea (as I said before), and I was as good a swimmer as any kid in Tel Aviv, even though I came from Jerusalem. I was forever trying to persuade Gabi to take me to the beach in Tel Aviv, and she would laugh at the way I started trembling with excitement even before we got there, like a fish running away from its Jerusalem aquarium, about to return to its natural home.

Poor Gabi would sit in an uneasy chair wearing her black dress and a white plastic noseguard, with suntan lotion smeared all over her body, even on her pocketbook. She looked like a ghost on the rollicking beach, she who loathed the sea and feared the sun, and was sorely tormented by the pretty girls passing by in their bikinis. Hither and thither her head would bounce between the twin paddles of grief and envy. "I'm the only person I know who gets seasick on the beach," she would grumble whenever a young girl wiggled by. "The Good Lord brought me to this world in order to set the upper limit of human suffering."

Dad didn't much like going to the beach, either. I don't believe I've ever seen him in the water (he can't swim, as I found out by chance one day when I was ten). But Gabi, for whom it was sheer agony, saw how happy I was in the waves and consented to take me to Tel Aviv at least once a month. That was our special fun day or, rather, my special fun day. I don't imagine Gabi derived much pleasure from those outings, though she didn't miss even one in five years, from the time I was eight: having hard-boiled herself on the sand, she would spend a couple of hours on her aching feet across the street from Lola Ciperola's, all without a grumble. From there we'd go to a restaurant where she would wolf down her food and then calculate on a paper napkin how many calories were hiding like stowaways in the harmless steaks and French-fried potatoes, which were not that fattening per se . . . and sometimes, after a few voracious bites, she would lean back and tap the rolls of fat over her stomach, murmuring, "Uh uh uh, Gabi, very bad for the 'roll call.' "

From the restaurant we would take a bus to our last, exciting destination: the chocolate factory on the outskirts of Ramat Gan. This was something else she and I had solemnly sworn to keep secret, our own sweet secret, and heaven help us if Dad ever found out how she was corrupting me.

One afternoon a month, at four o'clock on the dot, Gabi and I would embark on a tour of the factory. We were well-nigh guests of honor there after five years, sometimes the only guests, in fact, as we traipsed along after our sleepy guide, lapping up her description of how chocolate is made: the grinding of the cocoa beans, the melting of the butter, the stirring of the thick, creamy liquid in a vat . . .

The guide, a peculiar woman, was skinny as a pretzel stick. Everything about her betrayed an inborn antagonism to life's pleasures in general, and to chocolate in particular, yet she went about her job as obediently as a machine. She never varied her recitation, always told the same two jokes, and never thought to ask what had compelled us to trail after her once a month. On one occasion only had she departed from the regular route. We had been the only visitors that time, and when we got to the hall where the wrappers go on the chocolate bars, she turned to us and said, "Excuse me, but since you've been here before, would you mind skipping this part of the tour today? I have an important appointment at a quarter to five."

Gabi and I exchanged a look of shock: the packaging hall was one of the highlights of the tour! It was like visiting a dressing room before the actors go onstage!

Gabi narrowed her eyes and asked contentiously, "With whom? A man?"

"No," answered the guide, "with the doctor."

"Well, that's okay, then," Gabi forgave her, "but only this once."

And here let me pause a moment to make something clear: there are certain people in this world who are too coarse and vulgar and lacking in artistic flair to appreciate such a tour. Some who are quite fond of chocolate are interested solely in the finished product. In solid results.

Gabi and I, however, were entranced by the process itself: the pipes, the vats, the forklifts for moving sacks of cocoa beans, the giant drums where the beans were roasted before grinding, the great funnels through which the magical liquescence was poured, the shining beauty of a slab of chocolate before it is divided into bars and covered modestly, tantalizingly, first in shiny silver foil, then in a brightly colored wrapper— how lovely to behold are the cycles of life!

Forgive me for getting so carried away. I am aware of the ghastly possibility that among the readers of this book there may be one or two who are impervious to the charms of chocolate. Such people do exist in this world, and we must accept them with good grace as instances of a phenomenon that is not scientifically explainable. I even know one boy, without mentioning any names, who has since earliest childhood preferred salty foods to sweet. Seriously: he has a real craving for pretzels and potato chips and things. I must say I find his preference strange. In this respect, I fear we come from different branches of humanity.

Now, the salty branch, as everyone knows, is practical, devastatingly logical and decisive, leery of fantasy and deferential to fact. I have heard talk about hideous rites observed by their councils somewhere in the hills of Sodom which consist of immersing whole bars of chocolate in the Dead Sea! Too horrible, but then it's common knowledge that the faculties become impaired after years of grinding salt.

I, on the other hand, sometimes believe that (cherry-flavored) chocolate syrup runs through my veins. Whenever I have an important lunch date with some seeming adult, I know in my heart that the meal and conversation are the dues I will have to pay in order to get to dessert.

And when it comes, oh boy!

Chatting nonchalantly, I slide in a mouthful of chocolate mousse, or "sweet dreams" cake, or a little swan éclair, or creamy Himalaya snow peak . . . and my companions across the table never dream that somewhere in this mild-mannered fellow's memory lurk two figures: a child with short blond hair and a big woman in a slimming black dress, unabashedly slurping and smacking their lips and smearing themselves in a transport of bliss . . .

And here I beg to digress again and take advantage of this rare moment of sweet intimacy between writer and reader in order to disclose my final earthly request and spiritual testament:

To be buried in a chocolate coffin.

Let the earth be sweet.

First I saw the bulldozer, then I saw Felix. I caught sight of him before he ever noticed me. He emerged from a nearby alley just as I arrived at the beach. Limping like a beggar, he glanced around a few times with the air of a fisherman casting his net and taking everything in with his eyes . . . He certainly knew how to look, too: because when ordinary, innocent folks try to see what's behind them, they usually glance over their left shoulder. That's how it is. Try it and see. Which is why when a good detective is tailing a suspect, he hangs back to the right to avoid being spotted. Felix knew this, of course, and occasionally glanced to the right as well, thereby spying me in the shadows.

I guess he wasn't certain it was me walking behind him. All of a sudden he vanished. I couldn't see where. It was almost as though he had been swallowed by the sand, had faded into the darkness. That's what they used to say about him at the precinct—that he was as elusive as water: policemen and detectives by the hundreds, believing they had at last succeeded in nabbing him, would open their hands and find he had slipped through their fingers again.

Except for the one who clenched him so tightly that when he opened his fist, Felix Glick was still there.

I waited. Where was he? I hesitated a moment, then softly whistled "Your Eyes Shine." I saw something moving in the dunes, slithering like a snake between shadow and moonlight, and a moment later a faint whistle responded. That was the signal we seemed to have decided on without prior arrangement.

We approached each other through the darkness. "There," I said, pointing at the bulldozer nearby.

"That dinosaur," spat Felix. I couldn't tell whether he meant that the bulldozer was old or that it looked like a prehistoric animal.

It was small and sturdy, with a yellow shovel as big as its frame, upraised.

We were standing in a wide ditch scooped out of the sand, where apparently the foundations of a building would soon be laid. I still had no idea what we had come there for. We paced around in silence, surveying the area. There was a wooden fence around the ditch and a heap of iron rails next to a hacksaw. There was a little guard shack nearby, but no light was shining through the cracks.

We drew closer. It seemed to me that Felix was sniffing rather than looking.

"There's someone inside." He signaled with his finger. "Sleeping."

"How do you know?" I whispered.

"There was campfire here." He pointed at a small ring of embers. "Only one cup of coffee."

"Excellent, Holmes," said Gabi inside my head. "And how do you know he's sleeping?"

"I don't know, I just hope so," whispered Felix in reply. "Who am I, prophet Elijah?" We walked around the shack. There were no windows. This seemed to please Felix quite a lot. He gave me the thumbs-up. Now he began to search all around. He found a wooden beam and measured it against the door of the shack. Tiptoeing like a cat in a mouse's nightmare, he approached the door. A moment's silence, and then suddenly he forced the beam under the handle, turning the shack into a jail.

"Quick," he called, and I heard the power come into his voice the way it did in times of danger, and start to gurgle like a motor.

Felix hopped up on the bulldozer as though it were the back of a horse. He groped about and found two large nails and a pair of pliers.

I couldn't figure out what he was doing. It seemed that the person in the shack had woken up and was stomping around inside. Felix twisted the two nails together with the pliers. He made a little metal fork and inserted it into the double hole behind the driver's seat. The silence continued. I didn't know what to expect.

All at once the silence was shattered. Felix turned the improvised key and the bulldozer began to roar. The noise was terrible. No one in the city of Tel Aviv could sleep through this din, I thought. Felix jumped up on the seat and beckoned me to join him; I took a leap and—

He pulled the hand brake and released it; the bulldozer gave a jolt. To and fro we pitched, as though mounted on a camel that was rising off its knees. Felix tried pulling the two big levers in front of him, pressed down on the pedals with his feet, saw that it worked, and began to drive. The bulldozer obeyed at once, as though it could sense his authority. As we rolled past the shack, a dim light seemed to be shining through the cracks. I saw the door handle jiggling up and down. The guard was trying to get out. The door was jammed with the beam, though. He started pounding on it with his fists.

When you make a mistake, kid, you have to pay. That's the law of survival. Now go back to sleep.

Almost immediately we came to an embankment. It was huge, several meters high and many meters long. A wall of sand had been pressed into a solid rampart—the sand, apparently, scooped out of the ditch where we had stood before.

"This hill blocks view from Lola's window!" shouted Felix over the noise. "It hides sea from her!"

"But when they build a house here, it will hide it even more," I shouted.

"For three years they are not building!" he answered at the top of his voice. "They go away and leave everything behind like this, sand, bulldozer, even guard! They run out of money and take off with sea! Now hold on tight! Hi-deh!"

And with a terrible shout, he turned the bulldozer toward the hill and raced ahead full force. I bounced up. With one hand I grabbed hold of the hood rail and closed my eyes.

The shovel struck the middle of the rampart and broke it in two. After three years, the sand had been packed solid with salt and moisture, but the bulldozer smashed right through it. Suffocating clouds of sand blew up. My eyes, my nose, my mouth—everything was full of sand. Felix grabbed the gearshift and reversed the bulldozer. He maneuvered it boldly around and charged again.

The bulldozer was making inroads, raising the shovel, letting it down again, pounding the embankment with all its steely might. Huge slabs and rocks of sand broke off and collapsed all around us, rising up as dust to the sky. Felix threw his head back, roared like a lion, howled like a jackal, and screamed for joy. I punched his shoulder to remind him we were partners! He slid over in the driver's seat to let me step on the gas. The bulldozer rumbled and shook. I pulled out of the piles of sand cascading all around us, and again we rushed down the embankment, looking for a place to smash through. It was incredible, insane; we were like conquerors battering a stone rampart, and in the little list I kept in my head, under the heading of "driving experience" I added "bulldozer" after "locomotive." Felix was shouting at the top of his lungs, singing, I believe, new words to the old tune "Who will steal the train to Tel Aviv?" and belting out the answer, "We the pioneers will steal Tel Aviv!" Then he sang another song, "Blue sea below, blue skies above, demolish the harbor, blast the cove." And then I figured it was time to sing our anthem, and raising our voices with the clouds of dust and the pounding waves, we composed this little song:

> *Your eyes shine diamonds*
> *From the quay you wave farewell!*
> *They stole the sea!*
> *I'll bring it back!*
> *And your scarf you'll give to me!*

I'm not sure which one of us actually made it up. I began it, Felix took over, and a moment later we were both shouting it out loud. Felix waved his arms in the air, tears of joy pouring down his cheeks. Jumping around in his beggar's costume, he looked like some ancient pagan worshipping the moon, and I wondered whether perhaps he was so happy because throughout his lifetime of crime he had never done the kind of job he was doing with me, for a worthy cause, and so we danced, waving our arms and shouting together, and the yellow bulldozer joined in the spirit of things. Never in my life have I seen such a playful bulldozer. Maybe it was grateful to us for waking it from its slumbers. It cavorted around, slyly approached the rampart, and, at the very last moment, surprised it with a blow of its mighty shovel. It was as sweetly menacing as a baby mammoth, raising its snaggy shovel to the sky after every wallop and seeming to shake with bulldozer laughter. Sometimes we had to smack it in the ribs to quiet it down . . .

(All together now:

> *Hey, hey, Lola—*
> *Hey, Lola Ciperola!*
> *Hey, hey, Lola—*
> *Lola Ciperola!*)

The sky turned pallid and its color slowly drained into the sea. Light-blue stripes were visible through the breaches we had made in the rampart. I took a deep breath of sea air and felt the salty sting in my lungs. I hollered, I screamed, I can't remember what I did, I had conquered it! Now it was mine! The first kid ever! In the whole wide world!

At five in the morning the bulldozer stopped abruptly. Maybe it broke down or ran out of gas or something. The sky was turning bright around the edges, and white seagulls began to soar and screech. The rampart lay in ruins all the way down, and fast little morning waves were already nibbling at it, dragging the remains back into the sea. Felix and I were covered with sand from head to toe. I even felt the stinging over my eyelids. A mask of wet sand and salt had hardened over our faces, but his eyes shone through like the blue eyes of a very happy child.

Felix slipped his mud-cast hand under his torn beggar's shirt and pulled out a fine gold chain. A heart-shaped locket and two golden ears of wheat sparkled mysteriously in his sand-frosted hand.

"You're just like your mother." He laughed through the sand. "This is how she was at seashore. Crazy like you. The sea was her home. She was like fish in water."

He took an ear of wheat off the chain and caressed it with his fingers. "Now toss it," he said, putting it in the palm of my hand.

"Me?"

(Me?!)

"You're letting me give your sign?"

(He was letting me give his sign?)

"Yes. Please. It is right thing to do. Go ahead, please."

Light and golden. A tiny ear of wheat in my hand. I stood tall on the bulldozer. I saw he was giving me a special sideways glance, as he had the first time he saw me on the train. I tossed it high, to the sky, to the sea.

It hovered in the air and slowly twirled and flashed as it was swallowed by the waves. A white seagull swooped down after it. Maybe it caught it, maybe not.

We jumped off the bulldozer and started to run. We had to drop out of sight before the city woke up. I looked back with a twinge of sadness: our little bulldozer was parked on the shoreline, its shovel raised. We had awakened it from its enchanted sleep for a single night, but now it had gone to sleep again.

From the guard's shack we heard the sounds of banging and shouting. Felix hesitated, and then walked over to the shack. He loosened the beam over the handle. The banging inside subsided. Maybe the man was frightened. We hurried away, but before we left the beach, Felix stopped and pointed at the tall buildings.

"Look there, Amnon."

The shutters on most of the buildings were drawn. Tel Aviv was still asleep, innocently dreaming its last dream. But from one high window a sheer purple cloud was waving and quivering and coming alive in the morning breeze. It was Lola Ciperola's scarf, and now it was mine.

20

Do You Believe in Reincarnation?

and Also, I Make the Headlines

To begin with, I took a shower. It was the first shower I'd ever taken in Tel Aviv, and I must say it was just like Jerusalemites describe it: a heavy flow of water foaming down over your head, not the trickle-trickle of a Jerusalem shower, one quick spritz before the water gurgles back into the pipes. Anyway, I washed off the layers of sand that encrusted me and stood under the waterfall for another half hour or so until I was all calmed down. While I was in there, I remembered that I hadn't called Dad and Gabi yet, but as soon as I got out, Felix said breakfast was ready and that we'd better sit down and eat. Lola had fixed us a royal feast of omelettes and salad finely chopped and cocoa and applesauce, which in my opinion deserved at least second place on the YUMTUM scale (after our dinner at the restaurant). I told her she made salads just like Gabi, and Lola asked, Who's Gabi, and I answered with my mouth full (as befitted Gabi). I regretted that Gabi wasn't with me now, because I felt sure she and Lola would have gotten along really well on account of their similar views about life and men. And I also regretted that Gabi couldn't see me here, talking with a famous and important star. I'd been calling her Lola for quite a while, and she'd been calling me Nonny.

But Lola didn't seem famous or important around the house. She was a plain old woman without the layers of makeup, and without her voice sliding up and down so fast it sounded theatrical, and her melodramatic gestures. At home she was a woman of flesh and blood who spoke with a slight accent and made humorous comments about things, and had a pretty face and a supple body and age spots on her hands and a slightly wrinkled neck, which may be why she always wore the scarf.

With me she was gentle and solicitous. She would follow me wherever I went, sit down, and gaze at me. This was kind of weird, because until yesterday I'd been the one straining to catch a glimpse of her, and normally I had to pay money to sit and watch her, whereas here she was the one devouring me with her eyes.

"Let me know when you get tired of me, Nonny," she said. "I so enjoy looking at you."

"What's there to see?" I giggled with embarrassment.

"You're a nice-looking boy, not a boy beautiful, so don't let it go to your head, but you do have an interesting face. There are so many contradictions in you I'd like to understand better! And those ears— like a cat's. You're sweet when you smile, and I'm touched by everything you do. Oof!" She pressed her cheeks and shook her head, laughing. "What an old chatterbox I am. But you must understand me: the only children I come in contact with in the theater are grown women dressed up as children. I haven't seen a real child in a very long time. Tell me more."

"About what?"

"Oh, everything. About your friends, how your room is arranged, who buys your clothes, what you do after school. Do you like to read?"

First Felix and now Lola. It had been ages since anyone took such an interest in me. What had gotten into the two of them?

"So come help me with the pictures. I need someone strong to hand them to me."

She climbed up on a stepladder, and one by one, I passed her the pictures that had been hanging on the wall until the day before. She had spent the whole night taking them down, pulling out the nails and filling the holes with toothpaste, and toward dawn she had repainted the wall.

"All thanks to you. Because you helped me decide!" she said in greeting when we returned from the beach that morning. She was dressed in trousers and a man's shirt splattered with paint.

"For ten years I've wanted to do this, but didn't dare!" she exclaimed, waving the paintbrush and dabbling Felix white from head to toe. "For ten years I have been suffocated by those pompous faces, and by my own pictures in those dreadful poses. Into the storage loft with all of them! I want some fresh air in here!"

I stood below, handing up Elizabeth Taylor, David Ben-Gurion, even Moshe Dayan, and her laughter rolled over my head as she thrust them into the storage loft.

"I would call this a most successful diet!" she informed me, climbing down. "I'm sure I've lost at least a ton of façades and pretensions, and all in one night!"

"But the theater is your life!" I said, stunned and a little disappointed.

"Wrong, Mr. Feuerberg! My life is only now beginning. Today! And perhaps I owe it all to you!" She grabbed me and danced wildly around the room with me until we nearly fell down.

I'm going nuts, I thought, I don't understand anything.

But it sure is fun.

As we were eating our breakfast we heard the neighbors open their blinds, cry out in surprise, and shout for joy. More and more blinds were opened. People looked out and called to each other, astonished at the miracle that had taken place during the night. I could hear an old man downstairs explaining at length that the light of the moon the night before had exerted such a strong gravitational force that it drew in unusually big waves that flooded the rampart and eroded it. Another neighbor speculated that the municipality was planning to levy a new tax on the view, which is why they had quickly brought the sea back to the neighborhood . . .

"You heard right, boy," said Lola. "Entrance tests are not required for those who live in Tel Aviv." She came and stood between Felix and me and threw her arms around our shoulders. "It was a fine gift you gave them," she said, "even though they may never know."

I wanted to call home, but Felix started describing yet again how we had torn down the embankment, with the sand flying everywhere, and how we had locked the guard in his shack, and how . . . He looked like Dad does when he winds up a case. He spoke with pride, and with contempt for anyone who tried to stand in his way. At such times it was the sadness in Dad that faded, but with Felix it was some of his elegance. I observed him, thinking how much he and Dad both loved to win, and that it must certainly have been humiliating for him when Dad won the contest.

Lola said it was time for bed. She offered Felix the sofa in the living room and led me to a small room with a view of the sea.

"This room has the best view in the apartment," she said as she made up the bed. "Years ago, I would sit here for hours, looking out at the waves. Alone or with another. Even from afar, the sea has a calming effect on me, and now, thanks to you and Felix, I have it back again."

She stood a moment, leaning out the window. "From here the sea looks bluer, more open," she murmured, seeming to quote someone who had often said so.

Then she let down the blinds so the morning sun wouldn't disturb me. But her movements were sharp, as though she wished to keep out a painful memory. "Good night, Nonny," she whispered, and left the room.

Darkness. I lay on my back and tried to fall asleep. I could hear her speaking to Felix in a whisper, but I didn't catch what they said. It irked me that I'd forgotten to call home again. Oh well. Later.

The bed was narrow as a child's cot, but I felt comfortable, like Goldilocks in the baby bear's bed. I seemed to have caught a little cold on the job, and I had trouble breathing. Also, the air in the room was musty. You could tell it hadn't been used for a while, possibly no one had even been in it. There was a big wardrobe against the wall facing me, and pictures of scenery. I got up quietly for a better look: they were framed postcards of the Alps, the Eiffel Tower, the Empire State Building, a herd of zebras. I walked on tiptoe. I didn't want Lola and Felix to know I was up. Why was I so secretive, and from whom was I hiding?

There was a row of little dolls on the corner shelf, soldier dolls from various lands, dressed in traditional uniforms. Someone had apparently arranged them on the shelf that way many years before. I picked one up and it came apart in my hand. The bright red uniform practically crumbled. I felt bad about spoiling it, and began to worry that I might spoil everything I touched.

I hurried back to bed. It was dark in the room, but I stepped surely; everything felt familiar to me, like the rough tiles under my bare feet. It was as if I had been here before. But how was that possible? The first time I'd ever walked into Lola's apartment was yesterday! The buzzing between my eyes was about to begin again. I could feel it coming, like a motorcycle rounding the bend. Maybe I'd eaten too much for breakfast. I lay down. Sat up. Who's there? Only a shadow.

I pulled the covers over my head, over both ears, contrary to Dad's regulations. I left just a crack open to peep through. I examined the shadows. The wardrobe, various objects, the little soldiers on the shelf, the scenic postcards from all over the world. I began to feel cramped. The room was crowding in on me. I rolled over onto my back. No good. I rolled back onto my stomach. Took a whiff of the pillow. It smelled familiar. I knew that smell. What was the matter with me? Everything in the room spoke to me. Breakfast congealed in my stomach. I reached out listlessly and touched the wall, and my finger found a scratch there, shaped like a bolt of lightning, deeper by far than the one I had at home, so I guess whoever had slept in that bed must have tried very hard to keep from crying, and as I touched it I felt my finger turn pale. I quickly slipped my hand between the bed frame and the mattress. There I found what I had been looking for, what I'd been afraid to find, petrified gobs of chewing gum. It couldn't be, I thought, everything's the same as it is in my room. I poked around the mattress and found the hole in the cover, just where I knew it would be. Whoever had slept here before liked to dig his finger into the mattress right where I did. Please, I thought stupidly, don't let me find any raspberry candies in there.

I sat up in alarm. This couldn't be happening, I thought, it's too weird. Suddenly I stopped sniffling. I realized that this was exactly like the story Chaim Stauber had told me once about an Indian girl remembering who she'd been in her previous incarnation, and then taking her parents to a village she had never seen in her life and showing them exactly where she'd hidden a favorite toy one hundred years before she was born. But things like that could happen only in India. Not here. Not to me. What's wrong with me? I asked myself. Who am I? Frozen with fear, I unwrapped the candy and put it in my mouth. It was all dried up. Like a rock crystal. Even the mildew had solidified. I licked it and sucked it and rolled it around in my mouth until it got wet and remembered what it was. A fine thread of flavor, the memory of raspberry, melted on my tongue and spread through my brain. I sat up in bed and licked that candy, all mouth and tongue and memory. Everything vanished, except for the taste of raspberry melting in my mouth. Maybe that's how a baby feels, suckling its mother's milk.

I woke up from this sweet reverie, no longer tired. The room was calling me, emanating sound waves the way a hand transmits the sensation of pins and needles when it's fallen asleep and is trying to wake up. I quietly got out of bed, walked over to the wardrobe, and opened it.

It was a child's wardrobe. Nothing unusual here, I thought, trying to keep cool: from top to bottom, children's clothes. But I couldn't keep cool. Just the opposite, in fact; I had goose bumps all over. Children's clothes. A boy's or a girl's? I couldn't tell. Maybe both: there were dresses and skirts, and girl's underwear. But also a boy's shirts and trousers. Wide leather belts. Thick sweat socks. A boy's or a girl's? And the doll collection on the shelf—a boy's or a girl's? Dolls, yes, but they were soldiers. Or maybe a lot of boys and girls had come through this room, like me, lured here by means of tricks and excuses? And what happened to them? Where were they now? I ran my hand over a dress hanging in the wardrobe. It was cool to the touch, like the skirt Felix had given me today. The colors, too, were like the colors of the clothes he gave me, reds and purples and greens. Something's wrong here, I thought. Why had they put me in this particular room? Gabi never told me about a little boy or girl living with Lola. So to whom did the clothes in the wardrobe belong? And what was the connection between Lola and Felix? And why had Felix brought me here? I wanted to call home. I had to talk to Dad. Right away.

I heard footsteps approaching and jumped back into bed. I managed to cover myself just in time. Lola and Felix tiptoed into the room. I closed my eyes. I was cold with fear, fear that flitted batlike out of the darkness of translated fairy tales and unconfirmed police reports about kidnappers and what they do to children. With my last bit of strength I wrestled with that fear. It simply wasn't in their character. No? Why not? Maybe all kidnappers seem like perfectly nice people. They have to lure kids into following them, don't they? Maybe the two of them always worked as a team, and it was Felix's job to bring the victims here. And what did Lola mean about his crazy games, when she asked whether he had permission to bring me here? And where did they get all the children's clothes?

I peeked out and saw them standing over me. She was leaning against his shoulder, and he had his arm around her. They watched me in silence.

Lola sighed.

Then she pushed Felix out of the room and closed the door behind him. She sat down on a little chair near my bed and gazed at me, barely breathing.

I was so confused. I didn't have the strength to figure out what was happening around me. Felix had been a criminal at one time, maybe he still was, but I was the one who'd brought him here. I chose to come! And Lola? What was her connection to all this? If she was involved in a crime against me, then I wouldn't mind dying, because nothing would mean anything. I sighed with anguish.

Lola stood up and hurried to my side. She stroked my brow and wiped away the perspiration.

"Go to sleep now, I'll watch over you," she whispered. Her gentle hands tucked the blanket around me and fluffed the pillow. Of course, I knew all long that she could never be involved in wickedness.

Her eyes enveloped me with wistfulness, longing. I turned toward her. We gazed at each other in the dark.

"Don't be afraid, Nonny," she said in her haimish voice. "It's only me. Would you like me to go?"

"No, that's okay," I answered. But what did she want from me?

"Felix tells me you used to wait outside my house and that I never even noticed you," she said. "I'm sorry."

"It doesn't matter. I got to see you in your plays, too."

"So he told me. And what do you think of my acting?"

"It's wonderful. I thought . . . I think you're a really great actress, only . . ."

"Only what?" She leaned forward. Why did I have to open my big mouth?

"It's just that, well, here in your house, you seem, you know, more real."

I heard her chuckle in the darkness.

"Well, Felix thinks so, too. He says I'm only good at playing queens, but in the role of an ordinary woman, I'm quite a flop. He's been saying that to me for years. Maybe he's right."

I wanted to protest, to rush to her defense, the way I do when Gabi makes fun of herself for being fat. But I was just too weak.

"Tell me about yourself, Nonny."

"I'm a little tired now."

"How silly of me. I so enjoy being with you, having a little boy around, but here I am torturing you, poor darling. Never mind, I'll leave now. Go to sleep."

"No, stay! Please don't leave." Maybe I was afraid to be alone in that mysterious room, or maybe it was the wonderful feeling I had with her, like being with a grandmother.

Of course I already had Grandma Tsitka. A complicated relationship. She was the mother of Uncle Samuel and Dad and their three brothers, a tall, thin woman who wore her hair in a top knot, had a cataract over one eye, and bony yellow fingers. I'm sorry if this sounds like a police description of a missing witch, but that's just how she looked. Nor did she care for me very much, in general or in particular. No matter what I said or did, she always criticized me. The moment she saw me, she would fix me with her one good eye and start circling around, carping at me till I just couldn't take any more, and then I would burst out crying or throw a tantrum. I believe she detested me from the moment I was born, and I, for my part, stopped calling her Grandma at the age of three and insisted on using her first name instead. I had a special way of pronouncing it, "Tsitka," making sure she would hear exactly how I felt about her. Then, at the age of four—after Gabi read me "Little Red Riding-Hood"—I began having serious suspicions about Tsitka, and I told Dad I didn't want to visit her anymore, at least not until the hunter arrived and clarified a few points concerning her identity.

Dad never tried to intervene. He simply went along with whatever she said about me and tried to keep us apart. Sometimes I wondered at her readiness to cut off relations. But then Dad wasn't much of a family man. Nor was he particularly eager for me to make friends with Tsitka's other grandchildren, my seven cousins, all of them, without exception, typical Feuerberg-Shilhavs, who didn't seem to have much trouble suppressing their friendliness toward someone like me. We never met except at weddings and other family occasions, when they would sit with their parents all evening and eat with a knife and fork and speak only when spoken to. And because they were always giving me dirty looks and I didn't want to spoil their bad impression, I used to stand at the bar and pretend to gulp down one drink after another, until the waiter would call one of my uncles over to take care of the little shikker. Then, looking out of the corner of my eye to make sure Grandma Tsitka had a good view, I would march away with my head held high and pick a fight with the drummer.

Yet with Lola, a stranger, I felt good. Her gentleness, her unaccountable fondness for me—

"Tell me about you," I said, half dozing. "Not as an actress. About you."

"Finally, someone who understands." Lola smiled. She sat with her feet tucked under her, the way she liked, and reflected a moment.

"You're right, Nonny. The person I am and the actress are no longer one and the same. For years now I've been aware of the difference, and to tell the truth"—she moved closer and whispered—"I don't really enjoy standing in front of an audience anymore."

I was flabbergasted. What a scoop! "Lola Ciperola Hates Theater!" But she could count on me not to leak it to the press. This was private and confidential.

"How strange." She smiled. "I never said it quite that way before. So firmly. Being with you makes everything clearer somehow: what's important and what's not. And what to do with my remaining years."

I smiled a crooked smile. She was being polite with me.

"I feel like telling you about myself." She giggled. "So you'll get to know me better. I don't want to tire you, but I can't seem to hold myself back. Aren't I awful? Go on, say you're tired and that you've had enough."

"Tell me what you were like as a girl."

"Shall I really?" She was so delighted, I immediately saw how she'd been as a girl.

"But don't tell me—" I hesitated. I didn't know how to say it without hurting her feelings. "Don't tell me the things you say in your interviews. Tell me new stories."

She gazed at me and slowly nodded. "For that you deserve a great big kiss, Nonny, but I'll try to control myself. Suddenly I don't feel like talking anymore. Would you mind if I sang you a song?"

" 'Your Eyes Shine'?"

"No. A different song. One my mother used to sing to me when I was about your age, living in a faraway land where I was known as Lola Katz. I hadn't taken on my ridiculous stage name yet. But I had a dog named Victor. And two friends named Elka and Katya."

"Lola Katz? Is that your real name?"

"Fancy that. Are you disappointed?"

"No—I just—I mean, it's strange—because Lola Ciperola is a pretty nice name, actually . . ."

She smiled to herself, closed her eyes, and sang a sweet song in a strange language.

A few hours, or minutes, later I heard her murmur, "Sleep, my darling. There's still time."

But by the time I woke up it was evening. Everything was topsy-turvy. I lay in bed dreaming a little while longer. If I were home now, Dad would still be out and I would have the house to myself. I would play soccer or go through Dad's gun catalogues or trot the globe with my fingertips, trying different routes to different places, or do nothing at all.

Sometimes it seemed as though a whole hour had gone by and that Dad would be home any minute, but the clock maintained that only a minute had passed, so what to do now? I didn't feel like staying in the house. I didn't feel like doing homework without Gabi. I would go to Micah's as a last resort and hang around with him, and when my lies started gushing out, he would stare at me, his mouth agape, his heavy earlobes like sinkers, waiting for me to get caught up in my own lies, which would irritate me into provoking a fight out of sheer boredom, and eventually I would leave him, feeling hollow inside. Our friendship had long ago stopped being real; it was just that we had nothing better to do. After my bar mitzvah I planned to inform him that we were no longer friends. Enough is enough already.

If only I enjoyed reading—but I didn't, I preferred it if Gabi read to me. If only I played a musical instrument, like the drums—you don't need a good ear to be a drummer, just a sense of rhythm and plenty of energy, and I definitely had that. But Dad refused to buy me a drum set.

So where did those thousands of hours go? Those interminable afternoons of my childhood? How did I fill my life? For one thing, I remember, I used to try to identify the neighbors' cars by the noises their motors made. Or I would spend hours leafing through my missing-persons notices, wondering where they were now, and how I could organize them into my own secret service, since they had no connections anymore, they were lost, so why couldn't they join up with me and be my guards? Or I would roller-skate over to Memorial Park and see if I could remember the names of the forty fallen on the plaque. Or I would hang around, doing nothing, just existing and waiting for life to begin.

But it didn't begin. And when it did, with one genuine friendship, I blew it.

If today were a Wednesday, I would be creeping through the bushes about now, seeing Chaim's mother safely home from the shopping center. At six-thirty in the evening she would make her way back from the beauty parlor, and though I was in disgrace as far as she was concerned, I didn't like to leave her without protection. As her bodyguard, I would check for possible trouble sources in the vicinity, and plan escape routes in case anything came up, like a protest demonstration. Sometimes she would stop to talk to a neighbor in the street. I would stand alert, ready to leap into the fire if the neighbor attacked. Inside my head I would hear a voice blaring, "Draw! Fire! Shoot!" and steal a glance out of the bushes at her softly fluttering eyelashes. And sometimes when I hid close by, it seemed to me that I could hear her words.

The clock on the wall at Lola's showed a quarter to seven. I got up and took another shower, to wash away the perspiration of the sultry day. How can anyone stand to live in Tel Aviv, I wondered. Lola had already gone to the theater, leaving Felix a long list of "Instructions for minding the house, the kitchen, and Nonny." You might have thought I was three years old and made of glass. Felix was sitting in the living room, reading the newspaper by the light of the Chinese lamp. He was wearing a red bathrobe tied with a sash. His hair was freshly shampooed, combed in neat little white waves, yellowing at the ends. When he saw me, he stood up, folded the newspaper, and asked what I wanted to eat.

There was tension in his voice, I noticed. We set the table in the kitchen, neither of us speaking. I sat down. I got up. I wanted to call home. Felix said the omelette would be ready in a minute and it would be a shame not to eat it hot. I said I just wanted to tell them I was okay at home, it wouldn't take long. Felix said all the lines to Jerusalem would probably be busy at this hour. He spoke fast and sounded firm. I sat down again. Why would the lines be busy? He served my omelette, garnished with a crown of pimiento and a sprig of parsley, like an artist's signature. He must have missed the good old days, with thirty guests for dinner.

"Is okay this way, Amnon?"

"Sure. That's style, eh?"

There was a wan smile on his lips. I was alarmed. Whenever Felix was down like this, I felt as if someone were trying to blow out the candle we'd succeeded in lighting together. I reminded him how the night before we had charged on the bulldozer and made the rampart fall.

"So what you want to do tonight?" he interrupted absentmindedly.

I returned the question: "What do you want to do?"

"You can go home, if you want."

"What? Are you kidding? Quit now?" I was just starting to enjoy myself.

"We don't have to," he sighed. "You decide."

"I'd like to stay like this forever." I laughed. "Only, I have a bar mitzvah in a few days. What did Dad tell you? What did the two of you decide?"

"Once again, I tell you, Amnon: is for you to decide."

That was a strange answer. As though he was avoiding my question.

"Wait a minute: what if I decided that we should stay together for a week? Or a month? And that I won't go to school anymore, that we'll just roam around at night and do things?"

Gravely Felix answered, "For me that is greatest compliment."

But his answer sounded wrong. Dad would never let him keep me. A little warning bell started ringing inside me. People always say that it rings in their heads. With me, it rang in my stomach, just under my heart and to the right.

Felix wandered around the kitchen. He washed the glasses, he retied the sash of his bathrobe a few times. He opened the refrigerator and shut it . . .

I stopped eating and watched him. What was the matter?

"By the way, Amnon," he said, with his back to me, "there is something we must to talk about, you and I. Just we two. Before we go on."

"What is it? Is anything wrong?" Oh please, don't let anything be wrong, I prayed, don't let anything spoil this beautiful dream. Just a little while longer, another day or two. In any case, I had to be back by Saturday. Felix was searching for something. He found it on his chair. The newspaper. The folded newspaper. He threw it on the table, right into my plate. What was the matter with him? He indicated that I should open the paper and read. What was I supposed to be looking for? It didn't take me long to find out.

In big red letters the headline screamed: SEARCH FOR BOY'S KIDNAP-PER WIDENS.

And underneath, in heavy black letters: "Police have called for total news blackout. Kidnapped boy is reportedly the son of senior police officer."

Below was a picture of the engineer standing outside the train in the middle of a field. And then I read another line: "The father of the boy is organizing the search. The identity of the kidnapper is known. The boy's life may be in danger."

21

Quick on the Draw:

A Question of Love

I was very cold. That I remember. I felt cold all over, as if someone had snipped me out of a warm, glowing picture with a pair of frosty scissors.

"What's this?" I asked. Or said. I didn't have the energy to perk my voice up into a question.

"I tell you story," said Felix wearily. His eyes were closed.

"What is this . . ." I asked again, my voice trembling like the newspaper in his hands. The words "boy's life in danger" were flashing at me. On the table, between me and Felix, lay a large bread knife. I couldn't take my eyes off it.

"Did you kidnap me?" I asked cautiously. I couldn't believe it. I knew all along, only I hadn't wanted to understand.

"You might say that," he answered. He still hadn't opened his eyes. His face looked pinched and drawn.

"You actually kidnapped me?" My voice cracked.

"You choose to come with me," he said.

He was right. I was the one who'd approached him on the train and asked, "Who am I?"

"It is long story . . . very complicated," said Felix, leaning against the wall. "But if you don't wish to hear it, tell me now."

I felt numb. No emotions or sensations. I didn't want to exist any-more. Going home was out of the question. How could I go home to Dad after what I'd done? Had all my adventures with Felix actually been crimes? Yes, crimes. I had committed crimes. The buzzing bored through my head, directly into my left eye. I deserved the pain. But how did it happen? Was it coincidental? And did Dad plan any of the things I did? And if he didn't know, then he wouldn't come and leave a big fat tip for the big fat waiter, which made me Felix's accomplice in all those crimes. How could I have believed him? What's the matter with me? Who am I, indeed?

And why had I enjoyed it all so much?

"Why did you kidnap me?" I asked, carefully pronouncing the word "kidnap," which sounded horribly ruthless all of a sudden.

He didn't reply.

"Why did you kidnap me?!" I shouted. He shuddered, looking old and weak suddenly.

"Because . . . because . . . I want to tell you something," he said.

"Tell me what? Why are you lying?" I shouted, so loudly that I startled myself. The knife was very close to his hand.

"This is story about you, Amnon. Also about me, but mostly about you."

"And what are you going to do to me now? Ask Dad for ransom money?"

Now I understood: this was his revenge on Dad! That's right. He was a criminal, he had hinted as much, but I was too stupid to understand: he wanted revenge on Dad for arresting him and sending him to prison! But where was my guilt in all this? What had I ever done to him?!

And what about their secret agreement to train me as a criminal so I would make a better detective, what about their manly handshake? I had made it all up.

"I want nothing from your father. I do not need his money."

"What do you want from him, then?"

"His son."

"What for?!"

The question erupted from inside me with a howl, rending my heart in two. Because I had liked him and I believed he liked me, before I realized I was kidnapped. But everything had gone wrong, everything was twisted now. How could I have believed for one minute that Dad planned the operation, when, in fact, the only arrangements he and

Gabi had made were for a magician, a contortionist, a policeman in disguise, and a phony prisoner to come aboard the train—which is not a whole lot, compared to what I did with Felix.

"You kidnapped me for revenge," I said, spitting out the word with disgust. "To get revenge on Dad. That's why!"

He shook his head and closed his eyes. I had the feeling he was afraid to open them again, because he, too, was sorry everything was spoiled. "No, Amnon. I kidnap you only because I want to see you and be with you. This is not connected to your father. It is something just between you and me."

"Me? Come on! Why me? I'm not famous. I'm just a kid! You wouldn't get anything for me if I weren't his son!"

"Amnon, go if you want—you are free," said Felix. "I am not holding you against your will. But I want you should know: only you are important to me here. Not your father. Only you, Amnon."

"What, you mean if I want to, I can just get up and run away?"

"You don't must to run away. Running away is only when people are chasing after you."

"And you won't . . . chase after me?"

At last he opened his eyes. They were veiled with sadness, resignation. I believed his eyes, but I couldn't help remembering all the people he had fooled with those same eyes.

"The way you look at me now . . ." he said, pressing his head with his hands and shaking it, "this is my great punishment for seventy years of lies—your eyes, the way you look at me . . ."

I got up. My knees were trembling, and so were my arms. I tried to hide it from him. I didn't want him to see I was afraid. I walked away slowly, never turning my back. He groaned. I could see how much it hurt him that I didn't trust him anymore. How could I trust him?

"I'm going," I said.

"You decide. I always say to you, you decide when this game is over."

I backed off toward the door.

"I must to tell you important story," he said quietly. "Story about your life."

To hell with you and your stories, I thought. You spoiled the beautiful dream, and now everything seems ugly and frightening.

"I only want for you to know one thing," said Felix. "If you give me few more hours, not long, just until tomorrow morning, I can tell you this story."

"And if I don't? If I don't believe you?"

With every word I said he bowed his head lower, as though stricken. "Don't go. No one else can tell you this story."

"I bet you'd swear to that."

I bumped into the door handle. I was sure that it was locked, that the key was clenched in his hand, that he would dangle it before my eyes soon, smiling like a maniac, and that would be the end of me, as it was for the other children he had brought to this house. And then my picture would appear on a missing-persons notice, and the police would ask for volunteers to help search for me, and they would find my remains in the Jerusalem Forest.

"No, Amnon, I don't swear anything to you," said Felix softly. "To you I only promise."

But the key was in the lock. I turned it and the door opened. I skipped out, slammed the door behind me, and bounded down the stairs. I cleared three or four steps at a time. For a second I imagined he was hot on my trail, and I may have screamed. My hair bristled, my body bristled. But he wasn't running after me. I tore out of the building. It was dark in the street. Cars were passing with their headlights on. I rested against a fence, panting like a dog. All the while I kept thinking, I'm free! I'm free! But I felt no joy somehow, only terrible pain and humiliation. I remember that the air was fragrant with honeysuckle, that it seemed like a perfectly ordinary evening. No one could have guessed what I was going through then, and the fate I had eluded. A couple passed, arm in arm, and then a man with a dog. He carried the newspaper with the headline. What would he do if I stopped him now and revealed that I was the one, the boy the whole country was searching for?

The man walked past me, but the dog dawdled along and sniffed my shoes. It looked up suspiciously and started growling at me, as dogs are wont to do. But the man tugged at the leash and dragged the dog off before it could give me away.

I walked quickly up the sidewalk, thinking I would need a whole year's quiet to unravel the tangled events of the past two days. What shocked me most was that I had never realized what was going on around me. That while so many people were searching frantically for me, I had been lost in my own little fiction.

As usual.

Idiot. What was I thinking? That Dad would place me in the hands of a certified criminal so he could teach me some tricks of the trade, offer me a speed course in lawbreaking? My own father, who'd tried so hard all his life to abide by the law and fight against crooks like this Felix character.

What was the matter with me? How could I have made such a mistake? It was as if I'd been sidetracked in my sleep but went on smiling like an imbecile, believing everything I saw, when it was all a lie. A lie and a crime. And after so many lies, I had deceived myself.

The kiosk on the corner was still open. I glanced cautiously at the headlines as I scuttled by, all of them seemingly about me, though the only information they revealed was that I'd been kidnapped. They didn't even give my name, because the police were keeping that a secret.

Kidnapping. Kidnapped. Life in danger. I muttered the words to myself. They sounded tinny. They had nothing to do with Felix's treatment of me. And my life was not in danger. Why did the papers lie like that? To attract readers.

I crossed the street and hurried on, where I didn't know. To get away from Felix. To run as far as possible from the danger in him. What was he doing now, alone, in the kitchen? He had escaped, no doubt, slipped out like a shadow, and was already searching for another sucker.

I circled around, back to the street behind Lola Ciperola's house. I just wanted to see whether he would try to get out through the window. He didn't, though. I figured I'd better report to the police. I could ask to call from the kiosk. I didn't have any money on me, but maybe

I could explain to the man that I was the kid in all the newspapers, the victim of the kidnapping. Right.

I slowed down. Such things required serious consideration. I wondered whether Micah knew already, whether the rest of my classmates had guessed that it was me. The ones who'd never been my friends, who used to make fun of me and Dad and our silly detective games and the way we saluted each other, and the ranks he did or did not confer on me, the "police mascot," who couldn't even get accepted into the traffic patrol for reasons A, B, and C.

Let's hear what they have to say now. Like Mrs. Marcus, who was always so eager to have me expelled from school, maybe she would wipe her eyes and say, "No, he wasn't emotionally disturbed, he was a zigzag kid, that's all, with the soul of an artist, only we didn't realize it in time." And the other teachers would be on the phone to each other by now, saying, "It was him. Poor thing. Maybe we drove him to it. We should print up a nice little booklet in his memory. There was something special about the boy, though he could get a little wild sometimes."

I wondered what Chaim Stauber was thinking now, and if this would change anything. And whether he would discuss it at home.

I stuck my hands in my pockets to slow myself down. Why was I running? Look before you leap. But there I was again, in front of Lola Ciperola's house. The streets all looked the same to me. I walked down to the corner. I passed the newspaper headlines again. Maybe even Golda Meir had taken time out of her busy schedule to ask her special advisor on crime whether the police were making every effort to save the boy, and whether he would divulge the boy's name to her, in strictest confidence, of course, and the advisor would whisper my name in her ear, and the Prime Minister would say, "Aha!," neglecting, for the moment, other pressing affairs of state.

But what was Felix doing, all alone by the kitchen table? This man, the partner with whom I had just spent the two happiest days of my life, had entered the headlines and become a stranger and an enemy. As I walked away, I had seen the life drain out of him. Why was it so vital that I believe him? Why had he been trying so hard to show me a good time?

He'd offered to share my vegetarianism.

And I'd promised (in my heart) that I would be loyal to him.

I betrayed him. But he betrayed me first.

I sat on the curb, wondering what to do.

A police siren went off down the street. All I had to do was go over there now and I could be done with this. But then I would never learn the secret Felix wanted to tell me. And I couldn't ask him any more questions. Dad would never tell me the story. He didn't want me to know. Not even Gabi was allowed to discuss it with me.

And Felix said he had known Zohara.

He knew about her life in the mountains with Dad.

But what about the horses they kept there? And what was it like for them together?

He said he had kidnapped me so he could tell me the story.

The story. The story. There was no end to the buzzing of this story. For thirteen years the story had been silent, and now it wouldn't leave me alone.

But wait: the photo. The one he'd showed me on the train.

Oh, God.

In that photo of me and Micah, I was wearing a coat. Which meant Felix started planning this operation last winter. So much thought and effort had gone into it: and for what, so he could tell me a story? What about the Bugatti he had had shipped to Israel, and the Beetle that succeeded it? And maybe there was more to come. I had heard him say to Lola, This is Felix's final operation. His farewell performance.

He knew something about me. Something that was important to him. Otherwise he wouldn't have put so much into it. My story was important to him. And if he didn't tell it to me, no one would. Because no one ever had, not in thirteen years.

I'm not afraid of Felix, I told myself anxiously. I can go back now if I want, hear his story, then turn him over to the police.

That would be great, I tried to work up a little enthusiasm.

Father-detective catches a felon, and ten years later, son-detective catches same. Full circle.

What a crook, I fumed: how did he convince me that Dad agreed to all this? I asked questions and he answered. And, in fact, he hadn't lied to me. That was the strange thing: he hadn't lied to me once since we'd met. Except for that time with the gun when he was trying to make me laugh. And even then he wanted to tell me about himself. And everything he had told me was true (or so it seemed to me), as if he had to have someone, even if only a kid, with whom he could be totally honest.

But why me, the son of the detective who had apprehended him?

I decided to go back. Felix had never lied to me or tried to harm me in any way. He had made no attempt to stop me from leaving. Why did I not hear what he kept telling me, then? "You decide. The choice is yours." It was all up to me. If I had the courage, I would know everything. If I didn't, I could go home now to a hero's welcome for having escaped from the kidnapper. Only I would know the truth.

Slowly I climbed the stairs. Yes, I was coming back of my own free will. I would listen to his story and lure him into a trap. That's what I would do. That's how I would make up for all I'd done with him, and Dad would have to forgive me.

Just as I was about to knock on the door, I stopped. Be reasonable, I told myself, he has a gun. He's desperate. This is your last chance to turn back. If you go in now, you may never come out alive.

I knocked on Lola's door. There was no sound inside.

He's probably run away by now, I thought. That's typical. Yeah, well, was he supposed to wait patiently for me to return with the cops? He had run away, and now I would never hear the story. I felt a pang of regret. In part because the story had been lost to me forever and in part because I realized that I would miss that crook.

I touched the handle. The door opened. I squeezed in sideways so it would be harder to hit me. All of Dad's instincts were at work in me now.

Silence.

"Is anyone there?" I asked cautiously.

The curtain stirred and Felix emerged from behind it with a gun in his hand. I knew. I had walked right into his trap.

"You come back," he said, his pallor showing through the tan. His hand was trembling. "You come back alone, without police, right?"

I nodded. I didn't dare move, I was so frightened and angry at my own stupidity.

He tossed the gun on the carpet and covered his face with his hands. He pressed his eyelids. I stood perfectly still. I didn't make a lunge for the gun. I waited for him to get hold of himself, for his shoulders to stop shaking. When he moved his hands away, I saw his eyes were red and swollen.

"You come back," he muttered. "This wonderful, Amnon, you come back."

He tottered away, dragging his feet, and his hair was wild and sticky with perspiration. I waited for him to go to the kitchen. Then I quickly picked up the gun and put it in my pocket. Now I felt more secure. But my heart was beating faster than ever, I don't know why. I stood in the doorway to the kitchen. Felix was drinking a glass of water. He sat down with a sigh and rested his forehead on his hands. His face was deathly pale, as pale as the face of a corpse in a forensic photograph. There was a pen on the table and a sheet of paper with a few lines scrawled on it. When he noticed I was looking, he quietly picked it up and crumpled it into a little ball.

"You don't know what it means to me that you come back," he said.

"Were you about to run away?" I asked. There was still some harshness in my voice, but the hatred in it had dissolved.

"By coming back you save my life," he said. "Not that life of Felix Glick is worth very much anymore. But when you come back you make it worth something again . . . Do you understand what I tell you?"

I didn't understand.

"Five minutes later, and we would never see each other again," he said.

"The story!" I puffed impatiently. Again I regretted coming back. I had given up my chance to make a clean getaway, to go home and forget all about this bizarre episode. "You promised a story, tell it to me now!" If only I had walked up to the police cruiser in the street before, I could by now have been talking to Dad on the telephone.

"The story is about one woman," said Felix hesitantly. My heart was pounding. Zohara, Zohara, the blood throbbed in my temples. Felix reached into his shirt. Unthinkingly I touched the trigger on the gun in my pocket. My instincts were faster than my thoughts, unnecessarily so, it seemed. He wasn't going for a weapon. He was merely pulling out the gold chain with the one remaining ear of wheat and the heart-shaped locket.

With a flick of his finger he opened the locket, handed it to me, and said with a croaking voice, "This woman both I and your father loved."

There inside the locket Zohara was smiling at me, with her beautiful face and wide-set eyes.

22

The Bird in Winter

Once upon a time there was a little girl. On her sixth birthday, the little girl had a party. The guests gathered around the flower-festooned chair where she sat and lifted it in the air, once for each of her six years of life. But when they raised her high for the year to come, she announced with a beaming smile that she had decided to die exactly twenty years from the day. A hush fell over the crowded room. The girl gazed bewilderedly at the mute and pain-filled faces that surrounded her. Then she laughed and said, "Don't worry, there's still plenty of time!"

She had a narrow face with prominent cheekbones that gave her a hungry look, and her gangly arms and legs were usually covered with ugly scratches she inflicted on herself in her sleep at night or in her daylight reveries. She would sit for hours staring out the bedroom window through dark, half-lidded eyes, and even when her name was called, she didn't hear. At a later age, she would devour books, or rather, be devoured by them herself. She would read anything and everything, whether for children or adults, nurturing the precious secret that she was not a little girl at all but a spy sent out to the world from her favorite book of the moment, to try to live an ordinary life among ordinary people, and never be discovered. And if anyone discovered her pretense of being a real person in the guise of a little girl, a grave punishment would follow. I'm afraid she never confided in her diary what this punishment would be, but now that I'm older than Zohara

was when she died, I think I can guess: the spy would have to abide
with humanity forever.

When she was a little older, Zohara (or Pippi Longstocking or Anne
of Green Gables or Huckleberry Finn or David Copperfield or Dorothy
or Lassie or Romeo and Juliet—rolled into one) would write lengthy
descriptions in her diary of a place she called "the land of death," or
the land of the dead, and the families that lived there together, in death,
and she would draw pictures of the infants born there: little white babies with no eyes. Various doctors she was taken to could find no way
to cure her sadness. One doctor suggested that playing a musical instrument might help, so they bought her a recorder in a small music
shop in Tel Aviv, and though Zohara seemed eager to play it, usually,
after a few moments, she would withdraw in silence again, with the
recorder still in her mouth and her fingers fluttering over the holes to a
secret tune no one else could hear.

On her rare good days, Zohara would sing like a little sparrow,
happy to have survived the winter storms: all brightness, she would
chatter merrily and skip around, hugging her loved ones and pressing
her cheek to their beating hearts. On those days her face shone brightly
and the disfiguring lines of pain and anger vanished beneath her skin.
Dressed in clothes she was too young to wear—long scarves and gaily
colored hats—she would promenade with her mother through the
streets of Tel Aviv, like some rare postage stamp, taking in the looks
of astonishment on the faces of passersby, as though laying away sup-
plies for a long and lonely voyage.

On these good days, Zohara bubbled over with words. She needed
to talk, and would make up stories to tell her family, her classmates,
anyone with the patience to listen. In a lyrical language, like a little
poet, she would speak of the other worlds she visited, in former incar-
nations, perhaps, or of the tiny beings that floated under her lids and
performed her wishes, or about a certain young prince who lived in a
far-off country, the name of which she must not utter because it was
like a magic spell; the oracle of the realm had foretold that the prince
would marry a girl from Israel, from the little city of Tel Aviv . . . She

would say such things with the utmost gravity, her eyes half-closed and her lips pouting as though she were listening to someone inside tell her these things, which she in turn was bound to pass on to others. And so charming were the stories she told that no one called them lies but only fairy tales, Zohara's fairy tales; even at school none of her classmates called her a liar and would listen in wonder, with only the mildest reservations, unable to decide whether or not Zohara believed what she was saying herself; because if she didn't, how could she speak with so much authority, and how could anyone understand a girl who acts one way and then suddenly another. Let her decide once and for all who she is!

And there's another thing that pains me: when she was eight or nine, Zohara would choose a boy to love passionately, with all the devotion and grandeur of her soul. Of course, this was alarming to the chosen one. Who needed a crazy girl clinging to you like a pest, making the other children smirk at you with her heavy, grown-up love? But Zohara, undeterred, would write long letters, wait for hours outside the boy's house, and make a real fool of herself in front of everyone, though she seemed not to notice that he was trying to avoid her (if he was kind), or as happened more often, that he was laughing in her lovesick face, with vows of undying love prompted by his tittering friends behind the door. Zohara didn't mind. She had chosen him and was indifferent to their mockery. She knew that boys their age hated girls, it was a law of nature, though it was too bad the wonderful boy of her choice had yielded to convention. Still, Zohara was strong enough for both of them; her patience went beyond convention, beyond nature, even, she was a law unto herself, and would wait uncomplainingly for him to pass through this silly phase. She had no doubt that something of what she lavished on him sank in, that a word or a look of hers still sparkled in his heart of hearts when he was away from his mocking friends, and that someday, in a year or two, a great light would shine forth to her from his heart, which was all the more reason to rejoice even now and dance through the streets; life was so beautiful and she was a part of it, not as a spy, but as a girl of flesh and blood and soul!

And suddenly, as if by some feat of dark magic, her eyes would cloud over and the corners of her mouth would fall, and her face would grow so pinched she looked like an old crone who was weary of living.

The slightest thing would cause her unendurable pain: a broken pitcher, a man limping across the street, a promise unkept. Even in springtime when the world is in flower and children feel like the fruit and blossom of the trees, their bodies filled with juice, she would sit by the window, holding her hand up to the light to see her delicate bones and joints, and then burst into tears. Once in the middle of a lesson at school, she stood up, gaping as though she'd just wakened from a nightmare, and screamed, "But there's no fence! There's no fence!" When the teacher put her arms around her and tried to calm her down and find out what had frightened her so much, Zohara wriggled away from her and scurried around the classroom like a frightened animal, shrieking, "There's no fence, there's no fence around the world, what if we all fall off?"

But at the age of fourteen, when her doctors had given up hope, these grievous symptoms all but disappeared. Like magic. The doctors had no explanation for this. They mumbled something about puberty . . . the effect of hormones . . . The important thing is that she's better . . . And Zohara began to mature. The bitterly unhappy child was gone, to everyone's relief, and a young girl emerged to take her place: wild, mercurial, with a ringing laugh, an unquenchable thirst for the colors and pleasures of the world, growing daily taller and more beautiful, no, not beautiful, ravishing, with her jet-black hair and eyes, and the curving cheekbones that made her seem both fierce and refined. She outdid the boys in coarse language and scruffy clothes, her everyday trousers and ragged shirts. There was no mirror on the wardrobe door of her bedroom. "I just don't want to see myself, there's nothing to see!" She would goad the boys into foolhardy acts, and incite them cruelly against the other girls, the soft, feminine girls, who were terrified of her; she was rude to her teachers, and spent one day at school for every two at the beach, and her eyes sparkled, she was tan and muscular, with a swimmer's physique, fast-moving and frenetic, as if to make up for all the years of staring and inertia. She wouldn't touch a book if she could help it and risk falling foolishly into the snare of depression that lay between the alluring covers. Only the recorder beckoned occasionally, drawing her back when the seasons changed, but as she sat on the windowsill in her bedroom, pressing her lips to the mouthpiece, she would suddenly— No! Absolutely not! Because Zohara was the boss, it was she who would decide what to play and how to play it! And if the recorder defied her with extraneous notes and forgotten undertones, she would confine it to its velvet sheath, where it would have to lie in the dark until it learned its lesson.

All this occurred in the stormy days before Israel became a state and the Jews were trying to oust the British and teenagers like Zohara were joining the underground, performing heroic deeds, toughing out beatings, arrest, and jail. At school there were whispers, secret codes, and rumors. Everyone spoke the same language, but Zohara remained uninvolved. "Who cares about politics, I go to the beach to swim and sunbathe, not to help illegal immigrants off the boats," and once someone spotted her dancing at a café frequented by British soldiers, and when she received a gentle warning to stay away from the enemy occupiers of the land, she replied so coarsely that a classmate who was active in the underground said, "Forget about her, she doesn't belong anywhere. Just pretend that she fell from the moon."

And maybe he was right. In a little while we'll get to the part in my story where she ran across the moon and jumped down to earth, and it was to that moon and a certain lunar mountain that I owe my birth.

"I don't know anything about Zohara," I said again to Felix in Lola's kitchen. "Dad refuses to talk about her, and even Gabi is silent on the subject."

"I think," said Felix, "that Miss Gabi finds very nice, smart way to tell you about Zohara."

"But she didn't tell me anything!"

"Little by little you understand how much she tells you."

"Someone once said that she used to like strawberry jam."

"Did your father tell you this, or Gabi?"

"Neither of them. It was Tsitka, Dad's mother. I polished off a jar of jam, and Tsitka said I was just like her. 'Just like his mother,' she said in that voice, with her lips like a scar."

"And I can tell you, Amnon, that your mother loved anything sweet, but most of all she loved chocolate, she was crazy for chocolate."

Just like me.

And there was something about my bullfight that reminded Dad of her and made him mad.

"And you never meet anyone from your mother's family? Uncles, aunts, anyone?"

"She didn't have a family . . ." Or so I'd heard. Or thought. Or hadn't thought.

"Really? You have seen once somebody with no family at all, no uncle or distant cousin even, nothing? And what is her work, her profession? You never think to ask that?"

I was speechless.

"Now I tell you the story, Amnon. It will not be easy for you to hear. And it will hurt, too. But then you will understand many things you did not know before. I have to tell you, because you see—how to say it—this is why I wanted that we should meet."

"All right, then, tell me." What will be will be.

"One moment. Maybe you think it over first. Maybe is too much for you to know. What you don't know won't hurt."

But what I didn't know already hurt. I nodded at him to continue.

"All right," he said, sitting up in his chair, "I tell you before that I knew Zohara from when she was baby, because I knew her mother, too. Then I knew Zohara at your age. But I knew her best when she was eighteen. So pretty, and she was most wonderful girl I ever know, and believe me, Amnon, this old man," he said, pointing at himself, "know plenty of girls in his day."

"Did you . . . love her?" But I didn't have to ask. I could see it on his face.

"For me it was impossible not to love Zohara."

For me it was plain embarrassing to hear that Felix had once been my mother's boyfriend.

"But it was special kind of love," he said. "Love like in cinema!"

Worse and worse.

Then slowly, Felix unfolded the story of Zohara. He spoke simply, without drama, rarely flashing his eyes. I sensed how hard he was trying to be fair, to stick to the facts, even when they were incredible. He wanted me to hear it straight, minus any artifice on his part.

I couldn't say how long Felix spoke. I put myself completely in his hands and he took me around the world, in rickshaws, riverboats, and big airplanes. He told the story with care, and though every word was painful at first, turning my whole life inside out, I knew it was all true; still, now and then, I would find myself listening as though this were a very sad and beautiful fairy tale.

Once upon a time, in the city of Tel Aviv, there lived a beautiful maiden named Zohara. Zohara was a wild, fresh sea nymph. At sixteen she decided to quit school, and no one could say she knew less than other girls her age. By her seventeenth birthday she was the most beautiful girl in Tel Aviv, wooed not only by British soldiers but by a famous millionaire nearly twice her age, a Dutch conductor, and the center forward of the Tel Aviv soccer team. Zohara would have none of them. And why? Because she hadn't found anyone worthy of her? Or because she was afraid to love again as she had in childhood? At eighteen, she took her first trip abroad with the archcriminal Felix Glick, a man with mesmerizing blue eyes.

It was a two-year journey to exotic places, the faraway countries of an atlas smudged with fingerprints. For two years my mother and Felix Glick traveled together to places Zohara chose according to the incantatory power of their names: Madagascar, Hawaii, Paraguay, Tierra del Fuego, Tanganyika, Zanzibar, the Ivory Coast . . .

In luxurious hotel lobbies they would encounter characters who seemed to have stepped out of an old book: exiled princes, dethroned emperors, generals and mercenaries, failed revolutionaries, stars of the silent screen whose voices had proven too shrill for talking pictures . . .

"And I was there posing as art collector from Italy"—Felix smiled—"or curator of museum in Florence who ran away from Italian bureau of taxes, and Zohara—well, we tell people she is my only daughter, and sole heir to paintings by Picasso and Modigliani I keep in bank. This is what we do."

"Go on." I laughed, uncomprehending. "You mean Zohara was also a . . . uhm . . ."

"You must to listen now, and I will tell you."

During their sojourns in one city or another, they would stroll along the river, or hire a gaudy carriage emblazoned with imitation gold, and the devoted daughter would tuck an angora shawl around the knees of her would-be father to keep him warm. And thus, on their innocent outings, they might chance upon an exiled king who would happen to notice the white handkerchief dropped by the beautiful girl, run after the two of them, retrieve the hanky, kiss her hand, and tip his hat to her and her father. In the course of the conversation that invariably followed, the king would ask the modest gentleman and his beautiful daughter to join him for dinner at his hotel suite, and afterward, when he was mellow with wine and had fallen under the spell of the daughter's charms and the blue of Felix's eyes, he would invite them on a river cruise aboard his yacht.

At first they would demur, not wishing to be a nuisance. "Not at all! It will be a great pleasure, I'm sure!"

"But you are too gracious, Your Highness."

"Not in the least! Do come. We sail tomorrow."

And at last they would agree, and step aboard the luxurious yacht wearing tropical sun hats and carrying seven empty suitcases, to impress him with their wealth, and Zohara's recorder, purchased from a music store in Tel Aviv, to summon the nymphs of the sea.

"Always this story," said Felix, looking away. "Five times, ten times—it works same. Only places change, and different people, different pigeon every time. We hunt him—and he, you can be sure, was hunting us, but there was no huntress like your mother."

"What? What did you say?" I couldn't understand what he was on about. How did any of this concern my mother? I wished he would tell me about Zohara already.

Felix was silent a moment. He shrugged his shoulders.

"This is not easy for you, Amnon. It is difficult story. But I must to tell you. I promised her. She asked me to promise."

And I said, as though bitten by a snake, "Who asked? Who asked you?"

"Your mother, Zohara. Before she died. She told me to find you and tell you whole story before your bar mitzvah. She said you must to know everything about her. That is reason for all this."

"The reason for all what?"

"For this. For taking you with me so I can tell you story . . . Your bar mitzvah is any day now."

"Ah," I said, nodding slowly, "ah yes." But I didn't understand a thing.

"And I must to give you gift from her," he added carefully, "her present for your bar mitzvah."

"What present? She's dead, isn't she?" I could barely move my lips.

"Yes, she is dead. But before she died, she arranged it for you. Only I think is impossible to get it until tomorrow morning. Her present is in safe-deposit box she left in bank many years ago. This is why I want you should stay with me until tomorrow. If you go with me to safe-deposit box, I give you last golden ear of wheat. Then you can leave, forget about Felix."

My lips formed a pale smile. Forget about Felix. Oh sure.

"My mother—" I began hoarsely, and the two words nearly toppled me over, and filled my throat with honey and brine and other strange flavors.

"She was very special woman," said Felix, stroking my hand because he saw my distress. "Beautiful, wild, like tiger, and so young, she was queen of Tel Aviv. Whenever she crooked her little finger, twenty men were willing to kill themselves for her. There is nothing in this world she wanted and did not do, and there is no one in this world could tell her what to do."

I listened in amazement. My mother? Is that what she was like? Although I seldom imagined her, suddenly she was beyond imagining.

"And she was strong, Amnon, strong like only very beautiful people are. She was even, how to say it, cruel. Maybe she did not know her own power or understand danger of beauty. There are some whose lives were ruined because of her. Because they fell in love with her, and she played with them until she was tired and tossed them away.''

"Cruel?" It couldn't be. He must have been talking about some other woman, not my mother. He was lying! It was a fib from beginning to end! But his face spoke the truth.

"Yes, cruel, like kitten playing with mouse. The kitten does not know how strong its claws are. It thinks it is playing with mouse, but poor mousy is already dead.''

"But how did she marry my father? How did they meet? Tell me about that!" I felt an urgent need to change his story, or at least to bring Zohara closer to Dad. And normal life.

"Not so soon, Amnon." Felix sighed. "There is long way to go before she meets your Mr. Father.''

"Wait a minute," I shouted. "Is that why you kidnapped me? To get even with Dad for taking her away from you? Because she loved him more than she loved you?"

Felix shook his head. "I am sorry, Amnon! But you must to hear whole story! From beginning to end. In sequence. That is what she said! If not, you will understand nothing.''

Fine. I wanted him to tell me. That is, I did and I didn't. Actually, I didn't know what I wanted anymore. Everything he said turned my life topsy-turvy. And made it seem weird, too. And as soon as he finished telling me the story, I'd have to start getting reacquainted with myself. Nonny Feuerberg, a pleasure to meet you, or maybe not such a pleasure, at that.

"She was my partner. Yes, your mother. That is what she wished!" And then he added, as though justifying himself, when he saw the look in my eye, "That is life she wanted. She told me so. Is true!"

"A life of . . . of crime?"

He hung his head in silence.

"You mean my mother was a crimi— You're lying! You're lying to me again!" I shouted. I got up. I sat down. I stared up at the ceiling and down at the floor.

"Listen to me!" cried Felix. "That is what she wanted. 'Felix,' she said to me, 'they're all cowards, living hand-me-down lives!' And I said to her, 'Zohara, the life of criminals is very short! Any minute they can die!' And she answered that either way life is short, so why not live the time we have, whether it's years or months, as long as we live how we want! The grand life! The life of cinema!'"

So I had a criminal mother. That's what she was. That's what they had always tried to hide from me. A criminal mother. It happens. There are women's prisons out there, full of criminals. Still, how could it have happened to me? But why not? It had to happen to somebody, so why not me? And what did I care about her, anyway? I never even knew her. But I did care, she was the only thing I actually did care about just then. Or maybe Felix was lying. No, he was telling the truth. My mother had committed crimes all over the world. That's why Dad never talked about her, except for that one time after what I did to Pessia, when he yelled about the curse Zohara passed on to me.

But then . . . why did he marry her? How could my father have married a criminal?

I was the son of a policeman and a criminal.

I felt as if I would burst. As if I would split in two.

"Almost two years we were partners," said Felix. "Two years abroad, and everything was like dream. And then she was bored again. Always she was bored. But I never met anyone who enjoyed this work more than your mother. For her it was game, and always she was laughing."

I looked down at the checkered tablecloth. Square upon square, red and white. What more is there to say about squares? How I wished Gabi and Dad would turn up and hug me between them, with no one else around to see.

"I tell you now?" asked Felix cautiously.

23

Just Like the Cinema

● ● ● **A**nd at night, sailing down black waterways to the music of crickets and cicadas, under Madagascan stars, or a Zanzibari moon, the former monarch would reminisce about his beloved country, its lakes and mountains and the benevolence of his enlightened reign, cut short by the treachery of rebels who surprised him one day, though he had never harmed them, stormed his seventy-seven palaces, robbed him of his seven golden carriages, and even his prized collection of seven hundred pairs of shoes.

And the father-and-daughter impersonators would nod sympathetically and click their tongues over the treachery of the king's unworthy subjects who took revenge on his poor shoes; they were happy to hear, however, that the king had managed to escape from the thankless rabble with several pairs of gilded sandals, velvet pantofles inlaid with rubies, and also—he smiled with embarrassment, glancing around—some of the most exquisite treasures of the realm. But mum's the word.

And after many heartfelt sighs and heavy silences in tribute to the sorrows of the former monarch, the doting father with the streaks of greasepaint silver in his hair would tell about his peregrinations with his daughter and their escape from narrow-minded revenue agents, alluding casually to a certain collection of priceless paintings he kept in a Swiss bank vault, whereupon the roses returned to the faded royal cheek, and the father knew that the fish had smelled the bait and was even now circling around it.

And then, glibly changing the subject, the father would speak about his demure young daughter, the heiress to millions, as she fluttered her lashes behind an Oriental fan and inflamed the king with every blink of her eye.

And as the old man spoke, he had a fit of coughing so frightful that his devoted daughter spread the angora shawl over his knees; still, it persisted, an ugly, hacking cough he tried to bury in his handkerchief, and the king, who had already demonstrated his visual acuity when it came to handkerchiefs, glanced down at the spreading stain.

At this point the invalid father would ask permission to retire to his cabin and leave the fair lady and the fallen king alone together on the deck; and as he shuffled off, his wheezing cough would swell the sails, and the heart of the avaricious king as well.

Then the couple would continue the conversation, the king returning to his reminiscences about his youth and manhood and the spellbound girl hanging on his every word.

"But was she really spellbound or was she just pretending?" I asked Felix over the red-and-white-checkered tablecloth in the kitchen, because I was kind of spellbound myself.

"Yes and no" was his answer.

She was spellbound because everything there was like a dream—the river lapping by, the stars, the crickets, the bubbly champagne, and the melancholy king. And then again, she was not spellbound but, rather, lying in wait, like a hunter, or a panther, to shift the conversation to the desired tack.

And spellbound nonetheless, because more than any thought of wealth, she enjoyed the soft breeze blowing around her like a fabulous scarf as she performed her part in this play. For a moment she believed with all her heart that she was the sole heiress to the fortunes of a moribund millionaire, and her eyes would grow moist as she listened to the story of the king's travails, thinking, This is just like the cinema.

And the strange thing about it was that her tears—although engendered in fantasy—were wet and salty and real, and made the old king's heart flutter once, and then again.

After a sumptuous dinner on board his yacht, the king would ask the fair lady to play him a song on her recorder. Declining at first, she would eventually take the recorder out of its velvet sheath, lean back against the rail, and play popular Hebrew tunes like "Lovely Nights in Canaan" and "To the Fountain Came a Lamb"; and sometimes, taken in by her own magic, she would curl up with the recorder in her mouth, dreamily fingering the holes without a sound, yet drawing forth hidden overtones that would drip over the deck to the water below, where diaphanous river nymphs awoke from their slumbers and rose out of the dark waves, with their long seaweed tresses spread around them and the tide sparkling with the white, yellow, and purple of their eyes; and they would listen raptly, sighing.

And the king would clear his throat to rouse his sleeping flute girl (or so he imagined her), and eventually lost patience and shook her by the shoulders, and when she woke up in alarm, the king would peer into the dark abyss of her eyes and recoil, but very soon the lids would drop like a curtain and rise again over the shy and sultry eyes that he adored. And he would glance left and right to make sure they were alone, and whisper a secret in her ear.

Perhaps she has forgotten, says the dethroned king in a voice quivering with emotion, perhaps her heart does not incline to such earthly things, but he, the king, was fortunate enough to smuggle a number of treasures out of his country, including the pride of its famous mines, as well as several cases of diamond tiaras and crates full of gold ingots and golden scarabs and other provisions kings sometimes grab on the run, especially when they have just been dethroned.

All of this would be hers if she consented to marry him.

Marry him?

The fair lady batted her eyes and waved her fan, the fabulous scarf wafted around her, and the king's heart was already aflame. Maybe he was in love with her, or perhaps he realized the value of the paintings she would inherit after the lamentable death of her father. And he had a little plan to return to his kingdom, to buy off a few generals there and regain the throne, only for that he would need much money, generals cost dearly, and as he knew so well, a Picasso is sometimes worth more than ten diamonds.

"But I must consult dear Papa." She would flutter her lashes (it was fun to look at the world this way, through fluttering lashes that made the scenes flicker by as on the silver screen . . .) and the king said, "Just a minute," or whatever kings say, and ran back to his stateroom, which was next door to the captain's quarters, and there, with a trembling hand, he unlocked the safe hidden behind the portrait of his father, his grandfather, and his grandmother's father, and returned to her, flushed as a drunken moon, bearing one of the treasures, a ruby-red pomegranate plucked out of the black earth, and vivid flashes of the ripened fruit spurted out, red and purple, and cascaded into the black river below, and she stared at it openmouthed, for she had never before seen anything so beautiful, and as he fastened the pendant on a silver chain around her slender neck, his royal hand moist with perspiration and greed, though mostly greed, the girl was thinking of the glaring lights of distant Tel Aviv, where it was never quite dark enough for a moment like this, to see vivid flashes spurting into a river; in Tel Aviv there is no great river to reflect you with a former king helping you on with a ruby necklace. And a scrawny little girl of nine or ten looked out from deep inside her, an unhappy child with black eyes who couldn't lie, not to herself and not to others, and the adult Zohara pleaded with her to accept the glittering fruit, as a gift, or a bribe, or a potion to allay her fears, but the child shook her head with a decisive No!

Days passed. The journey was extended. Still, she was unable to make up her mind. The king had visited the sickly father in his cabin at least fifteen times, and couldn't help noticing, much to his sorrow, the fresh bloodstains on the embroidered pillowcase. And in the evenings His Highness would stroll around the deck with the girl, and then dine with her in his stateroom, regaling her with his anecdotes and fascinating reminiscences, and with gems and diamonds the size of wild berries, caressing her hand from time to time, in lieu of the kisses he longed to give her, but still she refused.

Then one day the girl's father took a turn for the worse, and he called her and the king into his cabin and asked his daughter to plight her troth to the eminent exile, and he made the king swear to care for his daughter like the apple of his eye, and in his last lucid moments he witnessed their vows of eternal love and loyalty, nor did he forget to

whisper the secret number of his Swiss bank account into the king's
ear, and the king was so excited he hurried back to his stateroom to
note the coveted number down in a little book, as well as on his stateroom door, and on the hand and forehead of the cabin boy who happened to pass just then, and he unpacked the ripest fruit and brought
it to the father's cabin, which filled to bursting with the vivid flashes of
broken light he now hung around the daughter's alabaster neck as a
token of their vows, what was his was hers, and what was hers was
his, forevermore.

Soon after, the girl's father was officially in the throes of death. His
daughter ran weeping through the corridors, and the captain radioed
the nearest city, whereupon an elderly doctor arrived on board accompanied by a stern-looking nun; they sat at his deathbed for a while and
then quickly left the yacht, wearing masks on their faces, protection, as
it were, against his contagious disease.

Only much later, when muffled shouts were heard from inside the
cabin, did the captain break down the door, only to find the elderly
doctor and the nun tied back to back, to their evident dismay, wearing
the clothes of the father and daughter, who had sneaked off the yacht,
disguised as the doctor and the nun, and were probably even now on
their way to the nearest airport, or already flying over the golden river-
boat, waving down at the old king, whose diamonds, pearls, scarabs,
and other beautiful berries were safe inside a secret pocket sewn into
the girl's suit, and she snuggled up to her invalid father, who looked
rather healthy as he roared with laughter. And this was one of his many
stories.

Felix was silent again. So was I. What could I say? It was very dark
out already, and there was still so much to hear. But I was frightened.
I suddenly felt her heartbeat in mine. That's what his story had done
to me: the boat, the black river, the king, the jewels, what they said . . .
her vitality coursed through me. The golden locket was open. Zohara's
eyes flashed vividly. "Look at me," they called. "Don't be afraid, not
of me or of yourself. You, too, are made of me."

"Ah, she was something to see," said Felix, with the wistful smile I knew by now. "Like princess in fairy tale . . . with clothes like nobody else . . . her dresses, her hats . . . like Purim all year long . . . and all the money, she gave it away . . . Money did not stick to her hand . . . Filthy lucre, she called it, money stolen from thieves, and I say to her, 'Zohara, my darling, there is no such thing as clean lucre and filthy lucre. Money is money, and what matters is what you do with it.' But for her—never! What she loved is acting. It hurt me to see how she threw it away! In the street, in darkened cinema, she would suddenly toss ten little diamonds up in the air, or from high in hot-air balloon, suddenly money would rain down . . ."

I shivered, enthralled. How well I understood that urge to wave my hand and throw down . . .

Felix and I jumped up in alarm. The loud ringing of the telephone tore us apart.

I was listening so closely to his story I forgot everything else—the kidnapping, the world outside, the newspaper headlines. Felix picked up the receiver and listened. Suddenly he beamed. "We will be right there," he said, and hung up.

"Come on, Amnon, we must to go."

"Where to? Who was that?" Because I had to be constantly alert.

"It is Lola calling from theater. I left our Rolls there. Lola is waiting for us."

"Our Rolls-Royce?"

"That is what I call it. Private joke. Come. Quickly put on Tammy's clothes and we go out. Lola said we are in all newspapers and maybe police are near. We must to run away. Till morning. Till we go to bank, for your present."

I didn't argue with him. I put on Tammy's clothes. But as I was getting dressed, I began to understand whose clothes they were and chills went up my spine.

Yes, at last I was beginning to understand, lousy detective that I was, not by thinking about it logically, but with my heart—because I had walked the paths my mother, Zohara, once walked when she wasn't much older than I was.

Because those were the rules of the story, the rules Felix had decided on so many months ago while he was planning this operation. And only now did I begin to understand the intention behind our journey: from the moment I met Felix and departed from the merry course Dad and Gabi had set for me, every step I had taken was predetermined, even when I chose it myself. Predetermined by Felix, who had led me here unwittingly. But even more, it was Zohara who had led the way, the Zohara within me, revealing herself.

I rejoined Felix wearing the old clothes, the red skirt and the green blouse. Their colors had faded over the years, the fabric no longer felt strange to me. The clothes caressed my skin, clung to it softly.

"These were her clothes, weren't they?" I asked.

Felix nodded.

"The clothes she wore when she was a little girl."

"*Nu*, yes, of course."

I remembered how he had looked when he first saw me on the train. And how his eyes had misted over when I put on her clothes in the Beetle.

"Do I resemble her a little this way?" I asked cautiously.

"Like two peas in pod."

24

The Detective's Son

We divided ourselves into two squads, one squad consisting of me and the other of Felix. First he explained how to get from Lola's house to the Habimah National Theater, and then warned me that detectives were moving in. His instincts told him that the place was crawling with cops. I asked how he knew that. "If I feel tickle like ants up and down my back, that is sign for me that police are near," he said. I, too, thought I felt a little tickle between my shoulders, as though someone were staring at my back. Maybe I was starting to develop anti-police tendencies myself.

Squad A went to the window to see if the coast was clear. Squad B was still working on his beggar's disguise. Squad A looked through the front-door peephole and reported all clear. Squad B reported that he would set off five minutes later than Squad A.

Squad A and Squad B stood facing each other.

"Goodbye, Amnon. Don't let them catch you. Be smart. You must still to hear story of how Zohara met your father, and also, there is present she gives to you!"

"You be careful, too."

"Shake my hand, partner."

Partner! I hadn't felt so proud since the day Dad promoted me to sergeant second-class. I reached out, we shook hands, and on a sudden impulse, the two squads hugged each other.

"See you," I whispered, thinking, Once this criminal was her partner, and now, years later, he is her son's. We've come full circle again.

"*Nu*, get out of here already," Felix grumbled, turning away for some reason.

Okay. My last night with Felix, the final chapter of our story begins.

Felix was right: the place was crawling with cops. I noticed this as soon as I left Lola's. Someone had made sure all the streetlamps in the area were turned off, and there were cruisers driving up and down with their dimmers on. Small groups of policemen stood on every corner, holding maps, examining the site of the operation. I could hear the whir of walkie-talkies in the dark, and I thought I saw a plainclothesman retreating behind a water tank on one of the rooftops. Or maybe not. It's hard to spot a lookout on a roof when it's so dark. I still couldn't understand how the police had guessed Felix and I were in the vicinity. Unless they'd found the ear of wheat I threw into the sea the day before, they had no reason to connect the bulldozer with the train hijacking! But the fact of it was that they had guessed something and were gradually closing in on the neighborhood. And maybe, I reasoned, they know something else, something Felix hasn't told me yet.

A young man walked by and plopped down on a bench. He looked too young to be so tired.

I glanced quickly at his feet. Shoes are the last item of a disguise a person will bother with. He was wearing the Palladium shoes issued by the Department of Criminal Investigation.

A little girl sauntered gaily by, her pigtail bouncing off her back. She stared pertly at the man through Zohara's eyes.

"Go away, little girl. Don't bother me," he snarled.

And she was such an obedient little girl.

I turned right, following Felix's directions. I could just imagine Dad organizing a search party now, hunched over a big street map of Tel Aviv, sending various teams out to wait in ambush. He had a real flair for ambushes. He always seemed to guess the criminal's escape route and where he would try to hide when pursued. Once he hid a detective inside a huge garbage bin, a kilometer and a half away from where an ambush was in progress outside a jewelry shop. The thief, who managed to slip by the detectives near the shop, streaked past three other detectives waiting along the route—the exact route Dad had anticipated when he plotted the chase—and dived into the stinking garbage bin, wearing a self-satisfied grin, when, much to his alarm, he heard the cuffs click shut on his wrists.

"A good detective thinks like a criminal."

But I was no longer certain which of the above pertained to me.

It was so dark out. And the whispers, the shadowy movements.

I had to keep reminding myself that from a purely professional standpoint Dad could count on me not to let him down. True, I was only thirteen, but I had nearly ten years of training behind me. From the age of three. That's what Dad wanted, because Mozart's father taught him how to play the piano at the age of three. He started off by training me how to describe people accurately. Sometimes he would play memory games with me: What color shirt was the bus driver wearing? Who was wearing glasses in the shop we just left? What had every child worn to nursery school that morning? What color dress was your nursery-school teacher wearing at your birthday party?

With a perfectly straight face. In dead earnest. Red with rage if I made a mistake. And whatever I didn't know one day, I had to make up the next. And there were punishments. But the worst punishment of all was his sneer of contempt when I failed.

And at the age of five: What's the license-plate number of the car parked in front of the house? How many traffic lights do we pass on the way to Grandma Tsitka's? In which hand does the new mailman carry letters? What kind of accent did the person who came to the door collecting for charity have? How do you jump-start a car? Why did you pull your blanket over both ears again last night, where's your vigilance? You're not going to get your allowance this week. Don't cry. One day you'll thank me for this.

I was running too fast, afraid I might give myself away.

For my tenth birthday, as I already mentioned, Dad gave me an IdentiKit. When I was twelve, he took me to the police firing range, for target practice, not with live ammo yet, only blanks, but from a real gun, a .38-caliber Wembley. Once a month we'd go there alone at night, just him and me, with warm leather flaps over our ears and a cold gun in our hands, the weight of it, and the blast that made me recoil, and

Dad's warm breath on my cheek as he guided my hand, and the tall green targets in the shape of a human body. "Aim at the head! Aim at the heart! Go on! Draw! Fire!"

A hundred times. A thousand times. Draw! Fire! You're walking down the street and somebody holds a knife to your back—draw! You're asleep in your bed and somebody breaks in and creeps into your room. Draw! You witness somebody snatching a boy and trying to shove him into a car. Draw! He tries to escape? Stand straight, spread your legs for balance, steady your right hand with your left, close one eye and aim, now fire! No good, by the time you moved, he could have killed you twice! Now draw! Always be the first to shoot and you'll live to tell the tale! Go on, draw! Let your instincts work for you! Time's a-wasting! You don't have so many years left to learn, pretty soon you'll be on the job yourself! You're twelve, kid! Draw! Fire!

When Gabi said I was spending too much time at the police station, "playing cowboys" and seeing things it wasn't good for a boy my age to see, Dad answered that this was the only way I would ever learn to overcome my weaknesses and develop into a strong and serious man. Because by "playing cowboys," as she so derisively called it, I was learning the most important lesson of life, the lesson about the eternal war between order and chaos, between law and the lawlessness that tried to tear everything down. Gabi listened patiently and said, yes, children make excellent detectives, because for them the world is one big riddle to solve, but every age has its riddles, and at his age there are other mysteries, including several about his own life; and Dad started blaring that she wasn't going to teach him how to raise his child, and okay, he may have made some mistakes with me, but to his mind, his greatest duty as a father was to train me for real life, for the war of survival. And Gabi said, "He'll turn out exactly how you're training him to be, and then you'll regret it."

A cricket chirred from a bush somewhere. A breeze blew in from the sea, and I happily inhaled the salty smell and drew strength from it. I stood up straight, with my head held high. This would be the night of my big test. I had to be as smart as he is, if not smarter. To try to think the way he does, and then to trick him. Knowledge is power, knowledge is powerrr! I understood his thinking and how he would go about such an operation. But he didn't know who I was anymore. He lacked up-to-date information on me. The Nonny he knew was a different boy. He was certain I would try to escape from Felix the first chance I got. He himself had taught me how to escape from kidnappers. But he didn't know me anymore. I felt strangely regretful for having run so far away, and I realized that maybe, for the first time in my life, I stood a fair chance of surprising him.

I started walking faster, attended by the fresh, caressing sea breezes. I could tell from the tingling in my back that very soon he would finish spreading his nets. I tried to imagine how he would present the situation to himself and to his detectives:

A. Felix kidnapped Nonny and is holding him against his will. B. Felix is hiding somewhere in the vicinity. D. Felix must be apprehended before he hurts Nonny.

But there was also a point C. which he couldn't say aloud, a most important point for him: they had to catch Felix before he told Nonny the story of Zohara.

I, in any case, was eager to hear the story from beginning to end. It was the story of my life and I had a right to know it. No one was going to interrupt this time if I could help it, not even Dad. Especially not Dad. No more secrets! No more cover-ups!

I felt like a knight striding bravely off to battle, ready to fight for Zohara and her story.

And if he tries to stop me, I'll run away.

And if he fights with me, I'll fight back. Once and for all, I've got to find out who I am.

Seems strange: I need the man who kidnapped me and I'm running away from the one who came to my rescue.

I was so nervous I forgot my disguise and walked briskly, holding my clenched fists out, not the walk of a sweet little girl. But Zohara was no sweet little girl either. I could just imagine her at my age. A pretty face, if a little sharp-featured, with flashing eyes. The kind of girl other girls hate and whisper about and the boys are a little scared of, too, and whom her teachers would try to transfer to a school more suitable for someone of her zigzag temperament.

And her mother?

Who was her mother? Of course she had a mother. And a father. Who were they? Why was I trembling?

I forced myself to slow down again. What was going on? How did Dad know Felix would hide in this neighborhood, of all places? What did everyone else know that I didn't? What did they understand that I didn't? It took every bit of strength I had to keep up my cover. Only years of training kept me sane. I walked past a police car parked at the curb. The policeman sitting inside it ignored me. With my eyes I followed a bird in flight from a cypress tree, say, to the power lines. Little Zohara taking an interest in our feathered friends. I look to the right, straining to see through the darkness. I knew it! There they were, those two men wearing dark shirts. They were standing on top of the highest roof on the street with a tripod set up for an infrared telescope.

Dad was tightening the ring around me. This was a manhunt, just like in the movies. A manhunt for Felix and me. He would search from house to house until he found us. I felt a chill up my spine. As though a strong, invisible net were hovering around me, waiting to swoop down and haul me off. I shuddered but kept walking. Please don't let them see the fear on my face. How did Dad think to look for me and Felix here, of all places? Why couldn't I break through the cement wall in my brain? The answer always seemed to be fluttering right in front of my eyes, yet I couldn't . . . Go on, keep moving, don't blow it now. In a couple of minutes the police will be everywhere. They'll spread out to every possible observation point. No one will be able to escape their scrutiny. All they had to do was sit tight, knowing that even an ingenious kidnapper like Felix will have to leave his hideout at some point, if only to buy food, or to move you, the victim of the kidnapping, somewhere else.

Dad's here already, I thought to myself. Of course he was. He wouldn't be holed up in some office at a time like this. He was here for sure, in a patrol car, reading a street map by the pale glow of his flashlight.

I could sense his presence. Stalking me. His muscular body bursting with energy. He was very close now. Watching. Waiting. I could feel him in the air, I could smell him there. Perhaps he was staring at my back this very moment. Those penetrating little eyes. Had he begun to wonder what really happened between me and Felix? Did he already suspect that for the past two days I had been purposely ignoring the silent cries his heart sent out to me? Did the furrow between his eyes grow suddenly deeper, as though someone had gouged it with a knife?

I started walking faster. My heart was pounding. I was like a hunted animal. A siren wailed somewhere and I jumped in alarm. No one noticed, though. Across the street I saw a policeman checking the papers of an old pedestrian. The pedestrian was furious and started gesturing excitedly. The policeman explained something, and the pedestrian immediately relaxed.

Get out of here. Beat it. Don't let Dad catch you. You don't belong to him. Not only to him.

I used every bit of know-how, every bit of training, everything he'd been teaching me since I learned how to walk. I took it all in at a glance, the phony license plates on the squad cars, the gleam of binoculars on the rooftops, the Palladium shoes worn by the young couple who'd just walked past me, arm in arm, and also, what was happening to me with Dad, or as opposed to Dad, and how both our lives were changing now.

I walked at a medium pace, taking notice of anything that might interest little Zohara. She was me. I found some pretext to look over my right shoulder. I checked the roofs. Lola's quiet neighborhood was bustling with mysterious activity. Everywhere there were cops rushing around, manning positions, getting their equipment ready.

I knew cops, I knew everything about them. I could smell their agitation in the air now. I hoped that Felix would make it out of there before they closed off Lola's street. I'd go nuts if they caught him before he could tell me the rest of the story. Before he could give me the present from Zohara.

I wondered what the present was. What could she send me from her land of the dead?

It was an eerie night. A light breeze shook the pointed tops of the cypress trees. Everything whished and rustled. I felt as though I were walking on air, detached from the world. As though I were missing, or lost. It felt strange, like floating in space. Maybe that's why the police have so much trouble finding missing persons. Maybe some missing persons don't want to be found. Because when you're missing, you are yourself alone. Free-floating through the world. You can choose what to be next. You are unique.

I was so alone at those moments. A tiny point in a vast world, me.

But who was this "me"? How had things gotten so screwed up that I turned into a criminal on the run from my own father? What was this powerful force sucking me further, deeper into the story?

I was plunging dizzily down, with no will of my own.

From the depths of my soul, an unfamiliar entity rose up to meet me, spreading like a cloud through my innermost recesses, whispering, "It's you, it's you on the run from Dad. You were always like this. You sensed it and it frightened you. And now you've learned the secret: this is who you really are. But only in part. Yet because of this part you will always be a bit of a fugitive, a bit of a criminal, and probably never your father's successor and the best detective in the world."

And along with this anguished whisper, I heard another voice inside, cackling fiendishly: "If you choose, you can follow in the footsteps of your mother . . . and Felix." And then I realized that maybe he had kidnapped me in order to pass on some of the tricks of his trade, his professional skills . . .

On the outside, I had my clothes for cover, and their softness pervaded me. They rustled to the rhythm of my walk. Once upon a time there was a woman named Zohara, and before that she was a girl. I still didn't know much about her as a girl, but her clothes communicated to me. They spoke right to my skin, her skirt and her blouse, and even the sandals that had absorbed the sweat of her feet.

I could practically walk there with my eyes closed. As though my feet knew the way from Lola's house to the Habimah National Theater. I simply stopped thinking and let Zohara's sandals whisk me there. And they did. They walked me down the sidewalk, aware of every pothole and street crossing and row of trees. Once when I tried to turn right, they forced me to go left. I never met such a determined pair of sandals. Twenty-five years had elapsed since they last took this route, but the memory was embedded in them. As I walked, they sent little messages through my feet, until finally I began to understand. I am so slow sometimes, it drives me crazy. Once there was a girl named Zohara. Don't you dare call her a girl, though, or she'll punch you. Zohara inhabited a lonely world, rejected by other children, a prey to grown-up thoughts, running for her life sometimes to fantasy and fairy tale, to the tiny creatures behind her lids that performed plays and films just for her. And what else? Oh yes, she loved strawberry jam and chocolate.

She lived in a tall building, and her bedroom looked out to where the sea was widest and bluest. She liked to hide raspberry candies inside a secret hole in the mattress. And to hang picture postcards from all over the world on the wall. And to collect soldier dolls from faraway lands. But why did she collect those dolls? Who gave them to her? And who sent the picture postcards?

Maybe it was her father. The father I hadn't thought of till now. Obviously she had a father, didn't she?

I reeled like a drunk. The sandals made me dance as though they had been possessed by a sudden joy. My eyes filled with silly tears. Ridiculous—me, a boy, crying like a girl. Like a girl trying not to cry, who scratched a lightning bolt on the wall to keep herself from crying. Why hadn't I seen what was going on during those two crazy days? The bedroom in Lola's apartment. The smell of the pillow and the clothes in the wardrobe. And the picture postcards from around the world.

Because I was afraid, afraid to know.

Lola sat up with me all night long. And she knew my birthday.

How could I have missed that?

And Dad had guessed that Felix would take me here, to Lola's house.

My route. The route that was planned for me in advance.

Like fate.

The story Felix was telling me.

I stumbled, I staggered. How many more surprises could I take, and what else would happen on this journey?

"There is little hill near traffic light, there, turn right, then left," Felix said in his directions.

I turned right, then left.

"Then look sharply to left."

I faced left, and looked up like an hour hand approaching nine o'clock.

There was a woman beside an electric pole, waving her scarf at me. It was Lola.

She was standing next to a motorcycle with a sidecar. I was struck by a long-forgotten memory: the motorcycle, the sidecar, the tomato plant. A wild stallion of a man who laughed like a horse, until one day he stopped and became very sad and law-abiding. But sitting on the motorcycle was Felix, wearing a peculiar pair of goggles and a leather helmet.

Naturally he'd made it past Dad's men. And naturally he had arrived here before me. He stepped on the gas and started her up.

Our Rolls.

And Lola Ciperola, the famous actress.

Who was Zohara's mother.

And Felix Glick, the man with the golden ears of wheat, who loved my mother.

But not like a lover, the way a man loves a woman. He loved her like a father. The way he would love a daughter.

Why hadn't I seen that before?

Felix was her father. Lola was her mother.

The golden ear of wheat and the purple scarf.

The parents of my mother, Zohara.

Both of them beckoning me to hurry up.

My grandmother and grandfather.

25

Zohara Sets Forth to Cross the Moon,

and Cupid Resorts to Firearms

We sped through the night on the motorcycle with the sidecar, me and Felix and Lola Ciperola. The wind slapped our faces and ruffled our hair, and we had to shout over the noise to hear each other. Felix drove, with Lola behind him hugging his waist, and I sat in the sidecar, snug as a bug. Then we changed places—I sat behind him, hugging his waist, and Lola Ciperola curled up snug as a bug in the sidecar.

On into the darkness we sailed. The city lights glared overhead, reflecting us in the smoky glasses of blind beggars and elegant display windows. The shadow of the motorcycle lapped up the sidewalks, the billboards, the benches where lovers sit, clinging tightly to each other; like a paper silhouette, we whizzed past the cafés, the sleepy boulevards, the late-night street sweepers, and a pack of dogs out on the town, barking boisterously as we rode by, a Dalmatian, a German shepherd, and the leader, a little white poodle, or a little dachshund, a huge Great Dane, and an ugly sheepdog, like delegates sent by the dogs of Tel Aviv to see us off on our nocturnal voyage in search of Zohara.

Perhaps I should begin with a description of the meeting that took place outside the National Theater, the meeting with my grandfather and grandmother, the incredible double gift I received for my bar mitzvah, without an exchange slip, of course.

I started walking up the street at an easy, casual pace, but a few steps later I broke into a run. Lola waved her scarf at me, in a self-restrained way at first, as befitting the first lady of the National Theater, but as I approached she started running toward me. No one in the street (or in the world) would have recognized her the way she looked then—wearing blue jeans, with her long hair down and no makeup. We flew into each other's arms. She could tell by the expression on my face that I already knew. We collided and hugged, and I burrowed my head into her shoulder. "You're Zohara's mother," I said, and she answered, "Yes, oh yes, and I'm so glad you found out. I couldn't keep from telling you anymore." My neck became wet after a sudden barometric drop outside the theater.

Felix stood nodding, with his hands on his hips. "Are you ready? Beg pardon, but we must to get moving! There will be plenty of time later for schmaltz and tears and coochie-coo."

"Aren't you the hero!" said Lola, wiping her nose. "I know why you're wearing that helmet, but I can see your eyes all the same!"

"He's my grandfather, I know that too now," I said to Lola, a little surprised at myself for running to her the way I had.

"If you dare call me Grandfather in public, I turn you over to police," grumbled Felix. "I am too young to be called Grandfather."

"Poor child." Lola wrung her hands. "To have Felix Glick for a grandfather."

"Why poor child?" protested Felix. "You know any other grandfathers who take grandchildren to hijack trains?"

He was right.

"I would be happy for you to call me Grandmother," said Lola, "and Felix will get used to it, too, eventually." Again I was enveloped in a cloud of her perfume. At last I have a real grandmother, I thought, a grandmother who hugs me, not a knitting-needle grandmother.

"So did you get married, then?" I blurted out, seeing that she was a woman of principles.

"Did I get married, he asks." She smiled. "What kind of question is that for a grandson to ask his grandmother?"

"No, because once you said that—"

She laughed. "Yes, Nonny, it's true, I like to be alone, to do whatever I please, that's the kind of woman I am, I've always been as free as a Gypsy, and if I love someone, I don't wait for him to come around, I walk right up and tell him so! And I did fall in love with this old man here." She patted him fondly on the helmet. "And I wanted his baby, but I refused to give him the keys to my life."

"For me, screwdriver is good as key." Felix laughed, and I was proud of Lola, my new grandmother, because I knew she would always be true to herself.

"Where did you find this motorcycle?" I asked Felix, and he smiled mysteriously, shrugged his shoulders, and muttered something about Felix the wizard, Felix the mastermind, and other little boasts and brags, intended mainly to annoy Lola. But Lola merely laughed as she massaged the back of his neck, and said, "Seventy years old and still behaving like a child!"

"Hi-deh." Felix stirred himself, and we were on our way.

I had so many questions to ask her. And him. Why hadn't she tried to contact me all these years? Did she know about me? Did she recognize me when Gabi and I met her in front of her house . . .

Gabi. Gabi Gabi Gabi.

How had she managed to conceal the most important things about Lola Ciperola from me? That she had been in love with Felix Glick. That they had a daughter, now dead, who had been, well, a criminal, and who also happened to be my mother. All these years Gabi had been throwing out subtle hints, insinuating that Lola Ciperola, and Felix, too, were important figures in my life and destiny, and planting little seeds of curiosity—with her talk of the purple scarf, and Felix and the golden ears of wheat, and her impersonations of Lola singing—all of which had sprouted in due course, a few days before my bar mitzvah.

How cunningly they had worked behind the scenes, Gabi and Felix, though neither was aware of what the other was doing.

And they had trapped me. But I wanted to be trapped, I wanted it badly.

I couldn't stop glancing at Lola and Felix, trying to get used to their being my grandparents. It still felt strange, because before I knew Lola, she had seemed so remote, and now all of a sudden she had entered my life, which made a huge difference, as big as the difference between someone called Lola Ciperola and a woman named Lola Katz, and I still didn't quite know how it would turn out for us, how close we would become, what it's like to have a real grandmother . . . And then suddenly our eyes met.

"Looking at you, Nonny," she said, leaning out of the sidecar, "I realize how silly of me it was not to defy your father. I never once attempted to meet with you."

"He wouldn't let you? Why not?" I shouted, not only because of the wind.

"After Zohara died, you see, he didn't want any contact with her past—God forbid anything of her character should rub off on her son, which is why he decided to put me out of the picture, too. Oh yes!" She tied her hair up so I'd be able to hear her better. "But enough of that! I have an agreement with you now, not with him. I would very much like to be your full-time grandmother. Am I hired?"

I laughed. All these women wanting to be my full-time mother and grandmother. I reached over to the sidecar and shook her hand. Of course she was hired.

"Here is diamond center," shouted Felix through his helmet, turning off at the intersection and zooming down a dirt path into a field behind the building.

And there he stopped.

The wind died down. Lola and I breathed a sigh of relief. Felix hopped around us, trying to pull off the leather hat with the ear flaps, which resembled a World War II aviator's helmet. The air was redolent of chocolate, and I knew where we were at once—at the fountain of the sweet secret Gabi and I shared, the wonderful chocolate factory, which, owing to our patronage, had greatly expanded over the past five years.

"How did you know I love to come here?" I smiled. "I never told you that."

"Told us what?" asked Lola, and then chided, "Come on, Felix. Get that silly thing off your head."

"That Gabi and I come here once a month, to the factory, to watch them make chocolate."

"Once a month?" Lola was astounded.

"We've been doing it for years. And then we go to your house and wait for you."

Lola looked from me to Felix and shook her head. "I want to meet this Gabi woman. She's simply marvelous!"

I didn't quite understand her enthusiasm. Aren't grandmothers supposed to worry about your teeth and disapprove of frequent visits to chocolate factories?

"Forget chocolate now!" exclaimed Felix, having finally managed to pull off the peculiar helmet; he added meekly, with an apologetic look at Lola, "Is my nose, you see, too hard to push through!"

Lola made a cruel snipping sign with her fingers, and Felix shrank in defense of his mighty schnozz. I got the feeling he'd always been a little scared of her.

"Forget chocolate now!" he repeated. "Look here, diamond center! This is where your story begins."

"My story?"

"Yessir! Here, many years ago, was diamond center of Israel! The building was full of diamonds, also guards, and cameras that can see a mouse move, and most up-to-date alarm system anywhere. To cut long story short, one day Zohara and I drive along this road, and Zohara sees it and laughs and says, 'What you think, Papineu,' that's what she used to call me, 'can I break in some night and climb up to the roof, and sneak out again without being caught?' "

Wait, slow down a minute. I felt like covering my ears. I couldn't get used to my own mother saying such things, the kinds of things you hear people in movies say. People without children.

Felix continued: "So I say to her, 'Zohara, darling, what for? If it's money you want, I give you as much as you need, and if you want big money and fun, like before, we go abroad, where no one knows us, and find some action there!' "

Lola put her arm around my shoulder. "Is this too much for you?" she whispered. "Felix likes to tell a good story, but sometimes he gets carried away."

"Carried away?" Felix protested. "I tell him story like it is, take him

where it happens, show him how it was, what it was. This is his life!
Is this wrong?"

I was beginning to understand why those two couldn't live together.

"Go on," I said. "I want to know."

"Aha—you see?" said Felix, puffing himself up. "Your grandson
wants to know! So, to cut long story short, Zohara says to me, 'Papineu,' she says, 'I don't want more filthy lucre, and I don't want to
swindle fools anymore. I just want to have some fun, to feel my heart
beat, because life is so boring now that we're home, I could die of
boredom here. What do you say I climb up to the roof and play my
recorder there, just one song, and then come down again without being
caught—what do you say, Papineu?' "

I looked up, tilting my head back to see the roof, which wasn't easy
to do while I was smiling. "Just to play her recorder?" A little tune was
trilling inside me.

"It was very stupid to break into this building," Felix continued. "If
there was big loot there, at least that is business, that I understand, but
just for showing off? Ah, Zohara. What I tell her not to do she does
on purpose. When I say, Zohara, darling, be careful!, she says, *Oi*,
Papineu, you won't let me do anything."

I watched him, thinking, Yes, that must be how they argued.

"Is better to talk to trees and stones." Felix sighed. "I say no, she
says yes, and in end we stop talking to each other. I was sure she forgot
all about it, thank God and good riddance; so I go abroad to work and
she stays here. But what happens? About two weeks later I get phone
call from your grandmother, telling me Zohara did it, what she said!"

"You mean she managed to climb up to the roof?"

"Of course, but don't ask me how, I don't know! Guards everywhere, and she goes right by them! But the camera catches her, and
then there is big hoo-ha, everyone jumps, alarm bells, guards, policemen, dogs . . . and Zohara is running! Running and laughing! But
instead of running away, she runs up to roof! Because she wants to play
her recorder there, yes? Because for her is one big game, yes?"

He shook his head. "But what happens after that, I don't know," he
said with a shrug. "Maybe you can tell me."

"Me? But how . . ."

"Is your story, no?"

How was I supposed to know? I wasn't even born yet! He pouted at me, and his bushy brows inclined at a sharper angle than ever. Where did she go? She climbed up to the roof just as she planned, but she'd planned something else, too. I smiled. No, impossible, she wouldn't dare play in front of all the police . . . ? But Felix closed his eyes and nodded vigorously. You mean she actually did it, she took the recorder out of her pocket and played?

"*Nu,* certainly, what you think?"

The moon shone over the tall building. I imagined Zohara standing on the rooftop, or even sitting on the ledge, dipping her feet in the sky, with the moonlight streaming on her hair and the police and their cars in the lot where we were standing now. As she calmly wiped the mouth-piece, I guessed what she was going to play, and I remembered the dreamy river nymphs and felt the throbbing in her neck.

Hush! The clear, delicate sound of the recorder. I could hear it floating down from the roof to where the policemen stood motionless, some of them shyly removing their caps as the tenuous little tune skipped like a goat-kid in the starry meadow around the flutist.

And they still didn't know it was a woman up there.

She played every note of the children's song. The policemen stood transfixed, as though hearing a hymn, a hymn to daring, a hymn to myth and madness. When she was done, she carefully wiped the mouth-piece and put the recorder back in its velvet sheath. What would she do now?

Because the spell had been broken and the commotion began, with detectives running everywhere, dogs barking, orders shouted over walkie-talkies, and she? What was she doing just then?

"You tell us," whispered Felix. "You know."

Me? How am I supposed to . . . ?

True, I knew her pretty well by then. When I shut my eyes tight, I could feel her buzzing between them, and I knew right away that she hadn't waited around for the police. "She escaped, didn't she?"

Yes, said Felix's eyes.

But where? There was no way down, and above her, only sky. So what did she do? What could she do? Jump up and grab hold of a passing airplane? Slide down a telephone pole? Felix smiled and said nothing. Lola observed me, tilting her head, as though following the progression of Zohara's thoughts in my face. I shut my eyes in concentration. I felt the point between them heating up. Zohara on the roof. My mother. Felix's daughter. I did come from a long line of clever crooks. Suddenly I was a member of a dynasty . . . so what would I have done in her place? Why couldn't I think of some really smart maneuver to get her out of there? Why couldn't I concentrate? Maybe it was the heavy smell of chocolate that muddled my thoughts . . . the fountain of the sweet secret we shared, Gabi and I . . . Once a month we came here . . . to the fountain came a little goat-kid . . . The smell drew me closer, whispering magic spells—

"There." I veered around, pointing at the chocolate factory. "That's where my mother fled to," and added earnestly, "She was crazy about chocolate, you know."

"At last." Felix sighed with relief, as if I had just made it through a tribal initiation.

Lola and Felix exchanged a smile, perhaps because I had called her "my mother."

She escaped to the chocolate factory.

Which is why Gabi—

Once a month for five years—

So many times, with unwavering devotion.

"But how does she get from diamond center to chocolate factory?" whispered Felix.

"How?" How indeed. The two buildings were wide apart, so a leap was out of the question, and climbing down—impossible, because of the policemen waiting below. But wait: "Were there any cranes around here back then?" I asked.

"There are always cranes around here," said Lola. "I think they use the buildings to erect the cranes, not the other way around."

So I knew.

Zohara leaped onto a giant crane that was standing right here, let's say. The arm of the crane was suspended over the roof of the diamond center. She extended her leg to check the distance: one little jump, about a meter, would take her there. Not very far, but there was a drop of many meters down. Felix was studying my face. I didn't say anything. The craziest thoughts were going through my head: Zohara braided her hair and stuffed the pigtail into her collar. She put the recorder in her pocket. It was life or death! And since death had never frightened her, she took a leap over the abyss and landed on the steel arm of the crane . . . I didn't even pause to let Felix confirm my guesses, my fantasies. I was as certain of them as if I had been with her at the time: I felt the thud of her fall, and her teeth snapping shut. She lay there a moment, stunned with pain, and maybe fear, and then began to crawl away . . .

Wrong. Sorry. If I had been there, I would have crawled away. But it was Zohara on the crane, and Zohara didn't crawl. Not ever. Slowly, tremblingly, she stretched herself and rose to her knees. Then stood up straight and started walking.

I gazed at the night sky. A long steel arm cleaved the moon in two. I imagined my mother walking across it. Traversing the moon, trying not to look down at the abyss below her, though perhaps she actually wanted to see it. And Felix, watching me, suddenly shivered.

And the police? What did they do? Did they aim their guns? Did they blow their whistles? I knew exactly how they felt, how bewildered they must have been to witness the tiny figure up there, the little reprobate who had broken into the fortress sitting on a ledge playing a children's song, and then setting forth to cross the moon, holding herself erect, like a tightrope walker, challenging something far bigger and grander than they were, with their guns and handcuffs and whistles, which may be why they barely moved but only raised a racket trying to decide what to do.

"But not all police!" Felix corrected my thinking. "There is one who understands where she is going. Only he, this one policeman. A detective."

Lola and Felix were gazing at me intently. It was my turn to take up the story again. To describe the detective. The only one who understood what Zohara was planning. I tried to envision a detective out of an American movie, good-looking with wavy hair and steely blue eyes. But it didn't feel right.

What could I do? I resorted to the model I had at home.

"This guy, the detective, isn't tall, but he's tough. He has a big head, hardly any neck. Real solid." Kind of shlumpy, too, I thought with affection, and a bit of a grouch, always looks as if his mind is elsewhere, a regular SOS, short for Sweaty Ornery Slob.

"That is so." Felix smiled. "That is just what he is like."

Go on, said Lola's eyes.

"He was the only one who knew what to do. He ran quickly and quietly over to the crane, and climbed up the rungs as though it were an extension ladder—"

This is good, I thought, feeling warm inside: he had plenty of experience with heights, climbing flagpoles . . . because on a certain night, four or five years earlier, he had scaled the roofs of five embassies and consulates in Jerusalem, and stealthily cut the ropes and tied others in their place, so that in the morning the Italian ambassador woke up under the flag of hostile Ethiopia, while the French consul, looking up from his croissant, nearly choked with horror to see his own domain flying the Union Jack! A moment later, nine frantic consuls and ambassadors were on the phone to each other, and the air was filled with angry words in a babel of tongues spitting diplomatic venom, while the rest of Jerusalem was in stitches, especially Dad, who had won his bet, and who now reenacted the vertical ascent and reached the arm of the crane only a few meters behind the mysterious tightrope walker, and, crouching a moment, glanced down and nearly fainted, then faced the intrepid thief herself, and knew that at long last he had met his match.

A match made in heaven, I thought, or at least pretty high off the ground.

One step at a time. The tightrope walker has nearly reached the edge of the steel arm that overhangs the roof of the chocolate factory. Dad tries to crawl forward, but fear and dizziness press him down against the arm of the crane. He decides to swallow his pride. And crawl. He can feel the vibrations of the fugitive's steps in his belly. They spread through his body with an inexplicable thrill. The tightrope walker turns around and sees the panting pursuer. Zohara smiles to herself, approving his courage and berating him for having to crawl. But did it really happen like this, or did I make it up? I didn't care. I wish it had, though. To this day, whenever I drive past the chocolate factory, I envision the two of them there, advancing silently across the arm of the colossal crane. High above the city lights, above the police, the first delicate strands of intimacy were woven between them, and maybe it was due to these that Zohara made haste, nearly bolted, in fact, while Dad crawled faster in pursuit; only, Zohara reached the edge of the arm before he did, and looked down over the roof of the chocolate factory.

I took a deep breath. "And then she jumped."

"But is very big jump down!" said Felix skeptically. "Four meters maybe!"

"Well, she jumped all the same," I insisted, "and nothing happened to her!"

"She always landed on her feet," Felix murmured wonderingly.

"It was night," I went on, unable to stop myself. The story virtually poured out of me, out of the place between my eyes, though I'd never heard it before. "The chocolate factory was deserted, and Zohara scurried around . . ." I could just imagine her scurrying around, looking for the exit, popping in and out of the huge facility, bounding through it on velvet feet. I saw all of this, with the feather-tickle in my brain, and I told them about it directly from the place of fantasy, only this time it wasn't a lie, it was my own story emerging at last like a tangled skein that had always been there but was suddenly unraveling, to bring Zohara back to life and set her dancing among the chocolate vats and stirring machines, and she would stop, unable to resist, stick her finger in, lick it, and laugh.

A heavy thud: a hulking body lands on the roof of the factory. It's the detective. The one and only. He rolls over, cursing, gets up, and cautiously enters the chocolate facility with his gun drawn. He peers around in search of the suspect. He's getting clear signals: warmth around the navel means a criminal is nearby. And he feels very hot, around the navel and everywhere else.

"Hey, you!" shouts Dad, and his voice echoes in an emanation of chocolate. "The place is surrounded! You don't stand a chance! Come out slowly with your hands in the air!"

The echoes fade away. Dad looks cautiously around. The smell of chocolate reaches his nostrils. Perhaps, for one fleeting whiff, he remembers his childhood in a similar factory, among machines such as this and sacks of flour and sugar. Cookies and chocolate together, yum! But he subdues all thought of this. In a profession like his, no distractions are permitted and any error might prove fatal. He treads carefully, his gun sniffing in every direction.

And then? What happened? My imagination suddenly switches off. The hot place between my eyes has grown cold. A red-black curtain waves in front of my mind.

"And then," said Felix, "she shot him."

"Shot him?" I gasped. It never occurred to me that she had a gun. "You mean to say that she shot Dad?"

"Yes, of course, with gun you have now in your pocket, Amnon. Gun you take from me belongs to her."

A woman's gun, I remembered. That's right. He examined one like it at a firearms exhibit once. Stroked it with his finger.

"Was he hit? Did she hit him?"

"In shoulder, I am sorry to say. She never shoots gun before in her life. She wouldn't kill even fly. But at your father, she fires one bullet. Maybe this was only joke for her, or maybe—who knows?"

"Maybe what?" I groaned. "Why on earth did she shoot him?"

"Maybe she felt that he was dangerous," said Lola simply. "Not as a detective, but as a man. Maybe she could sense that he would play an important part in her life, and it threw her into a panic."

I leaned back in the sidecar, allowed myself to flow. It would probably take me a couple of hundred years to digest all this. I buried my head under the seat, let my feet dangle over the side. Lola whispered something to Felix, and Felix sniffled. An airplane flew by. The antenna on top of the diamond center blinked red. The bullet on the chain fell out of my shirt and landed in my mouth. It was cold. Taken out of his body. Fired at him by Zohara. All my life I had been wearing it around my neck in complete ignorance. "Like Cupid's dart," said Lola, gently pulling me out of the sidecar. "Your father fell in love with her instantaneously."

"Because when she laughs as she fires the gun," explained Felix, "he hears that she is young woman."

Dad was stunned. I'm sure being hit by a bullet hurts about as much, say, as being gored by a cow. With his uninjured hand Dad grasped his shoulder to try to stop the bleeding. "What, you're a woman?" he asked in amazement.

And again he heard her laughter ring, deriding him. She fired again, but not in an attempt to hit him this time.

"You don't stand a chance against me," Dad called out to her, smiling against his will, and over against the pain shooting through him to his heart.

She fired yet again, shattering the big lamp over his head. He ducked and took cover behind the bags of coffee beans. Another shot. A cascade of fragrant brown beans flowed over him. He jumped back. Crouched down. She fired. He counted the shots, knew how many bullets she had left. Knowledge is power, only this time it seemed that the more he knew the weaker he became, and the more complete was his surrender.

They were alone together for what seemed like an eternity. She laughed and taunted him, hiding behind the machines, climbing on the forklifts, sticking out her rosy tongue at him from behind the assembly line where they make Cat Tongues, my favorite kind of chocolate to this day, waving her sweater from behind the sugar sacks, then vanishing as soon as he ran to her, reappearing somewhere else entirely, and carefully firing a shot over his head as part of the game.

He never stopped smiling. Against his will, despite new pain.

"That's how it all started," I explained, suddenly understanding. "She made him laugh."

"That's right," Lola confirmed. "No one could resist her when she wanted to amuse."

Yes, I thought. She's the only person who could make him laugh.
Poor Gabi.

"Once, when we were in Jamaica," Felix recalled, "Zohara was chosen Queen of Laughter for 1951! Three thousand dollars she won just for laughing!"

"And so they laughed together in the deserted factory," I continued, rejoicing at the thought of them, my father and my mother, chasing each other around the huge facility, young and happy, not as cops and robbers but as man and woman, and their laughter rang through the factory, her bell-like laugh and his husky horselaugh. I had never really heard him laugh wholeheartedly . . . "Until suddenly—"

Sometimes I think that was the moment it was decreed that I should become a storyteller. "Suddenly," I continued, strangely confident, "as she was running across a platform, she tripped and came tumbling down, and then . . ."

"And then . . . ?" asked Lola and Felix in unison, leaning forward.

"And then she landed . . . right in a vat of chocolate," I concluded with pride. It was three meters wide, three meters long, and two meters deep. A giant blade slowly stirred the sweetness. I had memorized the dimensions of all the vats. Gabi used to stand for hours by the biggest one, and silly me, I thought she was longing to dive into a sea of chocolate.

"Dad leaped in after her, uniform and all. He swam with all his might through the thick hot chocolate." I sounded like a sportscaster all of a sudden.

But then I stopped.

Because Dad doesn't know how to swim.

"True," Felix concurred. "He almost drowned!" And added chaffingly, in an aside to Lola, "What kind of detective drowns in chocolate."

"But Zohara did know how to swim," Lola went on, ignoring him. "She grabbed him by his wavy hair and dragged him all the way to the stairs inside the vat."

She grabbed him by his wavy hair.

And by his heart.

He had a full head of hair at the time. And a heart.

"Oh dear," said Lola. "It must be very hard for you to tell this story, and to hear it, too."

"Yes, it is," I said. "Or rather, it is and it isn't," I admitted, sitting in the sidecar again. "I had no idea I could tell this story."

"That is kind of story that comes out best," said Felix.

He was covered in it; there was chocolate all over him, on his eyes, his uniform, his gun. But his bachelor's heart was pounding like a drum: here was the one woman alive who could meet his difficult demands, a woman who had hunted down and fished him out . . . And Zohara stood there heaving with laughter, filled with a young girl's hope and admiration for his sturdy shoulders, his rugged body . . .

I see her as clearly as if I were there with them: lonely, unhappy, but covered with chocolate from head to toe. Her hair, her neck, her shoulders, her pointed ears, dripping long trails of chocolate. A bitter almond covered in chocolate.

"Like two chocolate dolls," whispered Lola, "a police doll and a thief doll."

"And they laugh together," grumbled Felix.

And how he laughed.

Poor Gabi.

She gorged herself on chocolate, but couldn't make him laugh.

"Put your hands in the air," said the detective doll, with his chocolate-covered gun.

Because he had counted the shots and knew she was out of ammunition.

"I like you," said the thief doll. Maybe she wiped a little chocolate off the tip of his nose and licked her finger. "I never met a man like you before. If you say pretty please, I'll marry you."

"All right then, pretty please—put your hands in the air," said Dad, who hadn't quite understood.

Zohara burst out laughing, because she thought that must be his special sense of humor.

⚍ 26 ⚎

No Two People Have Ever Been

So Incompatible

On the road again. We left the chocolate factory and headed north. I didn't know where we were going and didn't ask. On the way I changed back into my own clothes. I didn't need Zohara's anymore, now that I had her inside me.

The streetlamps flew by. The few people out walking stopped and stared. What a weird-looking trio we made, Felix in that awful leather helmet, leaning forward like a jockey in a race; Lola with her long hair flying like snakes; and me, far too young to be out at this hour of the night.

And of course the motorcycle also caught their eye: it was bulky and antiquated, and noisy as a tank. The sidecar seemed in danger of coming off any minute. One sharp turn and I'd be flying off alone, silent as a tomato plant, while Felix and Lola would continue on their way, clinging to each other on the motorcycle. Into the sunset.

I mean sunrise.

Occasionally I glanced over. Lola clung to him, her long gray hair covering both of them like a scarf. Felix didn't stop talking to her, shouting against the wind, and she shouted her answers into his ear. They may have been arguing, or just having a pleasant chat, but either way, you could see how close they had once been.

"That's only the beginning of the story!" Lola called over to me through the scarf of hair.

"I'm all ears!" I shouted in reply.

. . . Back at the chocolate factory, Dad spoke briefly to Zohara, explaining what she could expect: he was going to lead her out, make sure no one hurt her, and try to have himself assigned as her interrogator. She would say what she had to say, and tell him why she had decided to pull such a prank, when it was obvious that she came from a good family; maybe she did it on a dare, these things happen, no one understood that better than he did; and in return for her complete cooperation, he would see to it that she got off lightly, without the taint of a criminal record, so she could carry on with the normal life of a law-abiding citizen. And then, maybe, after it was all over, would she agree to go to the cinema with him?

Zohara was entranced. By his strength, his determination, his rugged manliness. By the way he came after her instead of waiting below with the other policemen. And because, while some suitors wrote high-flying love poems, and others threatened to jump off the roof if she ever left them, he was the very first man who had climbed to the heights in her pursuit and not abandoned her there. And Zohara, the woman who had spurned the advances of millionaires and soccer stars, gazed at my father, and her lips moved voicelessly. "Are you trustworthy?" she asked from the depths of her soul, and the vigor of his being roared out the answer with all the thunder of a regiment presenting arms, and Zohara was vanquished, taken by storm.

"A woman like Zohara," said Lola over the wind, "who lived in fantasy and often lost sight of the borderline between truth and fiction, would naturally be entranced by a man like your father. Maybe she thought he could help her find some peace of mind—"

Maybe Lola was right at that, because although he had been wild in his youth, and climbed up to those embassy roofs and cast the shadow of the Union Jack over French croissants, or squared wheels and lassoed zebras, he always knew where the border was, and the difference between right and wrong, fact and fantasy. It would not have perplexed him, for instance, to be asked who he was.

"Hey, cowboy." The chocolate doll smiled, unaware that this had once been his nickname. "Do you know what a catch you've made?"

And there and then, by the chocolate vat, she recounted a story abounding with the names of dethroned monarchs and exotic lands, etc., and sums of money and bank vaults in Switzerland. Dad just stood there with his mouth open, and she threw back her head and laughed at the sight of his blessed naïveté, the naïveté of an overgrown child, and I know that a cold sharp pain went though my father's heart just then, because a voice within him shouted, She's different from what you always imagined, she's not for you! And he could already hear his older brother Samuel berating him for falling so rashly in love with a criminal, and his mother, Tsitka, muttering, "Over my dead body you'll marry a criminal"; and he knew that his superiors on the force would suspend him from any operational responsibility on account of his criminal affiliations—he knew all this from the very first moment, and sure enough it all came to pass. Yet his heart was filled with the sweetest nectar of all, the nectar of new love, and he would not, could not, relinquish the only woman who had ever touched him so deeply; muscles he never dreamed were there now fortified his soul, the muscles of persistence and determination.

That's how it started. In those few moments his fate was diverted to another track, and even the cast of his features changed, becoming serious, somber, responsible, as though he had only then passed from youth into manhood. His neck suddenly thickened and lodged between his shoulders, and his shoulders grew broad over his chest in order to hold all the heart within him, to bear the new yoke; someone who had once danced with a refrigerator on his back could assume this enormous burden, the tumultuous life of the ravishingly beautiful woman who stood before him, because even while she spoke laughingly of the most odious crimes—hair-raising crimes!—he could hear her soft whispers, her pleas for help, and knew that she had been scrutinizing him to learn whether he would be a true detective and see through her pretenses into the lonely little girl, so bitter, so bright, searching for someone who would not fear her . . .

And of all my moments with Dad, of all the stories I ever heard about him, this was the one that made me love him the most (even though I wasn't with him at the time): the moment of his heroic effort to let go of all his little fears and rational considerations, and the tried-and-true course before him, and agree to take a dangerous and unfamiliar course.

In short, for giving up what was clear-cut and substantial in return for something as intangible as love.

Dad was assigned to interrogate her. For an entire month he went to see her daily at the jailhouse, and sat with her eight hours at a time, taking down her statement.

"It was no statement," grumbled Felix. "It was her confession." And he stepped angrily on the gas, jolting us back and forth.

"What do you want from the girl?" said Lola, poking him with her sharp nails in the best tradition of a knitting-needle grandmother. "She didn't inform on you! She never once mentioned your name! She wanted to purge herself of all her lies! To start over fresh. Can you blame her?"

"But why she must to tell him whole history of world going back to creation?" Felix ground his teeth and screeched down on the brakes. "Why she tell him every last secret?"

"Because that's the way she was when she fell in love." Lola sighed to herself, or perhaps to Felix. "She couldn't hold back any secrets from the man she loved . . ."

We rode on in silence for a while. Felix hiked his shoulders up to his ears, as though trying to ward off something Lola had hurled at him, something that I didn't quite understand. Then Lola sighed deeply and took up the story of that strange interrogation.

Zohara told Dad about the diamonds pouring like pomegranate seeds into the palm of her hand, and made frequent mention of remote islands and other places he had only read about in magazines, till everything sounded both real and surreal, he no longer cared which, because he felt she was pulling him by the hair on his head beyond his limitations, beyond all limitations, and something inside him cheered her on, while something else dug its feet in the ground with stubborn fear . . .

"It was a truly unique interrogation," Lola tried to shout through mantles of wind. "He wanted to know absolutely everything about her! It wasn't her crimes that interested him now . . . He had become fascinated by her character . . . by the riddle . . . Zohara . . ."

"He even came to interrogate Lola!" Felix shouted scornfully, driving so fast that the words flew away in the wind.

"Not to interrogate, to talk to me . . . in the kitchen, night after night

. . . for weeks on end . . . to ask what she was like as a child . . . to look at photograph albums . . . at her school notebooks . . . and sit for hours . . . He couldn't understand . . ." The wind brought tears to my eyes. The words she shouted sank into my ears. I thought about my father in Lola's kitchen, where I myself had sat only yesterday.

"And there was a trial." Lola continued shouting the story through the wind. "Your father promised the judge he would see to it that Zohara kept out of trouble. Thanks to him, the judge was lenient, and she was sentenced to two years in prison, which was very light considering what she'd done."

"Two years in prison?" I was astounded. "You mean they were separated for two whole years?"

"Oh no, Nonny, quite the contrary. It was a great love affair! Now we're getting there!"

"Getting where?"

But Lola touched her lips to silence me.

The wind died down. Once again the shades that passed before my eyes turned into familiar objects, a row of trees, a eucalyptus grove, a sand dune, a high fence. Felix turned off the main road with his usual finesse. The Rolls raised some dust, bumped over a dirt road, clattered through a eucalyptus grove, and stopped.

"Here," whispered Lola, "here, for two years."

We jumped off the motorcycle. I was still kind of shaky from the ride. We all staggered a little and held on to each other. Felix was struggling with the leather helmet again. Lola stood hugging me from behind with her cheek to mine.

"You'll catch a cold," she said.

"Already she is typical grandmother." Felix chuckled.

There in the moonlight stood an ugly rectangular prison, a women's prison surrounded by concrete walls and barbed wire. There were hexagonal turrets in each corner. Grim-looking guards marched across the roof. A searchlight revolved every minute or so and lit up the surrounding fields.

For two whole years my mother lived here.

Locked up, stifled, withering away.

"Oh no," said Lola, "within a month she was the leader of the joint, the representative of the inmates before the prison authorities. And besides, your father came to visit her every day!"

Yes, every day. He would finish work, say goodbye to his young secretary, Miss Gabi, and drive out to the prison. Here in this lot he would park his motorcycle (he had removed the tomato plant from the sidecar, having realized that the age of youthful high jinks was past). And he would sit motionless as a rock with his head cast down, take a deep breath, as he often did before going out to face the trials of life, dismount his motorcycle, and head for the visitors' gate.

Day after day. Nothing could stop him. Neither the weather nor the wrath of his superiors on the force. It was then, as he had foreseen, that they began to make trouble for him. They postponed his promotion. They curtailed his duties. He was told: "Leave her—and your advance up the ranks is assured!" But he continued to visit her. They exploded. "How can you ruin your whole career for the sake of some little criminal?" Dad listened. Said nothing. But at the end of the day he hopped on his motorcycle and rode out to the prison.

It was utterly senseless, utterly hopeless. It was unrealistic and unprofessional, and yet, I always remind myself, their love was born in a vat of chocolate, how could it be anything but senseless, and full of passion and remorse and sweet addiction and shame and guilt.

At six o'clock every evening he would meet her in the visitors' room, under the watchful eye of an armed guard. They would talk in whispers, head to head. My mother would tell him about prison life, about her cellmates, about her ongoing arguments with the warden and the guards. Dad would tell her about the homestead he was building for the two of them on a plot of land he had bought at the summit of the Mountain of the Moon on the Jordanian border: a wooden cabin, furniture he had made with his own hands, a pen for the sheep, a stable for the horses, and a chicken coop. He spent every weekend alone on the windy hilltop, building a nest where their love would grow. He bought lumber and tools, and pipes, and doors and windows, plus an old wooden plow, and seed and manure, and he started learning all about sheep and donkeys and horses . . . And when he came to visit Zohara he would show her the blueprints he had drawn, and where the sheep pen and the stable would be, and the plans for the fence he was putting up and the kitchen cupboards he was building. All the love imprisoned in him was translated into lumber, doorframes, and window cases. She was entranced by his thoroughgoing seriousness; his grave way of speaking about how high the stairs would be filled her with a serenity she had never known before. There was strength and responsibility in his broad shoulders and square hands, and Zohara imagined her perfect happiness in the wooden cabin with the three front steps, each one eighteen centimeters high.

"It will be just like the cinema." Zohara laughed, and her heart went out to him, her restless, easily bored, inconstant heart.

"Ai," sighed Lola, shivering.

"Ai," sighed Felix.

"No two people have ever been so incompatible," said Lola.

"To this day I don't understand what they saw in each other," said Felix angrily.

They were looking at me as if I held the answer. As if I were that answer.

I didn't know what to say. And I still wonder sometimes about the attraction between them, even though I'm the product of their differences and similarities.

"Your Mr. Father only thought they are similar," sneered Felix. I was beginning to realize just how much he disliked Dad. It's kind of complicated, having a grandfather who's the enemy of your father. "Your Mr. Father thinks just because he is making mischief in his army days or at shindigs in Jerusalem that he can understand Zohara. But she was too wild for him. If he was like cat, she was tigress."

Lola sighed. "He was simply too good and too honest . . . and also —how shall I put it—a bit too normal to understand the character of someone like her . . ."

She didn't say this sarcastically, but in a soft, almost regretful tone, and though I wasn't quite sure what she meant by it, I sensed that she was right; the bitterness of it trickled into my heart, and for the first time I began to question his skills as a detective, and to see that being a pro did not necessarily provide solutions to all the riddles of life and other human beings.

"I, too, am a little like . . ." I stammered, not knowing how to say it, ". . . like Zohara, what you said about her . . ." because I wanted to tell Lola everything about myself, the whole bitter truth, so there wouldn't be a single lie between us.

"You're Zohara's son and Felix's grandson," said Lola simply. "Naturally there's something of them in your blood."

This was new, I'd never thought of it like this before. So was it a good thing or a bad thing? Was I the way I was because of Zohara? But I barely knew her! What did it mean that I had something of her and Felix in my blood?

I stared at Felix in open-eyed amazement. He was standing tall, with his head held high, like a soldier on parade, looking somewhat anxious under my scrutiny, though, as if he felt guilty or apologetic, just as he had two days before after we broke into Lola's house, when he made his confession, as if he wanted me to forgive him for what he had passed on to Zohara and she to me . . . All this was getting too heavy and I glanced up at Lola, hoping she would come to my rescue with a kind word, and she understood, perfect grandmother that she was, and said with a compassionate smile, "Imagine how happy the two of them were when she was finally released."

I heaved a sigh of relief and so did Felix.

I could picture Zohara leaving the prison through the iron gate. Dad was waiting for her on the motorcycle, here in the parking lot. Okay, she's passed the gate, she's looking around. The guards are watching from the towers. Now Dad's getting off the motorcycle and walking toward her. They embrace, though it embarrasses him to do so in public, and then they . . .

But something was bothering me. I don't know, maybe it had to do with what had just transpired between Felix and me, or maybe I suddenly realized, to my deep sorrow, just how incompatible Dad and Zohara really were.

They hopped on the motorcycle and rode off to the Mountain of the Moon. Directly from prison, of this I was sure. They had nowhere else to go. Nobody wanted them anywhere. Zohara rode in the sidecar. I could see them moving into the distance. Perhaps there was a strong wind that day, too, making it difficult for them to talk to each other. Maybe they both fell silent, feeling shy now that they were alone together without the fairy-tale aura which had surrounded them before. No longer were they two dolls, policeman and criminal, whose love affair had been ignited by a gunshot and burst into flame behind bars . . . Now they were just two people, a man and a woman, feeling somewhat strange and extremely different from each other. How would they ever live there together, alone?

They were suddenly scared, and so was I. Zohara sank deeper into the sidecar. I could feel her, I could feel him, as if I had actually been with them on the deserted road with the wind in their faces. Quite suddenly their individual and very separate fates came into focus, and something inside her arched its back at him and hissed, while something inside him barked angrily at her . . . She groped for his hand, but he pushed her away with a tight-lipped scowl. Because it was against the law to drive with one hand.

"That's where we go now," whispered Felix. "We return this morning, in time to get Amnon's present from bank vault."

"Where are you taking us?" Lola asked. "I'm cold. I want to go back."

"To their cabin up on Mountain of the Moon."

Lola was astounded. "What?! All the way there? But it's so close to the border!"

"We must to go," insisted Felix. "I promise I show Amnon their whole life together tonight!"

"Felix," Lola cajoled him, "it will take hours to get there, and this old wreck is sure to fall apart on the way!"

"We arrive in just one hour! This Felix promises!"

The prison dogs had caught our scents, and our voices roused them, too. They started racing around like lunatics on their chains, barking themselves hoarse. Lola and Felix, nose to nose, stood rasping at each other.

She: "You want to make all the decisions, don't you? You want to plan out my whole life for me!"

He: "But you never listen! If only you listen to me, then you—"

She: "Thinks he knows better than anyone what to wear, what company to keep, which dramatic roles to accept! Mr. Big Shot!"

"Well, I really do know better." Felix laughed, stepping gracefully aside. "I even know what you are thinking."

"Oh, is that so?" said Lola, her face close to his. "Well, why don't you just tell me what I'm thinking, smarty?"

"You are thinking," said Felix, drawling out the words, "you are thinking that tree over there is real."

And he pointed at a large clump of bushes in the middle of the grove.

"You mean it isn't real?" I asked.

"Is not that what you think, Lolly?" Felix prodded her, cackling with delight and trying to pinch her chin till she was forced to turn her humiliated face toward him.

"And what have you hidden there? A new surprise? Oh, Felix, won't you ever grow up?"

I didn't wait around to hear the rest of the argument. I jumped up and ran to the tree.

From close up, I could see something hidden there. A huge thing someone had camouflaged with branches and shrubs. I lit into it, started clearing off piles of foliage and throwing them on the ground.

Very soon I saw what it was and could hardly believe my eyes. This was beyond my wildest imagination. How did he do it? When did he hide her here? Who helped him? Where on earth did he find her?

First I saw the shiny black door, then the heavy desert tire, and then the rounded fender, the one the English painted a white stripe on during the Blitz so pedestrians would see it coming . . .

I knelt beside her. My Pearl, our Pearl. The Humber Pullman we were forced to give Mautner, and which he overturned his first time out (Hallelujah), claiming she was cursed, and then promptly sold. And that was that, we forgot her, never mentioned her again, except now and then—when we flinched at the painful memory. And here she was, resurrected.

Filled with awe, I opened the door. I knew every centimeter of that car. Times without number I had buffed and polished the sleek chassis, the dashboard, the steering wheel. It was almost as though I had imprinted something of my personality in her. I was overwhelmed with nostalgia, the kind I always feel at the end of *Lassie Come Home*. I nestled luxuriously next to the driver's seat, wondering where she could possibly have been all this time and who had driven her, and whether she remembered the touch of my hands?

Felix walked up and looked in through the window.

"*Nu*, what do you say about your grandfather now?"

"Where was she? How did you get her here?"

"I thought if we start our trip in the Bugatti, we must to finish it in Humber Pullman. That is what I call style."

"But did you know it used to belong to us?"

He chuckled to himself, enjoying my admiration.

"Yes, that is what they always say," he crooned, putting his arm around Lola, who had come over to see. "Felix the wizard, Felix the magician!"

I told Lola about the Pearl, how Dad had found her by chance in a junkyard, nearly stripped, and brought her home in bits and pieces, and worked on her as though he were caring for a wounded animal, and how he and I had put her back together like a mosaic, and restored her dignity.

"Your Mr. Father would not let her out of yard." Felix laughed. "You hear that, Lolly? What is this, automobile or porcelain china?" He got in and invited us to join him. Lola stretched out in the back seat, I got in front. I knew there was no point in asking where he'd found her. He loved to shroud himself in mystery, even in cases less amazing than this. What did I care? Knowledge is power, but you don't need an explanation for everything. I didn't even ask. The searchlight whipped over us. The guards were becoming as edgy as the dogs. Maybe they thought we were planning a prison break. I could hear a loudspeaker blaring inside the walls. I looked at Felix. He looked at me. We felt the ants crawling up our backs. With a barely perceptible nod, Felix started the car. I counted under my breath as the engine gave three feeble hiccups that sounded so far away, no one would ever have guessed what was in those six cylinders. And then suddenly the motor started, and she trembled all over, like Sleeping Beauty when the Prince kisses her awake, and Felix released the hand brake, shifted into first gear, and with a mighty roar, the four desert tires, the kind Montgomery used against Rommel during the war, spurted out a stream of sand, and away we went.

Driving on and on.

Taking dirt roads through empty fields.

"You want to drive now?"

"What did you say?"

"You want to drive? That is what I said."

Did I want to drive?

"Felix!" my grandmother cautioned him, sticking her sharp finger between his shoulder blades. Sometimes she acted just like Tsitka. "Enough of this foolishness!"

"Let our boy drive. Where is harm? There is no police here. No people to see. And already he has driven locomotive!"

"Please, Lola!" I begged her. "Just for a little while!"

"Well, you hold on to his hands, then, Felix! I'm not happy about this!"

Felix winked at me. He stopped the car. We changed seats. I could barely reach the pedals. I stepped on the gas. The Pearl lurched forward. I slowed her down. I shifted gear. She obeyed me. She knew me. I knew how to rouse her and how to control her. All the moves were in my blood. The rounded top of the gearshift fit the palm of my hand now, so I could see how much I'd grown. Mautner could take driving lessons from me. I tried to think what Dad would say if he saw me. He would go nuts if I told him I'd driven her out of the yard. When would I tell him? Maybe never. Why go into all the details? I could hear my grandmother pleading from behind: "Nonny! Nonny!" Sometimes she shouted, "Felix, Felix!" I was bumping over a field of thistles, between the rocks, when suddenly I realized why you always see people steering a little to the right and then a little to the left, but the car goes straight ahead just the same, and then I felt the heat between my eyes. It ebbed and flowed. My foot pushed down on the gas, to fly away, to soar—

I stopped myself. I regained control. A moment before the eruption. I realized that I'd already lost the Pearl once because of my stupidity and I didn't want to lose her again.

"Your turn." I offered Felix my seat.

He looked at me, a little surprised. "This is it? I thought you will drive us all the way to Mountain of the Moon!"

"No thanks. I've had enough."

Lola squeezed my shoulder from behind. "Come, sit next to me," she said. I climbed over into the back and nestled beside her. I felt wonderful. As if I had fixed whatever it was that had gone wrong in my life. As if I had mastered something inside me. Felix was still watching me in the rearview mirror with a look of mild disappointment and surprise. Lola waved imperiously, and in the same voice she had used to tell the taxi driver, "Charge it to the theater!" she now commanded Felix, "To the Mountain of the Moon!" Felix obeyed.

27

The Empty House

The car glided softly into the night. The radio was playing American songs. Felix was driving. Lola spread out her purple scarf, now mine, and we snuggled under it together. We spoke in whispers so as not to disturb Felix, who had to concentrate on his driving, and also because we wanted privacy.

"Start asking," she said as we snuggled up. "We've lost so much time already. Ask me anything you want. I want very much to answer."

All right.

"When Zohara was a little girl, did she know that Felix was a— uhm—"

"Excellent!" she exclaimed. "Straight to the point, just like me. Maybe you did inherit something from me, after all, besides your acting ability."

"What, you mean I inherited it from you and not from—" I almost said "Gabi," which goes to show how hard it is to get rid of old beliefs.

"I certainly hope it's from me. Your mother was not a bad actress either! She had flair, she had feeling. As a little girl she practically lived at the theater with me. Oh my . . ." Lola laughed. "That child was utterly hypnotized, velvet curtains and masks, and kings and queens, and heroes and villains . . . My fellow actors called her the mascot of the Habimah Theater. Ah yes." She sighed. "I guess her talent stood her well enough, who knows how many people she swindled with it . . . But you asked me an important question . . ."

"Whether she knew he was a criminal." The word came out of my mouth more easily now.

"No, not only did she not know that he was a criminal," said Lola, "but until she was sixteen, she had no idea he was her father!"

"What?" I couldn't understand that at all.

"You're a big boy, Nonny, I can speak frankly to you, can't I?"

"Of course." But about what?

"There are all sorts of grandmothers in this world . . . You have one sort of grandmother on your father's side, I believe, and I'm sure she's very dear to you. But I myself am a different sort of grandmother."

"What do you mean, different?"

"I have different ideas, different standards of behavior— Everybody's different, right?"

"Yes," I answered, not sure what she meant, though she seemed cautious suddenly, worried about what I would think of her.

"There were always men around me, admirers and lovers . . . You had a pretty wild grandmother, I'm afraid . . ." She took a long look at herself in the rearview mirror. Felix glanced up for a moment, and there was a twinkle in his eyes. "For Zohara, Felix was just another uncle, a nice, rich uncle who sent her postcards and dolls from around the world. Whenever he landed in our tiny country he would spend time with us and everyone else—and then disappear, just another one of Mother's friends, but a very good friend, you see?"

"Yes," I answered. At least I thought I did. She really was a different sort of grandmother.

"And then, when Zohara turned eighteen, he sent a telegram inviting her on a grand tour as a kind of graduation present. The trip was supposed to last a month, but as soon as I read her first letter from Paris, I knew that she belonged to him." Lola glanced wistfully at Felix in the mirror. "You yourself have seen how charming he can be— especially when it comes to someone as volatile and impressionable as Zohara."

Or someone like me, I thought.

"Because the truth is, Nonny"—she sighed in my ear—"it wasn't just his stories and the things he could teach her that were so fascinating. It was what he passed on to her, in her blood, what she inherited from him. When the two of them were together on their grand tour, he let her see how truly similar to him she was, always had been, though she never knew it, or was afraid to be. And he showed her what she was, what she could be."

I sat up: this sounded familiar.

Felix stepped blithely on the gas. The Humber took off like a streak of lightning. I could just see the corner of his mouth in the mirror. He was smiling, pleased with himself. Lola saw him, too, and grimaced slightly. And then I realized that Felix's whole purpose in kidnapping his only heir was to reveal the hidden Nonny inside me, to rouse him from his slumbers so I would know he existed. So that some remembrance of him and of his character would survive.

And so I would know I didn't only come from my father's side of the family.

Boom.

My world kept changing. The events of the past few days were lit from a different angle every minute, as though reality was not at all solid and substantial but rather pliant, elusive, variable.

My head nearly burst with so many thoughts: What did Lola mean about Felix's blood running through Zohara and me? That I would grow up to be a criminal? That I was fated to become one? What if I didn't want to be one? What if I still wanted to be the best detective in the world? And what about Dad's blood running through me? Didn't that have any say in the matter? Hadn't he and Gabi raised me together? Did Zohara's blood outweigh all that? Is crime always stronger than the law? How many drops of criminal blood does it take to dissolve lawfulness? I shuddered. I could feel that blood circulating, hot, boiling hot, through my stomach, my chest, stinging my legs. I never thought you could feel it, that it had a character of its own, but maybe I had other drops of Zohara's blood in me as well, drops of the good things that were in her, like her imagination and the stories she told. Why not? The questions surged through my veins; my blood was raging, fermenting, as though someone were conducting experiments on it. But what would happen to me now? And more important, would someone remind me who I am?

"One thing is certain, you're not Zohara," said Lola sharply. "Don't ever forget that: you don't have to follow in her footsteps. It's up to you to decide."

"I'm not Zohara," I murmured to myself. "I'm not Zohara."

"Naturally you have in you something of her and something of Felix. But you also have in you something of many others, all the people on your father's side of the family, for instance, like the grandmother we spoke of, and your uncle, the famous educator Dr. Samuel Shilhav, right?"

For the first time in my life I could see that having a bit of Shilhav inside might not be such a bad thing; but I also felt the stirring of a new self-esteem, yes, a new confidence, because it wasn't just me on my own anymore against the tribe of Shilhavs. And I suddenly realized that I had always felt ashamed around them, like an insecure nobody, because they were this big family with strong ties and similarities, and I had to face them all alone, with no one on my side, like a foundling foisted on their family. And then I understood that they had been hostile toward me right from the start, even before I was born, on account of Zohara, but now with Lola, Felix, and Zohara on my side, the two clans could confront each other, the doctors, educators, and Tsitkas versus the actors, crooks, and storytellers . . . I shut my eyes tight and envisioned the scene, the two opposing sides—and me, adjusting my position till I was standing right between them. I listened inwardly: my position was still incorrect, so I backed up a little, half a step in the direction of the Felixes, and immediately felt calmer in spirit and more serene.

"You have a different sort of character," continued Lola, unaware of the little drill on the parade grounds inside me. "Only Zohara was Zohara. Don't ever forget that! Know her, feel her, but remember that you are a whole new person, an independent agent." I repeated her words under my breath and tried to engrave them on my memory. I knew that I'd be needing them a lot in the course of my life. "And now, Nonny, as an independent agent, I hereby order you to get a little sleep. We have a long night ahead of us."

I lay down with my head on her knees and closed my eyes. I tried to fall asleep, but couldn't. Thoughts were running through my mind at the speed of the car. Things were becoming clearer to me and more coherent. Okay, I was unusual. I had an unusual upbringing, an unusual father. He wasn't exactly my twin, and neither was she. I was an independent agent. I could be what I wanted to be. I would always have Gabi there to keep me on my path.

Oh, Gabi. Gabi Gabi Gabi.

The wise and subtle one, who had always maintained that I had the right to know about my mother, in spite of Dad's strict orders to the contrary, and had disclosed various things by way of little hints, and big and little deeds . . . I remembered her sitting by the sea with her plastic noseguard and tubes of sun cream, and standing in front of the chocolate vat, and then faithfully waiting with me outside Lola Ciperola's house—and I smiled. It was Gabi who had asked for the scarf and the golden ear of wheat, hoping to become as free and strong as Lola maybe, and a little wicked and fickle like Felix. To become like a blend of the two of them, like the product of their union, like—

In other words, to become like Zohara. So Dad would fall in love with her again—

But she's so unlike Zohara, I mused, and thank goodness for that. She's from real life, not the cinema.

The sky grew lighter. Soon it would be dawn. Lola's eyes closed. Perhaps she was drowsing, carried away by her memories and her regrets about Zohara. I lost a mother, I reflected, and she lost a daughter. That makes us partners in something important, something that no longer exists, but if we talk about it and remember it, she and I, it will come back to life. I, too, closed my eyes, and squeezed her warm hand.

The road raced by, and the Humbert Pullman hovered over it. A young couple had traveled this road together on a motorcycle with a sidecar. In time no doubt they stopped being afraid of each other. Vast spaces opened up. They started to talk. To rejoice over Zohara's new-

found freedom and the great adventure that lay ahead, and Dad's release from his job and family. The road rose steeply. The sky was
turning pale. It was the same hue as the night before, on the beach with
the bulldozer. The things I'd been through in the past few days! I remembered that little boy waving to his father and his Gabi from the
train. The kid who thought he was a pro. What a dope!, what a dope!

"Look," whispered Lola, "the Mountain of the Moon."

The mountain loomed in the early light, dark, crooked, and strange
to behold: one slope was smooth and rounded, the other was all jagged
cliffs. The car climbed the winding dirt road. Clouds of dust flew up
around us. Portly partridges scurried away from the wheels and stopped
to gape at us in amazement: it must have been years since a car had
gone by. The higher we climbed, the cooler and fresher the air was.
Below us lay the valley, veiled in morning mist, ribboned with green.

"There is Jordan River"—Felix indicated with his chin—"border
with kingdom of Jordan."

With one final roar, the Humber lurched forward and climbed to the
top of the mountain, where it rolled to a stop over a surface of rubble
and grass.

The Mountain of the Moon.

A chilly wind was blowing. The panorama faded in and out of the
mist. A bird of prey circled overhead, calling as it spread its wings in
flight. I felt cold and lonely. Lola wrapped our scarf around my shoulders. A tumbledown cabin stood there. No windowpanes. Weeds growing through the planks. The wind whistled with a chilling sound.

Slowly we approached the cabin, almost as though we were afraid to
get there. We climbed the three dilapidated steps. Felix pushed the door.
It creaked open and fell in with a crash. Everything had an echo, and
sounded bleak and forlorn.

We trod with care, raising dust with every step, keeping away from
the bare walls and the empty window frames. Yellow-flowered fennel
sprouted up between the broken floorboards. Lola clasped my
shoulders.

"Remember, they were happy here together," she said quietly, so as
not to break the silence. "They wanted a place of their own, without

intruders and gossip and the laws of the external world. A place where they wouldn't be hounded by the past."

"Look—" whispered Felix.

At the other end of the cabin there was a broken partition behind which their bedroom had probably been. The room was bare except for a big old stove that was so rusty it crumbled at the touch of my finger. Like the dolls in Zohara's room, I gasped, everything I had touched lately turned to dust. I would have to remember everything here.

"And look at this." Lola pointed.

There was a torn sheet of paper tacked up on the wall, flapping in the draft. On it was a faded pencil sketch of a man's face, and in the background a horse. It was hard to make it out, but all three of us knew at a glance whose portrait it was.

"She could really draw," I marveled.

"She could do anything she set her mind to," said Lola.

And that's how I wanted to be, too.

"Look at your father here," said Felix. He didn't say Mr. Father this time, and he didn't sound sarcastic anymore.

Dad looked young and handsome. He had thick, wavy hair, a smile in his eyes, and a smile on his lips. You could see from the picture that he was happy.

"Your father loved her. And she?" Lola asked with a sigh, and answered herself: "She loved his love, but whether she truly loved him, the way she had always dreamed of loving, I don't know . . ."

Now I'm going to write something I can only guess about, based on what Lola told me, and I hope this is how it really was: Zohara was happy there with Dad. At least in the beginning. She wasn't spoiled: she would take the sheep out to graze on the mountain, clean the stable, cook for the two of them on a kerosene burner. And she loved their little home.

As the days went by, she felt that her soul was being gradually cleansed, purified, and the old adventures dropped away like layers of dead skin, like somebody else's stories. They would spend their evenings watching the sunset and eating their simple, healthy supper in silence. Sometimes they would ride the horses out to the edge of the cliff. Together. They spoke very little. Words were superfluous there. Occasionally Zohara would play her recorder.

I'm only guessing. Probably their life was a lot more exciting than this, only I'm too unimaginative to be able to describe it. I'll just have to make do with the imagination I have, because Dad never told me how it really was. Even after my adventure with Felix, Dad kept silent about it. There are lots of other things I don't know, and will probably never know.

"Once I came to visit them," said Lola. "I spent a whole week here, and later, back in Tel Aviv, I remember thinking, Those two have created their own Garden of Eden. Adam and Eve. Without the snake."

"You visited them here? They let you come?"

"Why, they invited me. They wrote me a nice letter saying they wanted me to meet my grandson."

Me.

So I was born here?

"Didn't you know? I see he didn't tell you anything," she said, and nodded with a doleful sigh. "I told you, he wanted to wipe out the past, so you wouldn't find out! So it would be as if he were your only parent."

"Zohara was smart, she knew your Mr. Father will want to wipe her out of his past," muttered Felix. "And that is why she asked me to take this trip with you. She knew!"

"Take a good look around you, Nonny," continued Lola, breathing deep. "Here, in this cabin, in this very room, you were born. Without a doctor or a midwife. Your father couldn't get Zohara to a hospital in time, so he delivered you. He cut the umbilical cord himself." She hugged me from behind and pressed her cheek to mine. "This is probably the most beautiful place in the whole world to be born." Her voice began to quiver. "It was so primeval, the father, the mother, and the child. Right about now, at four-thirty in the morning, exactly thirteen years ago, less a few days."

I was overwhelmed.

"I can't go on," said Lola suddenly, and left the hut. Felix hurried after her.

It was difficult for me, too, but I wanted to stay a little longer. To be with them again. In the Garden of Eden. I knelt down and touched the wooden floor, the rusty nails, the marks left by the legs of the bed. Then I sat on the floor, quietly concentrating. I had never concentrated so hard in my whole life.

The echoes were fading, all the echoes that had been there since Zohara died and the whispering and secrecy began. Those bewildering echoes I was always trying to understand, to imitate, to obey.

I stayed inside a few minutes more. I found a bent spoon, the strap of a knapsack, a broken picture frame, an old box of matches, a woman's shoe, a man's faded handkerchief. I picked them all up and put them in the bedroom, next to the stove. I tidied up the cabin.

"With you she was happier than she had ever been in her life," Lola said to me when I went outside. Her eyes and nose were red. Felix's nose looked red, too. "She would romp around with you as though you were a couple of puppies. Here, look, this is where your father put the sandbox. Two days after you were born, he built a sandbox for you! And this is where she used to set down your blanket, because it is sheltered from the wind, and she would roll on the ground with you, and your father would stand there, laughing."

Presents, such presents I was getting for my bar mitzvah.

The sun came up and tinted the valley gold. Sometimes I think it was the open spaces I knew as a baby that make it hard for me even now to stay in a closed room for any length of time. In the early-morning light, at the edge of the cliff, I saw a fluttering patch of color, a shred of fabric on a thorn. It was a faded red or purple. Perhaps one of her scarves had caught on it as she galloped her horse toward the cliff. I didn't dare approach. Not because of the cliff.

"You grew up in the Garden of Eden," whispered Lola.

"But not for long," Felix murmured. "Zohara brought the snake with her."

When was it roused, that snake? With the poison of wanderlust, the longings for a serpentine flight. Why couldn't she just stay happy there? With him?

"It's not easy to tell, and even harder to hear," said Lola. "Make a fist, Nonny. Here it comes."

And she told me. Zohara grew more vexed and unhappy by the day. The landscape was monotonous; the sheep were boring; she was tired of working in the cabin and in the field, tired of smelling sheep dung on her clothes.

And my father?

There was something about him that drove her crazy, I don't know what, exactly. When I try to guess, it hurts too much. Maybe he was too taciturn. Maybe he bored her. I'm trying to see it from her point of view, because it always helps to look at things from a different angle. Maybe his eyes appeared small and greedy to her all of a sudden. He had this strange way of caressing an object, handling it with delight, as though forcing it to admit it belonged to him and that he had the right to touch it any way he wished. Maybe that's what got on her nerves. It makes me sad to speculate like this. I guess I'm like him in certain ways, and the older I get, the more like him I become.

And maybe it irked her that he was unwilling to make a complete break with his old life: that he had promised his mother to phone her once a week from Tiberias; that he just had to buy the Friday paper; that life wasn't worth living without an after-dinner bottle of malt beer; that he was addicted to the soccer matches on the radio—and once he bought an enormous armchair at the flea market, upholstered in chintz, and it reminded Zohara of a fat woman she knew named Dobtzi (Dobtzi, of all names!) and she started screaming at him, what was he doing, they had sworn to create their own Garden of Eden here, to be free as Gypsies without burdens or possessions, and now it seemed he had dragged his materialistic bourgeois soul up here with him. Her face was terrible in wrath, with her long black hair like flying snakes and her cheeks hollow as though after an illness: how dare he suppose his soul as great as her own! She had hoped he would walk alongside her in the sky—walk, not crawl! But look at him! How could he ever understand a person like her! He with his limited little soul, the soul of a boy who grew up in a cookie bakery! "Dobtzi! You big Dobtzi!" she screamed, and flew at him with her fists and nails, and Dad grabbed hold of her carefully, but with an iron hand, and she went wild, imprisoned by him, gasping for breath, for freedom, for release . . .

The fresh air turned stale between them. The valley contracted at the sound of their screaming from the mountaintop. Zohara felt Dad watching her. She remembered his promise to the judge—to see to it personally that she stayed out of trouble. Maybe he should never have made such a promise: because of it the judge commuted her sentence, but he turned Dad into her warden.

"Stop following me around," she would hiss at him.

"I'm not following you around. Just tell me where you're going with the horse."

"Wherever I please, Sergeant Feuerberg. I'm a free woman."

"Zohara, my darling, we're so close to the border. There are smugglers out there, and armed infiltrators, and you're alone."

"I am not alone. I have myself and my gun."

"What am I going to do with you, Zohara? What can I do to make you happy? Tell me. Teach me. I'm a good pupil!"

"Oh yes," said Zohara, mounted on her horse, as though she were seeing him for the first time. "You are a good pupil," she said pityingly. "And you certainly are diligent," she added with a note of irony, then turned on her horse and galloped away.

"Sometimes she would disappear for a few days," Lola recounted. "She would sleep in the hills, in the caves, who knows? She would come back starved and covered with scratches. Where were you, Zohara? But she wouldn't speak. Sometimes she would ride to Tel Aviv on the motorcycle and spend the night at my house. She would go dancing, get drunk, come home or not come home . . . He would arrive to take her back. Terrible fights . . . Zohara screaming that she didn't want to go back . . . that she didn't belong anywhere. Neither here nor there . . ." Lola spoke softly, with her head bowed. I drank in her every word.

"And then once she set off on horseback and never returned. That was the end," said Lola abruptly. "Maybe she crossed the border and was shot by Jordanian soldiers. Or maybe she fell to her death from a cliff. Maybe she was murdered by infiltrators. The army made inquiries.

They searched all over the area. Your father's army friends stole over the border at night and searched there, too. Nothing. She had vanished. Suddenly she was gone."

"Suddenly," sighed Felix. "All her life is like that: suddenly."

I looked out at the golden panorama. I didn't want to look, but I couldn't help it. And I felt Zohara riding toward them. Maybe she had galloped her horse over this very cliff. And all the while I kept hearing the question she had once asked as a child, Why isn't there a fence around the world to keep people from falling off? There is no fence. That's just it. You have to be careful and stop before you get to the edge.

She was twenty-six, the age when she had planned to die. But how could she have left us? I asked myself. Why didn't she think about me, and about what it would be like for me without her?

"But before that, before she did . . . what she did, she called me on the telephone," said Lola, her lips trembling. "It was a brief farewell with a single telephone token . . . 'Mother,' she said to me, and I could tell immediately from the sound of her voice that that was it, she was gone. 'Mother, last time I was in Tel Aviv I left something there for my son, for Nonnik.' "

Nonnik?

"Is that what she called me?"

"Yes, always Nonnik."

Nice name.

"It was a present for you, she said, but you weren't to open it until your bar mitzvah."

Nonnik.

So, I had a new name. No one had ever called me Nonnik before.

What a happy name.

"But what's the present?" I finally dared to ask her.

"She said it was a secret. A surprise. She loved secrets and surprises. She said you had to go with Felix to take it out."

The words "secret" and "surprise" made me tremble. "And that's the present she left in the vault at the bank?"

"Yes, she wanted to give you a surprise, like a grownup: a safe-deposit box in the vault. Why do you jump like that? She wanted something reminiscent of her adventures that only you could take out. Those were the instructions she left with the guards."

Only Nonnik may take it out, said my mother.

Maybe she didn't know how to be a good mother, but she had thought of my bar mitzvah even then and how I would feel and how I would miss her. She knew. She had a strong feeling for me, and I mustn't forget that.

"For you, she leaves present," Felix grumbled, "for me, only your Mr. Father."

Because Dad had vented all his rage and pain over her death on Felix. He had begun to suspect a mysterious link between Zohara and the legendary Felix Glick. Before then, he'd had no idea that Felix was her father. She had never told him, nor had Lola, and he had never asked. Maybe he didn't want to know. Rumor had it that Felix and Lola were lovers, but then again, she had so many lovers . . . Dad came down from the mountain. He left the cabin to the looters, to the shepherds in the surrounding villages, and to the infiltrators and smugglers from across the border. He spoke to his former chief on the force and asked to return to the police department. For three months he shut himself up in the tiny office they assigned him, and sat there working, morning, noon, and night. Gabi would bring him sandwiches, make him coffee, and watch the baby. That's when she fell in love with him. Maybe it was the pacifier in his holster, or whatever it is that makes people fall in love. Dad read through Zohara's case file again. He even flew abroad to speak to Interpol, and talked long distance to the police in Zanzibar and Madagascar, the Ivory Coast and Jamaica, who gradually filled in the picture of her grand tour of crime with Felix Glick.

"And all this time," said Felix with genuine amazement, "I am quietly working overseas. I know nothing. I sense nothing. I am busy taking banks, stamp collections, diamonds—earning my living—while he, your smart Mr. Father, is spreading his net around Felix Glick."

For Felix had become his greatest adversary, the epitome of crime. The serpent that gave Eve a taste for sin. He wanted to catch him. To stop his insidious activities, and his forked tongue and its half-truths.

Day and night he worked like a turbine: he had at least two hearts when he loved Zohara. At least two brains when he hunted for Felix Glick.

"One day I am back in Israel to visit, and next thing, hop, I am arrested."

He was furious, his eyes flashing at the memory of that humiliation. "A fifteen-years sentence I get. And six months ago I am released for lousy health and good behavior. I am in for ten years, and he is to blame!"

"No, you're to blame," Lola corrected him. "But enough about that. We all paid a heavy price. All of us. Including Jacob."

My father's name sounded gently familial when she said it.

We went back to the car. I took one last look at the valley. At the secluded cabin. This is where I began my life. Here I was happy before everything went wrong. I wanted to run to the cliff and get the fluttering shred of cloth, but I didn't dare. I picked up a stone instead and put it in my pocket, a smooth gray pebble shaped like an egg. To this day I have it. I keep it on my desk.

We drove away in heavy silence. At some point I fell asleep, and woke up just as we were entering Tel Aviv. When I rubbed my eyes, it all came back to me. What we had done that night, the longest night of my life, and what we were about to do. Meanwhile, as I yawned and stretched, the word "bank" recurred to me, putting me on the alert: bank and Felix—that pair of words sounded ominous.

"Did you say we were going to the bank?" I inquired.

"The bank. Yes. Good morning."

"To get my present from Zohara?"

"Yes, and then you also get the golden ear of wheat I promise to our Miss Gabi."

"Will it be hard to take it out of the bank?"

"Not at all, taking a bank vault is easy."

I can't do this, I thought. I wasn't born to rob banks. The furthest I'll go is hijacking trains, but a person has to know his limits.

Lola was sleeping at my side. I tried to appeal to Felix's conscience: "I'm too tired to rob a bank now."

Dead silence. He was pretending to be a careful driver again. I tried
to appeal to him as a grandfather. "Look, I'm really tired. I've had a
hard night."

"It is not work you have to do," he grumbled. "It's not crime. You
will walk in and take your package and then I give you Felix's last
golden ear of wheat."

"Without shooting a single guard?" snapped Lola, awakened by her
sharp grandmotherly instincts.

"Without shooting."

"Without crawling through a tunnel?" I asked.

"Why tunnel? What is this? We walk into bank, I tell you, you tell
your name to vault guard, we go into room, open box, take present,
and—"

"Good day, thank you, and shalom," I chimed in.

He smiled in surprise. "Exactly so," he said.

There was another silence.

"Look me in the eye, Grandfather."

I looked into his eyes in the rearview mirror. They were as innocent
and blue as the eyes of a baby.

28

This Is Too Much

At eight-thirty that morning Grandfather Felix parked the Humber Pullman on a quiet side street, not far from the theater. Lola Ciperola (Katz, to me), the first lady of Israeli theater and winner of the award of distinction in the performing arts (my grandmother), crossed the street and walked into the bank with wind-tousled hair and wearing a pair of dirty, faded jeans; and in spite of Felix's slurs, she succeeded perfectly in playing the part of a woman of the people. Not a queen, not an empress, not a goddess or a tragic heroine raising her hands on high or covering her eyes with grief, but a simple Jewish grandmother who wished to deposit five pounds into her account. Only, because of the heat, or her advanced age, or perhaps in order to distract the crowd from the old man and the boy who were slipping in behind them, she collapsed in a heap on the floor, moaning and groaning, and snorting most inelegantly.

It was the best role I'd ever seen her play. I had never enjoyed a character so much, and sometimes I think her success was due to the events of those two days, and because she had suddenly become a grandmother . . . Too bad I didn't have time to stand and watch. A large crowd had gathered around her. People were shouting, giving advice, calling for help, while we two stole down the spiral stairs and into the vault.

The only one down there was an elderly guard, who was nibbling a cheese and tomato sandwich. I told him my name. It was a tense moment. His newspaper lay folded on the table before him with my picture smeared all over the front page. And my name as well. They had finally divulged it! I goggled at the headline with pride. AMNON FEUERBERG KIDNAPPED! it said. That was the most famous day of my life, but just then my publicity might have ruined everything. The guard opened a large notebook and began to leaf through it, muttering my name over and over, with yellow crumbs in his mustache. For a moment his eyes rested on the newspaper. He read my name aloud from the newspaper but didn't notice any special resemblance. He continued leafing through his lists of names until he finally found mine.

"Here we are, Amnon Feuerberg. Authorization to take out mother's safe-deposit box. Oho! That was a good long while ago, thirteen years! Time for the safety-deposit box's bar mitzvah!" And he sprayed the newspaper with cheese crumbs as he laughed at his own little joke.

"Go right in. Is this your grandfather?"

Yes. He really was my grandfather.

Why is it that the truth can sound like such a lie!

The guard jangled through a pile of keys. He opened one iron door for us. And then another. He closed it behind us and left us alone.

"You have ten minutes," he said, and we could hear him shuffle back to his chair and his sandwich.

We were inside a small room. Four walls covered with safe-deposit boxes from floor to ceiling. Rectangular gray boxes. Each with a little round dial bearing numbers from zero to nine, and a small, arrow-shaped pointer. Felix immediately found ours.

"Ten minutes," he said. "In ten minutes Lola must to get up off the floor. That is very short time. Do you think you can do it?"

"Do what?"

"Open box."

"If you give me the key, I can."

"Well, you see, that is problem." Felix cleared his throat. "There is no key."

I stared at him. "What do you mean, no key? How are we supposed to open it?"

"You must to do it alone. Without key," he said, shrugging his shoulders again. "You must to guess five-number combination, and then, chop-chop, we open it." I gave him a long, hard look.

"It is secret combination," he added, as if that solved anything. "Like special password, this number Zohara wants you to guess."

"Just a minute." I was becoming annoyed. "You mean to say she didn't tell you the secret number?"

"No. She only said you will guess it when time comes." Again he shrugged his shoulders. "I know it is problem, sure I know!"

"Wait! Wait!" I shouted. "You think I can guess all five numbers of the combination in the right order?"

"*Nu*, sure, and better hurry."

"But that's impossible!" I blew up at him, feeling cheated and disappointed, because right in front of my nose here, behind this armored wall, was the only present my mother had ever given me and now I would never be able to get to it!

"It's impossible to guess five numbers like that!" I shouted in a whisper so the guard wouldn't hear me. "My chances of hitting on the right combination are less than one in a million!" Why had she done this to me? Why couldn't my family give nice, normal bar mitzvah presents?

"Yes, yes, don't shout. Very difficult, I know. But you must to remember it is your mother who chooses numbers for combination, right?"

"So?"

"So . . . that is it! She is your mother! You are her son! Her only son, blood of her blood!"

For some reason I was touched by this, though it didn't make sense. But I had lowered my expectations of things making sense over the past few days. It's true, I thought. I am her son. I'm the only person alive with her blood in his veins. And she's not alive, so I'll have to try.

"Okay," I said to Felix, "I'm ready. Keep a lookout and don't let anyone bother me."

I shut my eyes and gradually cut myself off from my surroundings.

From the guard munching his sandwich on the other side of the iron doors. From Felix, who was gazing fondly at me. From my grandmother

Lola, still sprawling on the floor upstairs, trying to gain precious time.

And from Dad and all the things he would say to me when we met up again. And how I'd explain. And what about Gabi? Was she still with him, or had she left him forever? Did I have anyone to go home to?

Five numbers.

Zohara. Zohara. I've worn your clothes. I've slept in your bed. I've eaten the raspberry candies you hid in your mattress. You had black hair. You had dark, wide-set eyes. I inherited the wide-set part, but not the black of them.

Hello, Zohara, this is Nonnik. I know more about you than I knew two days ago. But that's still not much. Lola will tell me about you later. I'll ask her about the kind of girl you were, and how you felt at the theater when you saw your mother acting onstage, just like me; I want to know more, I want to know everything: what you liked to eat besides chocolate and jam, and what your favorite movies were when you were my age, and what your favorite color was (blue, like me?), and how different my life would have been if you hadn't left me.

Zohara, you probably always wore pants. I'm sure the skirt Felix gave me to wear was your party skirt. Maybe you hated it. You were a tomboy, weren't you? A real tough cookie.

1.

"One," I muttered with my eyes shut. I just blurted it out. I had forgotten all about the numbers. But as soon as I said it, I just knew that was the first number Zohara would have chosen. Because it was the first of all the numbers, and also because the shape was right for her, a single line. I heard Felix move the pointer on the dial.

I immersed myself in Zohara again.

She grew up, and still she was lonely. But she was popular now. Because she started to blossom. People couldn't help noticing her beauty, and those incredible eyes and the way they sparkled with the magic of Zohara. Deeper and deeper I plunged, not thinking in words anymore. I'm only adding the words now, but at the time I dove way down under them to a place of inspiration, where I writhed and tingled inside, as though seeking the center, my point of origin.

Zohara was becoming a woman. More feminine, but wilder than ever; shapely but a real whirligig. Sweeping her admirers from party to party, indifferent to them all, flirting with them all, yet always lonely, even as the belle of the ball. She flashed through the night like a bolt of lightning, ever the ringleader of their shenanigans, their wagers and their cruel but hilarious pranks, and always unpredictable: a woman, but, like Felix, a curved line with a little zigzag—

2.

"Two," I said.

I could hear the pointer click in the lock.

And then Felix arrived on the scene and took her off to Paris. She didn't want to go home, so they continued on a tour of exotic places where exiled monarchs rode in gilded carriages and stolen diamonds were reflected in the black river and there were sea captains and nuns, and Zohara floated among them and from one to the other, swirling in circles where the figments of her imagination merged with the sights she saw around her, till she could no longer distinguish between dream and reality, and everything swirled like the smoke rings from the old king's pipe, and she closed her eyes and surrendered to the pleasure of inventing a fiction more sinuous than a snake, and learned that she, too, like her father, knew the trick of fusing true stories with the lies people believe; and all the while she was swirling down, down, down . . .

8.

"Eight."

The pointer moved.

I was getting tired. This process was killing me. The moment I closed my eyes, I went into trance. I was afraid of this moment. My heart was heavy, plunging deeper into an abyss of black quicksand.

"I can't go on," I whispered to Felix. "I think I'm about to faint . . ."

"Keep trying," he pleaded. "Don't stop yet!"

Rows and rows of numbers floated before me like a giant account ledger, where the sixes and sevens and eights danced by, confusing me, tempting me to choose them, but I shut my eyes and squeezed them as hard as I could, searching for Zohara in their midst . . .

I saw her with Dad in their happier days together. He and she on the round side of the mountain, and Zohara at dusk, watching the pure and glorious sun go down, her belly swelling with me inside! Nonnik! She washed herself in a metal basin, and even though she didn't truly love Dad, she tried to be happy in the warm nest he had built and feathered for her, and perhaps this was the last time she made a sincere effort to be happy for his sake, content within the small circle of their home . . .

0.

Zero? But my lips were hesitant. It wasn't actually zero. Not a perfect zero. It was round, yes, but with a swelling, like a pregnancy? Yes, and yet not a zero! Not empty the way zero should be! Because something was amiss there; something was kicking and writhing inside the zero, trying to break out of it, something that even then, during her happy days with Dad, was sharp and cutting, pushing through the peace of her pregnancy and the feathered nest—onward and upward!

5?

"Try five," I muttered.

"Just one more number," whispered Felix. "Is time for last number."

This is ridiculous, I brooded; here I sit with my eyes shut, looking serious, and making a complete fool of myself as I try to guess five arbitrary numbers someone thought up thirteen years ago. I mean, really.

And I was so tired, I felt as if my soul had been drained out of me.

But again, the moment I looked inward, I could feel her loneliness slinking around me. Her baby was born. And she loved it, that's certain. But later it was like waking out of a dream. She looked around at the bald hills. Dad bored her, though she didn't like to admit it. And disappointed her a little. She already knew, already felt that she didn't belong here or anywhere else, and sometimes she would gallop to the jagged side of the mountain, to the edge of the cliff, and look down at

the vastness calling her to fly down, like an anguished bird, to speed
herself out of her life like an arrow released . . .

7, I thought.

"Seven," I said.

"Are you sure?" whispered Felix. "Think carefully. This is last number."

"Seven," I said.

Silence.

And then I heard the pointer turning around the dial.

And a little click, like a key turning in a lock.

And Felix's breathing.

A small lid creaked open.

I opened my eyes. Felix was there, his white hair standing on end. In
his hand he held a long wooden box with a note stuck to it.

"You did it," said Felix faintly. My mouth was dry. I was wearier
than I'd been the entire trip. All I wanted now was to curl up and go
to sleep, even on the floor. To be no more.

"You read her from inside," said Felix, croaking with astonishment.
"That is blood talking."

He handed me the box. On it was a note in a shaky young hand:

"For Nonnik, a bar mitzvah present. With love, from your mother."

"Should I open it?" I asked in a whisper.

"Not here. There is no time. We must to get out of here. You can
open it later."

I put the box in my pocket. The minute I touched it, my strength
flowed back to me. Felix closed the safe-deposit box, this time forever.

"I can't believe how dumb I am," I said when I had finished. "I
should have guessed immediately that those would be the numbers she'd
choose."

"Why is that?"

"Because it's the date of my birth. The twelfth of August, '57."

Felix pronounced the numbers: "One and two and eight and five and
seven! Bravo!"

He looked at me and I looked at him, and we both started laughing.

"You see that this is most important day for her," he said. "Remember that."

"Let's get out," I said, "before anyone notices we're down here."

"Wait, Amnon. Felix makes promise, Felix delivers."

He pulled the fine chain out of his shirt, took off the last ear of wheat, and gave it to me. All that remained was the heart-shaped locket. He weighed it in his hand, looked at the bare chain. "That is all." He tried to smile, but his face fell. "No more ears of wheat."

I held the little ear of wheat in my hand. I slipped it on my chain, next to the bullet.

We walked out through the first iron door. Then the second. And then we noticed—simultaneously—that something wasn't quite right. We exchanged looks: the guard had left his table. Felix recoiled. He stood against the wall, narrowing his eyes like a panther. The cruel line over his lips turned white.

"They caught me," he rasped, and grimaced at himself for having been outsmarted. "*La dracu!* They caught me, damn them!"

He squeezed his way behind the iron door, as though trying to vanish into the wall. His eyes darted hither and thither. Beads of sweat broke out on his forehead. He was in a full state of terror now that he couldn't move, or change, or get away.

As we turned to the staircase, a gun barrel appeared. There was no time to waste. No time to think. Everything depended on my speed and my professional skill. I drew the gun, my mother's pistol, and cocked it, spreading my legs for balance and supporting my right hand with my left. I raised the gun to eye level. All that took less than a second. I didn't have to think after the hundreds of hours of training of my instincts. "Don't think. Act!" he had taught me. "Let your instincts work for you! Draw!" I closed my left eye. I focused a little over the gun barrel facing me.

The man holding it was careful not to show his face. He moved cautiously and slowly down the stairs. Hearing his steady, circumspect steps, I knew that this was a real professional. But I wasn't afraid. My thousands of hours of training with Dad had prepared me for this moment. My finger was on the trigger, poised.

Then the hand that held the gun came into view.

Thick and tan.

And then the face.

Broad. And the rugged body. The head attached to it by a minimal neck.

"Don't move! Police! Glick, two steps to the right. Nonny, throw me the gun."

Dad looked weary and unshaven.

≈ 29 ≈

Will Wonders Never Cease

Now what?

"Don't think! Draw!" How many hundreds of times had I heard him shout that at me. "The first one to draw will live to tell the tale to his grandchildren!" But I was the grandchild here! "Let your instincts work!" Which instincts exactly had he been shouting about during all our years of training? The instincts of a pro or the instincts of a son? And what about the instincts of a grandson who wants to defend his grandfather?

(From his own father.)

What a situation!

"Throw down the gun, Nonny," said Dad again, tense and quiet.

His gun was shaking. So was mine. We traced a wobbly circle over the other's body. Suddenly Dad's eyes nearly popped out of their sockets.

He recognized the gun in my hand.

The woman's gun with the mother-of-pearl handle. Zohara's. The one which had wounded him once before and changed the course of his life.

I could see the memory strike him from out of the past. Suddenly they were face-to-face again in the chocolate factory . . . I was forgotten for the moment. He didn't even see me: their guns took aim at each other. Only the two of them existed just then. And I, too, was losing my grip: the two guns were engaged in a snaky dance of defiance, of push and pull.

"Throw it down now, damn it!"

He shouted the words in despair.

But I didn't throw it down.

To this day I feel bad when I remember that moment. The older I get, the less I think about myself just then and the more I think about Dad. About what must have gone through him when he saw his son pointing that gun at him. As if all those years he'd been with me and taken care of me were wiped out the moment I picked up her gun.

As if she had beaten him twice.

"It's okay, Dad," I whispered. "Don't worry. I'm not going to shoot."

"Lower the barrel now, relax . . . and drop the gun."

"Okay." I slowly lowered the barrel.

And stopped. "But what will happen to Felix?"

"Glick will go back to jail, where he belongs."

"No." I raised the gun again. "No. I refuse."

"You—what?"

I recognized that expression, and it scared me. His face went red, his eyes turned small and mean, and the horrible exclamation point between them stood out like a wand or a stick waving over me.

"I said I refuse. Let him go."

"Nonny, don't be crazy! Throw that gun down right now."

"No. First promise me you'll let him go."

His face looked distorted with rage. "He kidnapped you, do you understand me? He kidnapped you!"

"No, it wasn't a kidnapping," I said.

"Shut up!" he roared. "I didn't ask you!"

"Let him go, or else—" I started to say, and a red fog spread over my brain.

"Or else what? What will you do to me?" said Dad, jeering at me, furious, his gun trembling in his hand.

"Or else I'll . . . I'll shoot!"

"Shoot who?" they shouted in unison, Dad and Felix.

"H-h-him . . . ! Felix!" The answer came to me.

I tried to understand myself.

"I don't get it," said Dad. "You want to shoot him?"

"I don't care! I don't care about anything! Not about him and not about you! You're both driving me crazy! Let him go or else I'll shoot him!"

The fog thickened. The events of the past few days were like a whirlpool in my brain. I'll shoot him. I'll shoot myself. I'll shoot all three of us. We'll have a general massacre, verging on mass murder. First I'll commit suicide and then I'll run away. I'll fight good, I'll fight evil. I'll live beyond good and evil!

I screamed, I blurted out incoherent words, I kicked the wall, I banged my head against the iron door. Mount Feuerberg was erupting! Anyway, I wanted Dad to watch me explode so he'd understand how dangerous I can be when I'm angry.

I don't know how long I raved like that, but there's one thing I'm sure of: at that moment, the moment I turned it into an act, I lost my ability to go wholeheartedly berserk. (Is that what Lola meant when she said, "Those who use emotion to make other people feel lose it for themselves"?)

"Wait a minute!" shouted Dad through the clouds of my theatrical fury. "Why do you say it wasn't a kidnapping?"

He sounded less sure of himself. Maybe my act had worked, after all.

"It's the truth!" I stamped my foot, but a little less vehemently, the kind of stamping that could start negotiations. "I went with him of my own free will! He didn't kidnap me!"

"What do you mean? Explain!"

"It all started with a mistake," I said. "I got into the wrong train compartment for the game you arranged."

Dad was listening morosely. "And what the hell was he doing on the train?" he said, tracing a circle of disdain around Felix with his gun.

Felix, who until that moment had been crouching as though frozen in mid-flight, now slowly stood up, relaxed his tense muscles, smoothed down his hair, and said sweetly to Dad, "What is problem, Mr. Father? I only want to look at him, what is wrong with that? Maybe he is not my grandson."

I was shocked when he smiled like that and pointed broadly at me as though showing off his own creation, because I realized how much he had managed to change me and distance me from Dad in only a few days. And maybe this was his greatest revenge.

I was so shocked; in fact, I couldn't move. Because if this was true, then he had done something extremely devious and cruel. He had used me against my own father . . . On the other hand, if he hadn't kidnapped me, I would never have heard the story about me and Zohara or gotten the present she had left me; on yet another hand, even if Felix had started out intending to get revenge, in the end he did what he did for my sake, as a partner, or a friend. And most of all—as a grandfather.

Dad gave a groan, pounded the wall with his fist, and roared at Felix: "Nonny is not your anything! You'll never come near him again, you hear? Not you and not that old woman up there doing a melodrama on the floor."

"But Lola is my grandmother!" I yelled, affronted.

He turned slowly toward me, like a weary bull. "So you know now. They've told you everything."

"Yes, everything. About my mother and about you. But don't worry. That won't change anything."

"It's no use . . ." muttered Dad, his gun drooping down with his head. "I didn't want you to know. You're too young for that."

All his anger suddenly vanished, and he sat on the stairs with his gun hanging down between his knees. At last I could look at him to my heart's content and try to read the story of the past few days in his face. He was staring out, holding his head in his hands. I searched his features for a trace of the young man who had jumped up on the crane that night and almost drowned in a vatful of sweetness; the young man who had visited Zohara in prison every day and built her a palace on the Mountain of the Moon; my father, who had delivered me with his own two hands and cut my umbilical cord.

But I couldn't find him.

His face was sealed. The face of a man who must constantly compress his lips to keep the memories from bursting out in a tidal wave. And he apparently succeeded: they didn't burst out. Not then and not ever.

When I was younger, I could feel them bubbling up inside him, like molten lava. Nowadays I'm barely aware of them. He succeeded too well.

All I could see was the face of the policeman, the professional. The one who had been punishing and torturing himself for the past twelve years for having fallen in love with a criminal, for having followed her on the journey she proposed, a journey beyond the laws of ordinary people. The man who cruelly refused ever to forgive himself for one great error, what he considered to be a great error; and with him, as we know, to err was unforgivable, and to punish himself he renounced anything that could bring him joy or relief or consolation.

He was his own prisoner, a prisoner of his character.

"I was planning to tell you everything, Nonny," he said gravely. "I just thought I should wait till you were a little older, that's all. I was afraid you weren't—uh—mature enough yet to hear about the whole mess. Now you know, and I'm sorry."

"Yes, but I'm okay, nothing's happened."

A lot had happened, of course, but this was not the right moment to go into troublesome details.

"He treated you well? He didn't harm you?"

"Felix is great, Dad." You're very much alike, I added silently.

Dad looked at Felix, Felix looked back at him, and I understood, in spite of my youth, what was passing between them as they gazed into each other's eyes. There was more than enmity between them. A special destiny bound these two men who had loved the same woman.

"So what will we do now?" asked Dad. "The police have been chasing you all over the country." He sighed. But it seemed to me that he was purposely saying too much. "And I came here alone because I figured that your final stop"—here he stared hard at Felix—"would be to pick up the present Zohara left for Nonny . . ."

"You come here alone?" There was a spark of interest in Felix's eyes. His tongue ran quickly over his bottom lip.

"All by myself," said Dad, staring at him blankly. "Why, did you want to make a proposition?"

"Lord, no. Who is Felix to make proposition to Mr. Father? Is just something I am thinking."

"Let's hear it."

"I am thinking perhaps we do like so: I pull out gun, yes?"

"Then what?" said Dad.

"Then I hold gun to Amnon's head and say, If Mr. Father does not let me go, I shoot, yes?"

"And then what?"

"*Nu*, you have no choice, so I get away."

Another silence. They didn't need too many words to understand each other. "You mean"—Dad chuckled heartily—"you mean, you beat me? You know what the press will make of that? And the police?"

"Who cares about police?" asked Felix with a grin. "Forget police. You catch Felix once, now you catch him twice. No other policeman ever did half so good. Think about that."

"But if I let you go, who'll know I caught you?"

"Ah, but you will know," said Felix, looking pious. "And your Amnon will know, and that is what is important, yes?"

Dad nodded and nodded. He was always quick to make up his mind.

"Oh well," he sighed. "Any other solution would hurt us all. Especially the boy. Go on, tie us up."

He rose to his feet, put his gun back in the holster, and took his belt off. Felix and I watched him tensely. I was still holding the gun, because what if he jumped me? Dad halted halfway to the stairs. He saw the expression on our faces and my gun following his movements, and he heaved a sigh.

"Ah, Nonny," he said with the trace of a bitter smile, "I know you're only doing what any professional would do in this situation, but for some reason, that really depresses me."

Now I was sure he wouldn't try to surprise us, and put the gun back in my pocket.

Dad smiled wryly, and said to Felix: "In the end, what we teach them, they use against us, eh?" and Felix nodded.

Dad drew nearer, looking big and sweaty and unshaven, the perfect

SOS. We hadn't seen each other for three days. I wanted to jump up and hug him and shout for joy that it was ending this way. But we didn't even shake hands. Maybe it was better that way, man-to-man. Felix asked us to enter the vault and sit back-to-back. He tied us tightly to each other, humming as he worked, and the mark over his lips stood out again, the way it did each time he tied somebody up. He finished tightening the belt so I wouldn't be able to undo it, and I could hear Dad rasping at him not to tie it too tight. "Don't hurt the boy," he said.

Then Felix pulled Dad's handcuffs out of his pocket and cuffed his hand to mine. Hearing the cuff clicking around Dad's wrist, I remembered the prisoner on the train and how he had turned into the policeman's jailor. What a weird trip this had been.

Out of the corner of my eye, I saw Felix leaning over Dad. "She was very special," he said. "I know you really love her. But enough. You must to forget the dead. Life goes on. Nonny is good boy. He needs to have a mother. Listen to me, Mr. Feuerberg: old Felix knows many, many women in his day—but no one, ever, like your Miss Gabi. She is very smart lady. Think kind thoughts of her. Forgive me if I am mixing up in your private affairs. Thank you and goodbye."

I could feel Dad breathing against my back. I was afraid he was about to explode. Felix circled the parcel he had just tied together and leaned over me with a smile; at first it was the old mesmerizing smile that turns everything blue, but then suddenly he wiped it off and gave me another one, from the heart.

"We have good time together, eh?"

I nodded.

"You are kid like nobody else. You are like crook and you are also good. Big jumble! Now that I see you, there is nothing more I need, because now I know: Felix will live on in this world." He sniffled loudly. His blue eyes were red at the rim. "Okay, enough. I must to go now. Urgent business elsewhere. Maybe I see you again sometime. Maybe not. Maybe one day you meet Grandfather Noah in street and say hello. Anything can happen in this world. But most important is that you know Felix now, and I know you." He reached out gently and touched the golden ear of wheat on my chain as though bidding it farewell, too. "And also, is important that I know Lola will be watching over you, to make sure you don't turn out, God forbid, like Felix, except in little ways, so you remember there is more to life than rules, that in this life there must to be room for rules you make yourself!" And then he drew closer and, before I knew it, kissed me on the forehead.

"And remember, Nonny: life is the light between darkness and darkness. And you have seen better than most the light of Felix passing through this world."

A flash of blue and he was gone.

We sat in silence, Dad and I, back-to-back.

Where do we begin?

Where do we be-ga-be—ga-be—ga-bi.

"So how's Gabi?" I ventured.

Silence, then a sigh. "Waiting at home."

"Is she going to leave us?"

I heard him rub his whiskered cheek against his shoulder.

"She gave me an ultimatum. I have till Sunday to decide."

Just as I figured. Yes, I knew everything.

Neither of us spoke.

And then he grumbled, "Do you still have the gun?"

I felt my pocket with my elbow. It was empty except for the folded scarf. Felix, that scoundrel, had picked my pocket while he kissed me! I wanted to laugh, but stopped myself out of respect for the feelings of my father, to whom I was very much attached.

And suddenly Dad said, "Do you realize it's only a few more days till your bar mitzvah?"

I just couldn't hold it in anymore. The laughter blared out of me. Dad sat in silence, his broad back sturdy and still. I laughed from the pit of my stomach and from my toes; I laughed back and forth and to and fro . . . and then I felt him kind of move, kind of shake behind me, trying to stop himself with all his might, until finally he roared with laughter, pitching me from side to side like a boat in a storm, like someone trying to waltz with a refrigerator on his back. I guess you could say I had just made him laugh for the first time in my life. The first, the only, and the last time: that's three times, all in all.

He did have a laugh—a real horselaugh!

"Things get so complicated sometimes," he said when we had both calmed down.

"I missed you," I said quickly.

"So did I," said Dad, and that was all I needed from him.

A few minutes later I was able to talk again. "I was in the newspaper," I said.

"Oh, is that all? The whole country was up in arms on account of you. And in the end you say it wasn't a kidnapping."

"Because it wasn't."

"I'm going to get in trouble because of this mess. As usual. Never mind, though. One reprimand more or less won't make much difference."

I said nothing. I had already decided for him about the police. I didn't care whether they came to my bar mitzvah or not. Who needed their presents? I had plenty of presents now.

"So I'll get in trouble," he said suddenly, tightening the muscles of his back till I was lifted off the floor. "I've been in trouble with them for the past twelve years! For twelve years I haven't gotten any kind of decent promotion. They throw only the most piddling cases my way. What more can they do to me?"

We heard the wailing of sirens in the street. A loud commotion, shouted orders.

"They've arrived!" Dad was fuming. "I told Ettinger to be here at 0900. I didn't tell him why. Looks like we're going to have a hot time now." Then he added the amazing words: "I hope at least your grandfather got away."

That evening we went out to a restaurant, Gabi, Dad, and I. It was the happiest dinner of my life, though I must admit, the meal at the restaurant with Felix was a little more elegant. As we were tucking in, I told them everything, or almost everything—or actually, very little, because the minute I started talking I realized I couldn't tell them the main thing, because the main thing was kind of vague and didn't make much sense. I felt like someone waking out of a dream, trying to convey that dream to the people around him, only to feel it fading away.

But one thing was still solid and substantial: the gift that had been sent to me out of the dream, and which was sitting on my lap. I held it tightly, and it's been with me ever since. Too bad I don't have a good enough ear to play the recorder, the simple wooden recorder Zohara left me. But whenever I feel sad or lonely, I sit on the windowsill, with my legs dangling out, put the recorder to my mouth, and listen for the undertones.

Later we discussed Dad's future on the force, and it turned out he didn't have one.

"I'll submit my resignation tomorrow morning. Look—uh—Gabi, I want to start a new life."

Gabi blushed red and stared down at the tablecloth. Suddenly I understood something: that he didn't say "uh—Gabi" to annoy her. He was just pausing to make sure he didn't blurt out another name accidentally, the name that was always on the tip of his tongue.

"It was a mistake, staying on the force for so many years after what happened with Zohara," he said, and I knew I had guessed right. It also made me feel good to hear him utter her name so freely.

"My real life was right here all along, only I didn't see it. I buried myself in hard work and wasted a lot of precious time."

I listened openmouthed. I had never heard him talk this way before. It was almost as if Gabi had written the speech for him. Gabi, by the way, was silent almost all evening. She seemed to be waiting to hear his decision.

"The past few days have taught me what's important, and who's important, and about the kind of life I want to live and what's really right for me. I wanted to use this evening—to make a change," he said.

He groped for something in his pocket, a little square box, the kind widowers take out of their pockets in the movies when they want to propose to their children's governess.

"Wait, Dad!" I shouted. "Don't spoil it for me!"

I pulled the wrinkled scarf out of my pocket, like a magician pulling a scarf out of his sleeve, and I was a magician, too; I spread it on the table, purple and sheer, and waited for all the heavy breathing to subside, and then, with forced composure, set the golden ear of wheat in the middle.

"This is for you, Gabi," I said. "I did it all for you."

Gabi covered her red face with her hands, and the tears began to flow.

"Don't cry!" I implored her in a whisper. "You'll ruin everything!"

"Let her cry," said Dad. "They're tears of joy."

Apparently something had changed between them while I was away.

Gabi ran her fingers over the scarf and she clasped the ear of wheat. "Now I have everything," she said. "Everything I need to make a wish. Will wonders never cease?"

She bit her trembling lip and looked bravely at Dad. She shut her eyes tightly and made a silent wish.

As she was wishing, Dad opened the little box and placed a beautiful, shiny ring on the table. People sitting nearby us dropped their forks and watched.

"What do you say—uh—Gabi, if you're not too busy next week, will you marry me?" asked Dad shyly.

He sure knew how to propose, my dad.

"A ring," murmured Gabi. "A diamond—you shouldn't have—"

With trembling hands she picked up the ring, smiling apologetically at Dad as she struggled to get it on her finger. She tried a thinner finger, but that didn't work either, and Dad cleared his throat and scowled at the other tables, until finally she managed to slip it on her little finger, she would never be able to get it off again, and Dad forced himself to smile and said, "That's so you can go on twisting us all around your little finger."

She glanced at me and then at him and started to laugh. It was a new sort of laugh, low and mysterious, like the burbling of a secret joke inside her throat, and for a moment I had a strange and probably ridiculous thought—that maybe Gabi had played a slightly larger role in my kidnapping than I first supposed. Maybe she hadn't been working alone but in secret association with a cunning, slightly crooked partner, someone who—but no—impossible—it couldn't be!

I looked back at her, intrigued, amazed: was it yes or no? Her face gave nothing away. I never did find out the answer to my question, and consequently deposited it in the bureau of questions I delight in musing about without ever wanting to know the answer, because while it's true that knowledge is power, mystery has its own special sweetness.

Then Gabi turned to Dad full face, turned to him with radiant joy; for a moment her inner beauty really did light up her face, and she said in a clear, ringing voice, "Yes, Jacob, I will marry you."

And she looked around with girlish pride at all the people in the restaurant, beaming from ear to ear, beaming at everyone, at me, and at Dad, and said tenderly, "Oh, Jacob—"

Then she stood up and hugged him around the neck. The waiters and the other customers stared unabashed. I, as usual, wanted to bury myself. First Felix and Lola, now Dad and Gabi. There was apparently something about me that made men and women throw themselves at each other.

I looked down, I looked up. "Jacob," that's a nice name, I thought. I wanted to tell them to call me Nonnik from now on. Then I ran out of things to think about. Gabi, all in tears, reached for my hand behind Dad's back and pressed it thankfully, and then she raised it in the air and traced two words, like a secret message from her to me:

AT LAST!